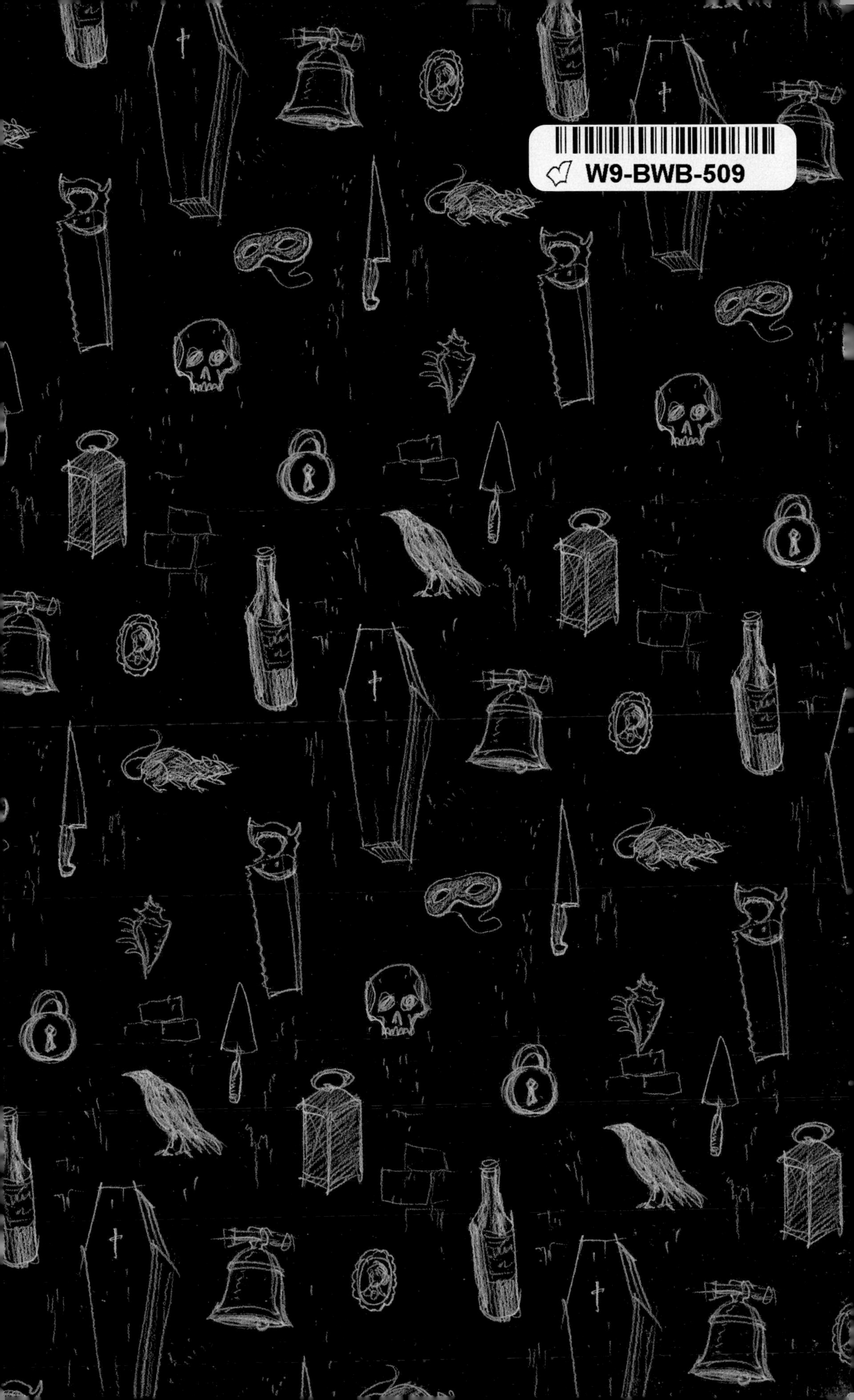

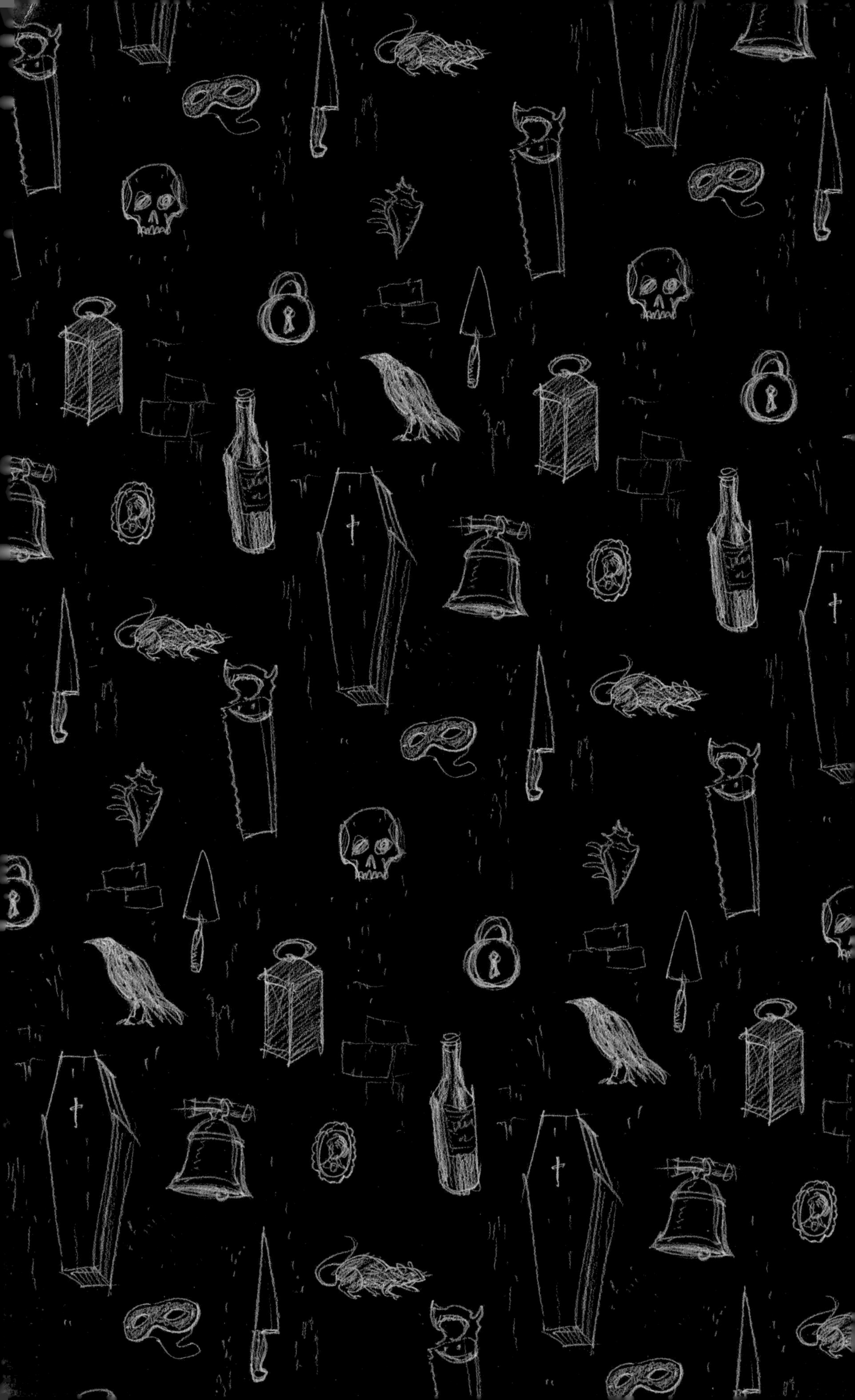

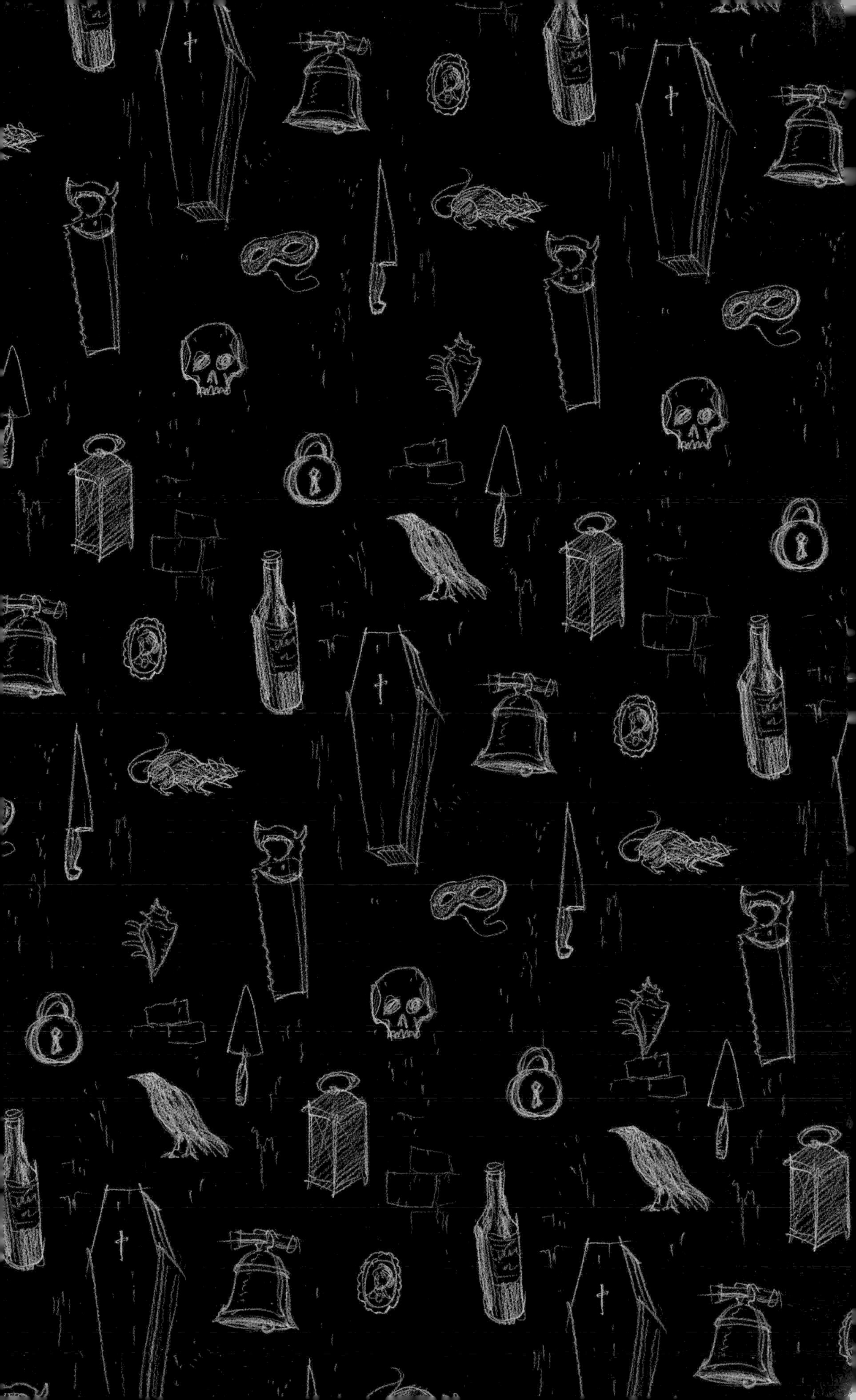

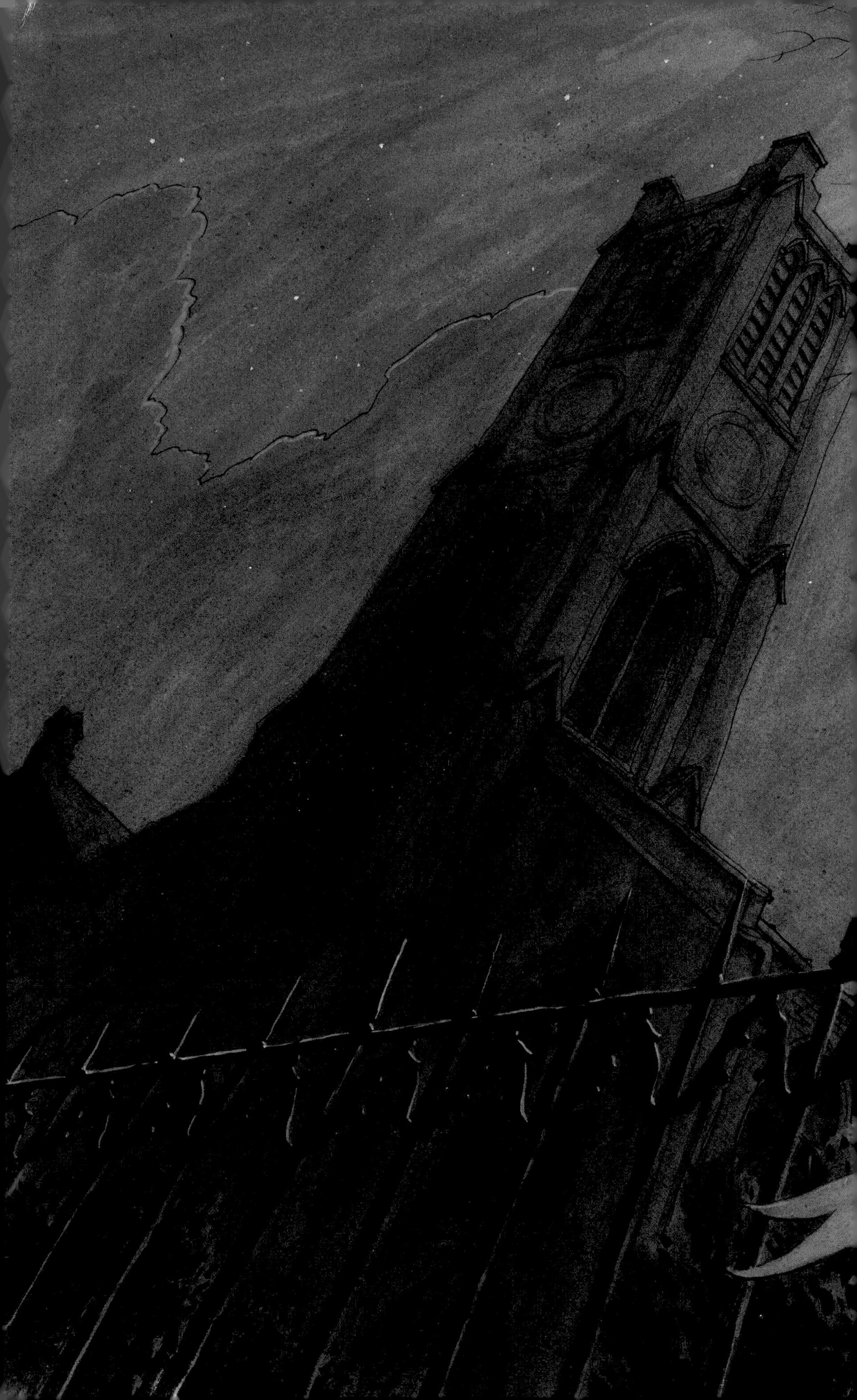

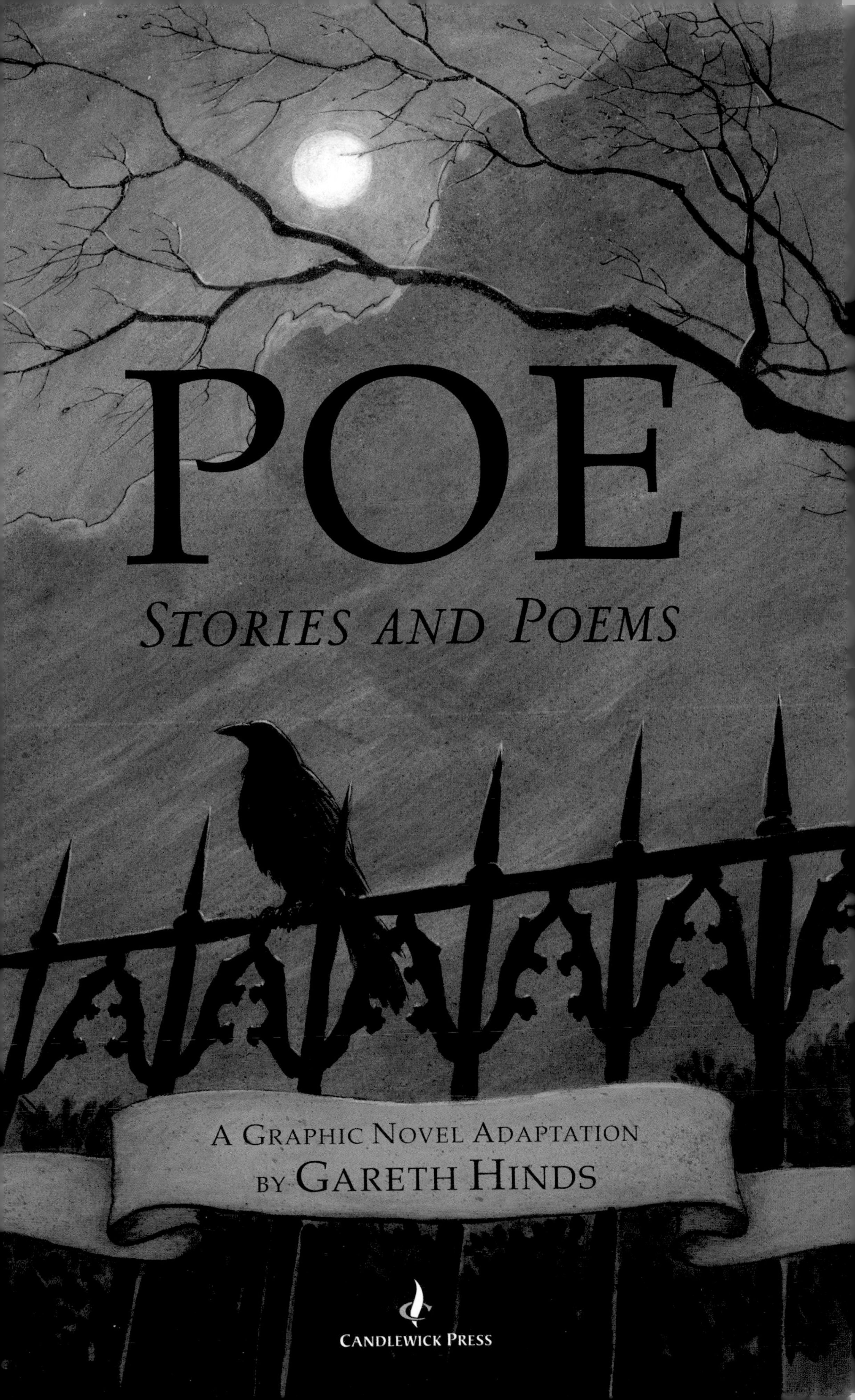

POE

Stories and Poems

A Graphic Novel Adaptation
by Gareth Hinds

Candlewick Press

THE POE CHECKLIST

Poe had some favorite themes he used to achieve his sense of horror. Here's a key to some of the recurring motifs, which you'll find listed at the start of each story.

ANGELS & DEMONS

CONFINEMENT

CREEPY ANIMALS

DARKNESS

DEATH

DISEASE

FIRE, BURNING

GUILTY CONSCIENCE (OR LACK THEREOF)

INSANITY

MURDER

PREMATURE BURIAL

SCARY SOUNDS, HYPERSENSITIVITY

CONTENTS

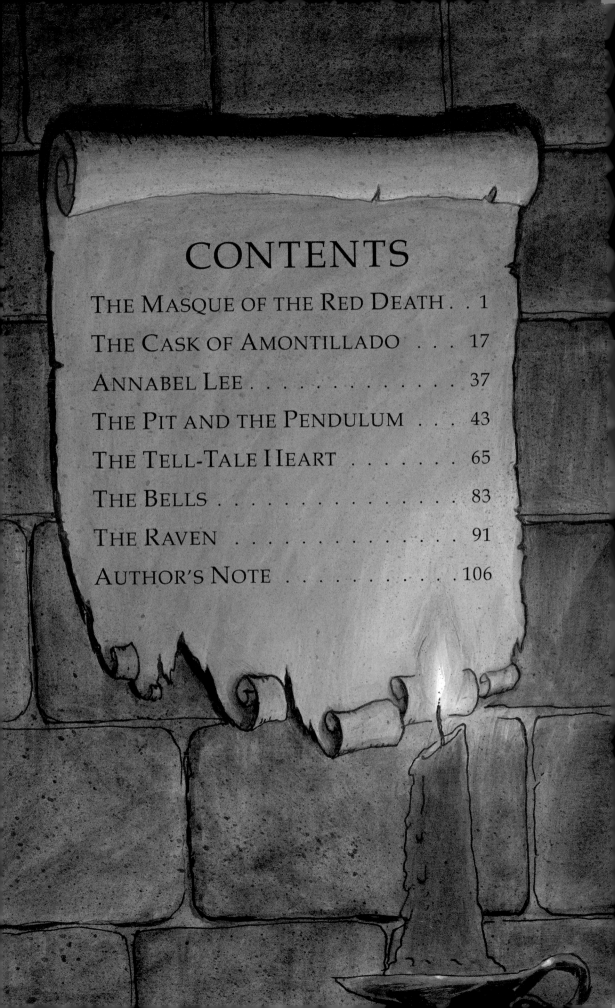

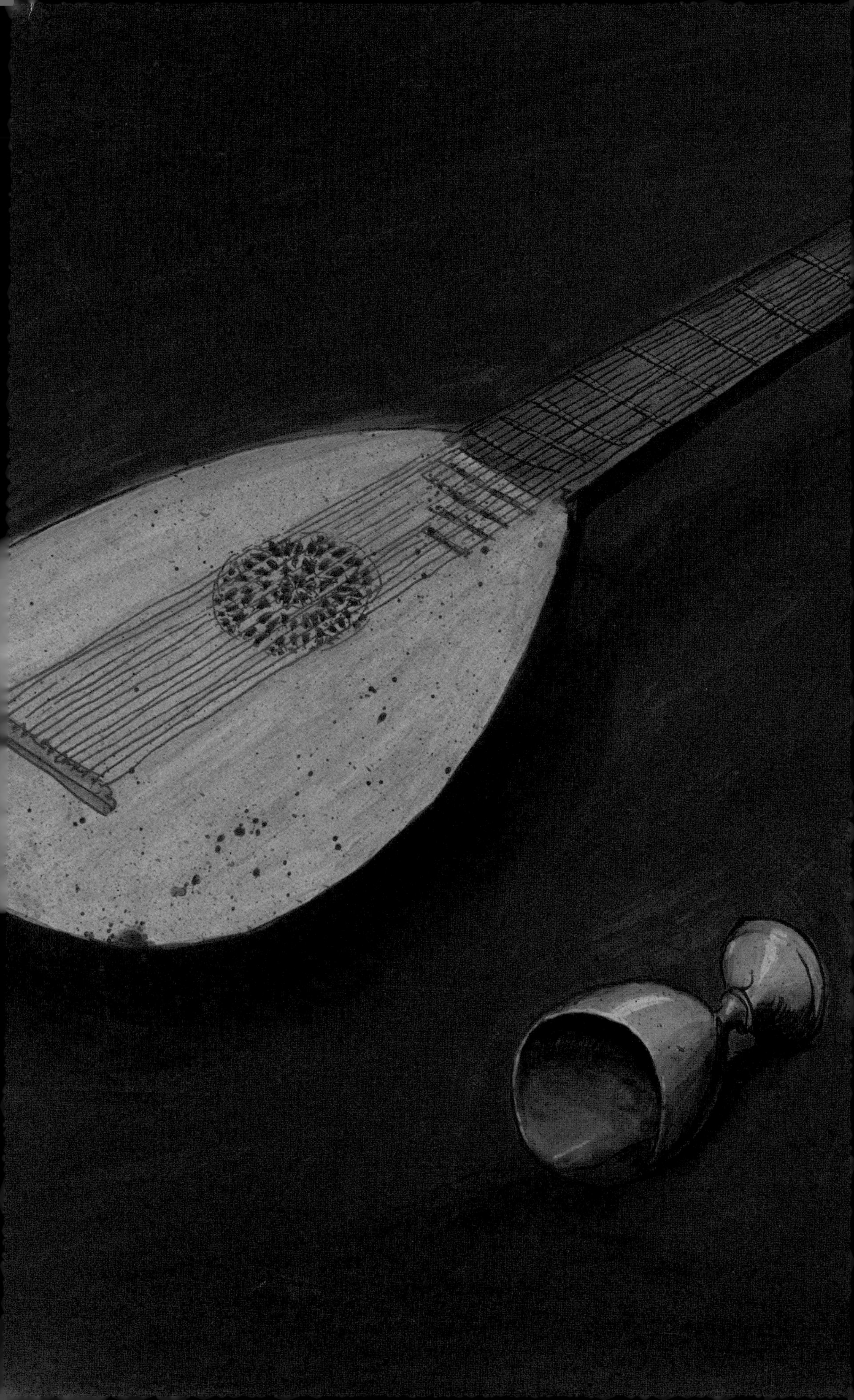

The MASQUE OF THE RED DEATH

1842

 DEATH   DISEASE   SCARY SOUNDS

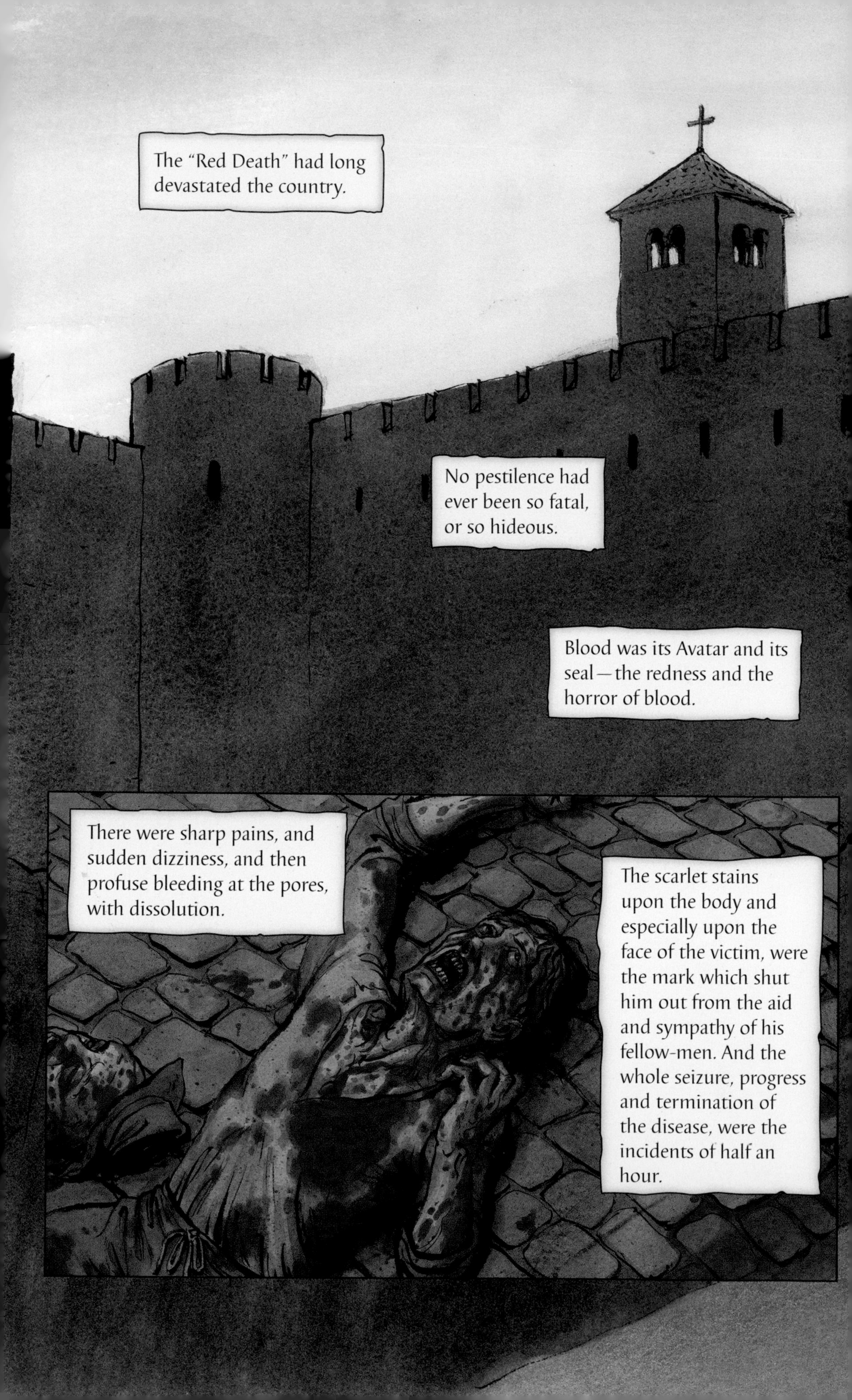
The "Red Death" had long devastated the country.
No pestilence had ever been so fatal, or so hideous.
Blood was its Avatar and its seal—the redness and the horror of blood.
There were sharp pains, and sudden dizziness, and then profuse bleeding at the pores, with dissolution.
The scarlet stains upon the body and especially upon the face of the victim, were the mark which shut him out from the aid and sympathy of his fellow-men. And the whole seizure, progress and termination of the disease, were the incidents of half an hour.

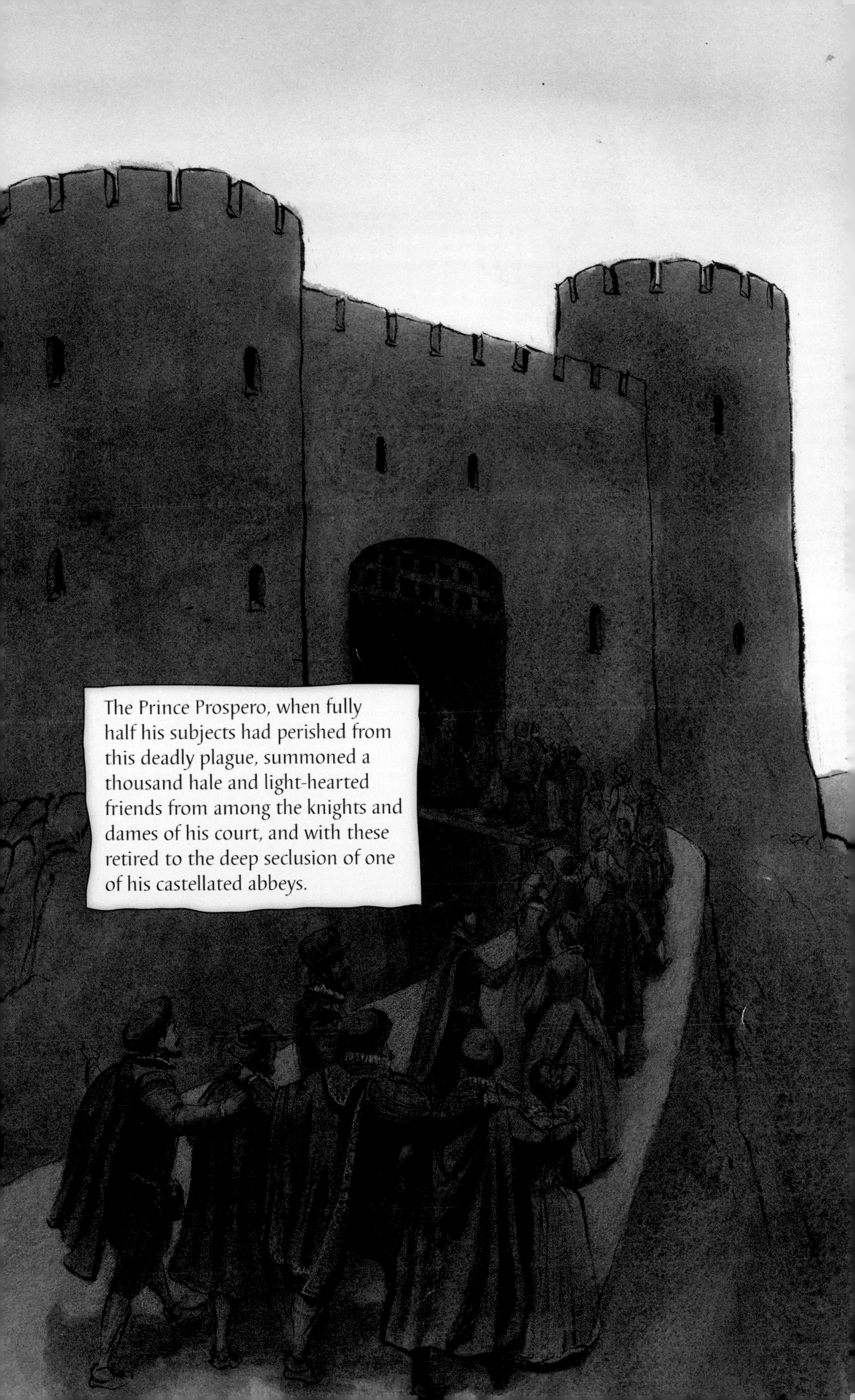
The Prince Prospero, when fully half his subjects had perished from this deadly plague, summoned a thousand hale and light-hearted friends from among the knights and dames of his court, and with these retired to the deep seclusion of one of his castellated abbeys.

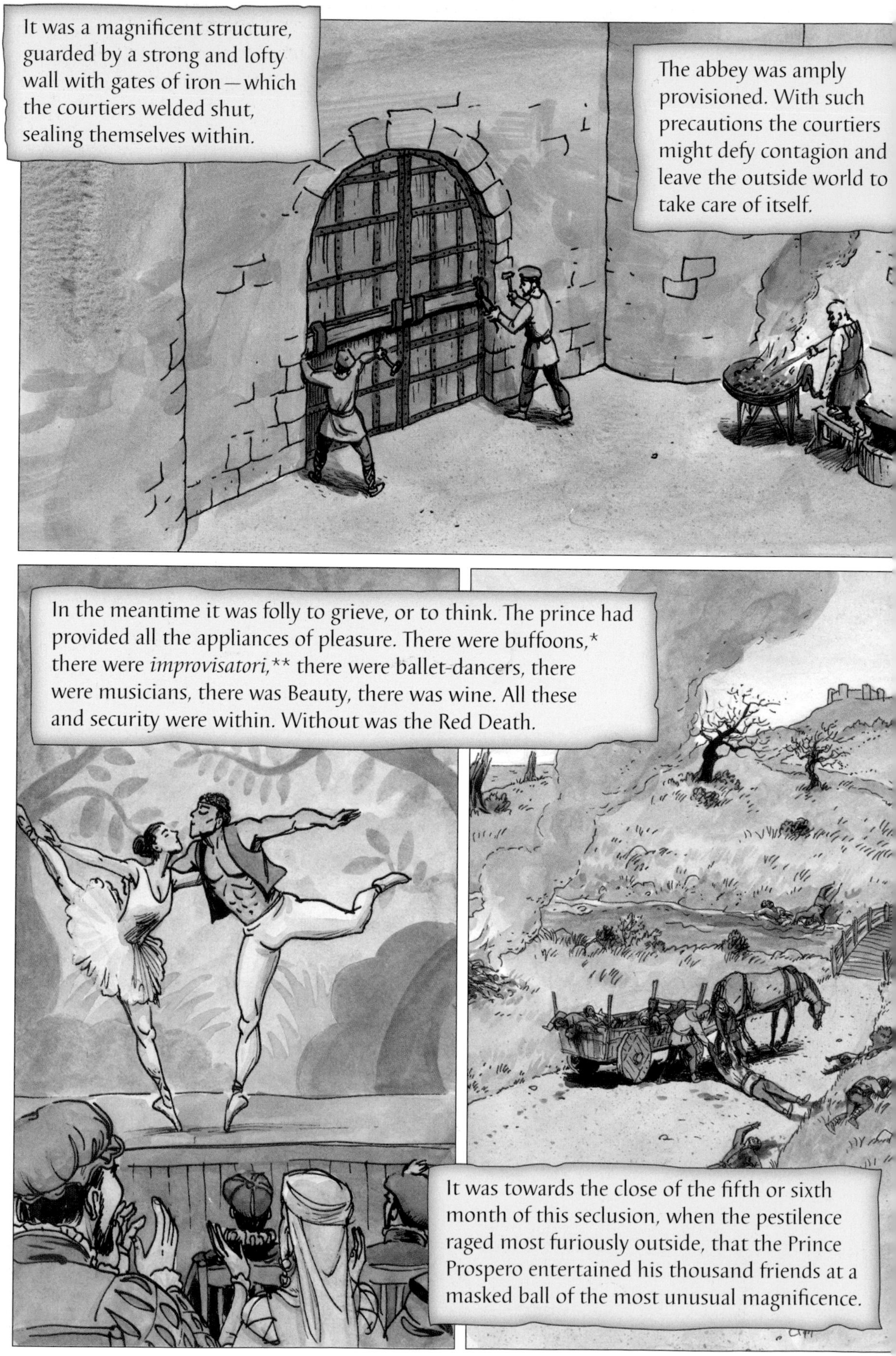
It was a magnificent structure, guarded by a strong and lofty wall with gates of iron—which the courtiers welded shut, sealing themselves within.
The abbey was amply provisioned. With such precautions the courtiers might defy contagion and leave the outside world to take care of itself.
In the meantime it was folly to grieve, or to think. The prince had provided all the appliances of pleasure. There were buffoons,* there were *improvisatori,*** there were ballet-dancers, there were musicians, there was Beauty, there was wine. All these and security were within. Without was the Red Death.
It was towards the close of the fifth or sixth month of this seclusion, when the pestilence raged most furiously outside, that the Prince Prospero entertained his thousand friends at a masked ball of the most unusual magnificence.

*clowns **Italian improvisational poets

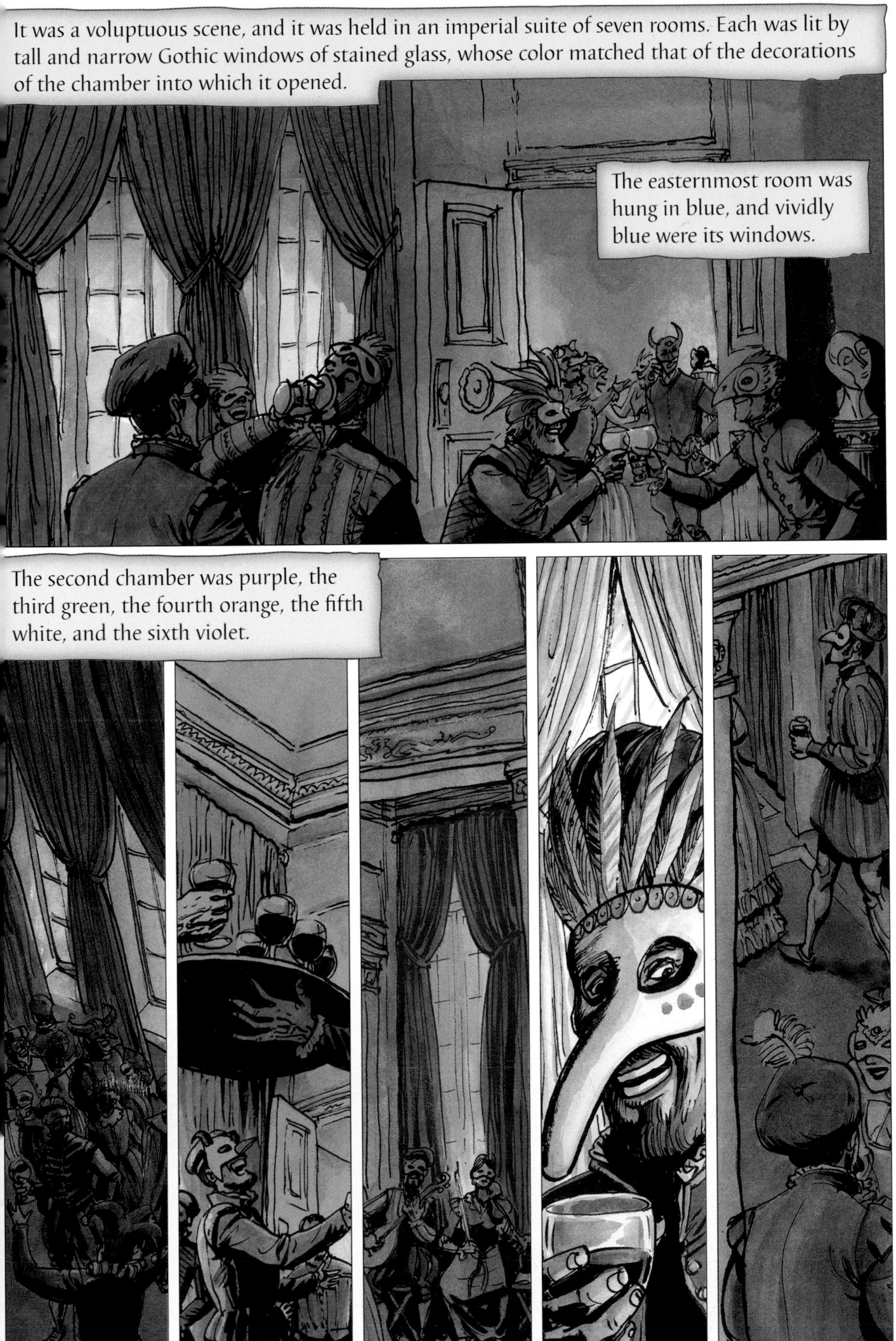
It was a voluptuous scene, and it was held in an imperial suite of seven rooms. Each was lit by tall and narrow Gothic windows of stained glass, whose color matched that of the decorations of the chamber into which it opened.
The easternmost room was hung in blue, and vividly blue were its windows.
The second chamber was purple, the third green, the fourth orange, the fifth white, and the sixth violet.

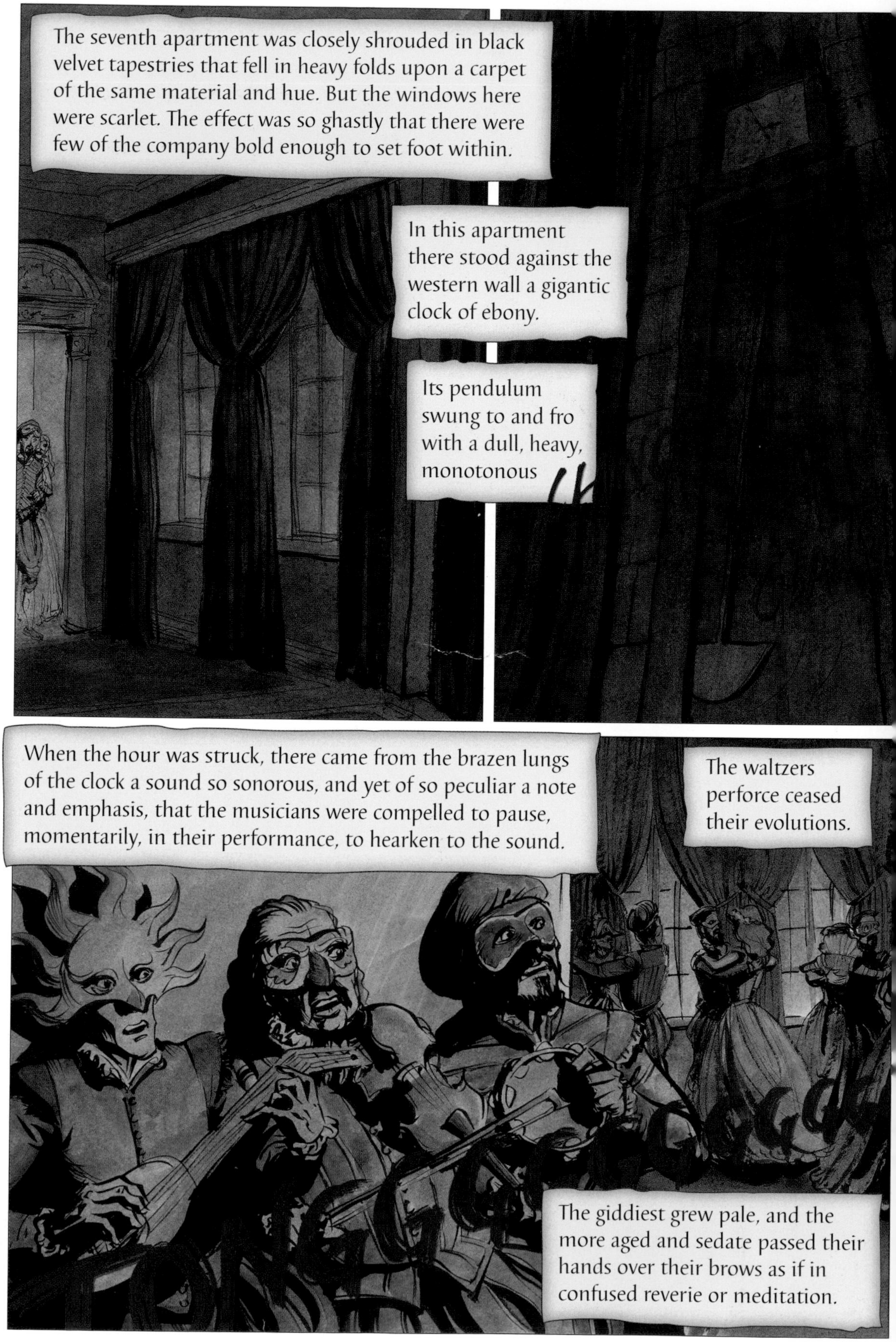
The seventh apartment was closely shrouded in black velvet tapestries that fell in heavy folds upon a carpet of the same material and hue. But the windows here were scarlet. The effect was so ghastly that there were few of the company bold enough to set foot within.
In this apartment there stood against the western wall a gigantic clock of ebony.
Its pendulum swung to and fro with a dull, heavy, monotonous
When the hour was struck, there came from the brazen lungs of the clock a sound so sonorous, and yet of so peculiar a note and emphasis, that the musicians were compelled to pause, momentarily, in their performance, to hearken to the sound.
The waltzers perforce ceased their evolutions.
The giddiest grew pale, and the more aged and sedate passed their hands over their brows as if in confused reverie or meditation.

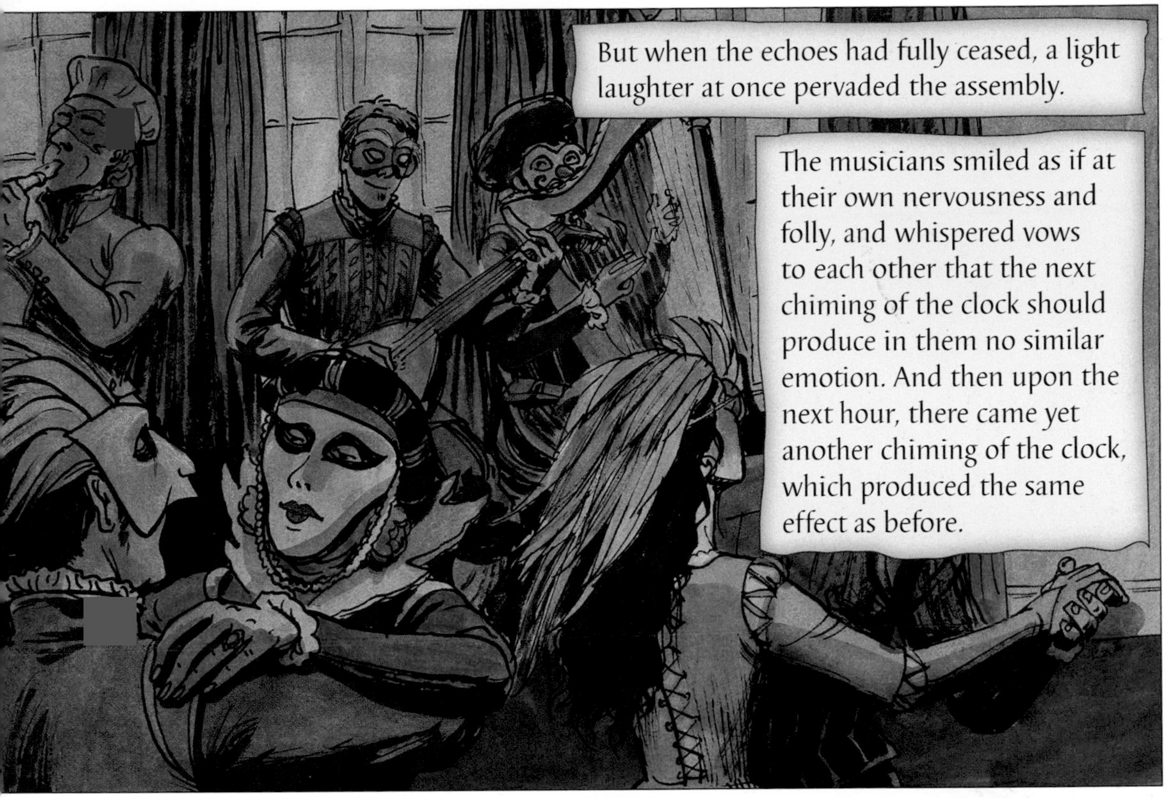
But when the echoes had fully ceased, a light laughter at once pervaded the assembly.
The musicians smiled as if at their own nervousness and folly, and whispered vows to each other that the next chiming of the clock should produce in them no similar emotion. And then upon the next hour, there came yet another chiming of the clock, which produced the same effect as before.

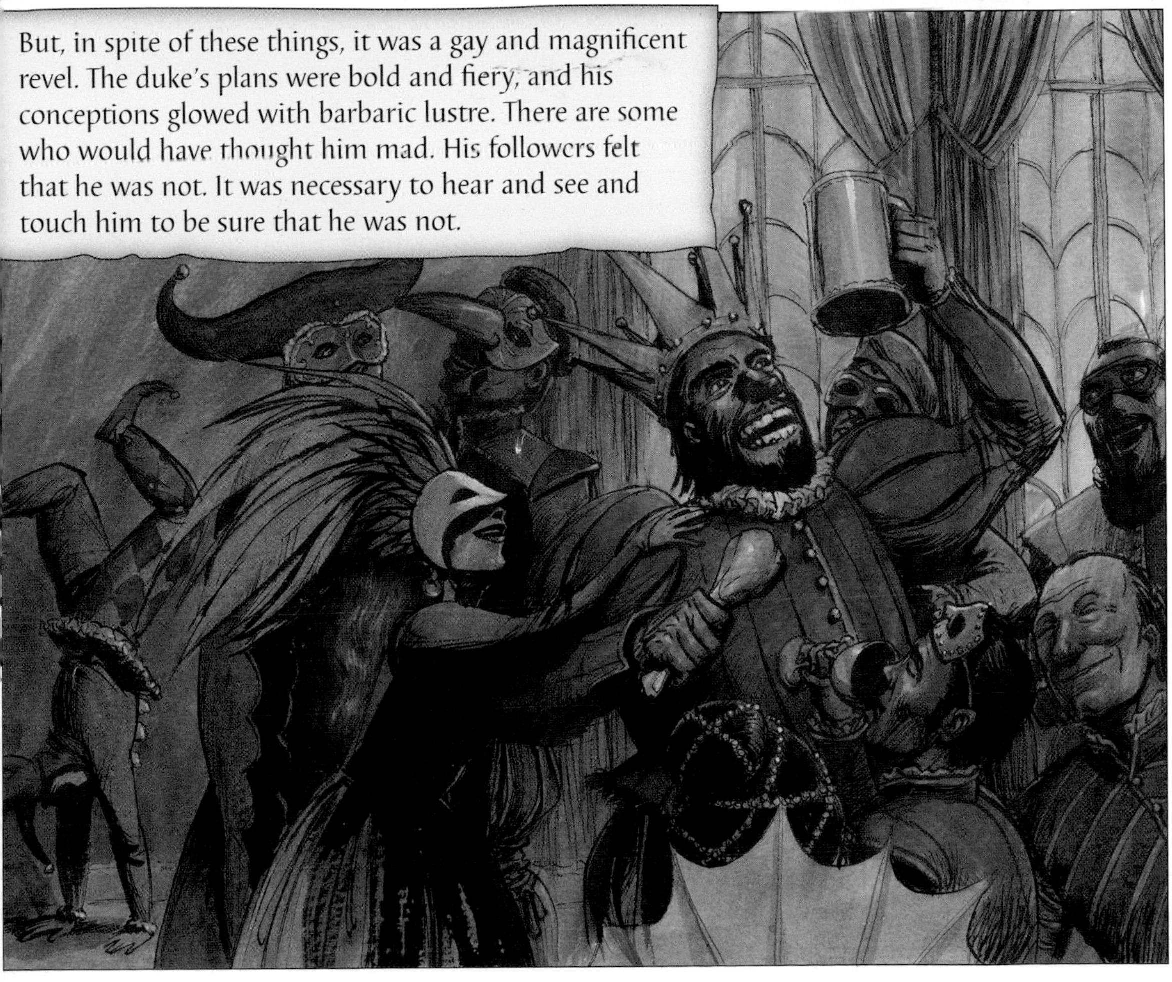
But, in spite of these things, it was a gay and magnificent revel. The duke's plans were bold and fiery, and his conceptions glowed with barbaric lustre. There are some who would have thought him mad. His followers felt that he was not. It was necessary to hear and see and touch him to be sure that he was not.

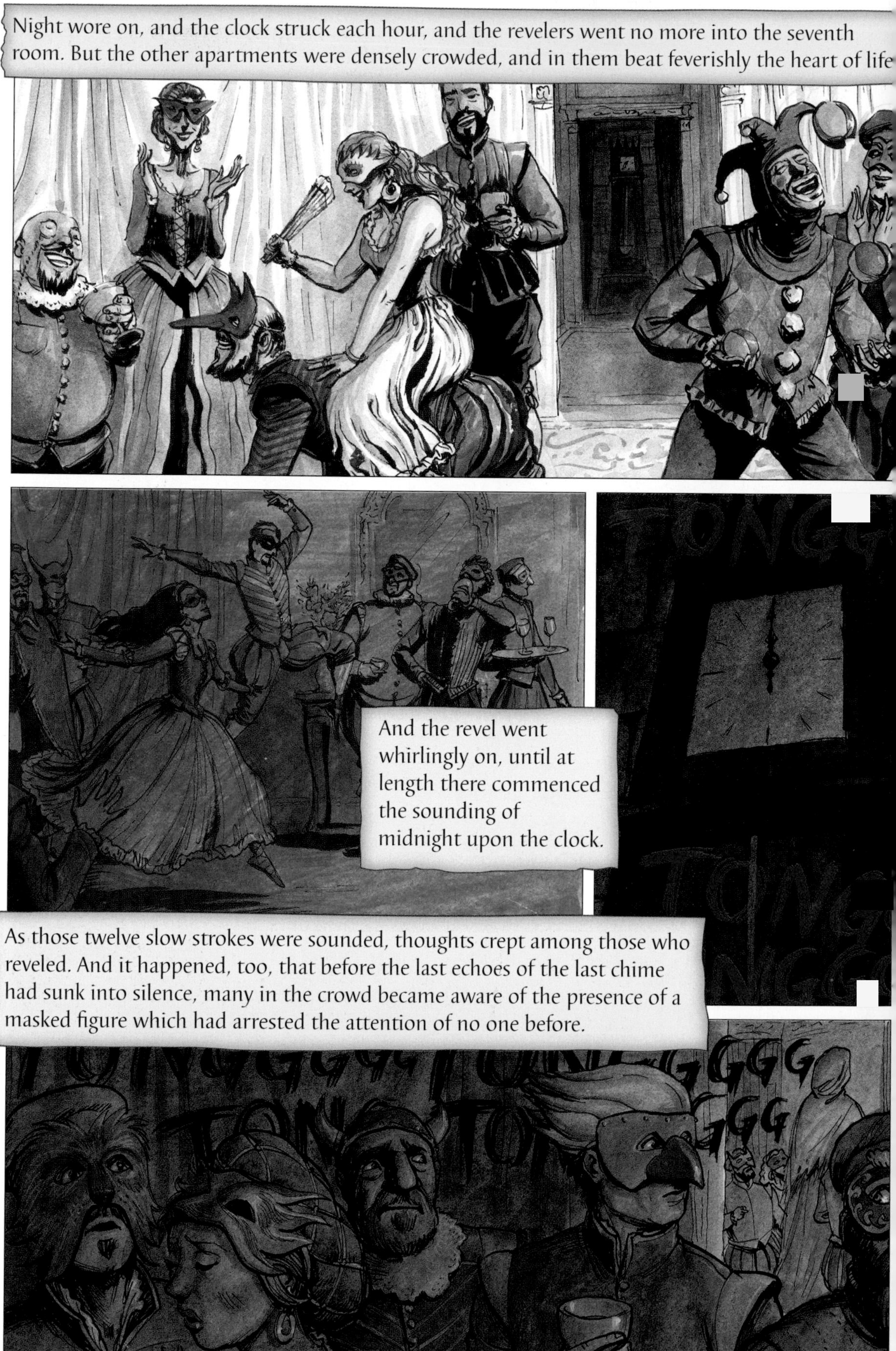
Night wore on, and the clock struck each hour, and the revelers went no more into the seventh room. But the other apartments were densely crowded, and in them beat feverishly the heart of life
And the revel went whirlingly on, until at length there commenced the sounding of midnight upon the clock.
As those twelve slow strokes were sounded, thoughts crept among those who reveled. And it happened, too, that before the last echoes of the last chime had sunk into silence, many in the crowd became aware of the presence of a masked figure which had arrested the attention of no one before.

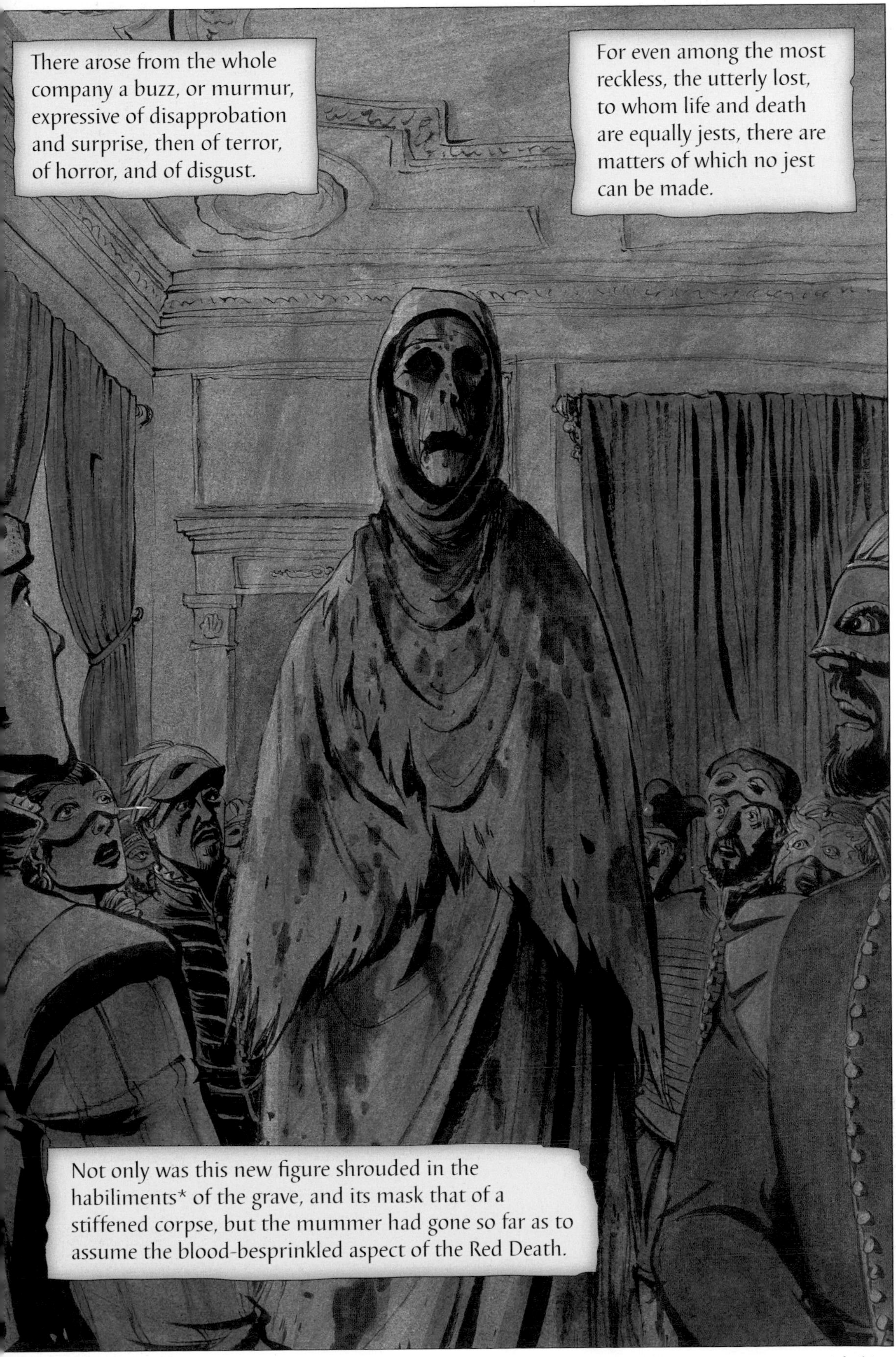
There arose from the whole company a buzz, or murmur, expressive of disapprobation and surprise, then of terror, of horror, and of disgust.
For even among the most reckless, the utterly lost, to whom life and death are equally jests, there are matters of which no jest can be made.
Not only was this new figure shrouded in the habiliments* of the grave, and its mask that of a stiffened corpse, but the mummer had gone so far as to assume the blood-besprinkled aspect of the Red Death.

*clothing

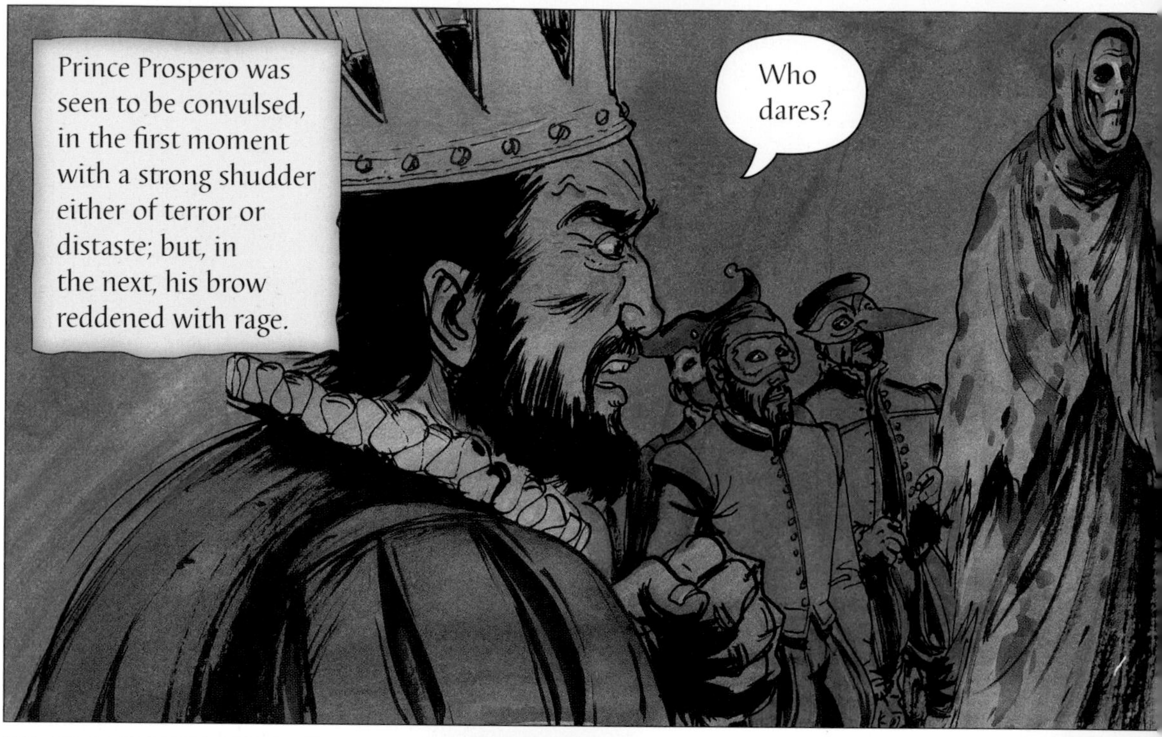
Prince Prospero was seen to be convulsed, in the first moment with a strong shudder either of terror or distaste; but, in the next, his brow reddened with rage.
Who dares?

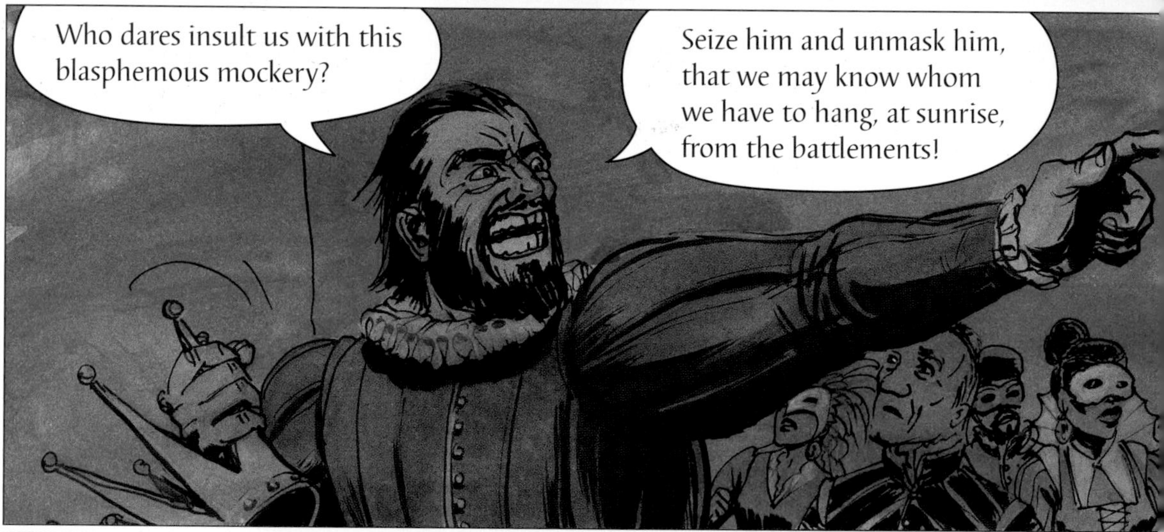
Who dares insult us with this blasphemous mockery?
Seize him and unmask him, that we may know whom we have to hang, at sunrise, from the battlements!

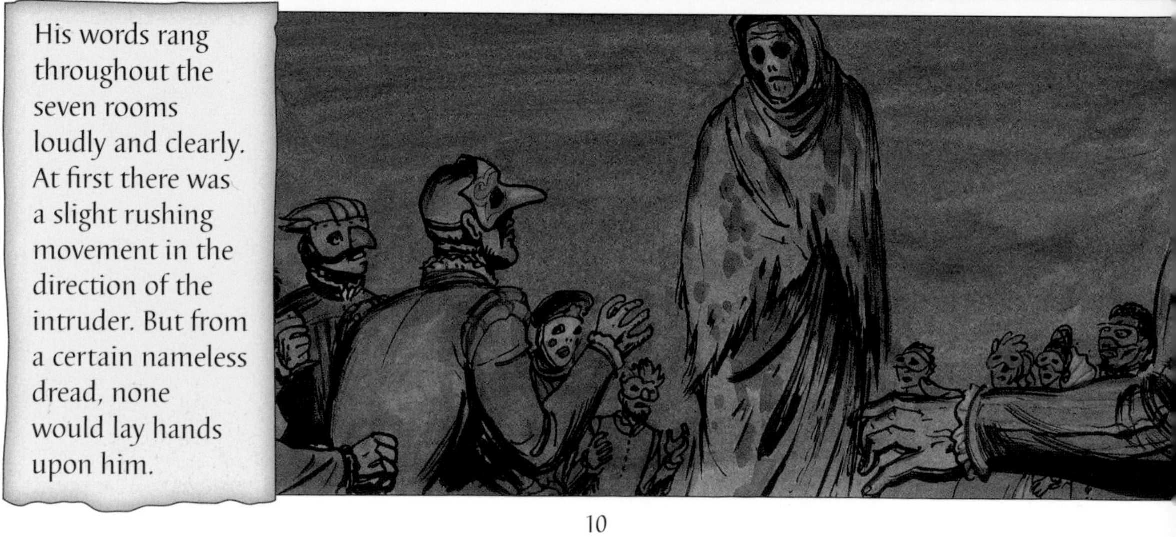
His words rang throughout the seven rooms loudly and clearly. At first there was a slight rushing movement in the direction of the intruder. But from a certain nameless dread, none would lay hands upon him.

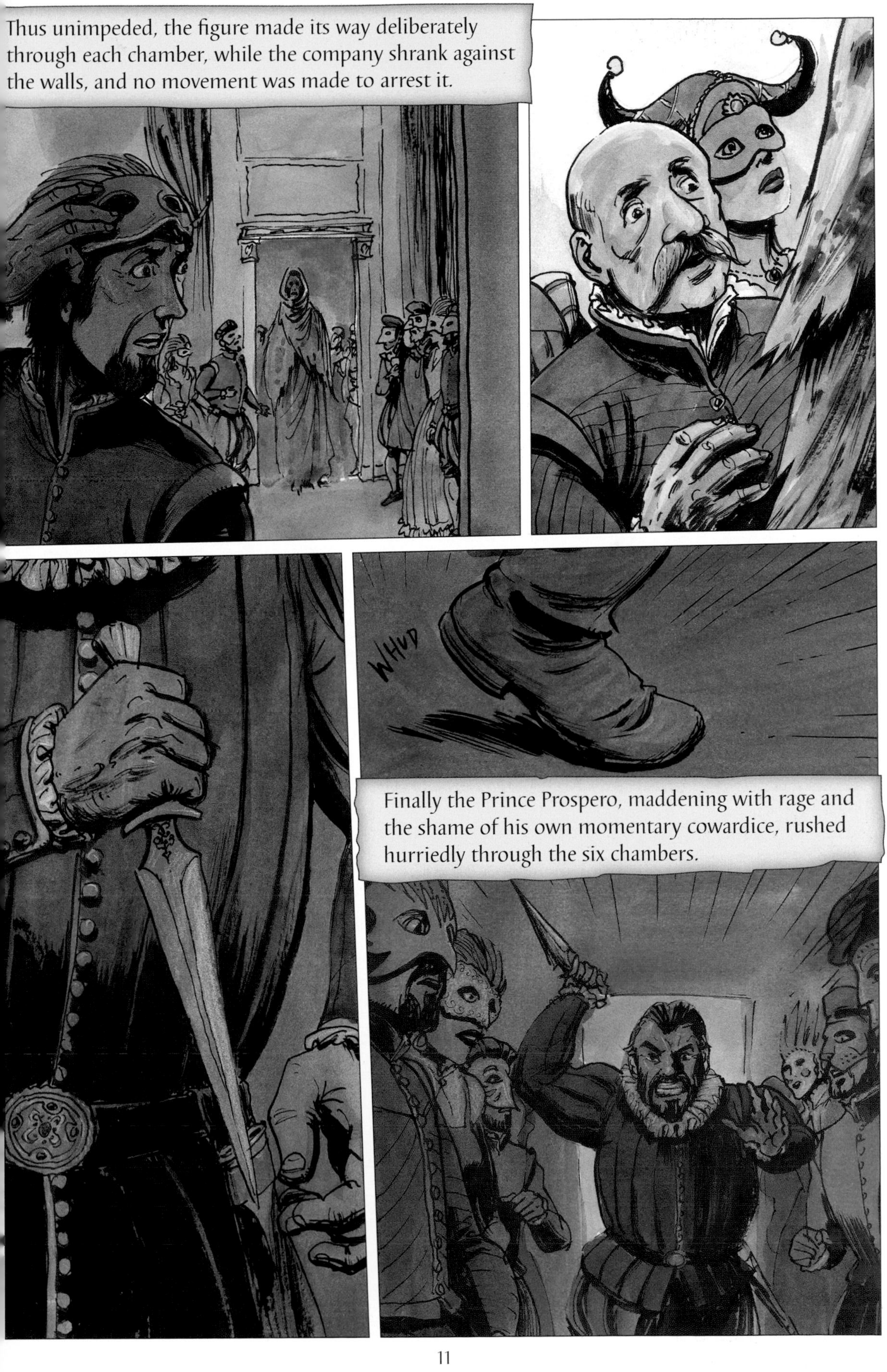
Thus unimpeded, the figure made its way deliberately through each chamber, while the company shrank against the walls, and no movement was made to arrest it.
WHUD
Finally the Prince Prospero, maddening with rage and the shame of his own momentary cowardice, rushed hurriedly through the six chambers.

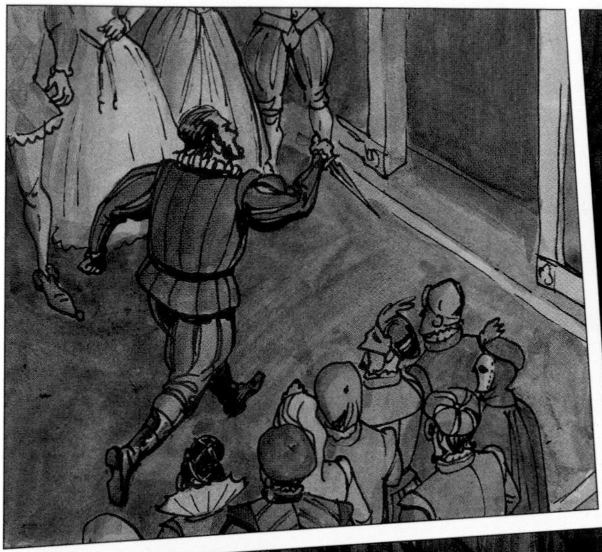

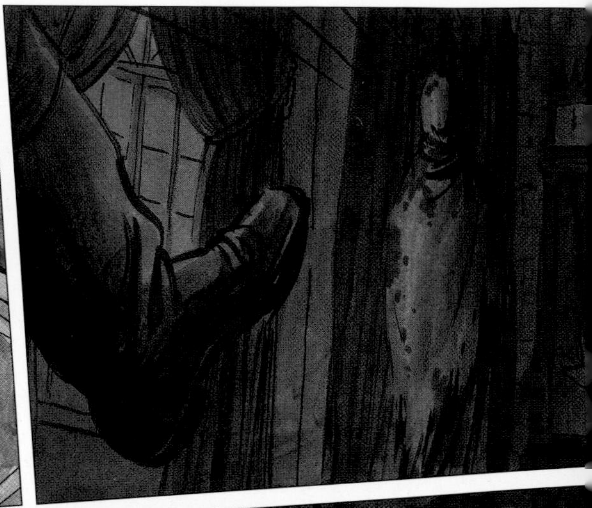

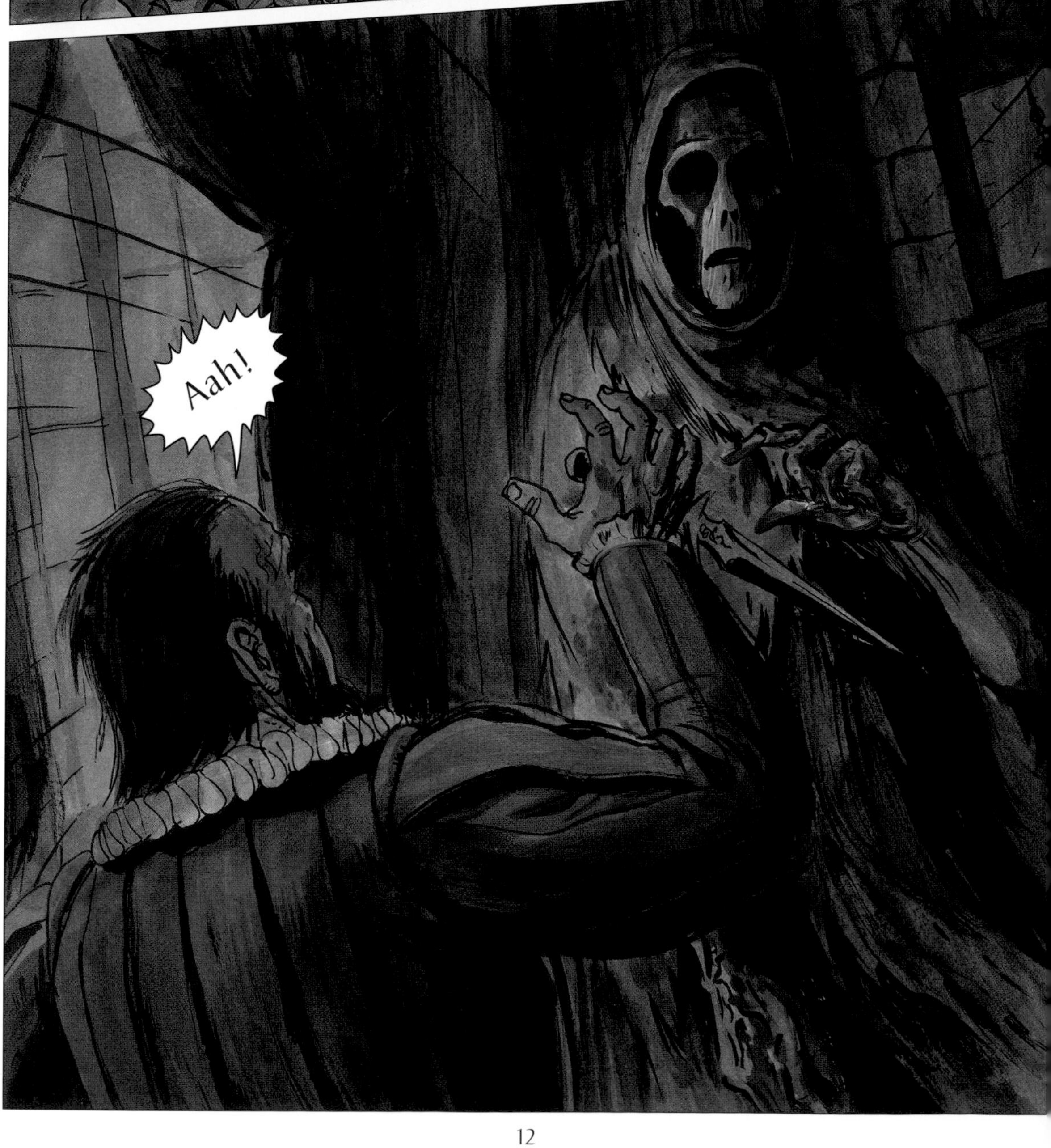
Aah!

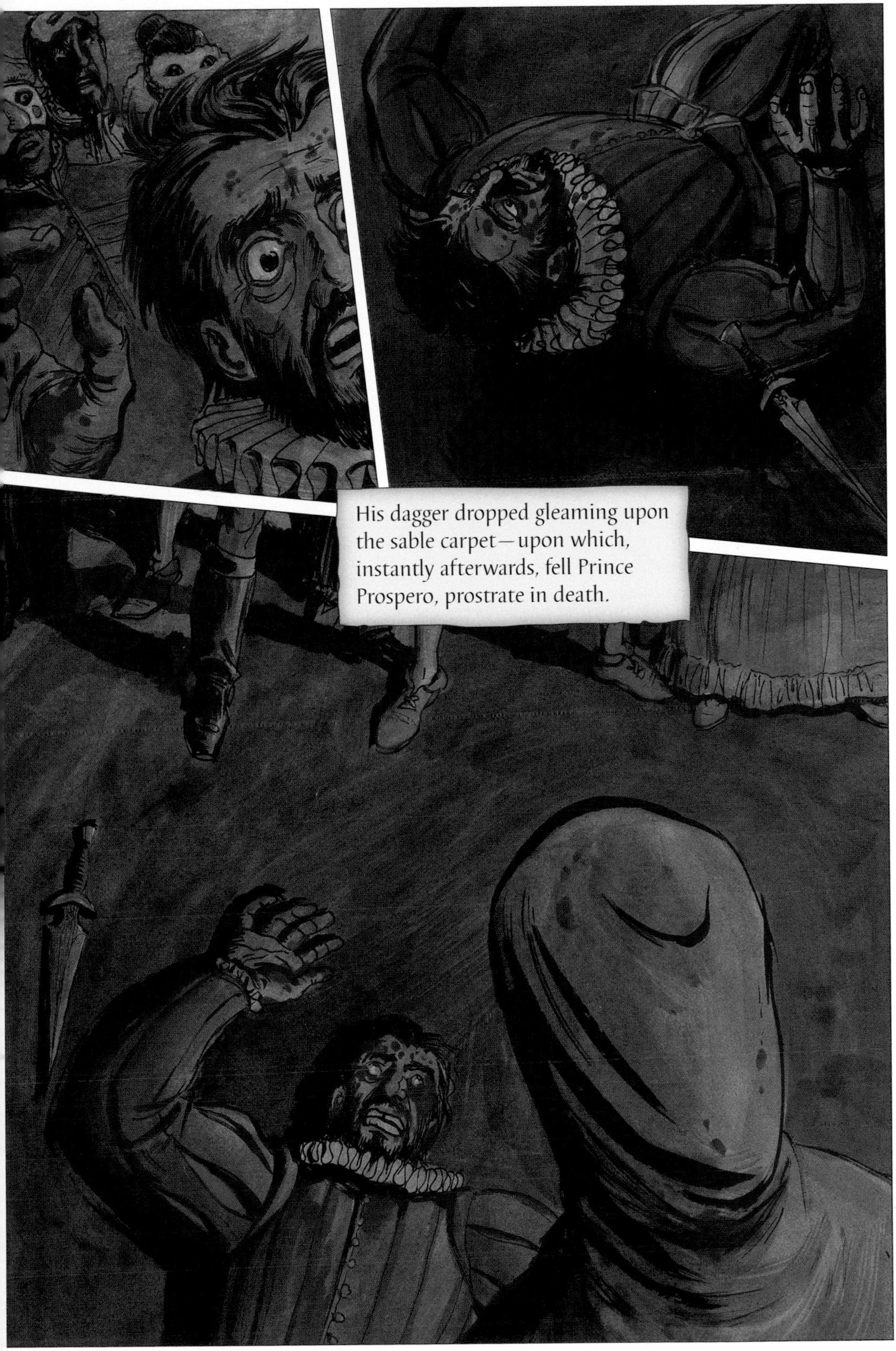
His dagger dropped gleaming upon the sable carpet—upon which, instantly afterwards, fell Prince Prospero, prostrate in death.

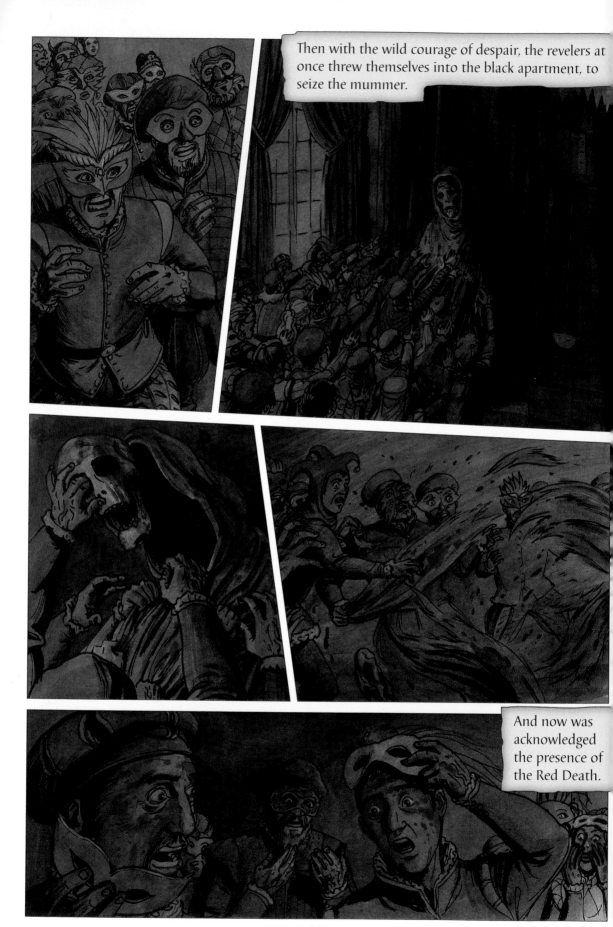

Then with the wild courage of despair, the revelers at once threw themselves into the black apartment, to seize the mummer.

And now was acknowledged the presence of the Red Death.

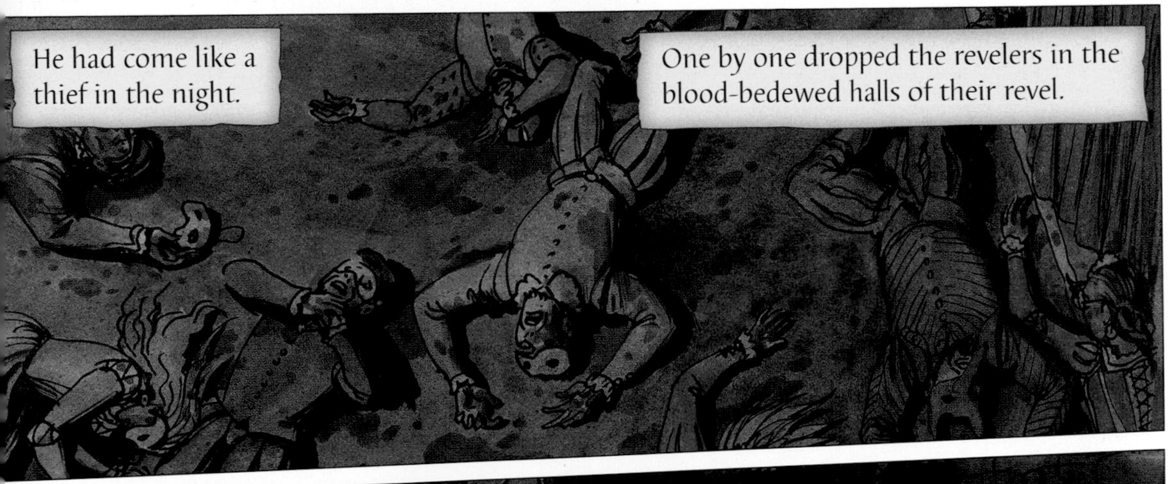
He had come like a thief in the night.
One by one dropped the revelers in the blood-bedewed halls of their revel.

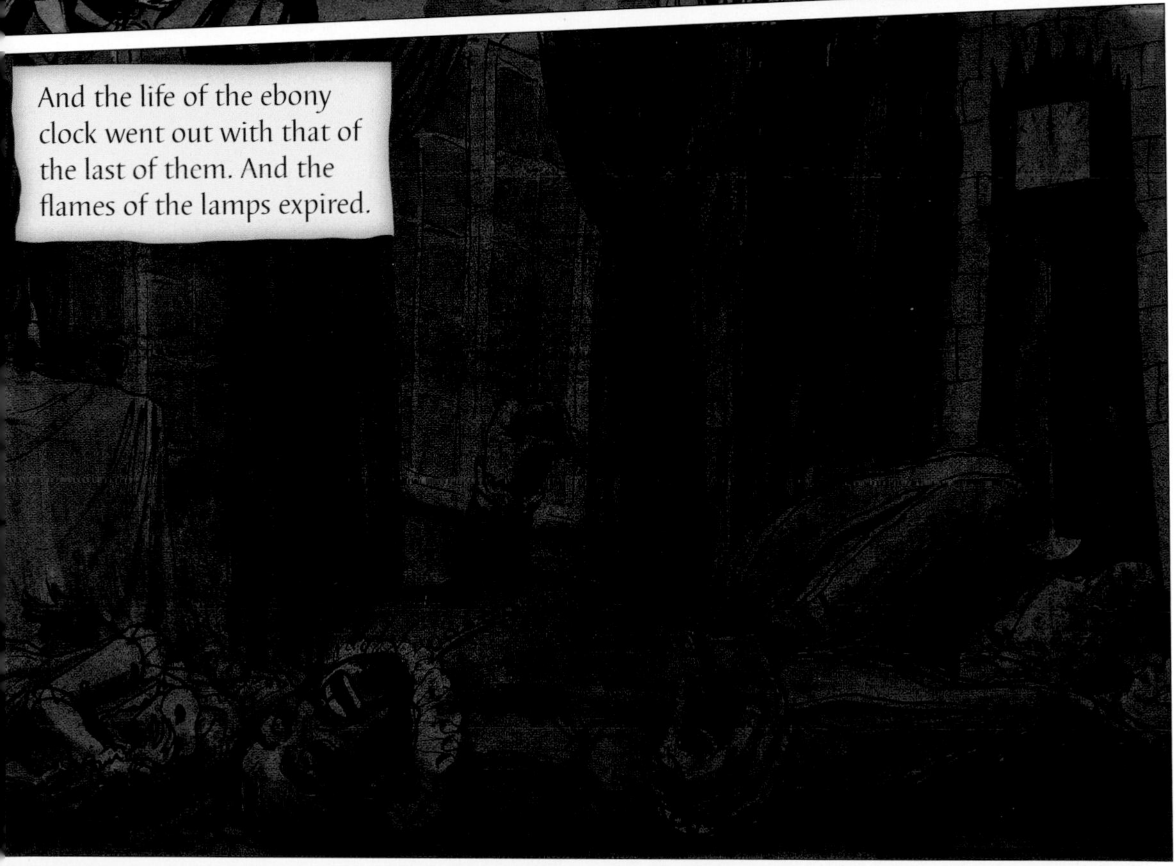
And the life of the ebony clock went out with that of the last of them. And the flames of the lamps expired.

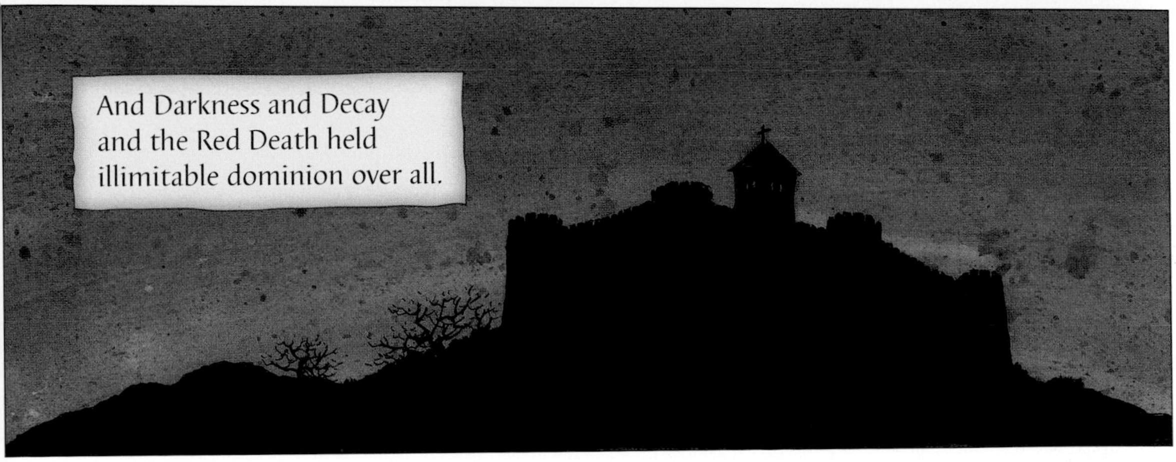
And Darkness and Decay and the Red Death held illimitable dominion over all.

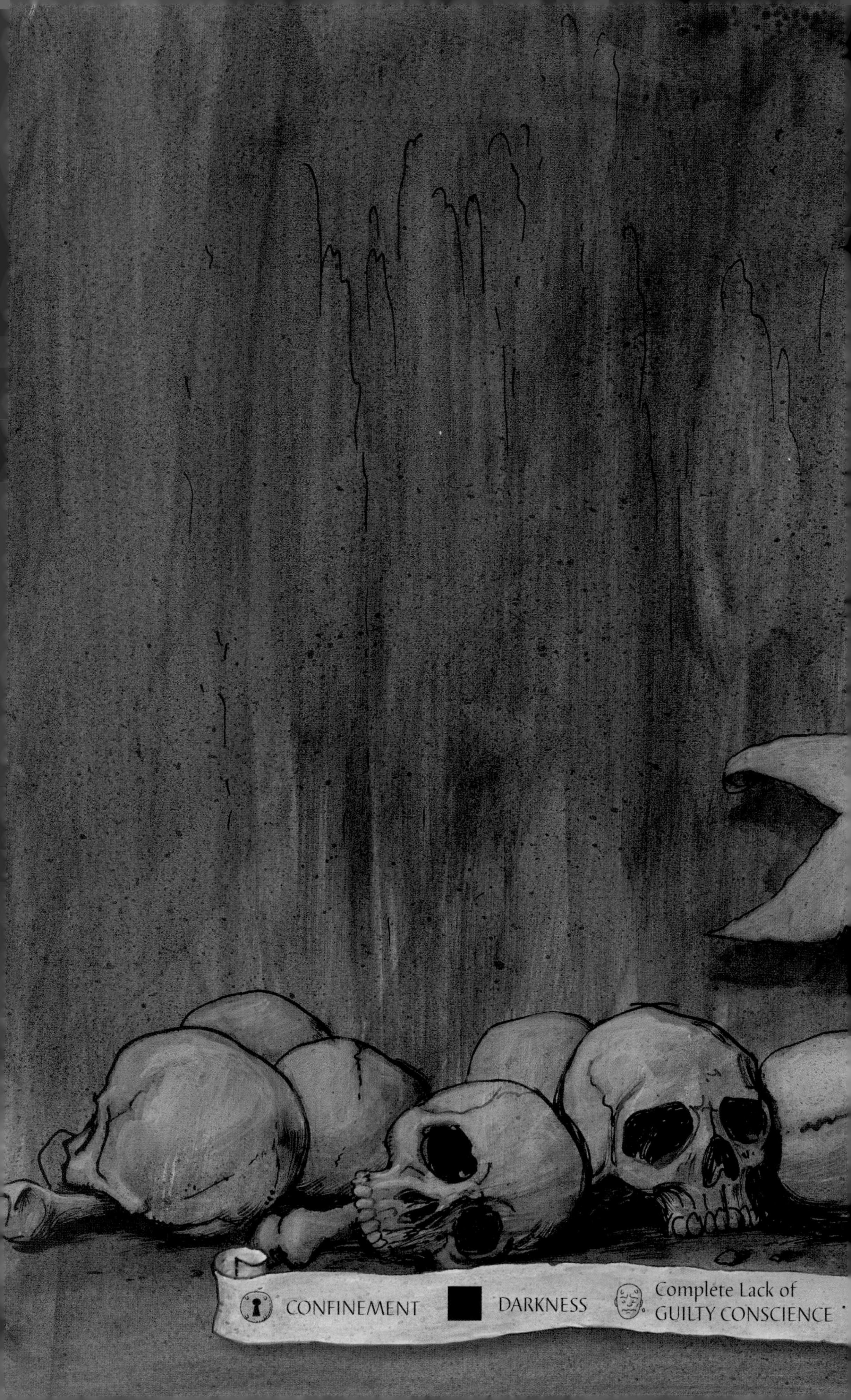
CONFINEMENT
DARKNESS
Complete Lack of GUILTY CONSCIENCE

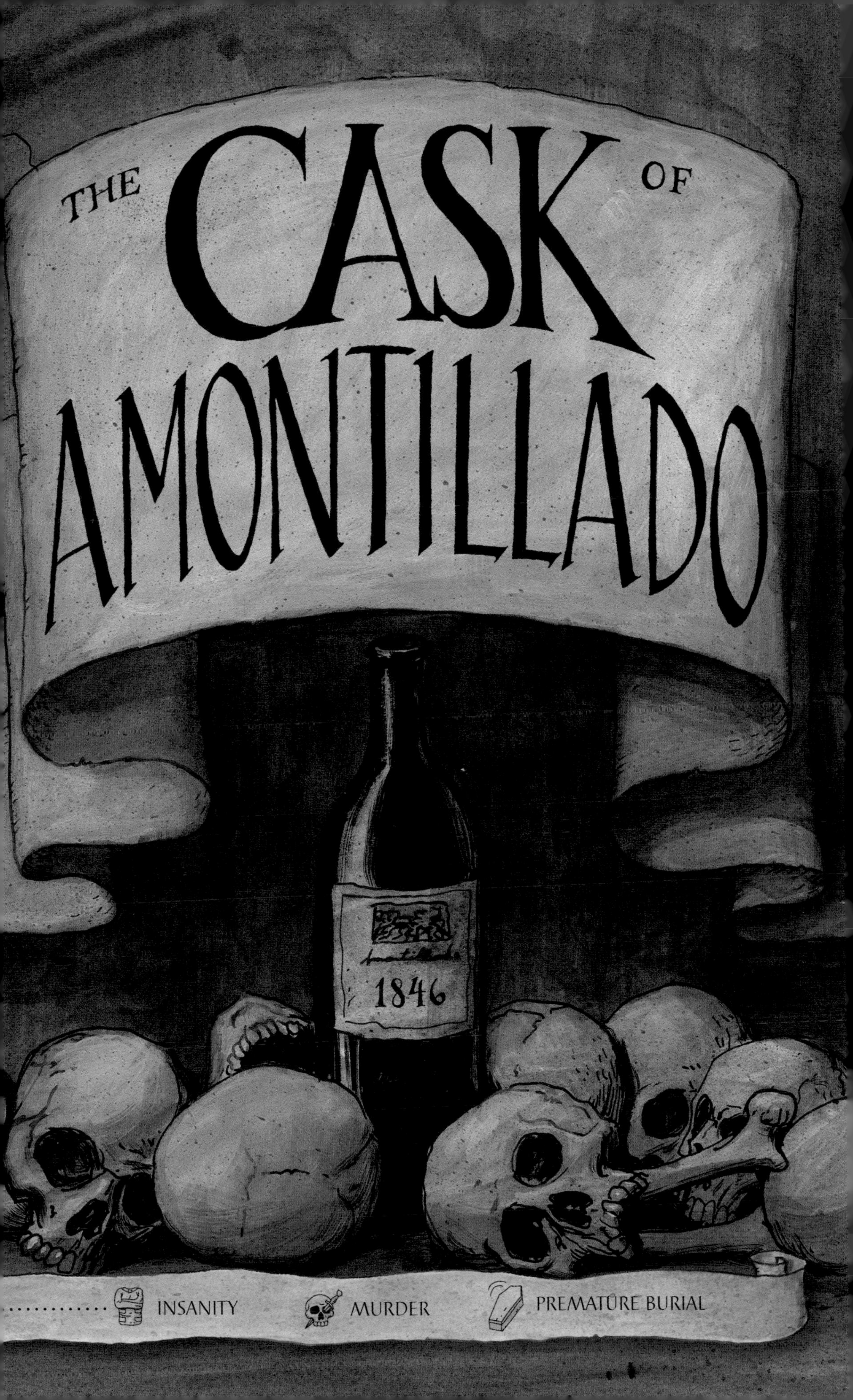
THE CASK OF AMONTILLADO
1846
INSANITY
MURDER
PREMATURE BURIAL

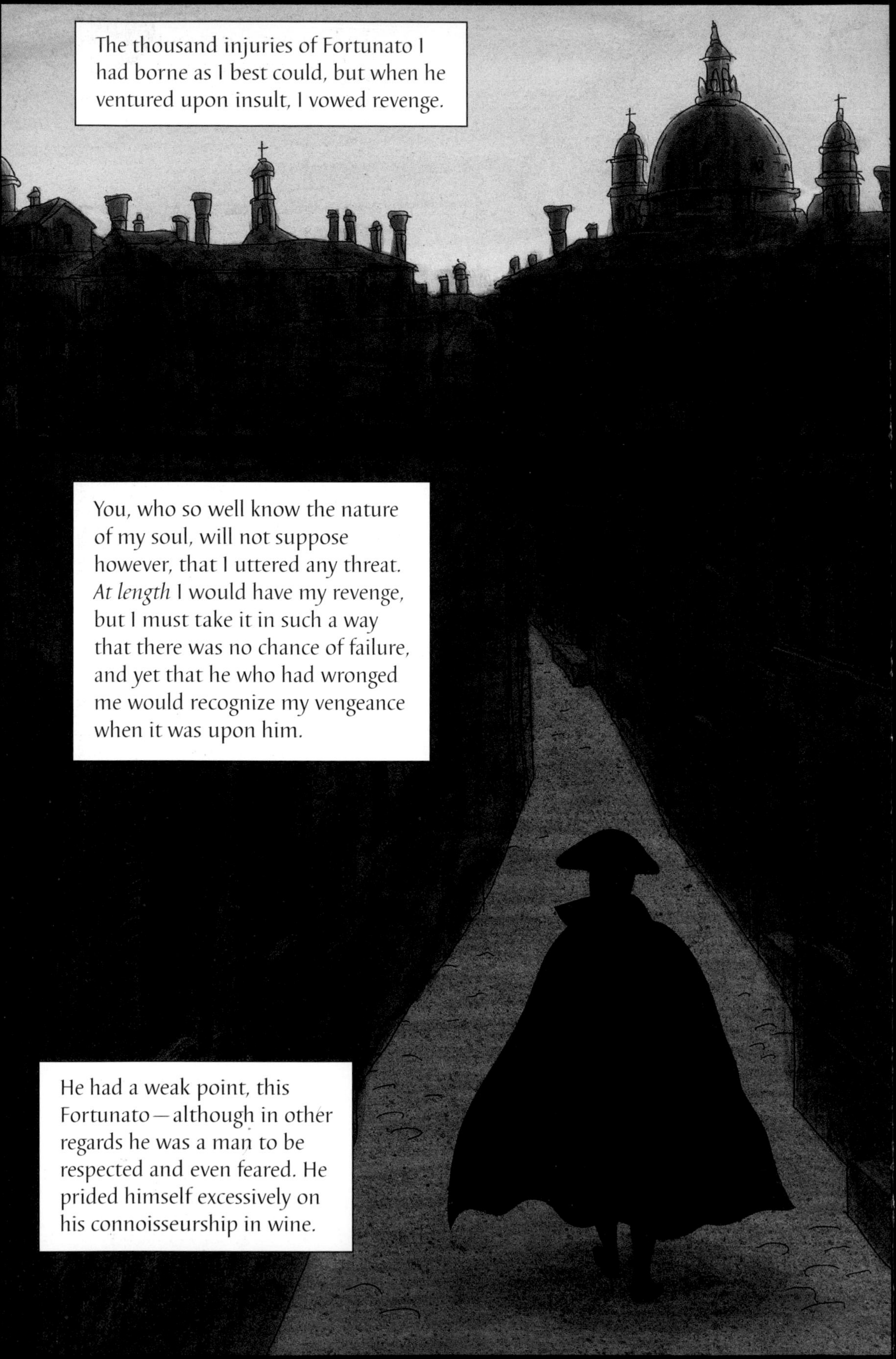
The thousand injuries of Fortunato I had borne as I best could, but when he ventured upon insult, I vowed revenge.
You, who so well know the nature of my soul, will not suppose however, that I uttered any threat. *At length* I would have my revenge, but I must take it in such a way that there was no chance of failure, and yet that he who had wronged me would recognize my vengeance when it was upon him.
He had a weak point, this Fortunato—although in other regards he was a man to be respected and even feared. He prided himself excessively on his connoisseurship in wine.

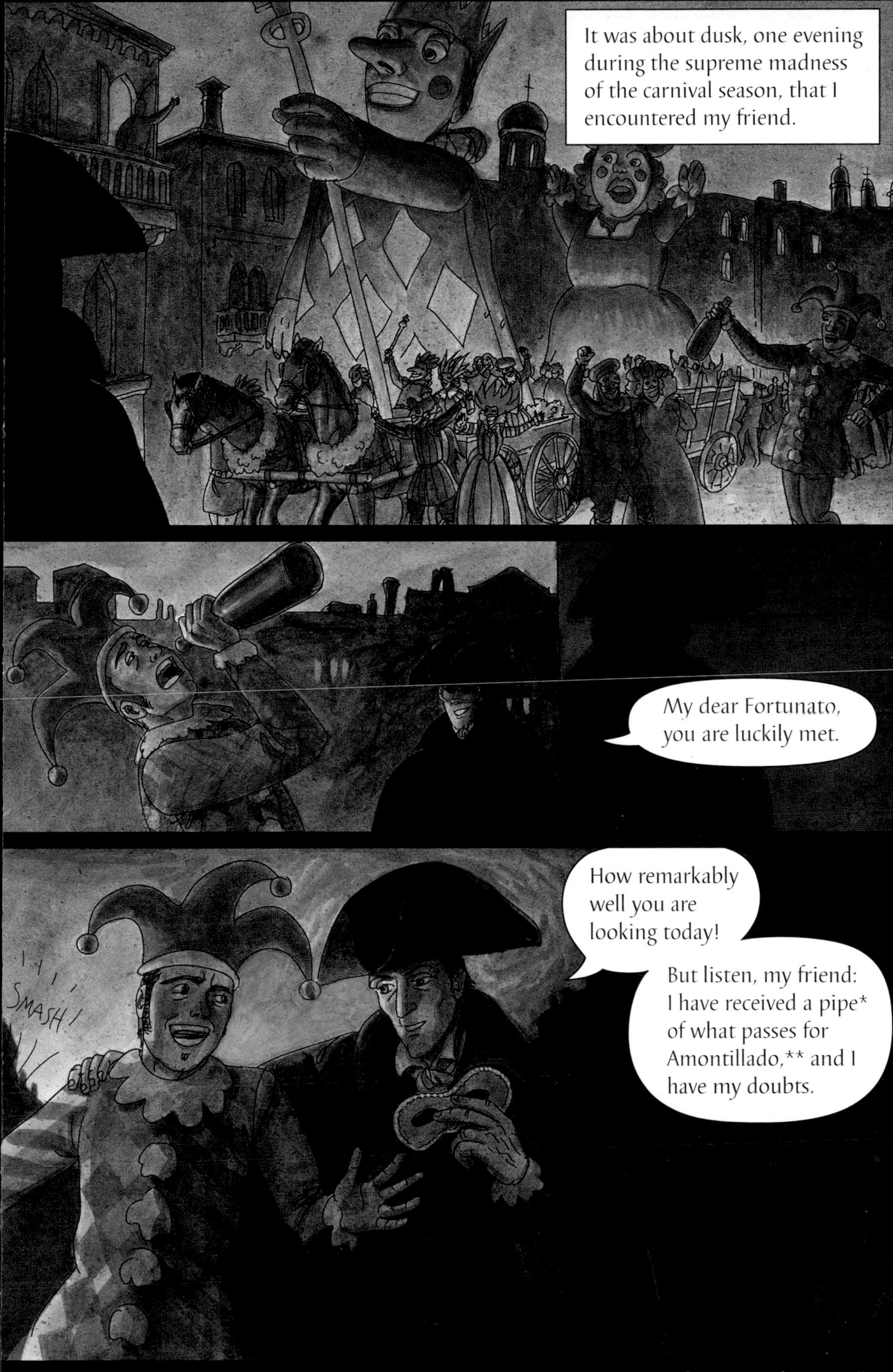
It was about dusk, one evening during the supreme madness of the carnival season, that I encountered my friend.
My dear Fortunato, you are luckily met.
How remarkably well you are looking today!
But listen, my friend: I have received a pipe* of what passes for Amontillado,** and I have my doubts.
SMASH!

*a measure of wine, more than 100 gallons.

**a type of sherry wine, named for the Montilla region of Spain.

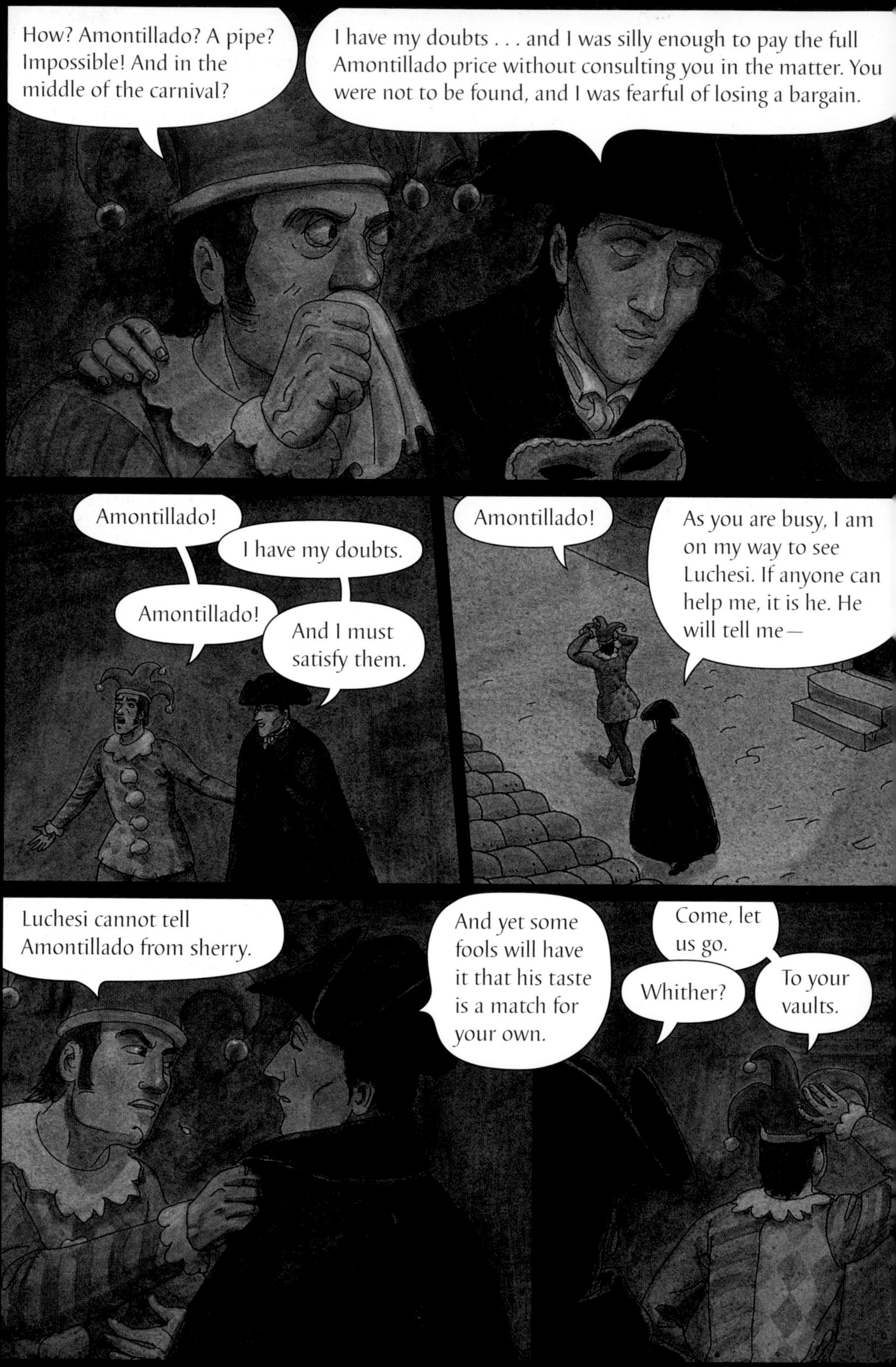
How? Amontillado? A pipe? Impossible! And in the middle of the carnival?
I have my doubts . . . and I was silly enough to pay the full Amontillado price without consulting you in the matter. You were not to be found, and I was fearful of losing a bargain.
Amontillado!
I have my doubts.
Amontillado!
And I must satisfy them.
Amontillado!
As you are busy, I am on my way to see Luchesi. If anyone can help me, it is he. He will tell me—
Luchesi cannot tell Amontillado from sherry.
And yet some fools will have it that his taste is a match for your own.
Come, let us go.
Whither?
To your vaults.

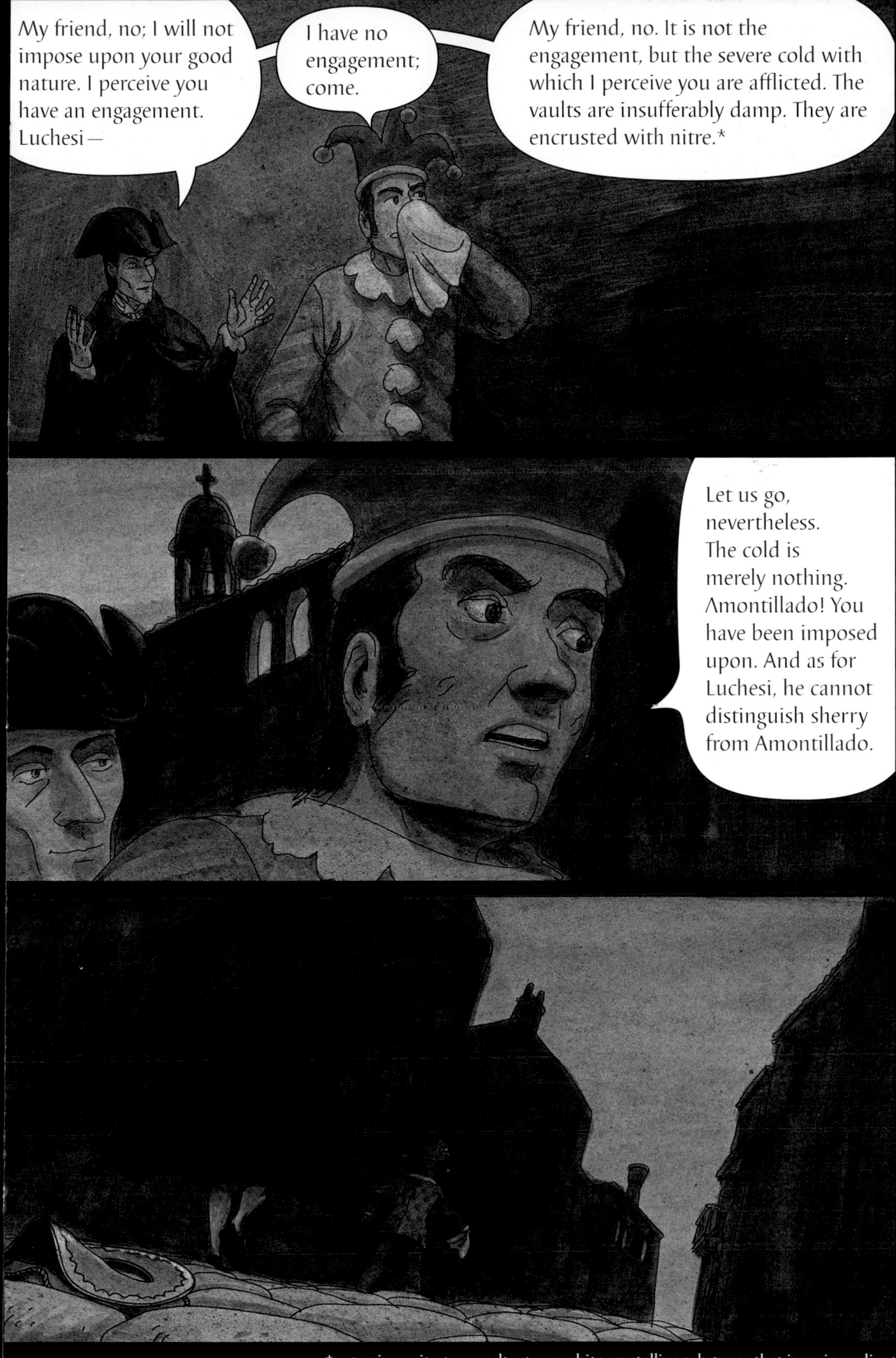
My friend, no; I will not impose upon your good nature. I perceive you have an engagement. Luchesi—
I have no engagement; come.
My friend, no. It is not the engagement, but the severe cold with which I perceive you are afflicted. The vaults are insufferably damp. They are encrusted with nitre.*
Let us go, nevertheless. The cold is merely nothing. Amontillado! You have been imposed upon. And as for Luchesi, he cannot distinguish sherry from Amontillado.

*potassium nitrate, or saltpeter, a white crystalline substance that is an ingredient in gunpowder—and to which it is implied that Fortunato is allergic

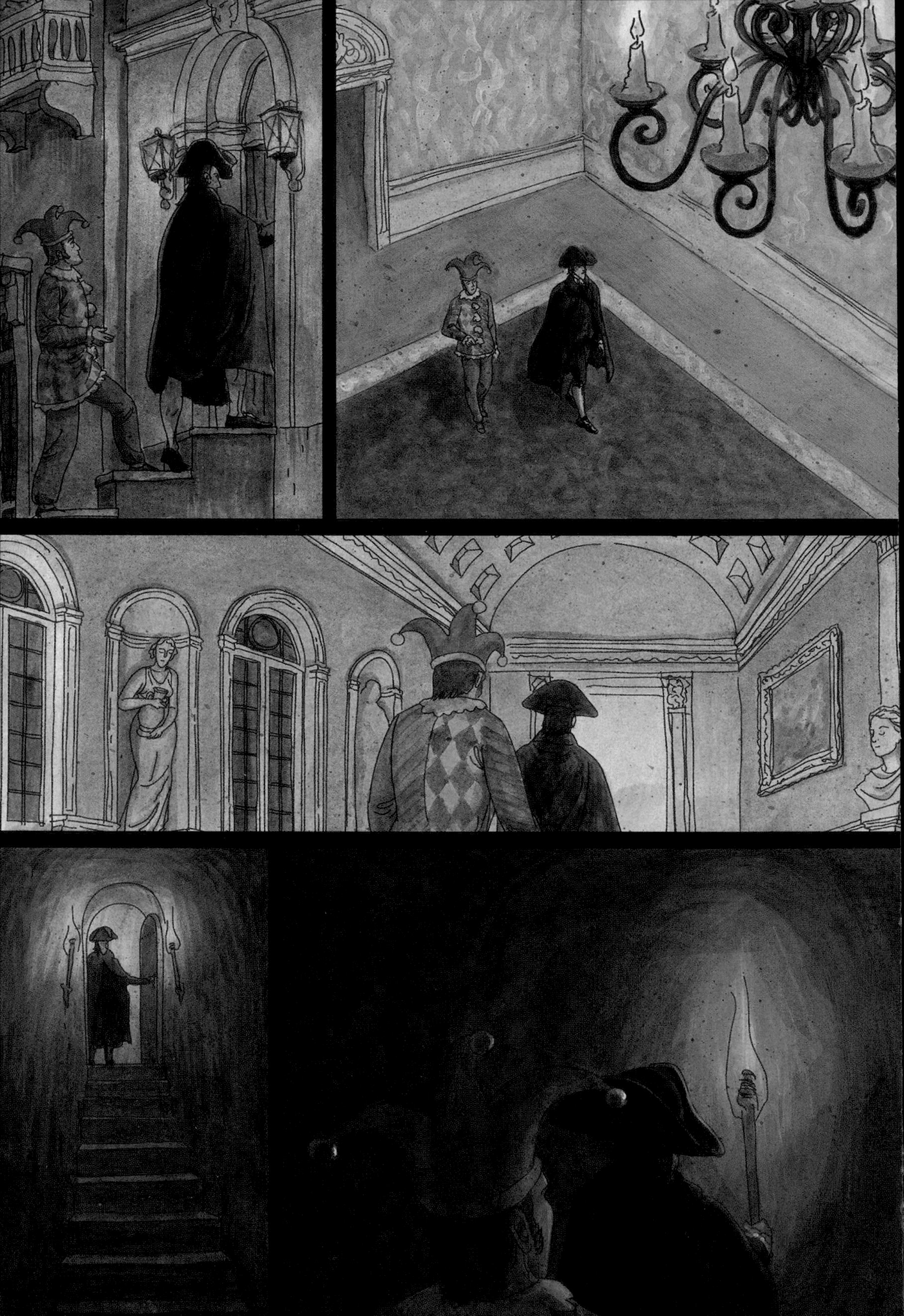

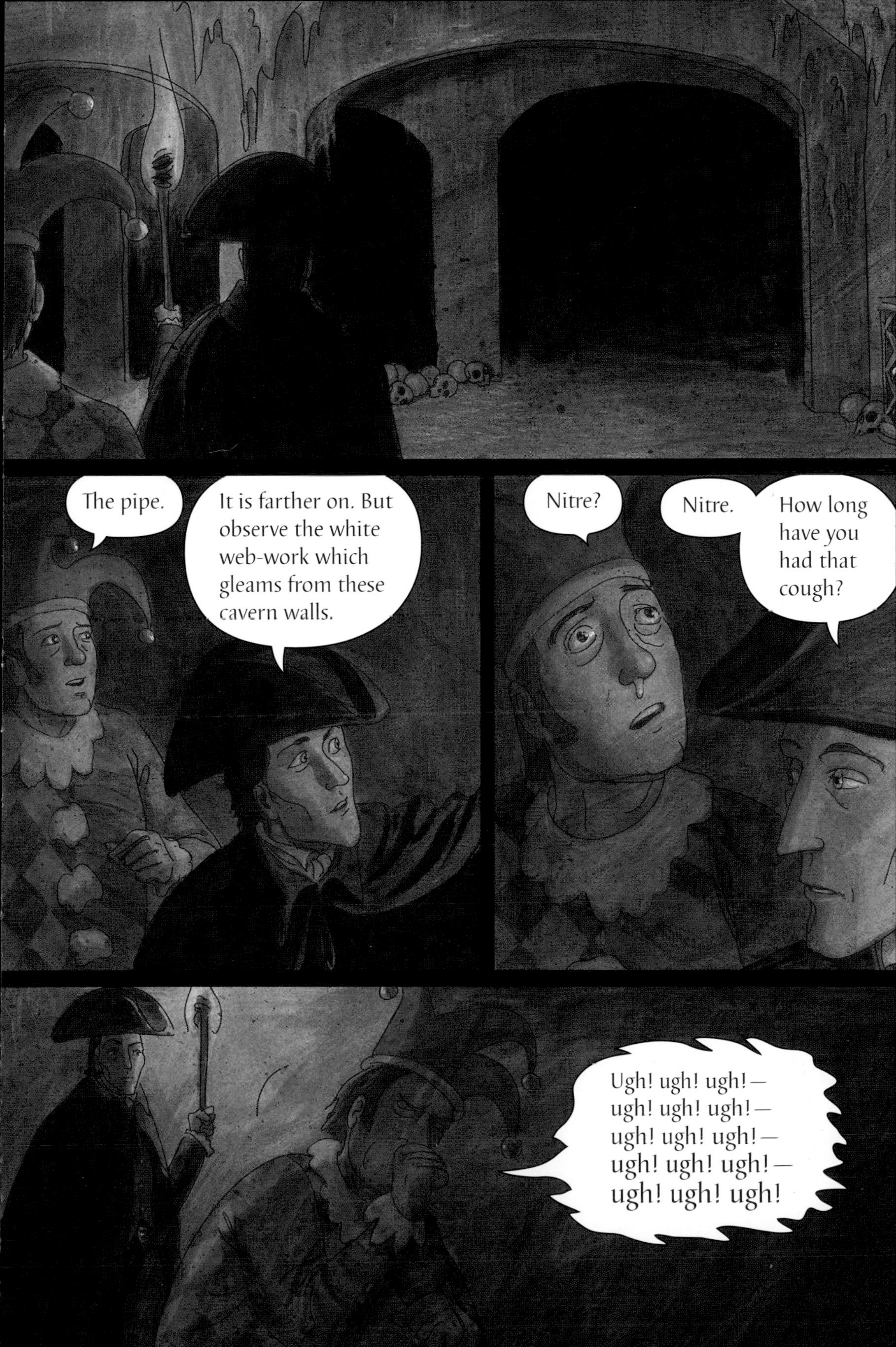
The pipe.
It is farther on. But observe the white web-work which gleams from these cavern walls.
Nitre?
Nitre.
How long have you had that cough?
Ugh! ugh! ugh!— ugh! ugh! ugh!— ugh! ugh! ugh!— ugh! ugh! ugh!— ugh! ugh! ugh!

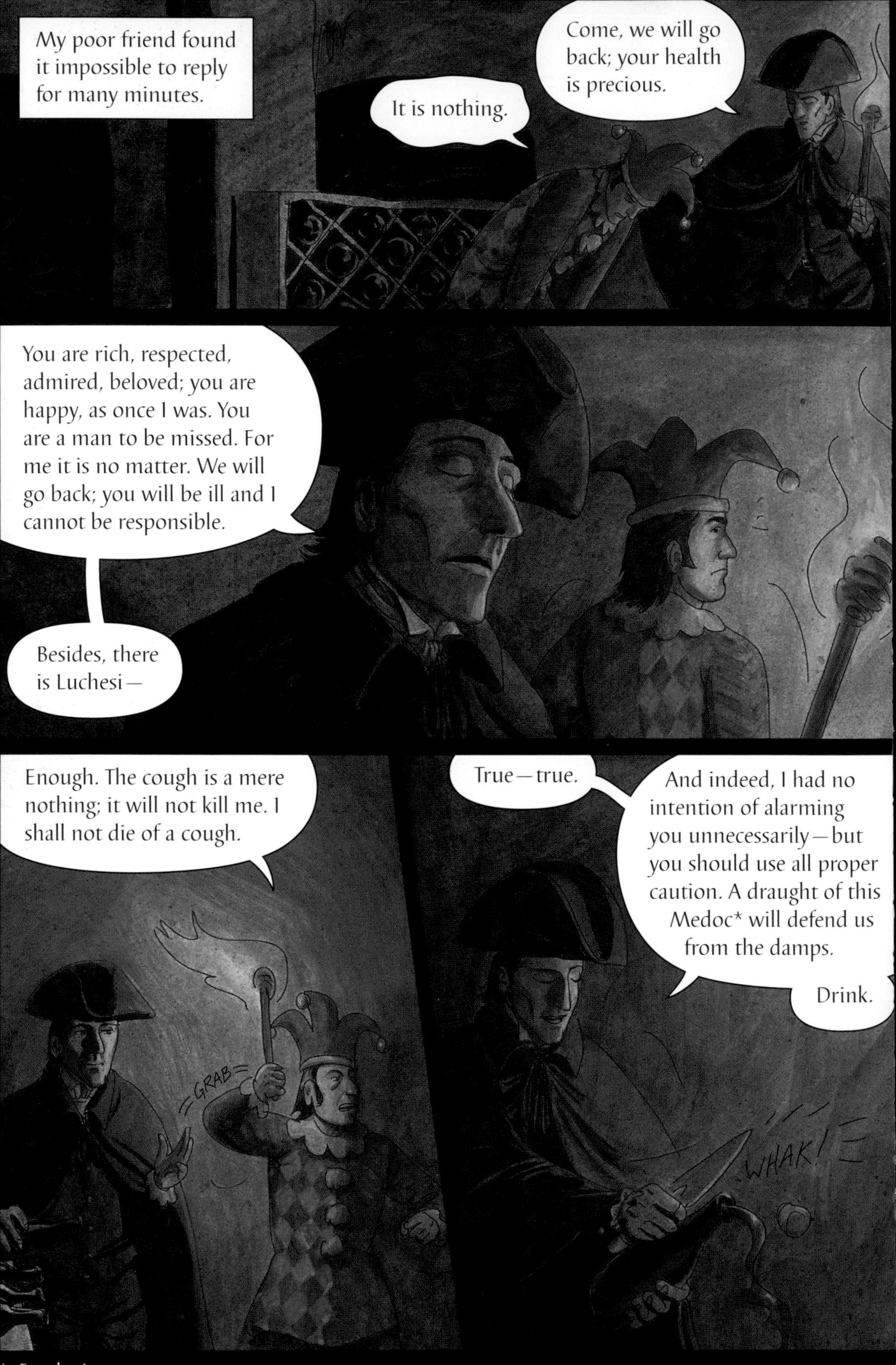
My poor friend found it impossible to reply for many minutes.
It is nothing.
Come, we will go back; your health is precious.
You are rich, respected, admired, beloved; you are happy, as once I was. You are a man to be missed. For me it is no matter. We will go back; you will be ill and I cannot be responsible.
Besides, there is Luchesi—
Enough. The cough is a mere nothing; it will not kill me. I shall not die of a cough.
GRAB
True—true.
And indeed, I had no intention of alarming you unnecessarily—but you should use all proper caution. A draught of this Medoc* will defend us from the damps.
Drink.
WHAK!

*a French wine

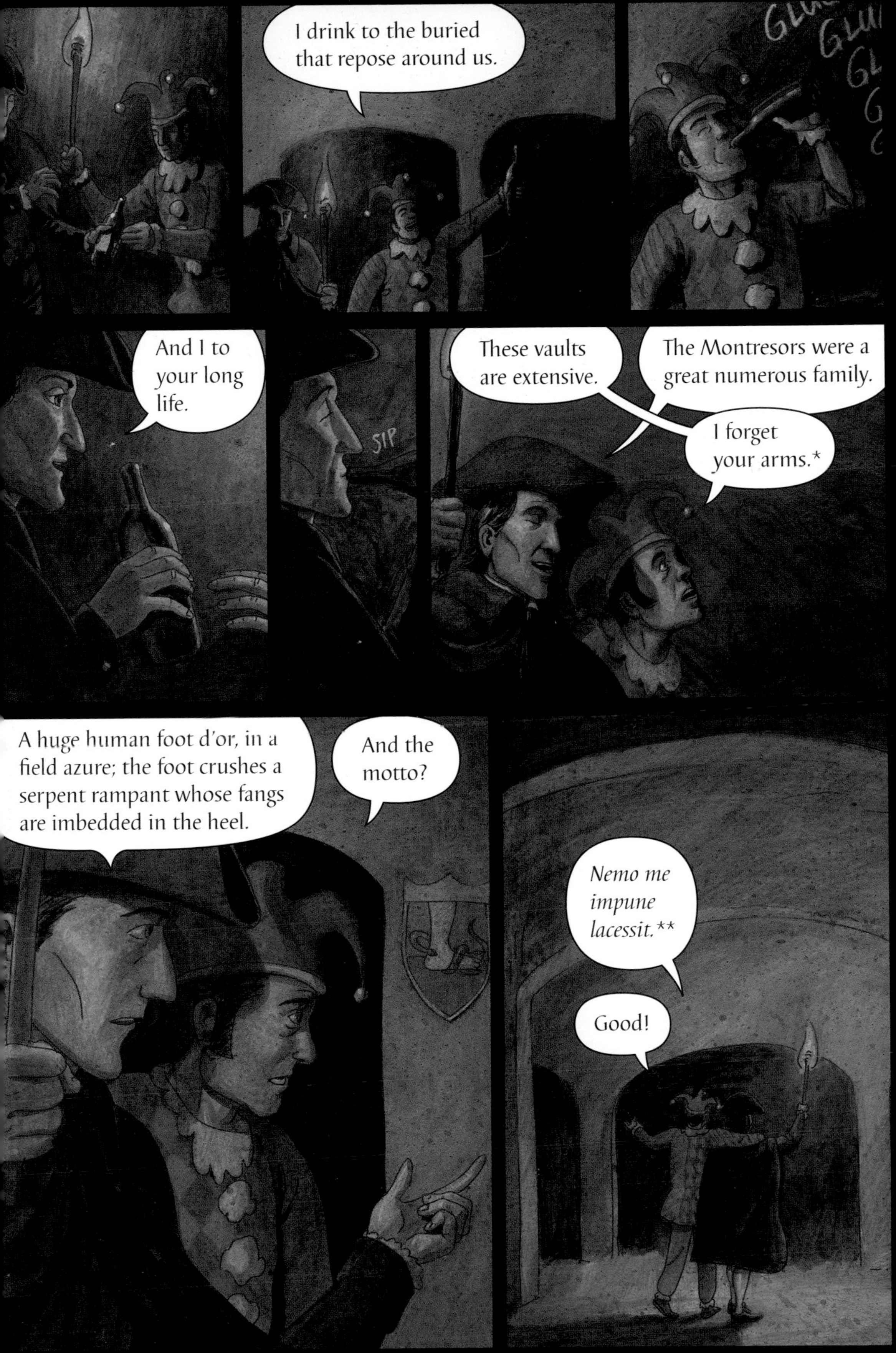
I drink to the buried that repose around us.
And I to your long life.
SIP
These vaults are extensive.
The Montresors were a great numerous family.
I forget your arms.*
A huge human foot d'or, in a field azure; the foot crushes a serpent rampant whose fangs are imbedded in the heel.
And the motto?
*Nemo me impune lacessit.***
Good!

*noble families were distinguished by their coat of arms, a symbolic image drawn on a shield.

**"No one attacks me with impunity."

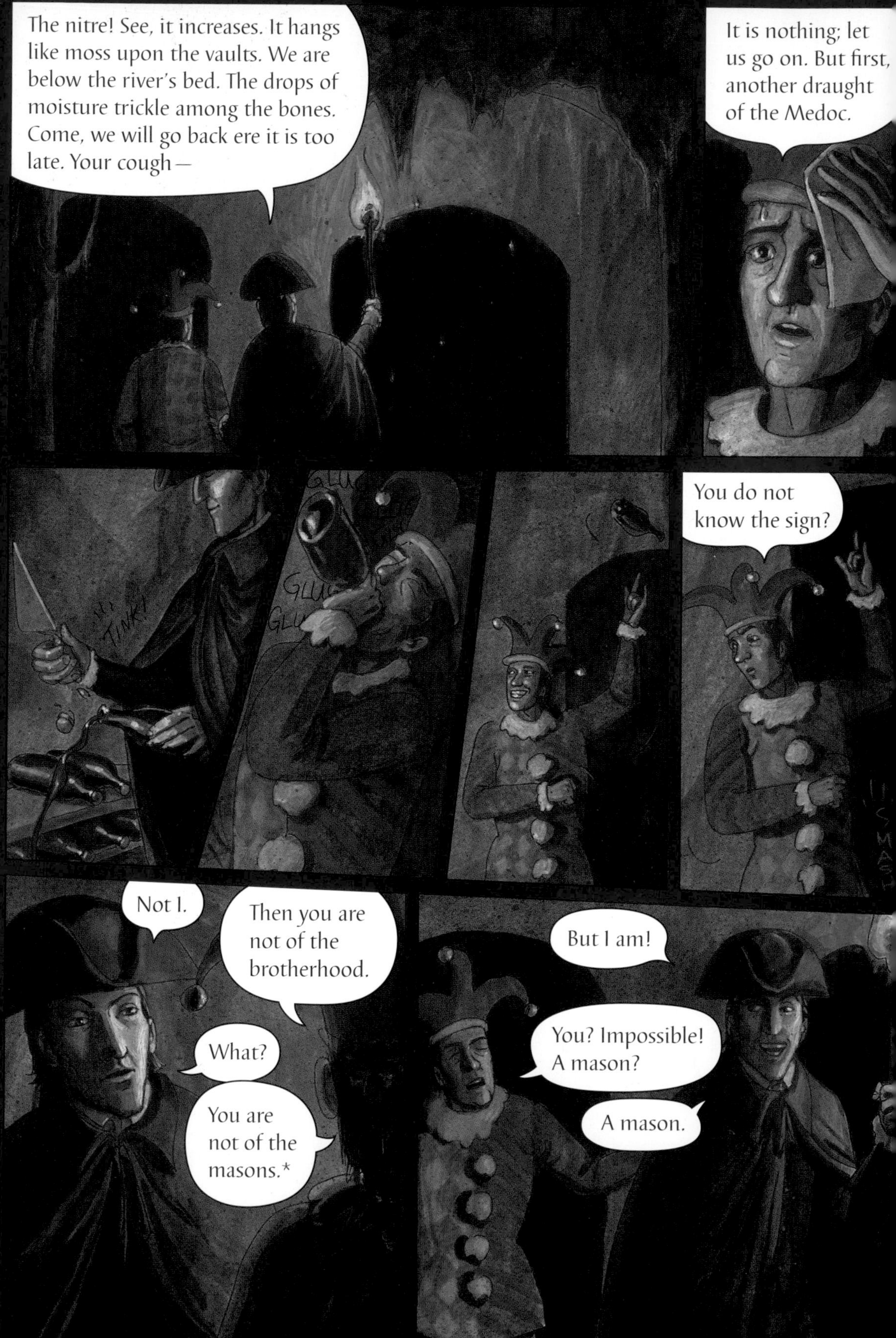
The nitre! See, it increases. It hangs like moss upon the vaults. We are below the river's bed. The drops of moisture trickle among the bones. Come, we will go back ere it is too late. Your cough—
It is nothing; let us go on. But first, another draught of the Medoc.
You do not know the sign?
Not I.
Then you are not of the brotherhood.
What?
You are not of the masons.*
But I am!
You? Impossible! A mason?
A mason.

*the Freemasons, a secret society that grew from small guilds of professional stonemasons into a worldwide social organization

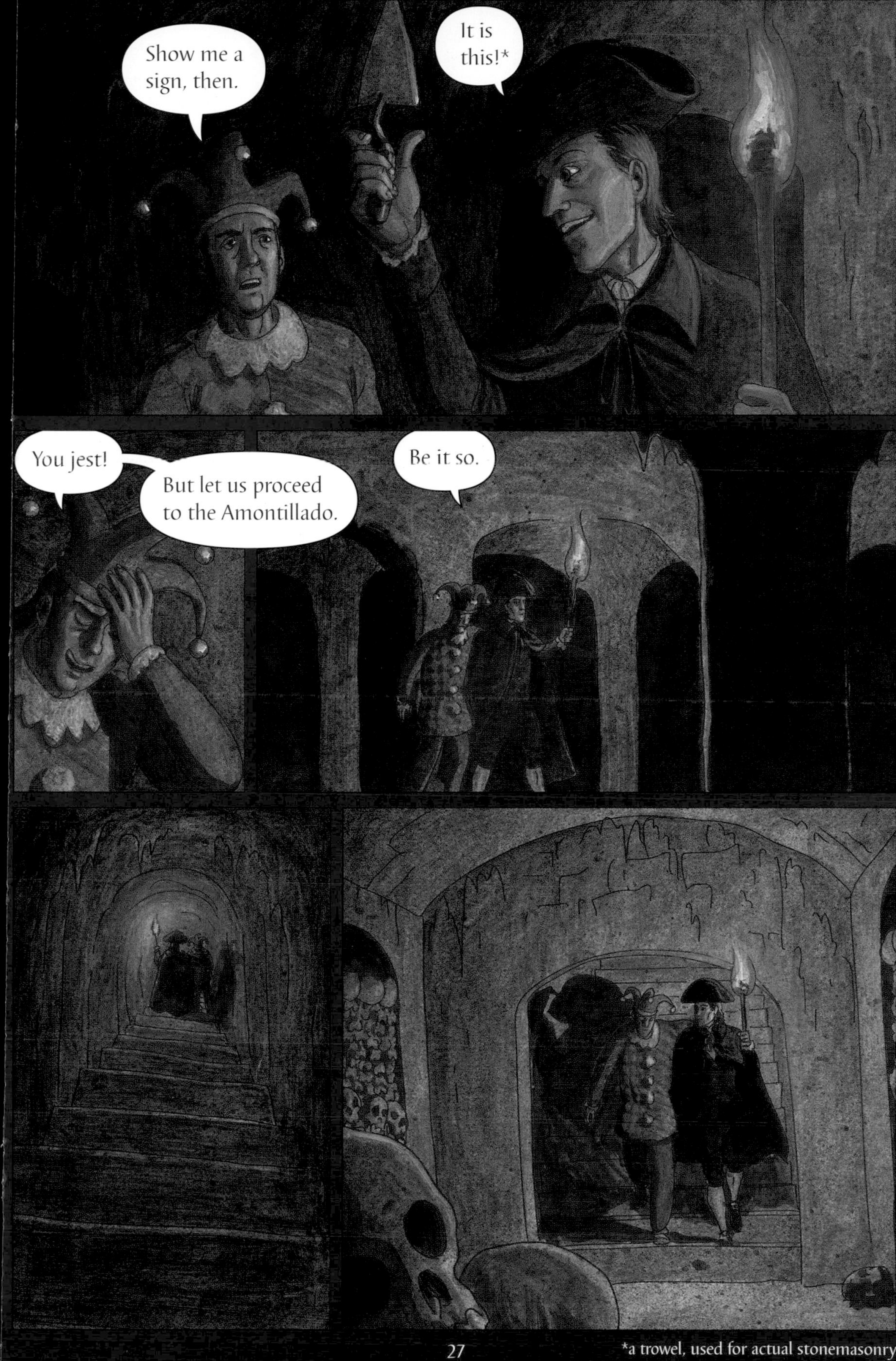
Show me a sign, then.
It is this!*
You jest!
But let us proceed to the Amontillado.
Be it so.

*a trowel, used for actual stonemasonry (laying bricks and stonework)

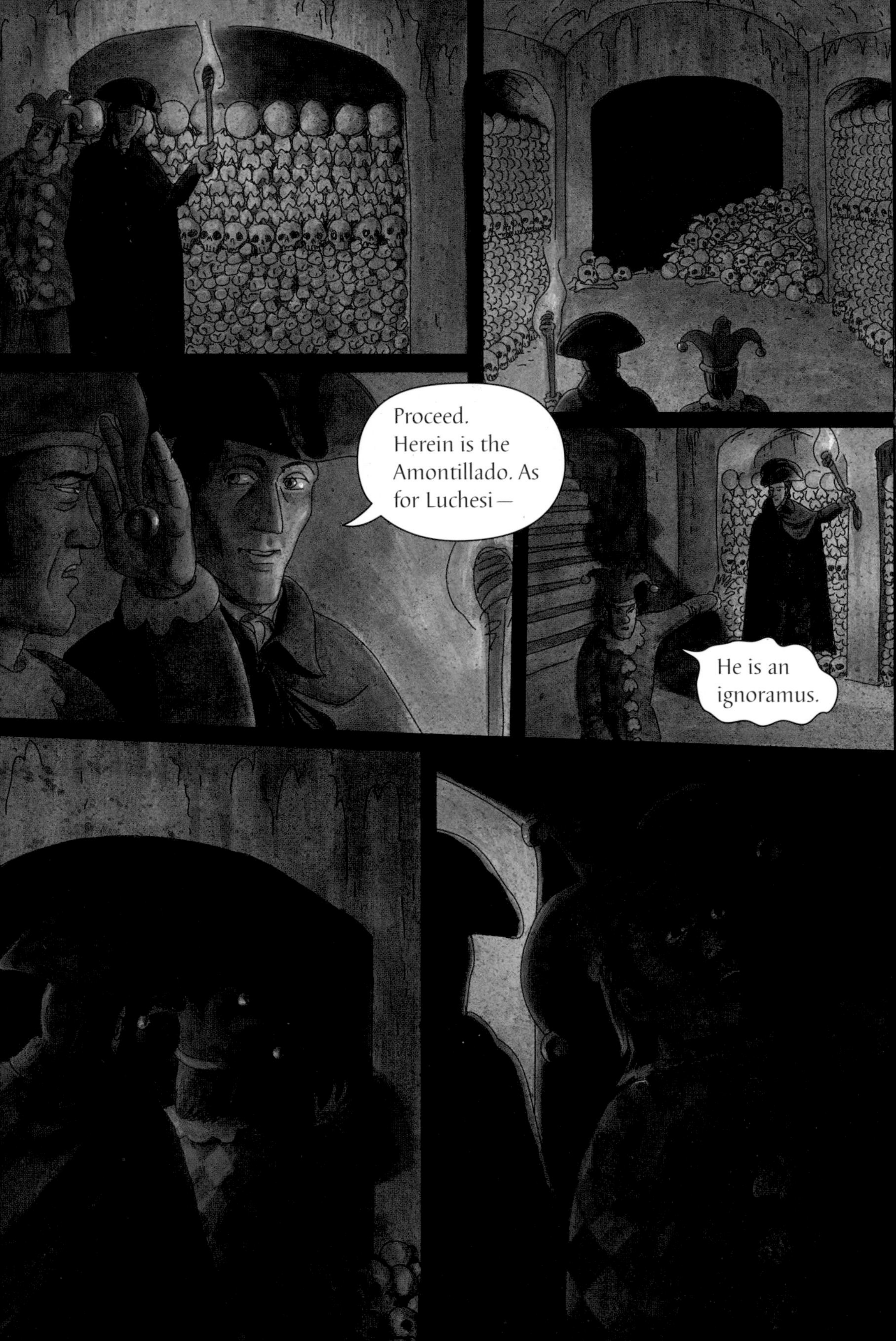
Proceed. Herein is the Amontillado. As for Luchesi—
He is an ignoramus.

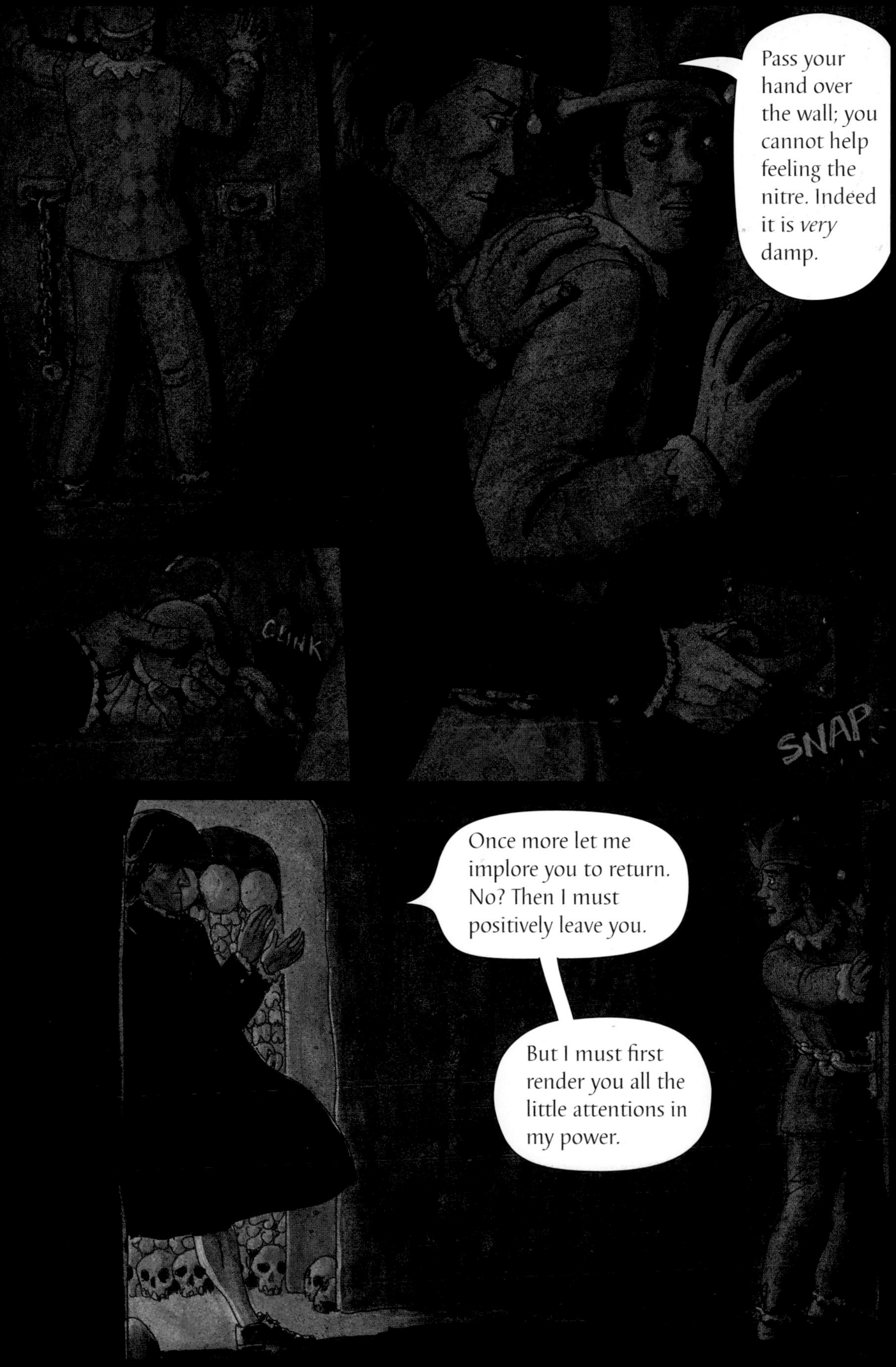
Pass your hand over the wall; you cannot help feeling the nitre. Indeed it is *very* damp.
CLINK
SNAP
Once more let me implore you to return. No? Then I must positively leave you.
But I must first render you all the little attentions in my power.

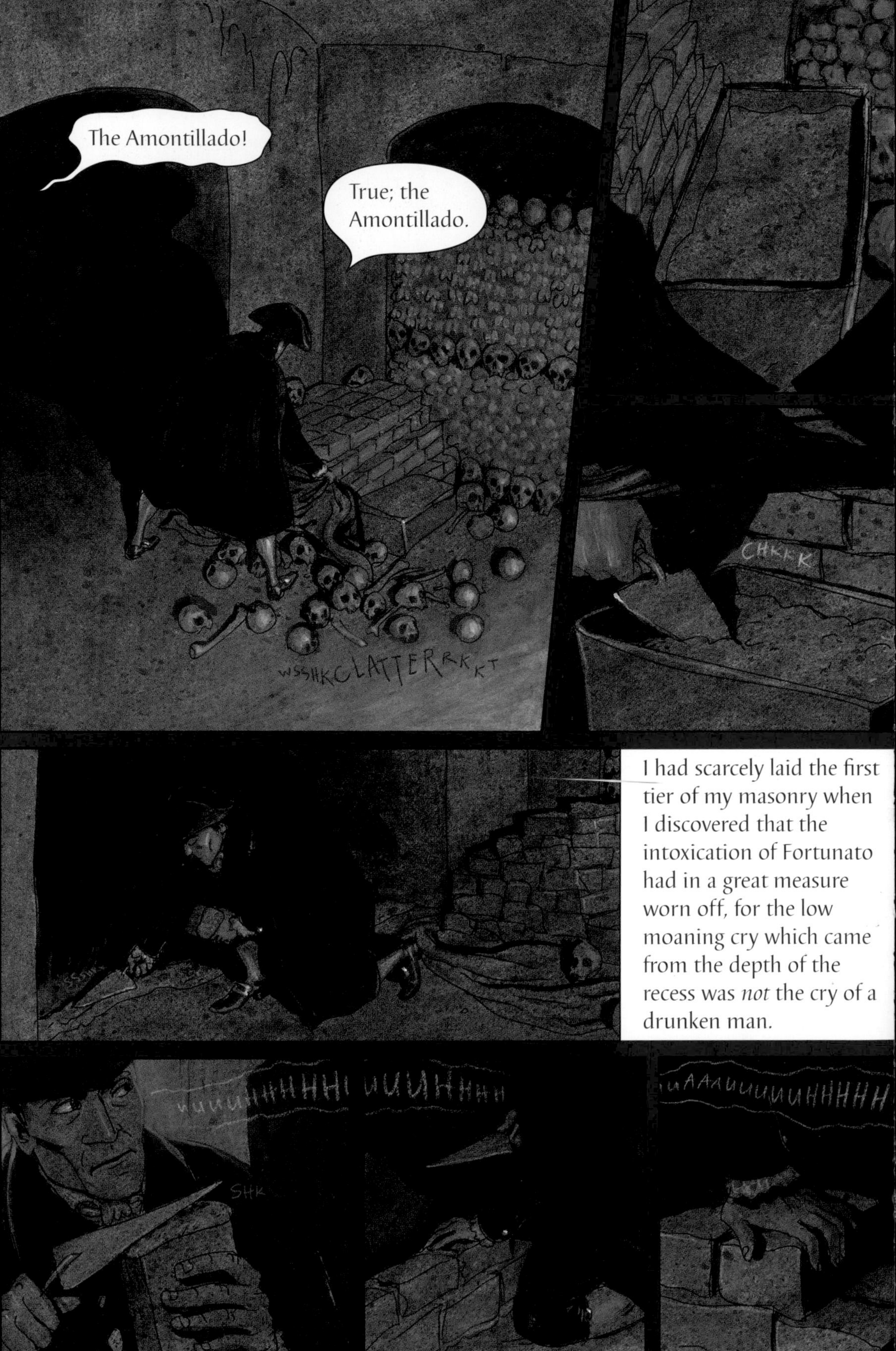
The Amontillado!
True; the Amontillado.
WSSHKCLATTERRKKT
CHKKK
I had scarcely laid the first tier of my masonry when I discovered that the intoxication of Fortunato had in a great measure worn off, for the low moaning cry which came from the depth of the recess was *not* the cry of a drunken man.
SHK
UUUUHHHHHI UUUHHHH
UAAAUUUUUUHHHHH

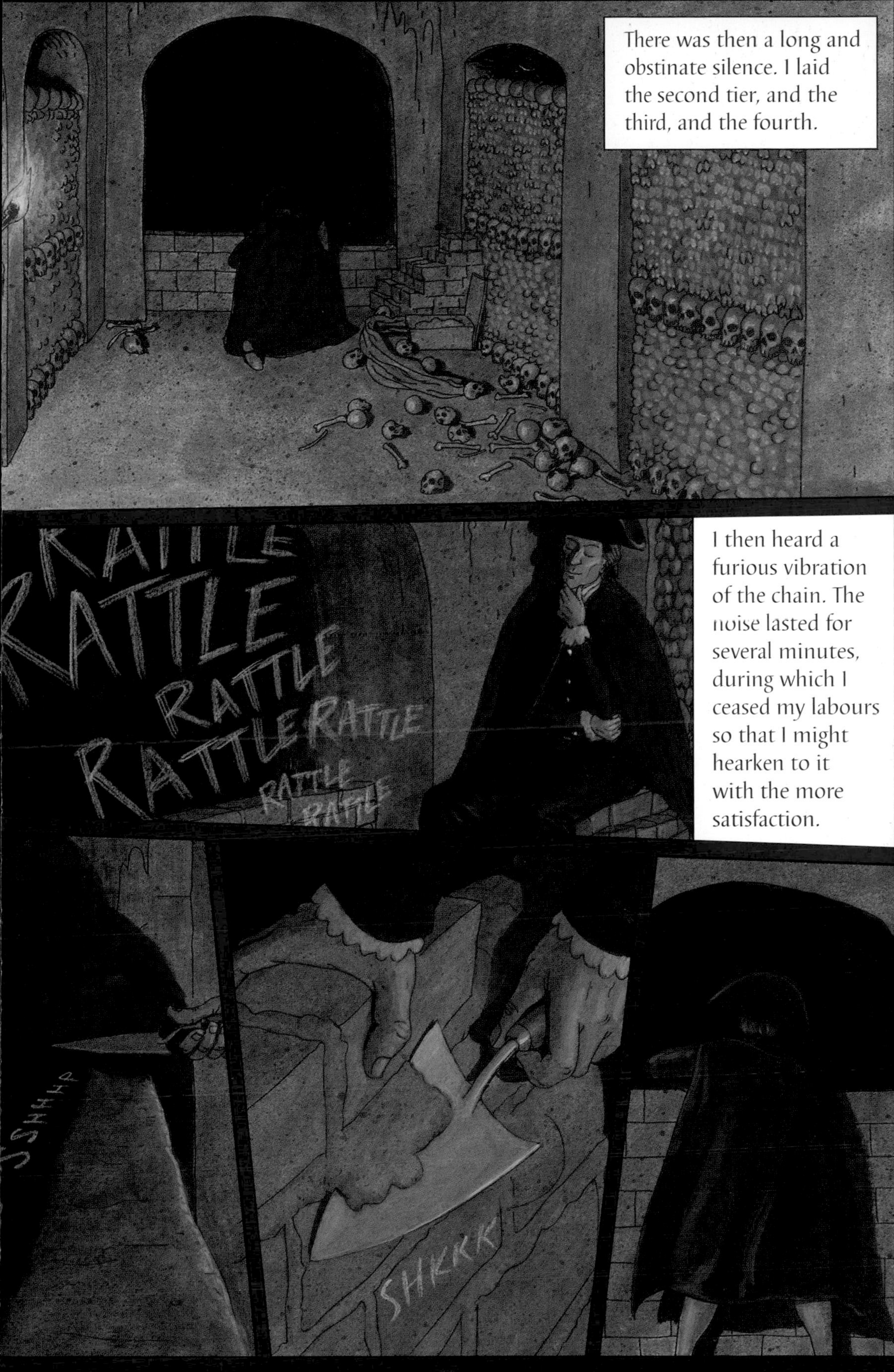
There was then a long and obstinate silence. I laid the second tier, and the third, and the fourth.
RATTLE
RATTLE
RATTLE
RATTLE RATTLE
RATTLE
RATTLE
I then heard a furious vibration of the chain. The noise lasted for several minutes, during which I ceased my labours so that I might hearken to it with the more satisfaction.
SHKKK

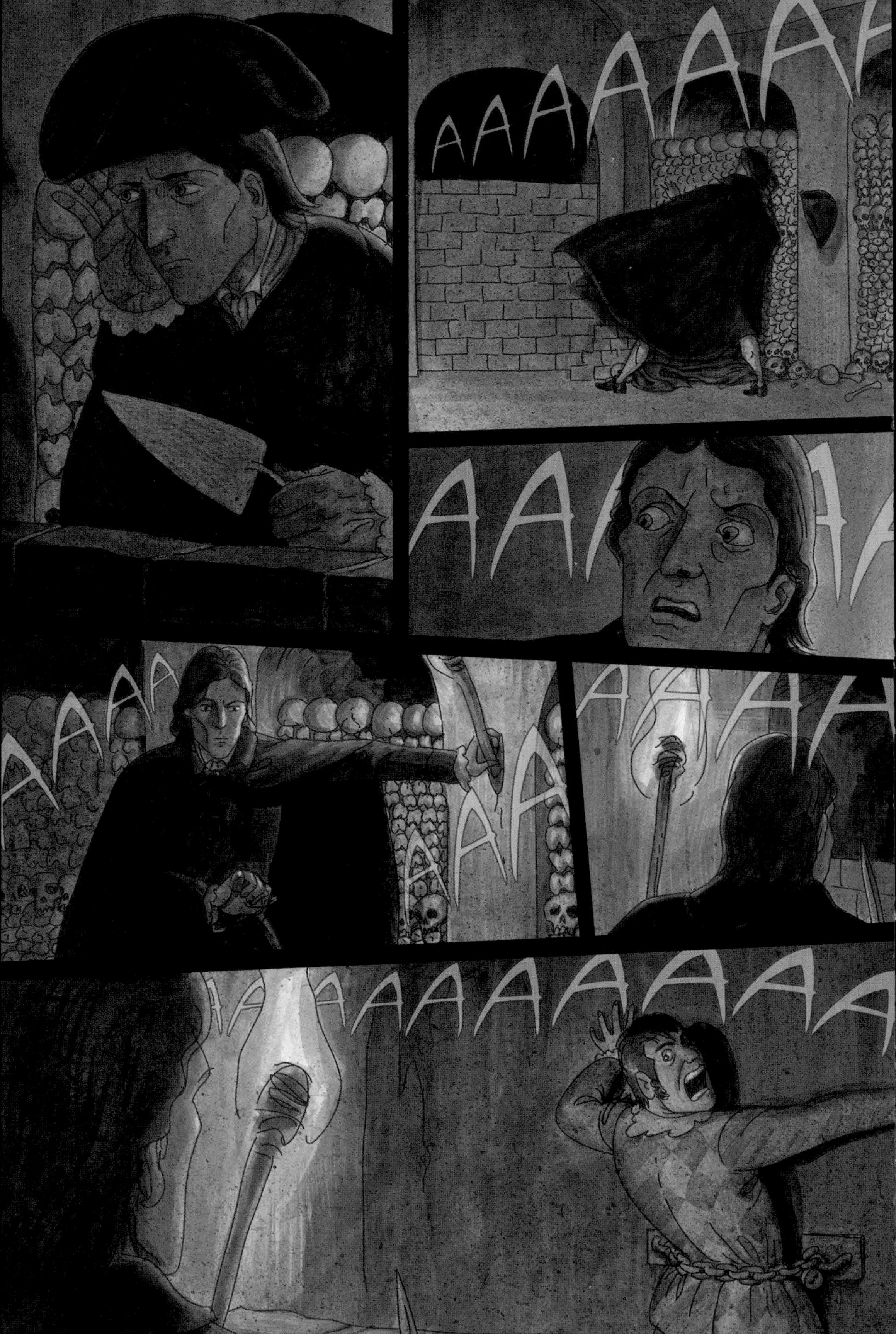
AAAAAAA
AAAAA
AAAAAAAAA
AAAAA
AAAAAAAAAAAA

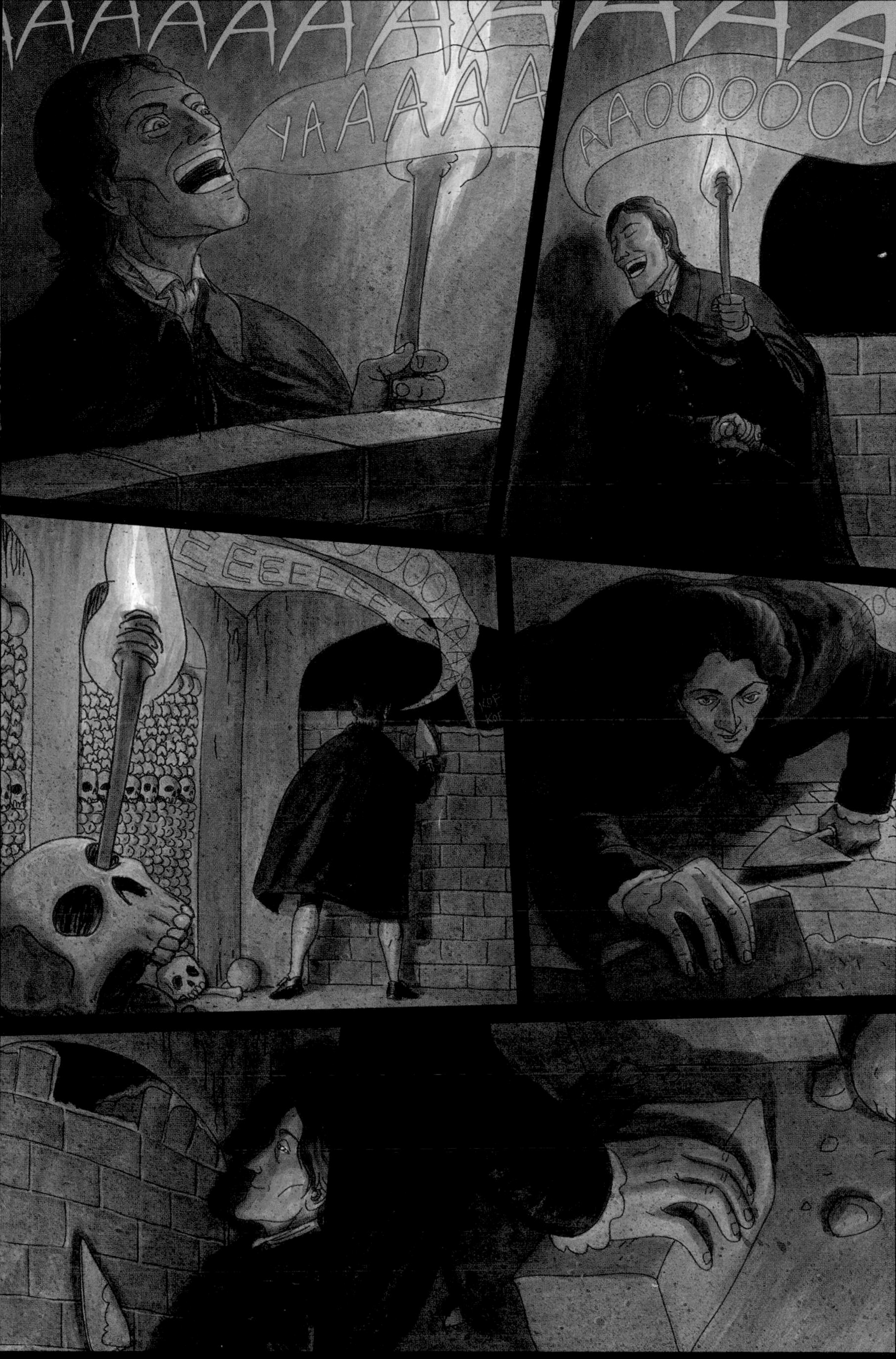

AAAAAAAAAAAAAA
YAAAAAA
AAOOOOOOO
EEEEEEEEEOOOOOAAAA
KOF KOF

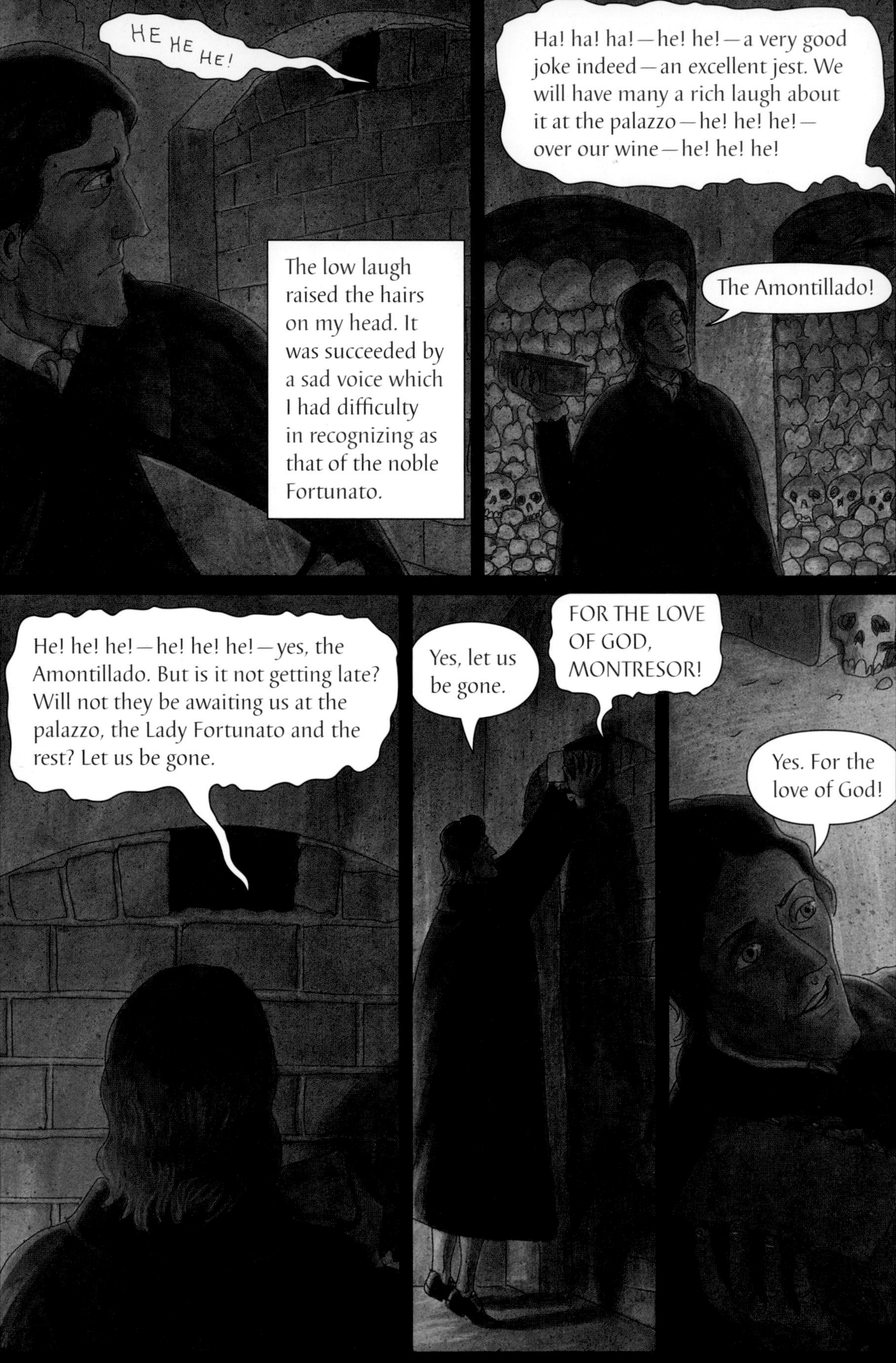
HE HE HE!
The low laugh raised the hairs on my head. It was succeeded by a sad voice which I had difficulty in recognizing as that of the noble Fortunato.
Ha! ha! ha!—he! he!—a very good joke indeed—an excellent jest. We will have many a rich laugh about it at the palazzo—he! he! he!—over our wine—he! he! he!
The Amontillado!
He! he! he!—he! he! he!—yes, the Amontillado. But is it not getting late? Will not they be awaiting us at the palazzo, the Lady Fortunato and the rest? Let us be gone.
Yes, let us be gone.
FOR THE LOVE OF GOD, MONTRESOR!
Yes. For the love of God!

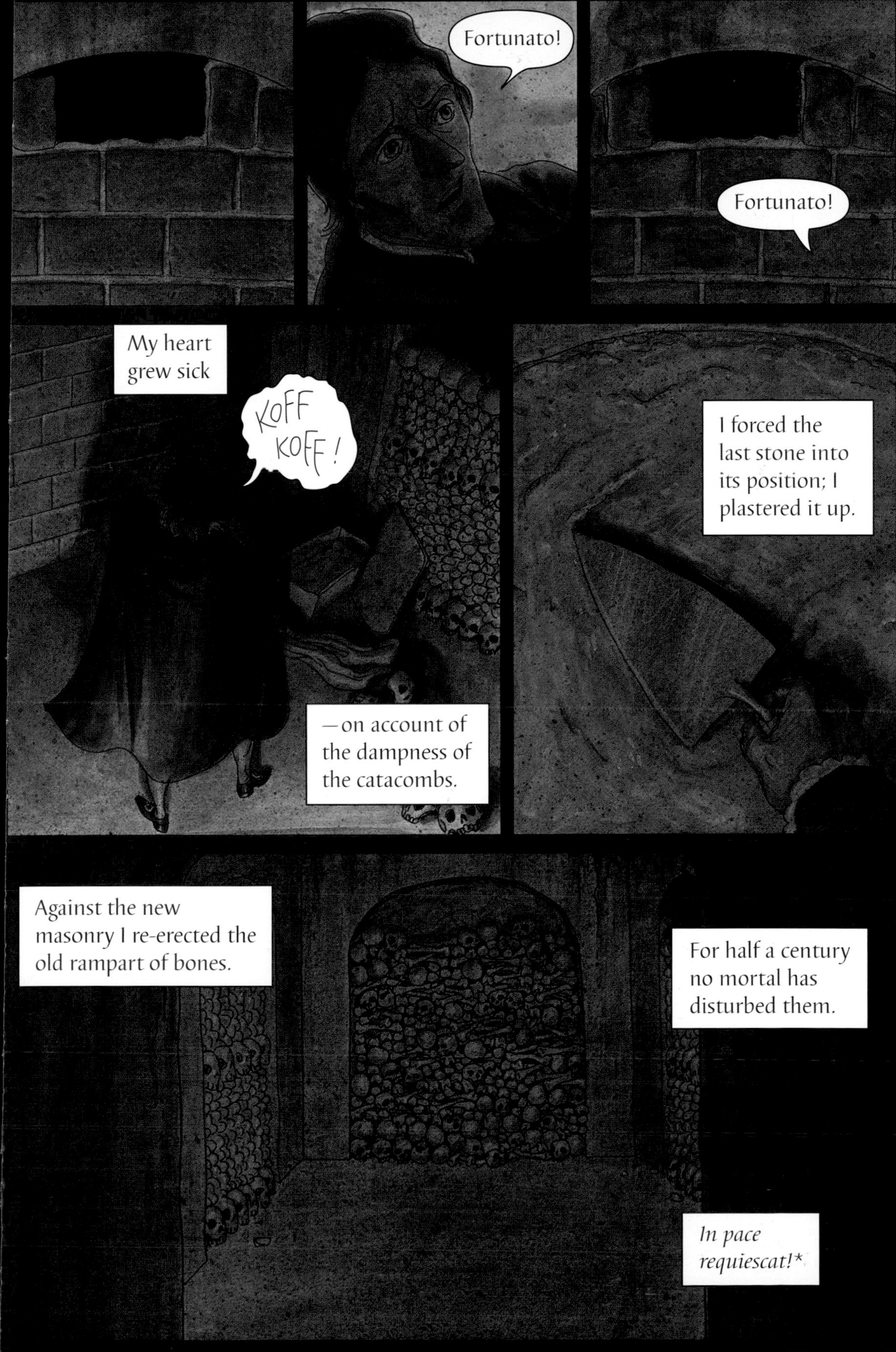
Fortunato!
Fortunato!
My heart grew sick
KOFF KOFF!
—on account of the dampness of the catacombs.
I forced the last stone into its position; I plastered it up.
Against the new masonry I re-erected the old rampart of bones.
For half a century no mortal has disturbed them.
*In pace requiescat!**

*"Rest in peace!"

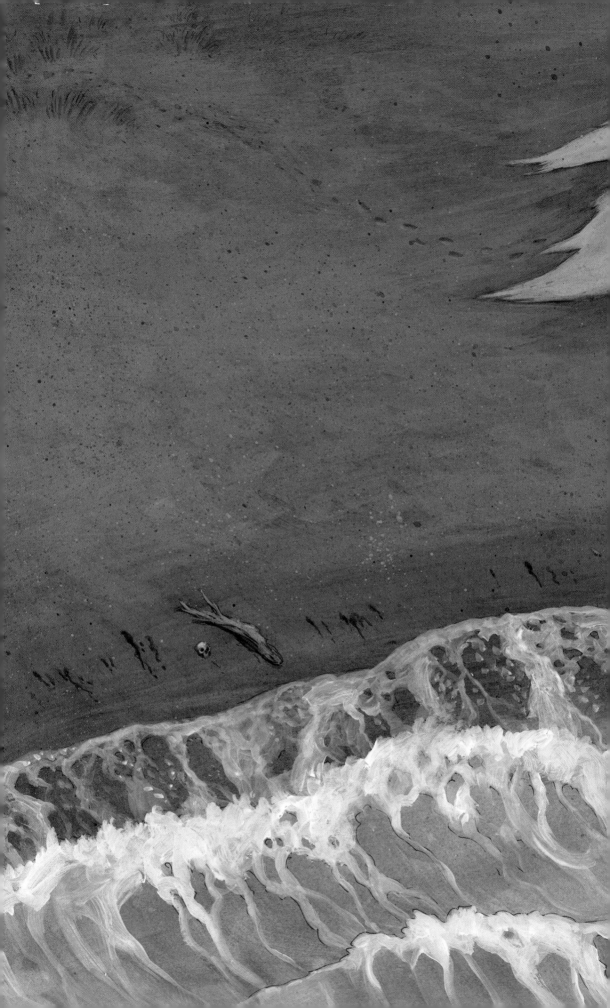

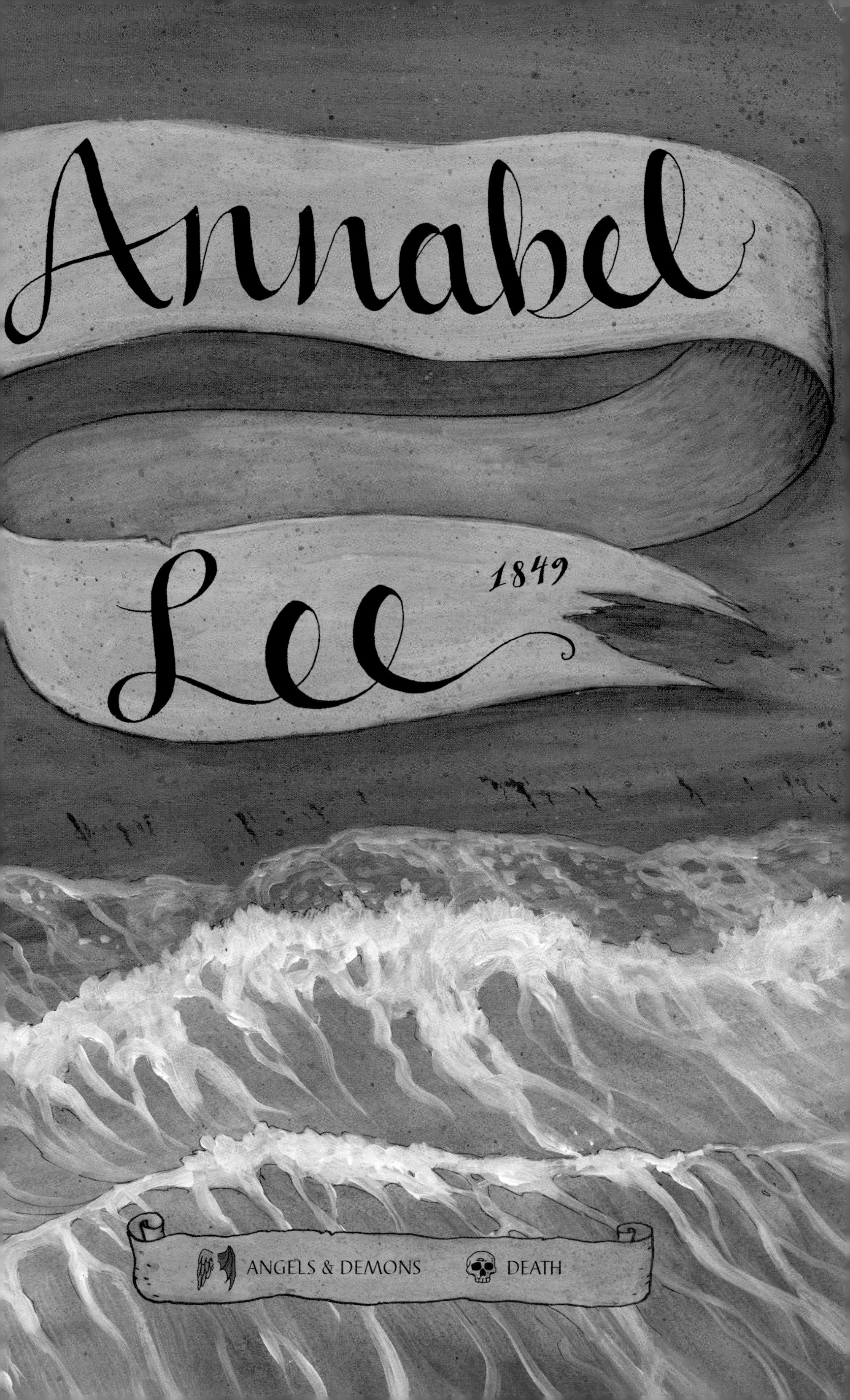
Annabel
Lee
1849
ANGELS & DEMONS
DEATH

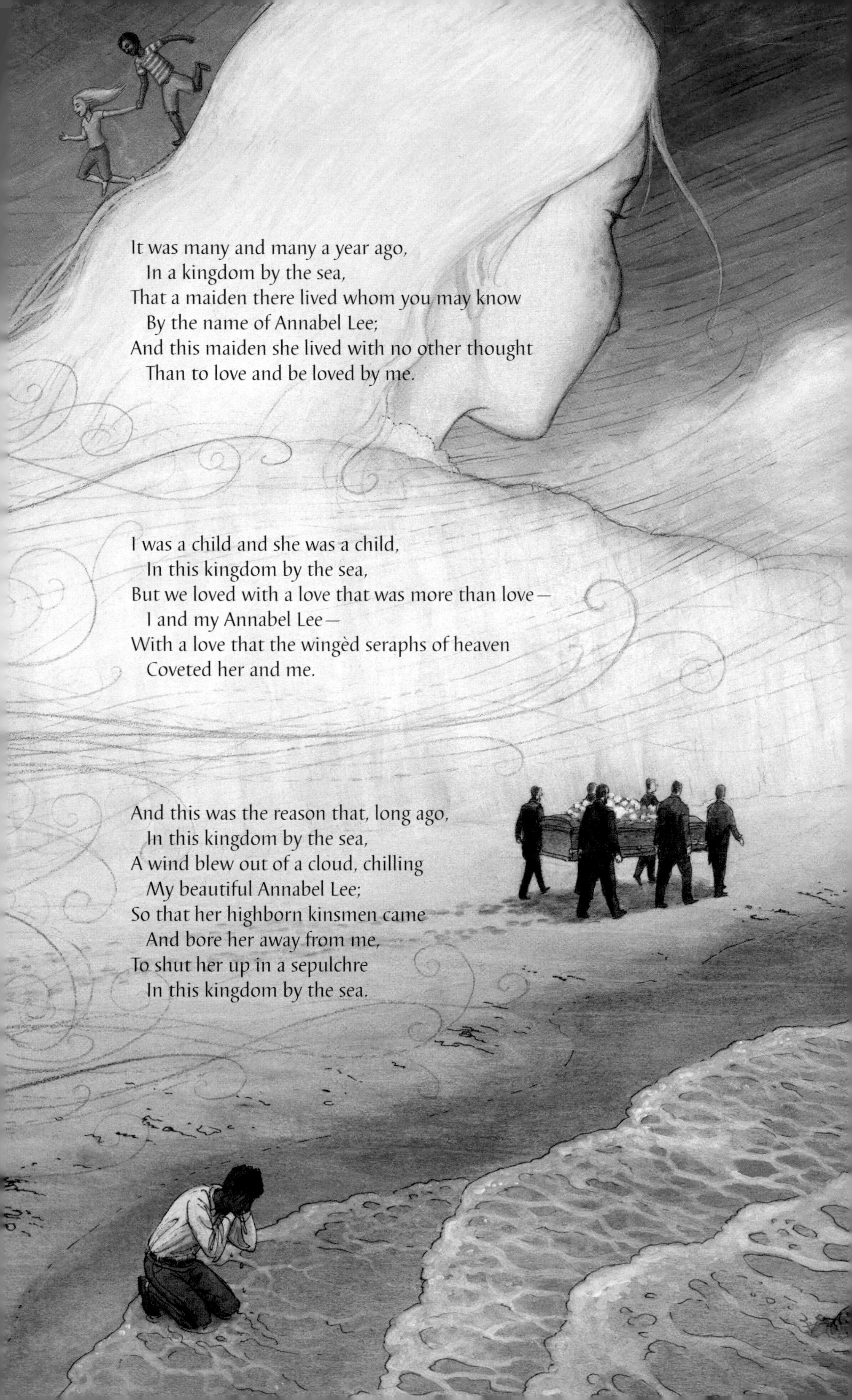

It was many and many a year ago,
   In a kingdom by the sea,
That a maiden there lived whom you may know
   By the name of Annabel Lee;
And this maiden she lived with no other thought
   Than to love and be loved by me.

I was a child and she was a child,
   In this kingdom by the sea,
But we loved with a love that was more than love—
   I and my Annabel Lee—
With a love that the wingèd seraphs of heaven
   Coveted her and me.

And this was the reason that, long ago,
   In this kingdom by the sea,
A wind blew out of a cloud, chilling
   My beautiful Annabel Lee;
So that her highborn kinsmen came
   And bore her away from me,
To shut her up in a sepulchre
   In this kingdom by the sea.

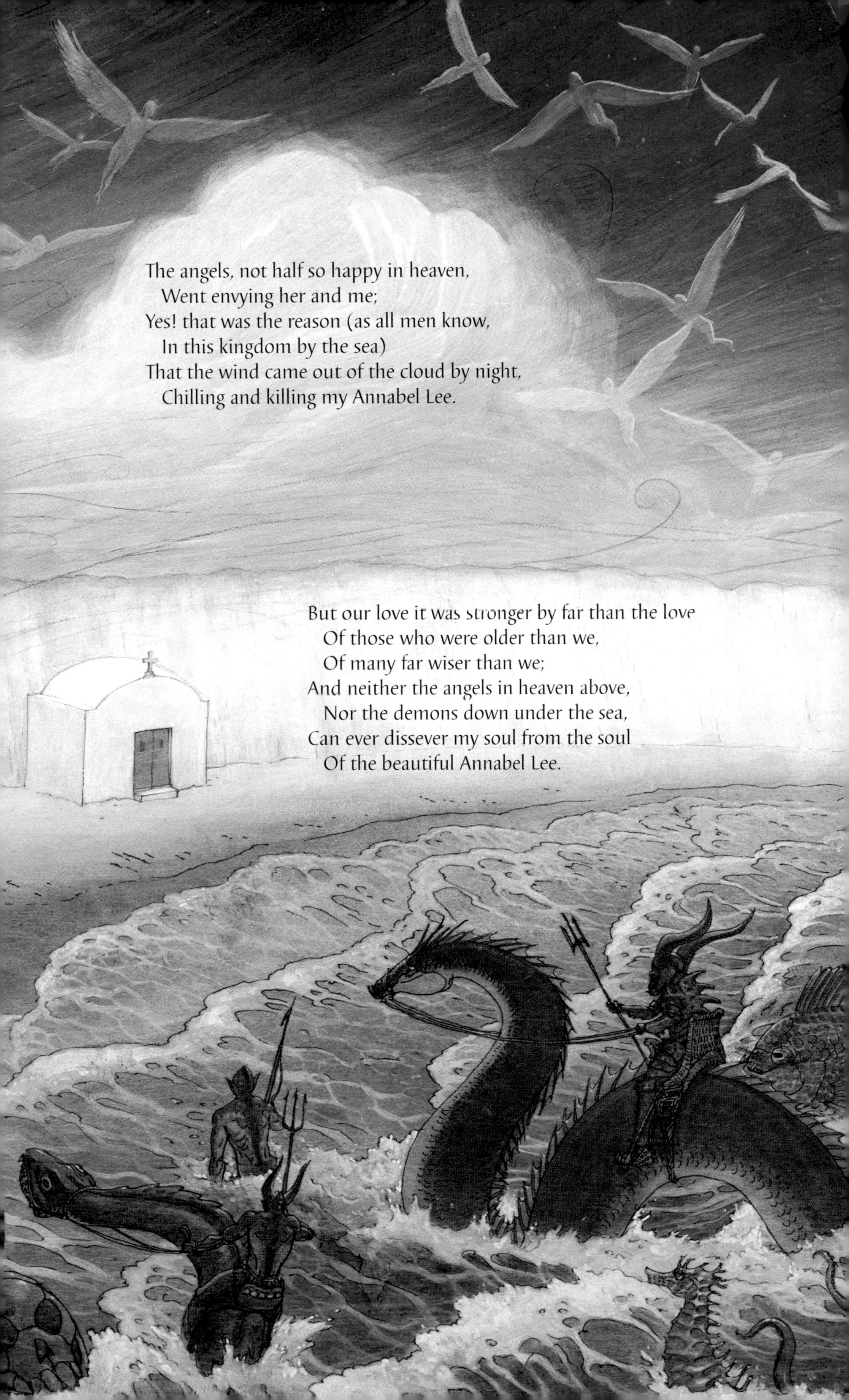

The angels, not half so happy in heaven,
   Went envying her and me;
Yes! that was the reason (as all men know,
   In this kingdom by the sea)
That the wind came out of the cloud by night,
   Chilling and killing my Annabel Lee.

But our love it was stronger by far than the love
   Of those who were older than we,
   Of many far wiser than we;
And neither the angels in heaven above,
   Nor the demons down under the sea,
Can ever dissever my soul from the soul
   Of the beautiful Annabel Lee.

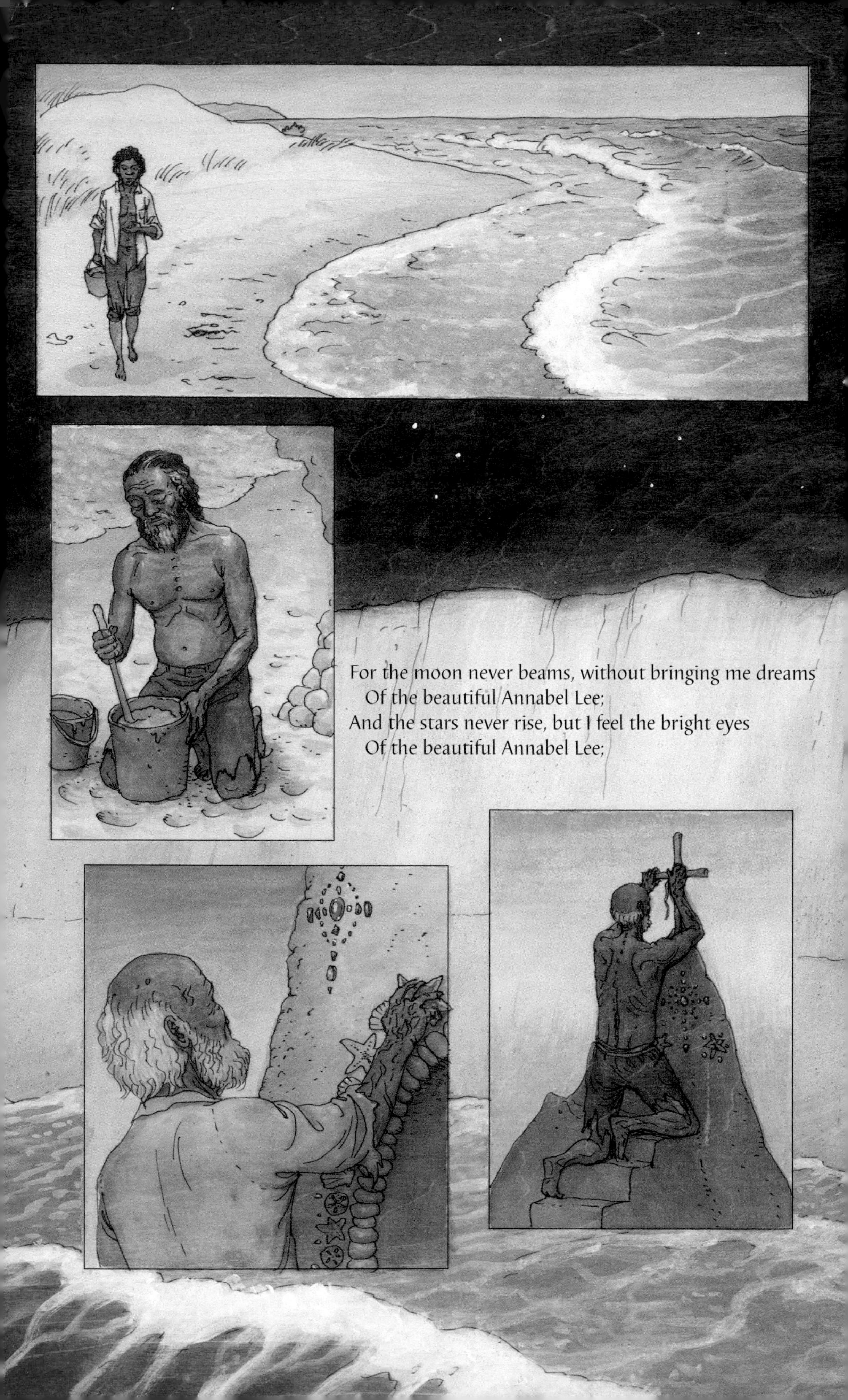
For the moon never beams, without bringing me dreams
Of the beautiful Annabel Lee;
And the stars never rise, but I feel the bright eyes
Of the beautiful Annabel Lee;

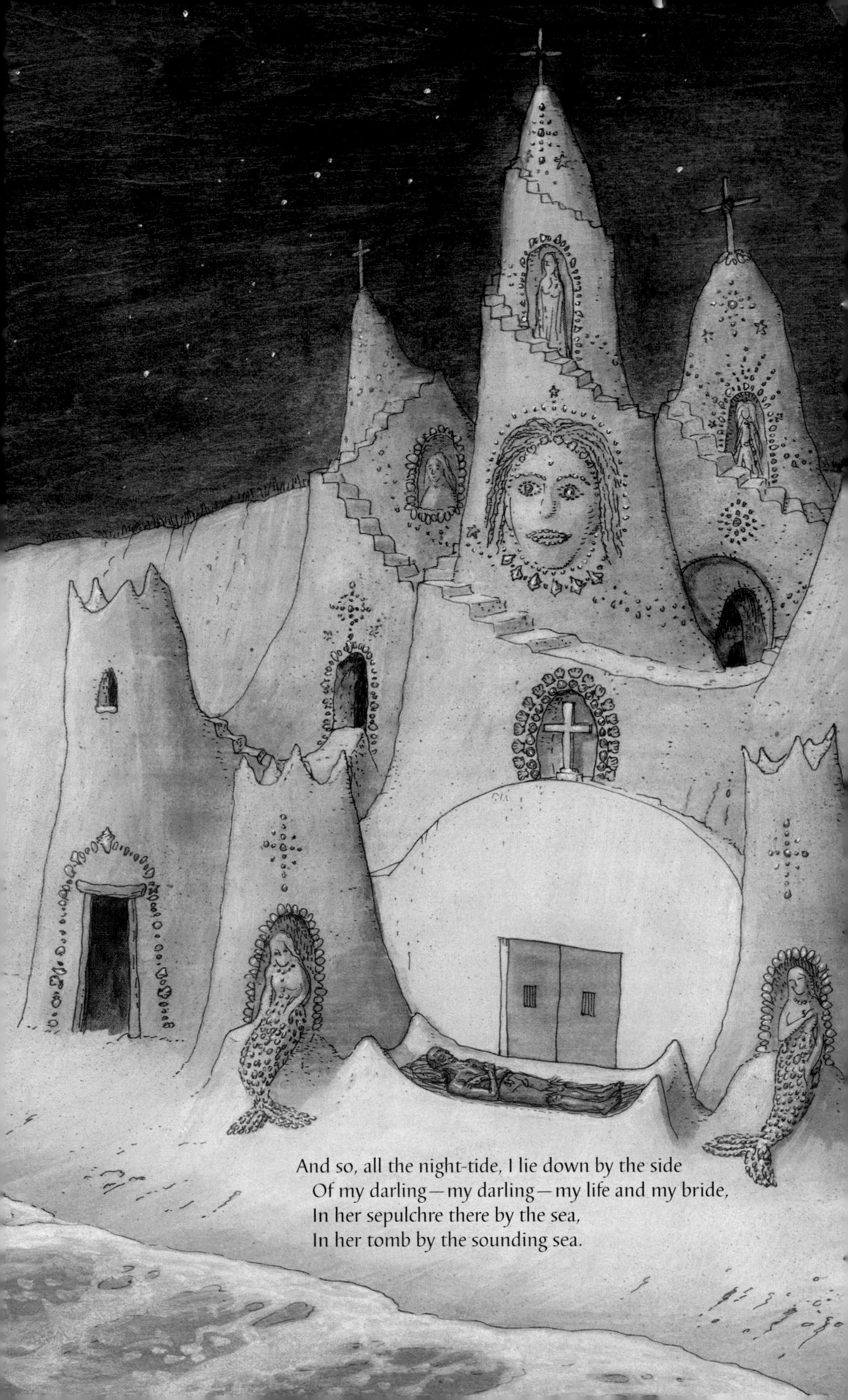

And so, all the night-tide, I lie down by the side
  Of my darling—my darling—my life and my bride,
  In her sepulchre there by the sea,
  In her tomb by the sounding sea.

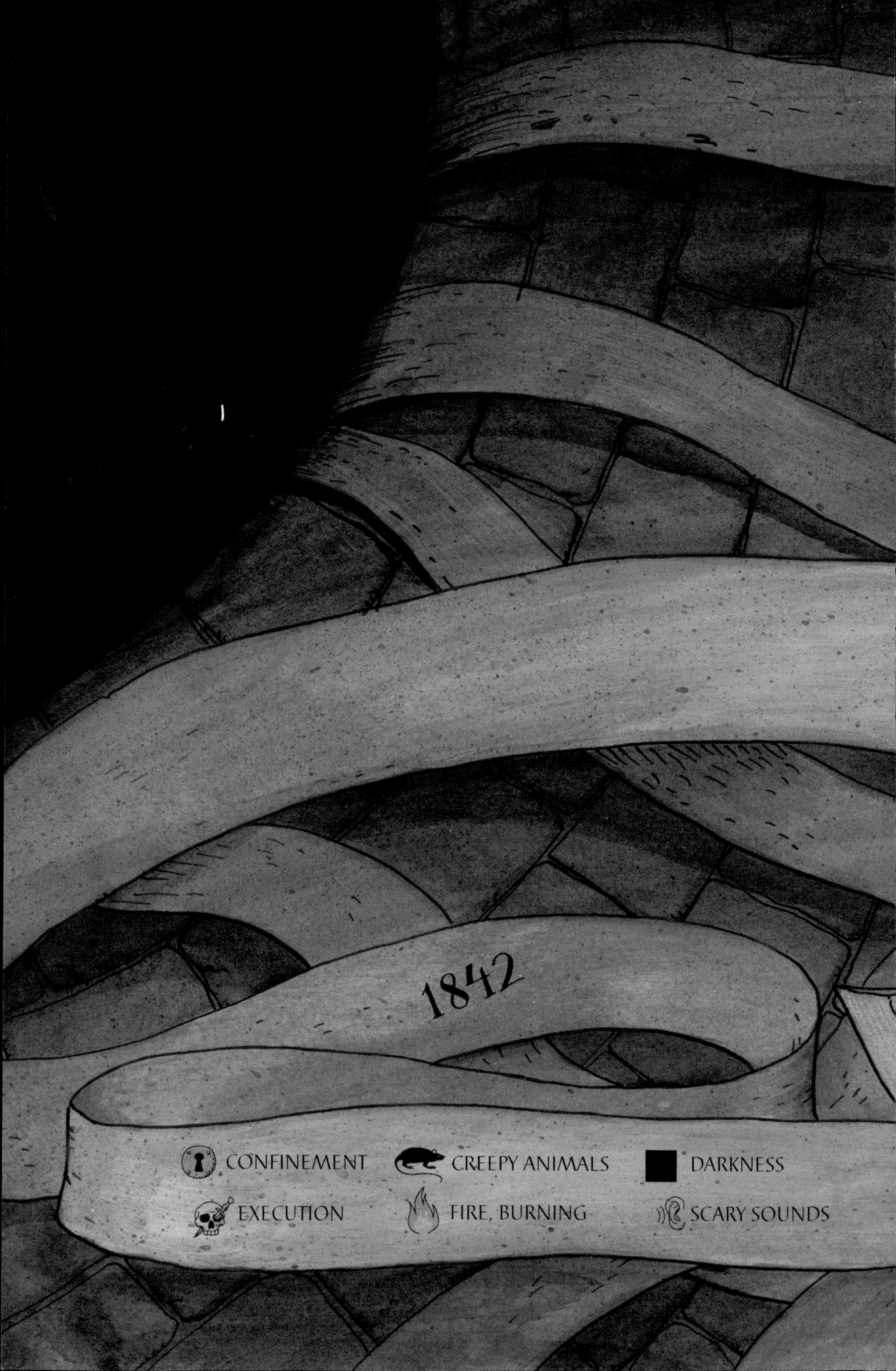
1842
CONFINEMENT
CREEPY ANIMALS
DARKNESS
EXECUTION
FIRE, BURNING
SCARY SOUNDS

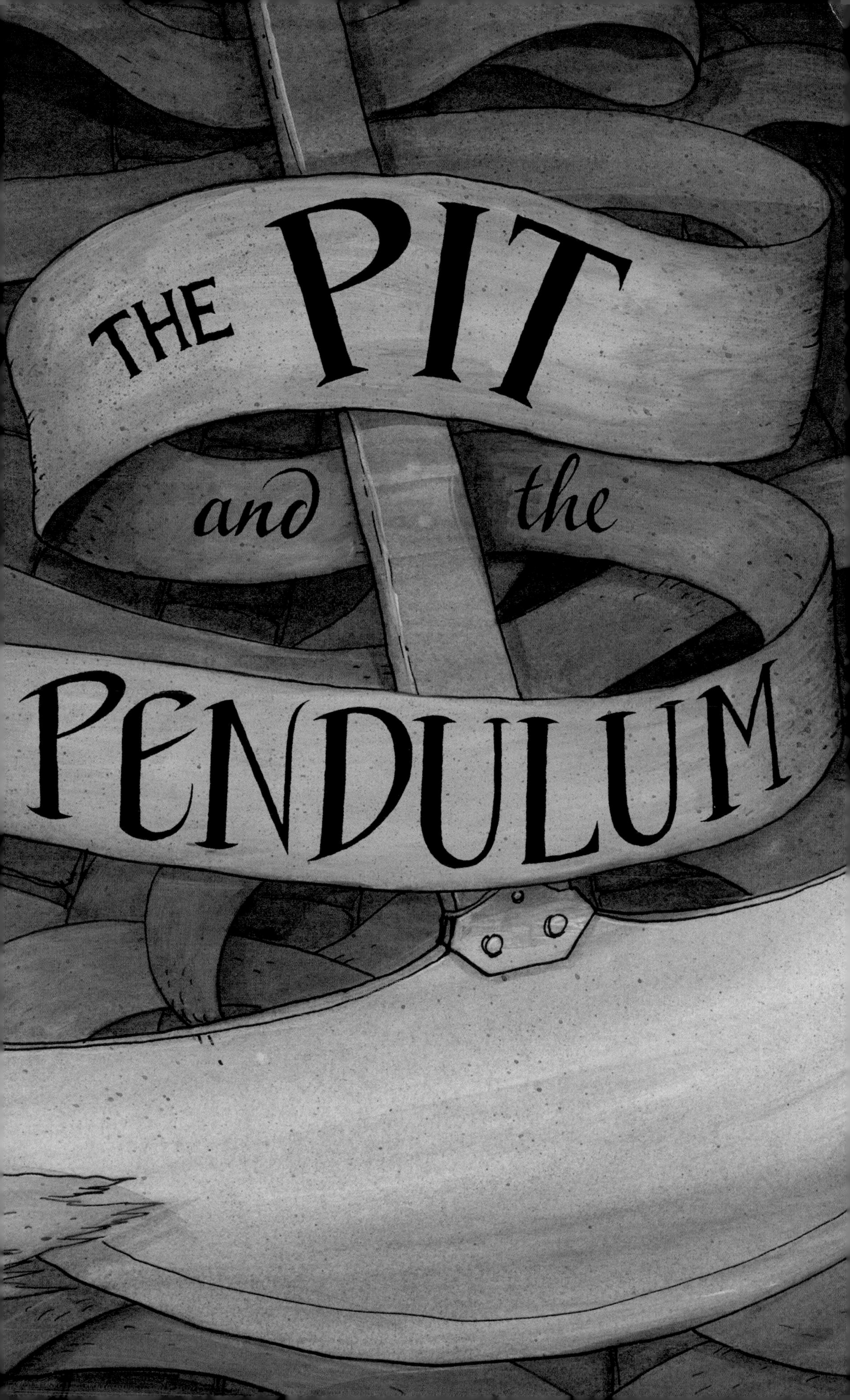
THE PIT
and the
PENDULUM

I awoke to impenetrable darkness. I could see not an inch. Was I blind? Was I dead?

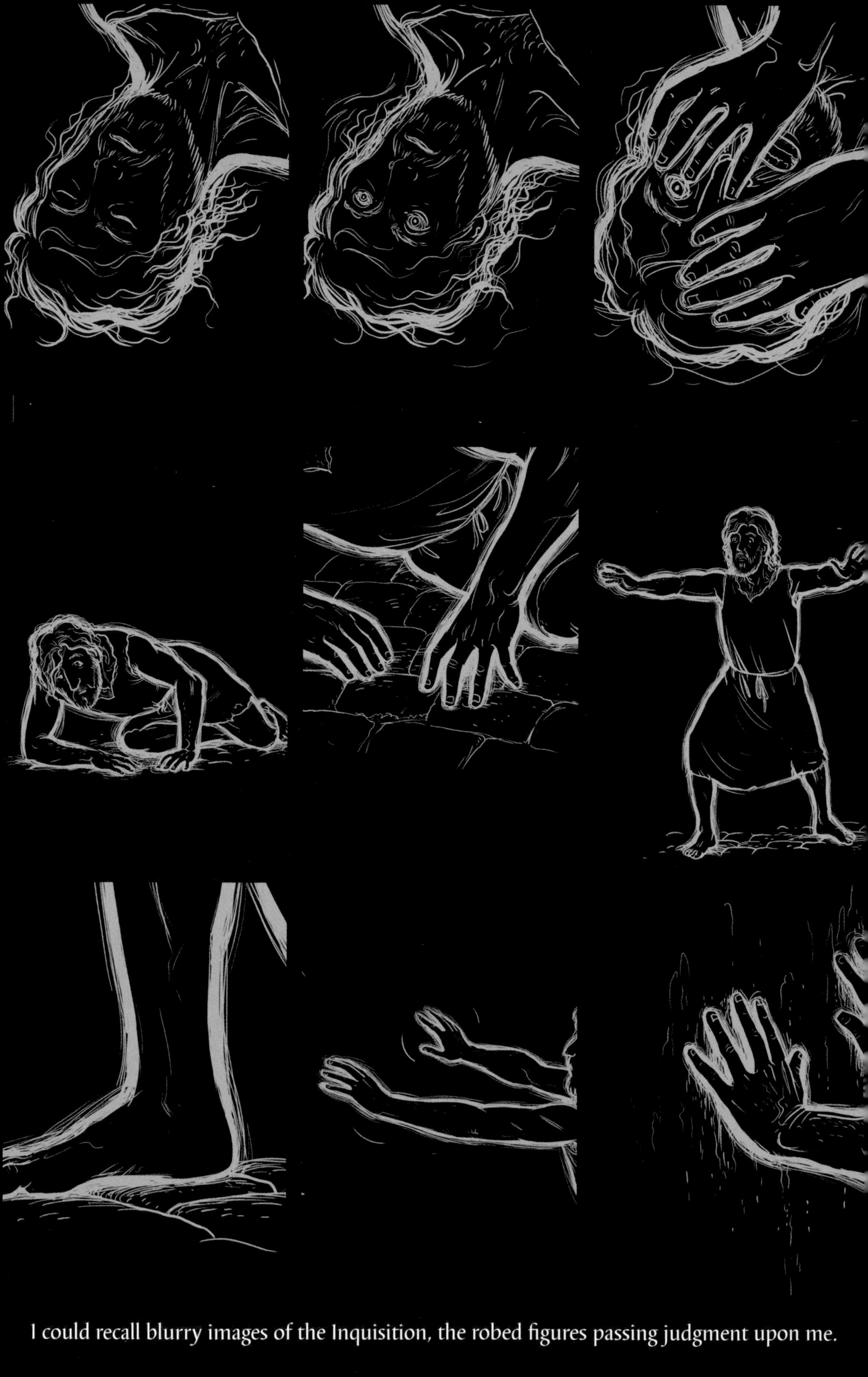

I could recall blurry images of the Inquisition, the robed figures passing judgment upon me.

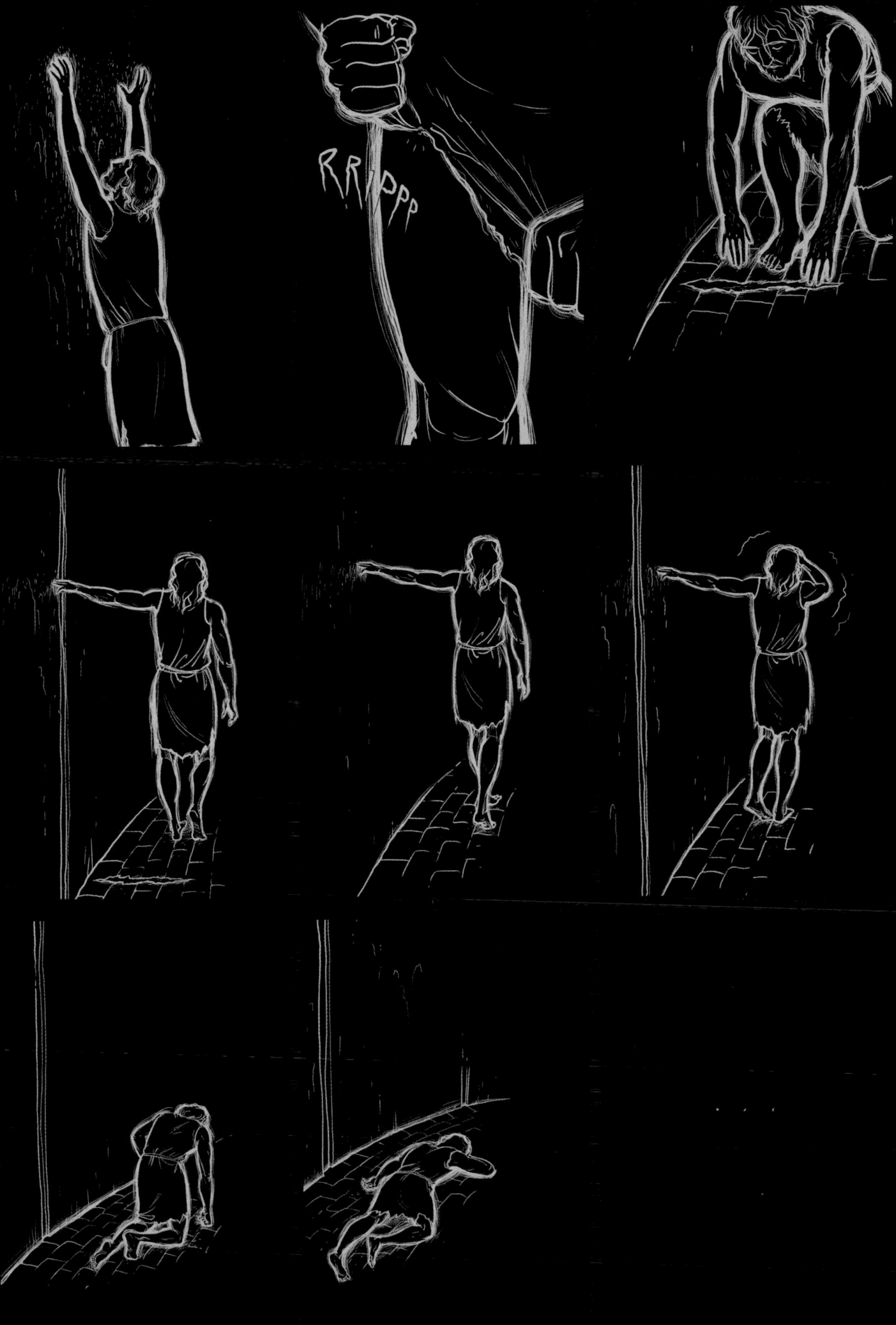
RRIPPP

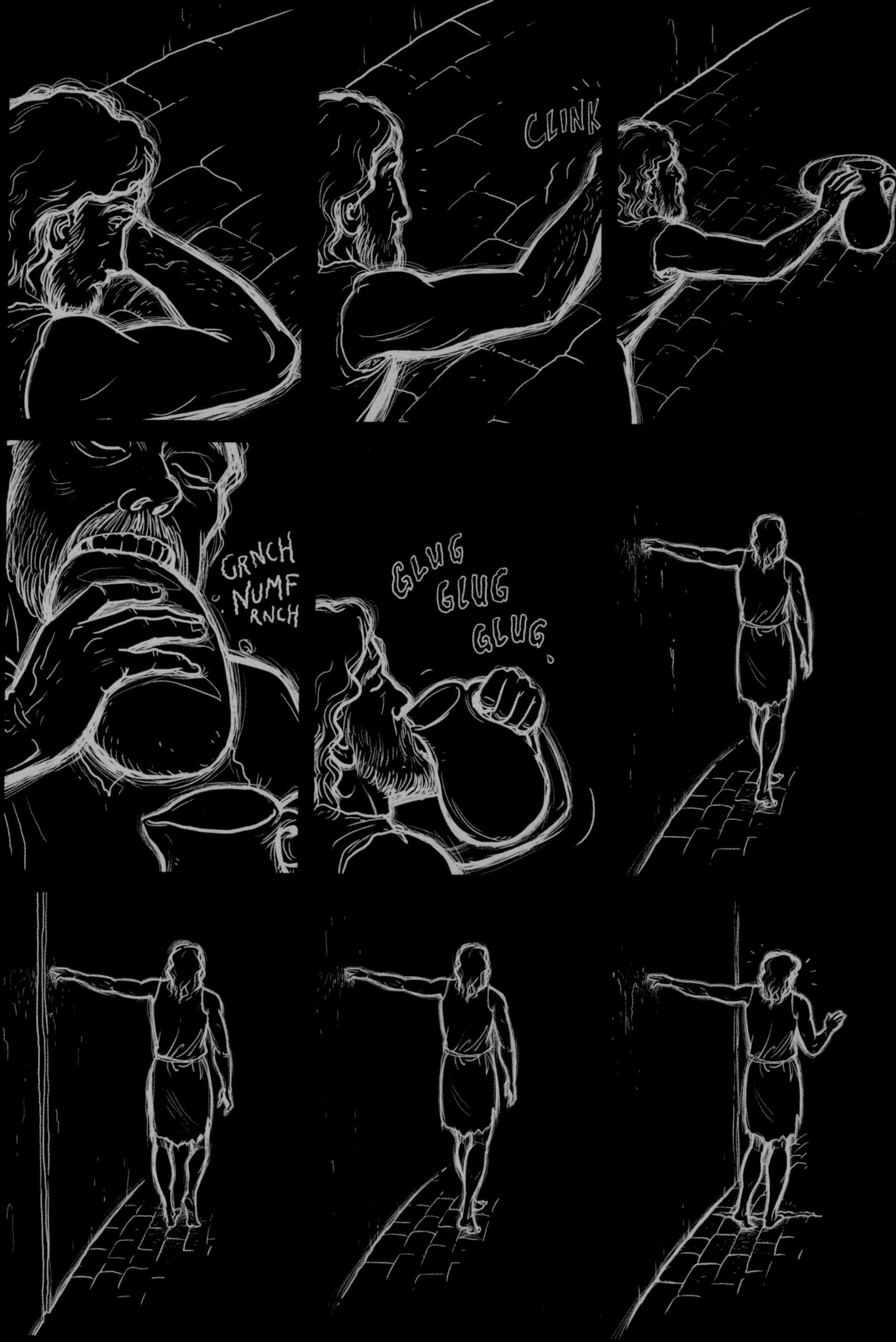
CLINK
GRNCH
NUMF
RNCH
GLUG
GLUG
GLUG

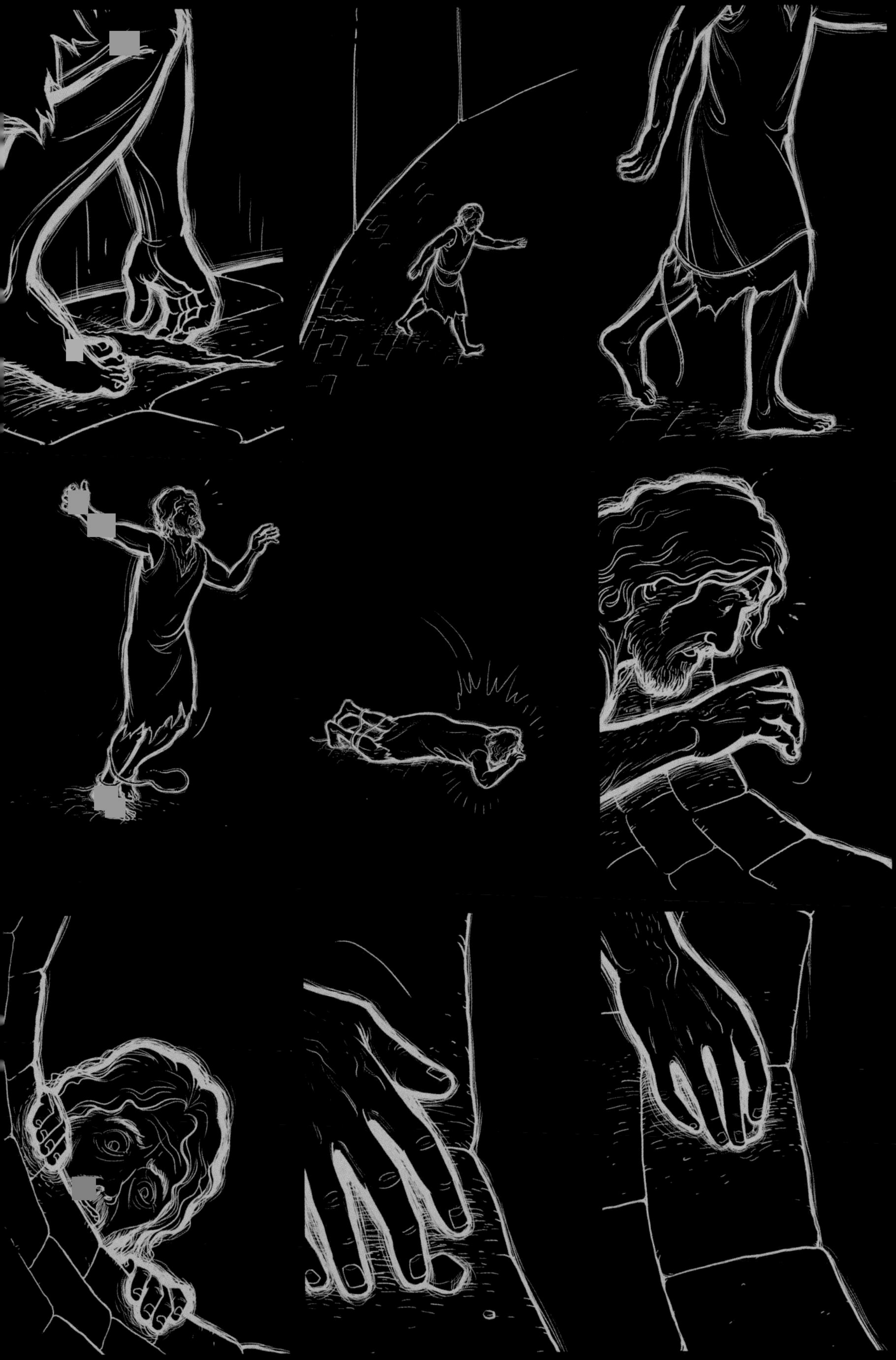

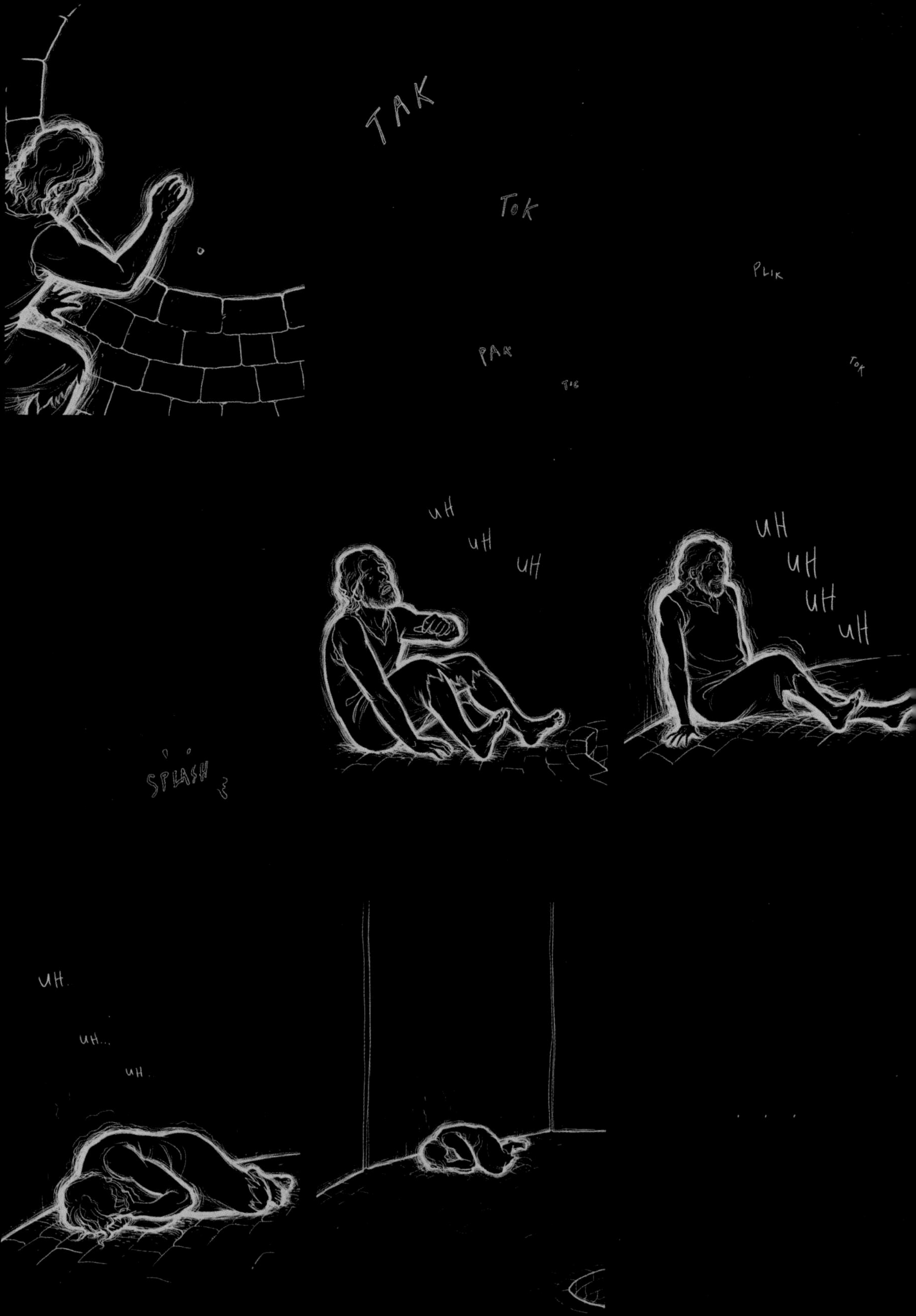

TAK
TOK
PAK
PLIK
TOK
SPLASH
UH
UH
UH
UH
UH
UH
UH
UH.
UH...
UH.

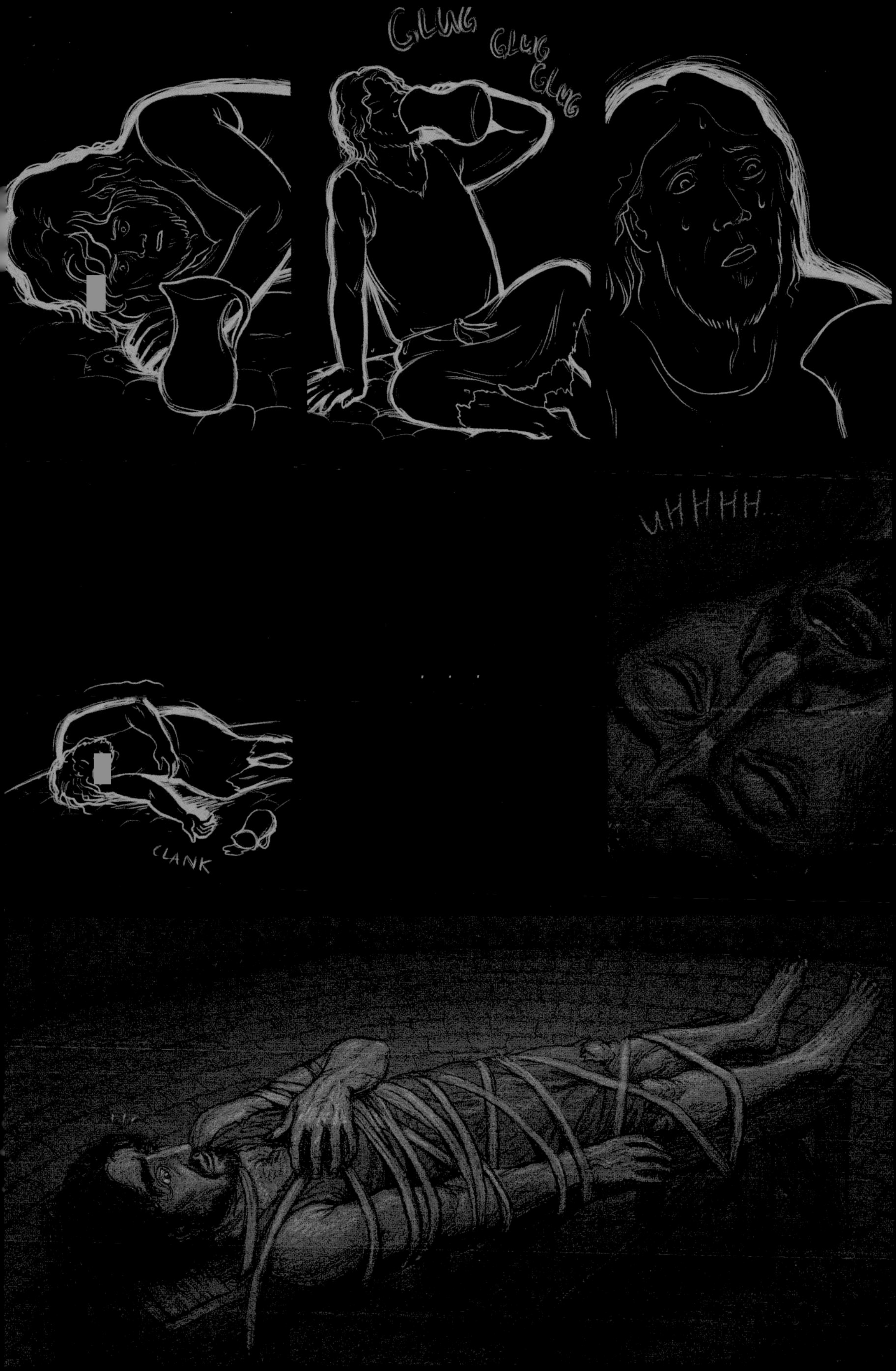
GLUG
GLUG
GLUG
CLANK
. . .
UHHHH...

Light! It was dim, but at last I could see my surroundings.

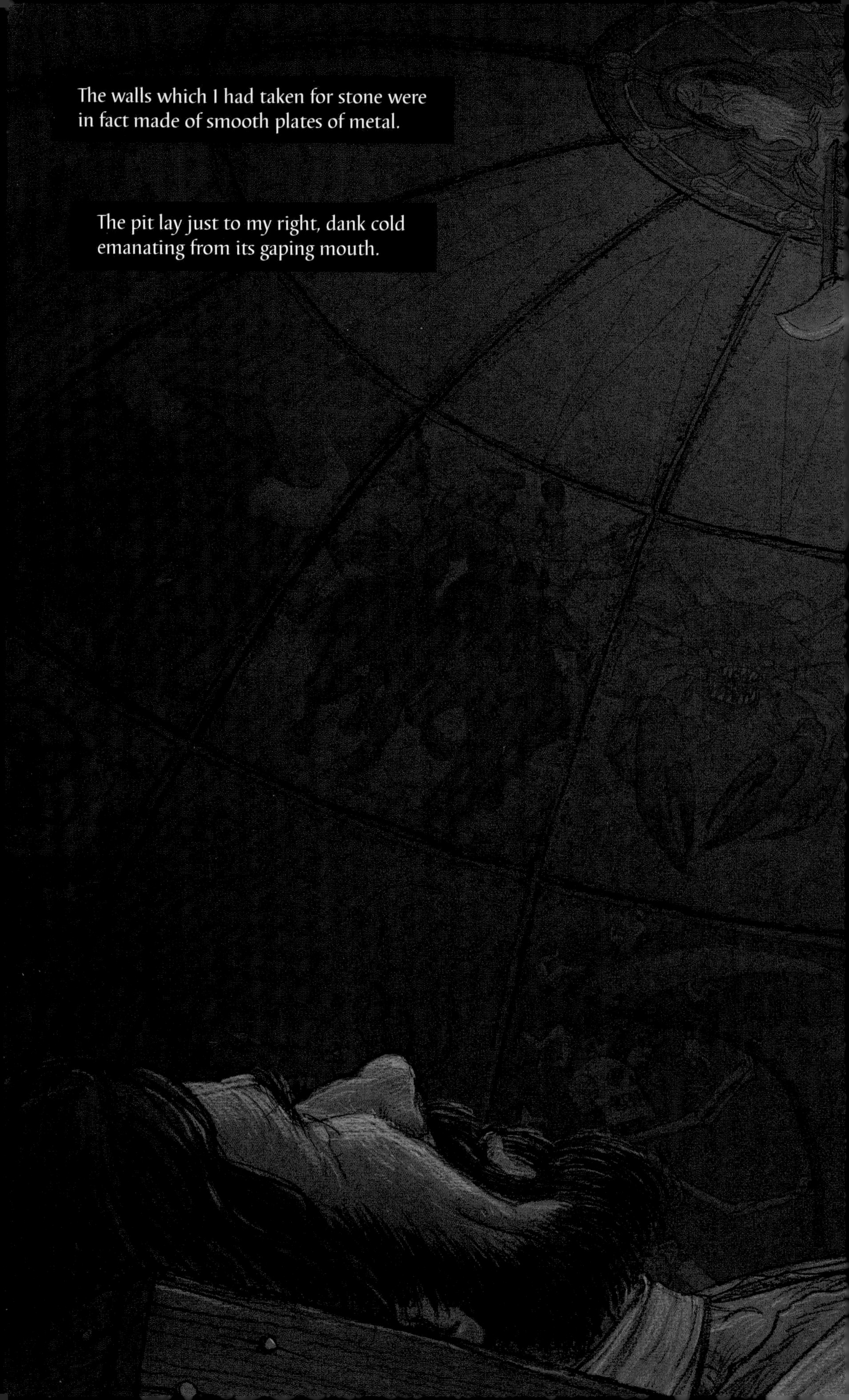
The walls which I had taken for stone were in fact made of smooth plates of metal.
The pit lay just to my right, dank cold emanating from its gaping mouth.

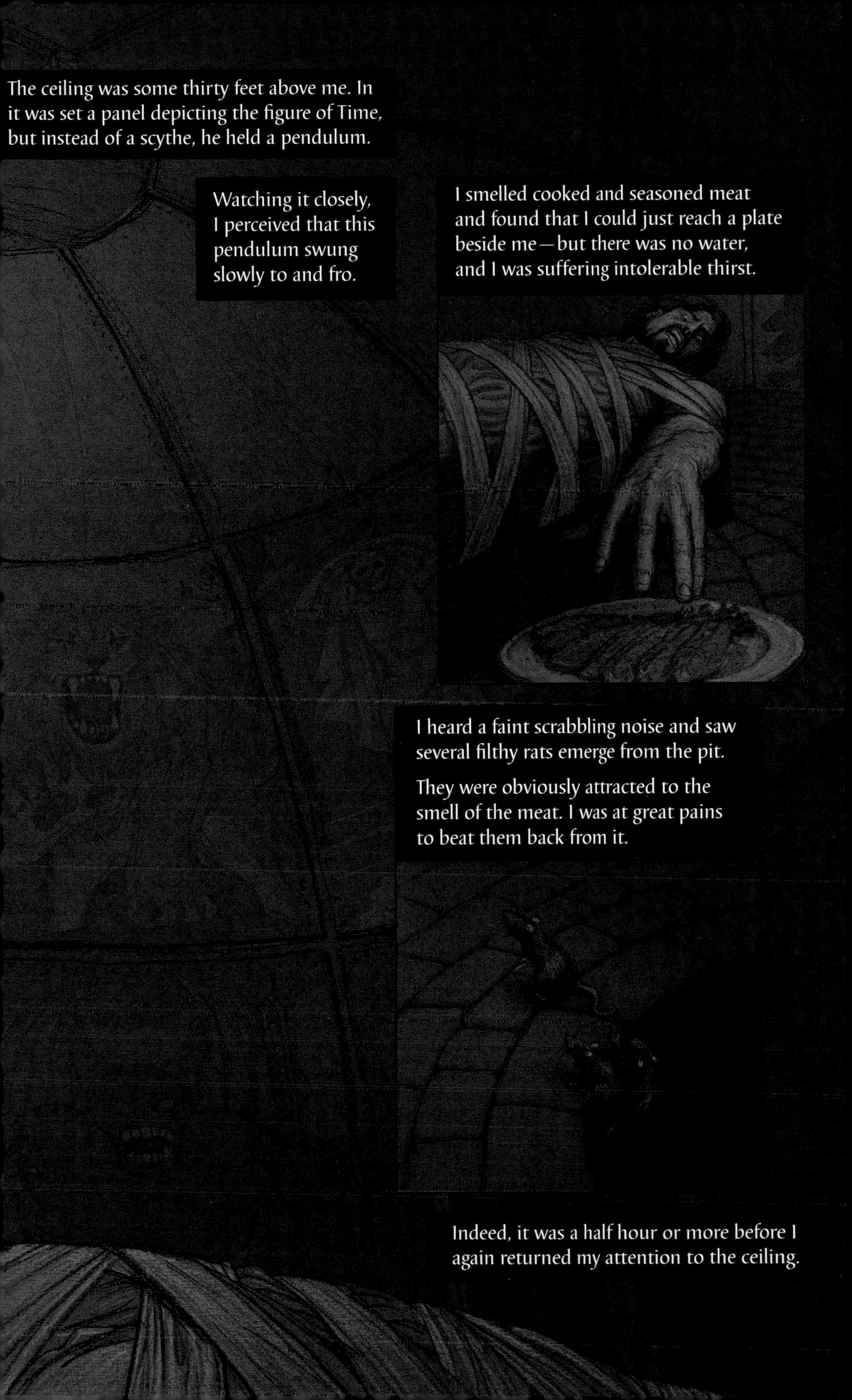
The ceiling was some thirty feet above me. In it was set a panel depicting the figure of Time, but instead of a scythe, he held a pendulum.
Watching it closely, I perceived that this pendulum swung slowly to and fro.
I smelled cooked and seasoned meat and found that I could just reach a plate beside me—but there was no water, and I was suffering intolerable thirst.
I heard a faint scrabbling noise and saw several filthy rats emerge from the pit.
They were obviously attracted to the smell of the meat. I was at great pains to beat them back from it.
Indeed, it was a half hour or more before I again returned my attention to the ceiling.

The sweep of the pendulum had increased by nearly a yard, and its velocity was much greater. But what mainly disturbed me was the idea that it had perceptibly **descended.**

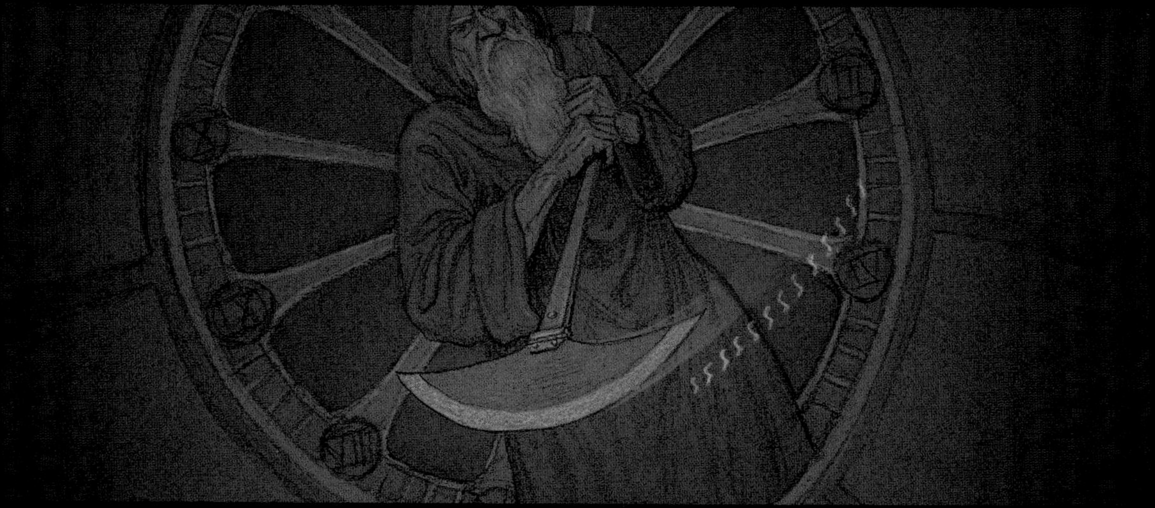

Also, I now clearly perceived that it ended in a crescent of glittering steel, its bottom edge evidently as sharp as a razor. The whole heavy arm **hissed** audibly as it swung through the air. I could no longer doubt the doom prepared for me.

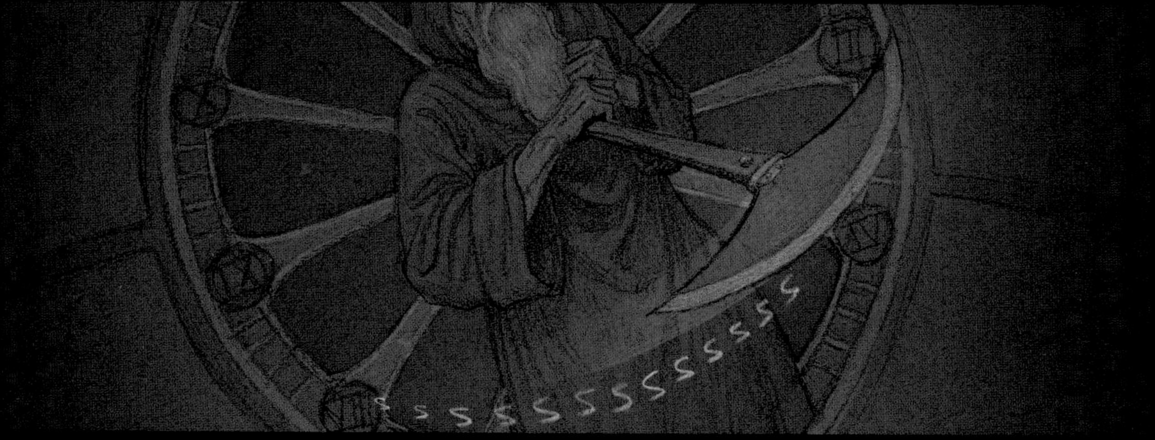

Having by chance escaped plunging into the pit, now a different and a milder destruction awaited me. Milder! I half smiled in my agony as I thought of such an application of that term.

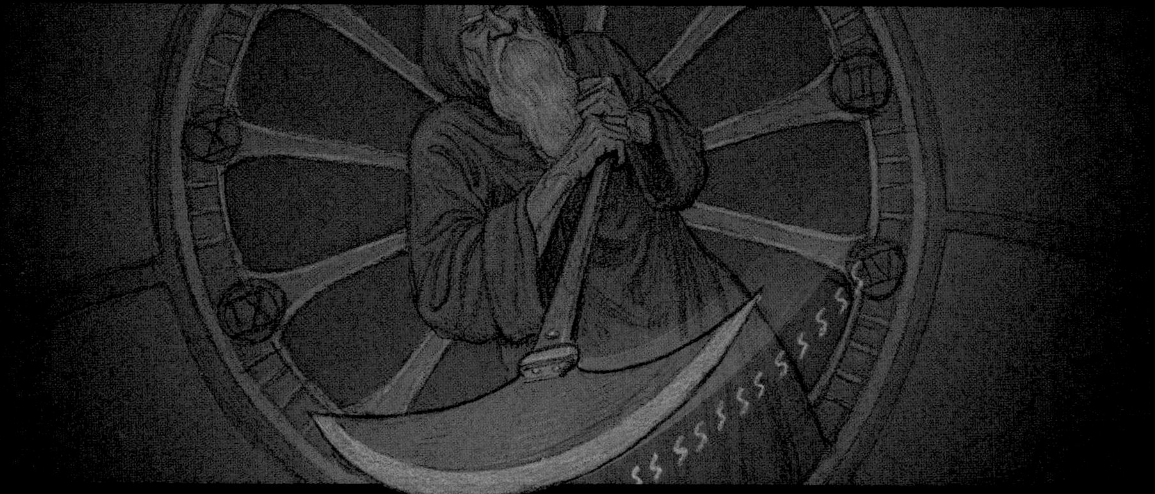

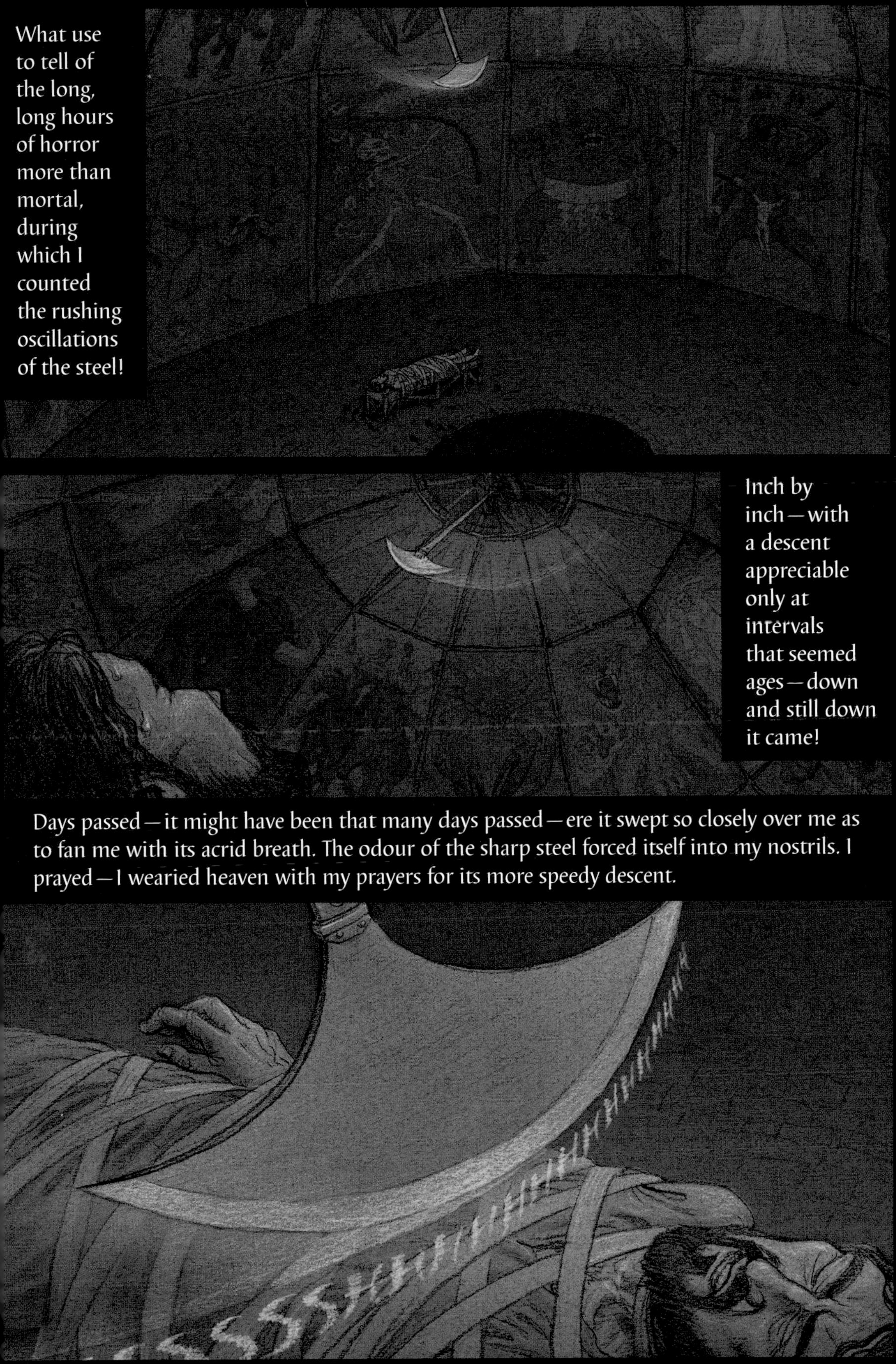
What use to tell of the long, long hours of horror more than mortal, during which I counted the rushing oscillations of the steel!
Inch by inch—with a descent appreciable only at intervals that seemed ages—down and still down it came!
Days passed—it might have been that many days passed—ere it swept so closely over me as to fan me with its acrid breath. The odour of the sharp steel forced itself into my nostrils. I prayed—I wearied heaven with my prayers for its more speedy descent.

Still its hissing vigor increased with each lengthening sweep of the steel.

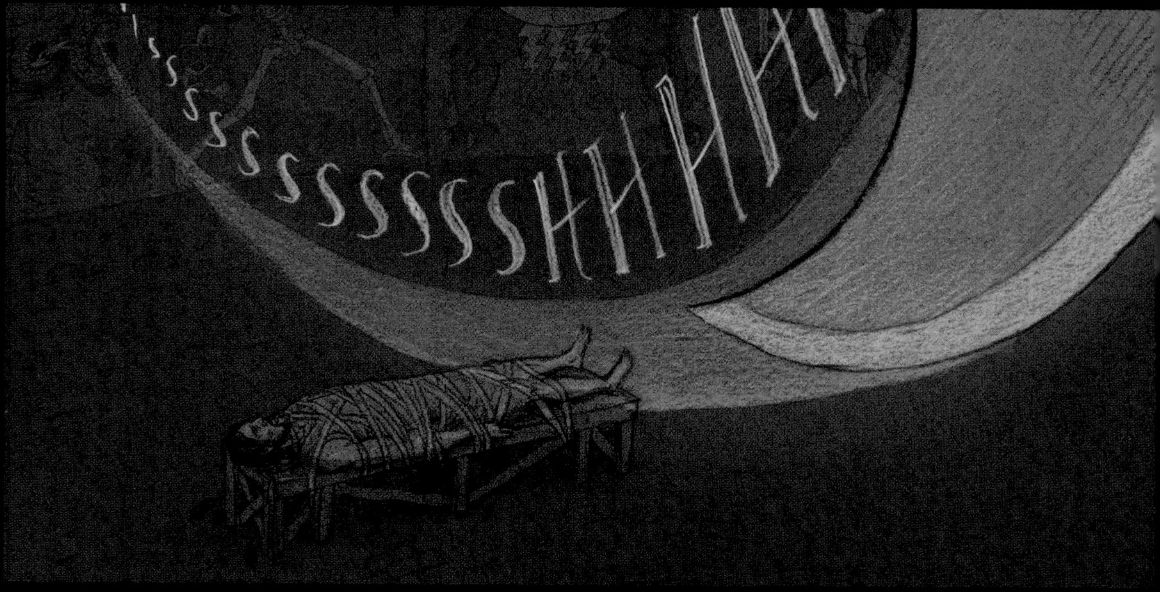

I saw that the crescent was positioned to cross the region of my heart. It would fray the cloth of my robe; it would return and repeat its operations — again — and again.

For a time I grew frantically mad and struggled to force my breast upward against the deadly scimitar.

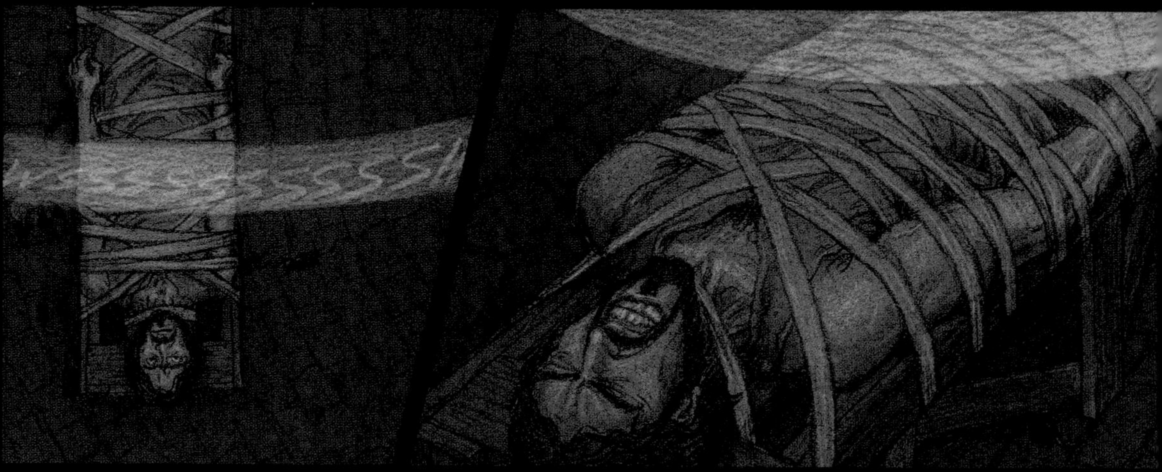

Then I fell suddenly calm and lay smiling at the glittering death as a child at some rare bauble.

There was another interval of utter insensibility. It was brief, for upon waking, there had been no perceptible descent in the pendulum.

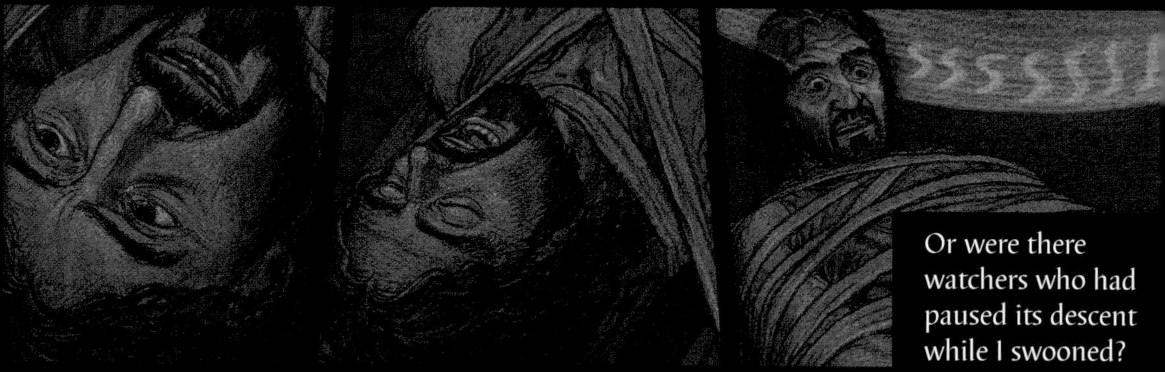
Or were there watchers who had paused its descent while I swooned?

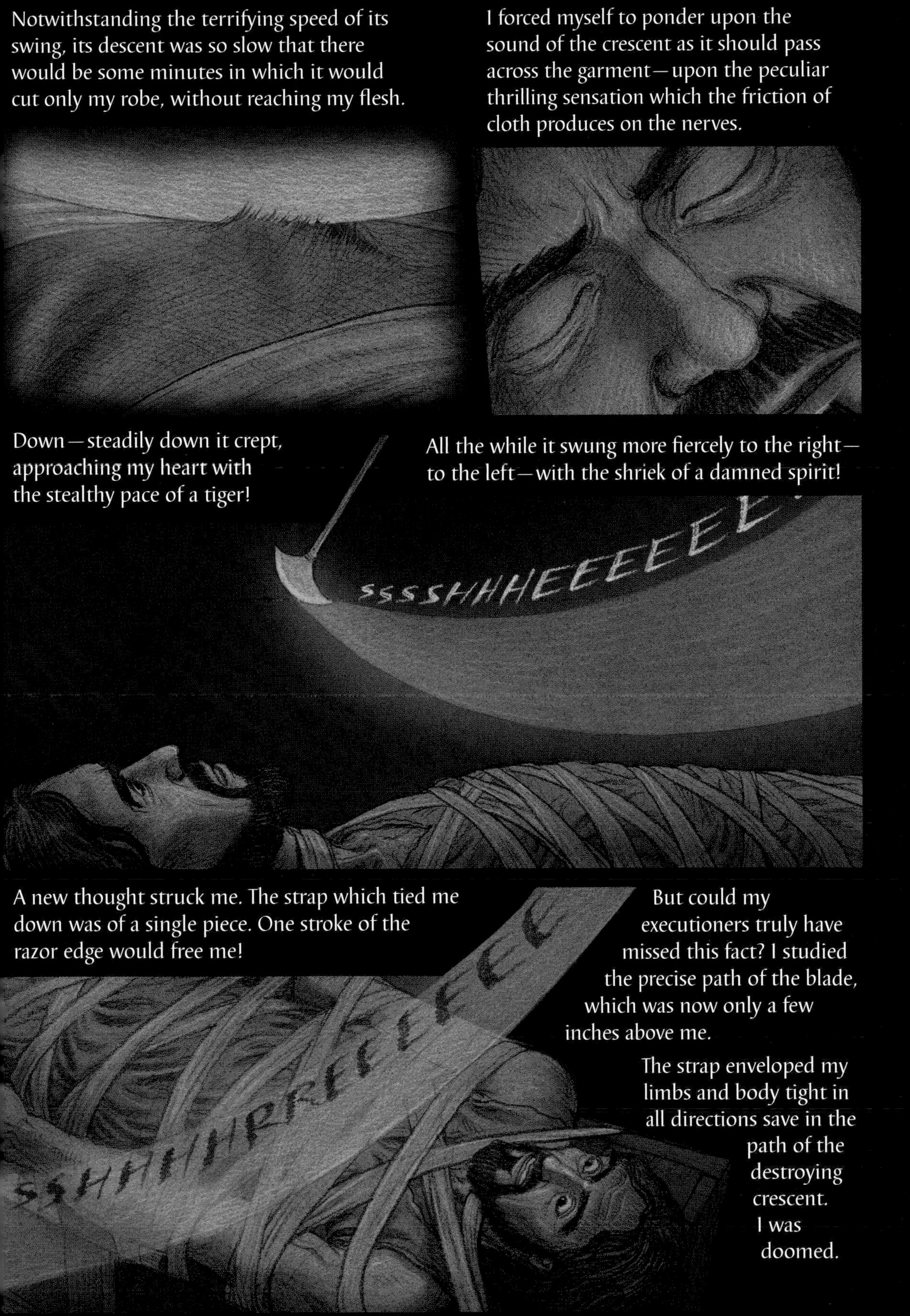
Notwithstanding the terrifying speed of its swing, its descent was so slow that there would be some minutes in which it would cut only my robe, without reaching my flesh.
I forced myself to ponder upon the sound of the crescent as it should pass across the garment—upon the peculiar thrilling sensation which the friction of cloth produces on the nerves.
Down—steadily down it crept, approaching my heart with the stealthy pace of a tiger!
All the while it swung more fiercely to the right—to the left—with the shriek of a damned spirit!
SSSSHHHEEEEEEE
A new thought struck me. The strap which tied me down was of a single piece. One stroke of the razor edge would free me!
SSHHHHRREEEEEE
But could my executioners truly have missed this fact? I studied the precise path of the blade, which was now only a few inches above me.
The strap enveloped my limbs and body tight in all directions save in the path of the destroying crescent.
I was doomed.

Or was I . . . ? I had been mechanically waving the rats away from my food, yet they had devoured nearly all, and bitten my fingers as well. Now I wiped the oils and juices from the meat, as well as the blood from the bites, upon the strap that bound me.

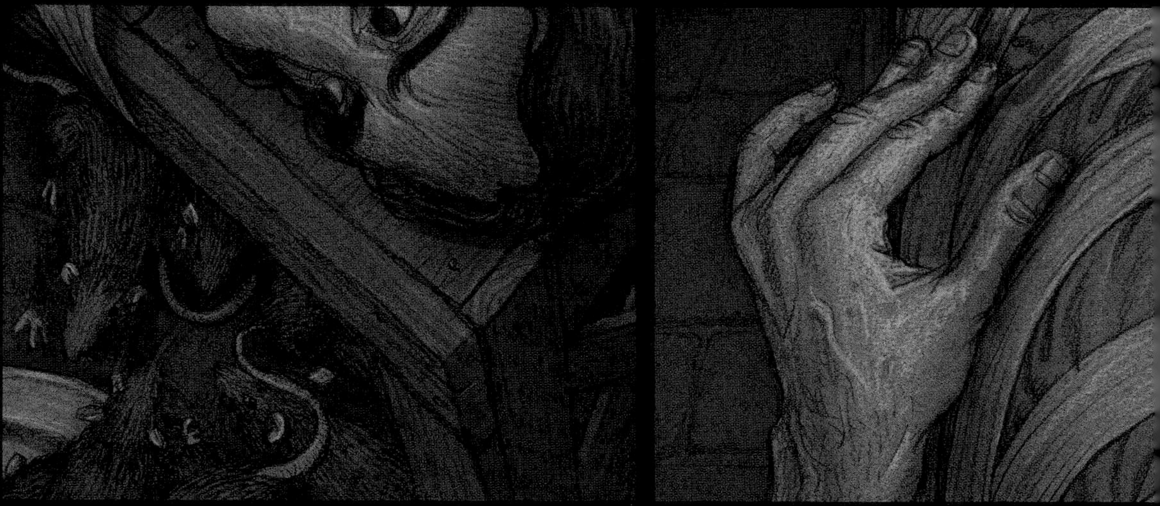

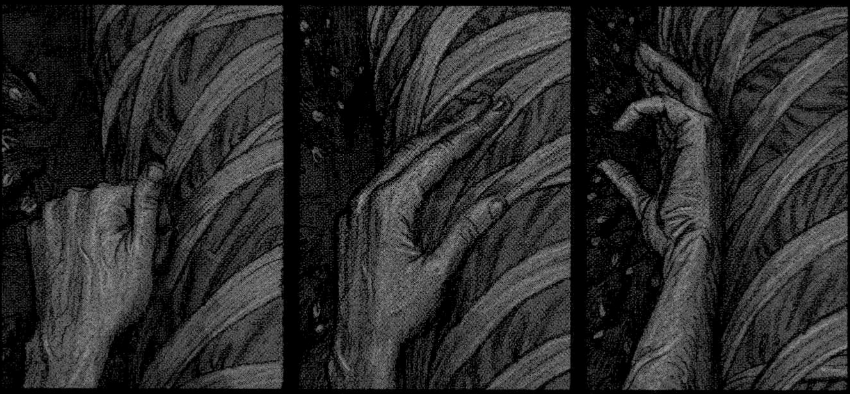

I had not counted in vain upon their voracity. As soon as I fell still, they swarmed upon me in a hideous multitude. The pendulum disturbed them not at all. Avoiding its strokes, they set hungrily upon the strap.

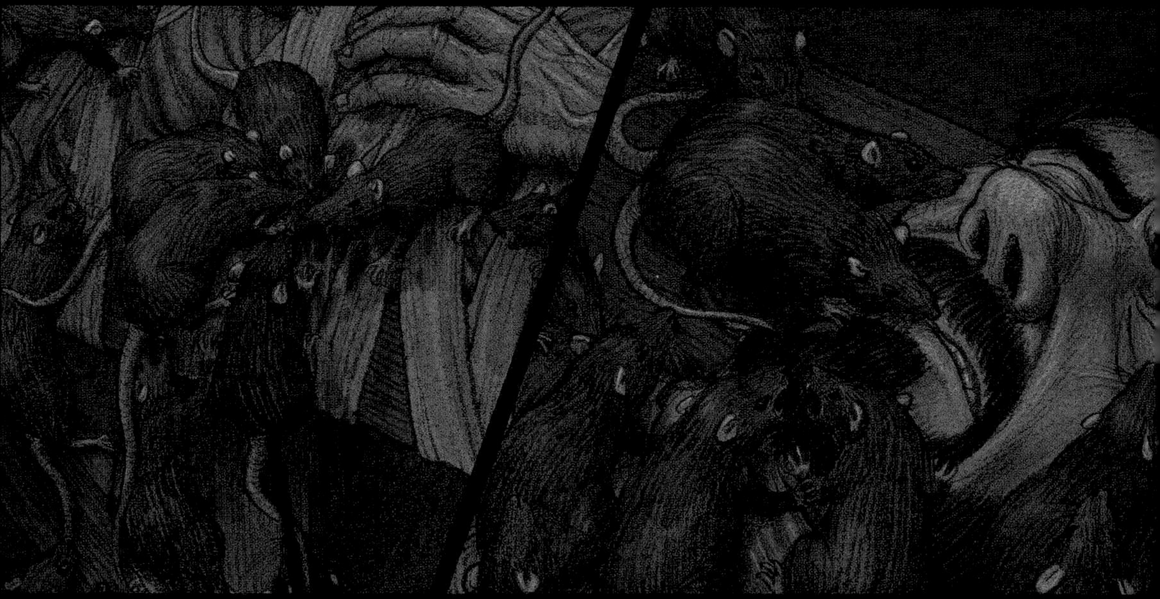

They pressed upon me in ever-accumulating heaps. They writhed upon my throat; their cold lips sought my own; I was half stifled by their thronging pressure. Yet I perceived a loosening of the strap. I knew that in at least one place it must be already severed. With a more than human resolution I lay still.

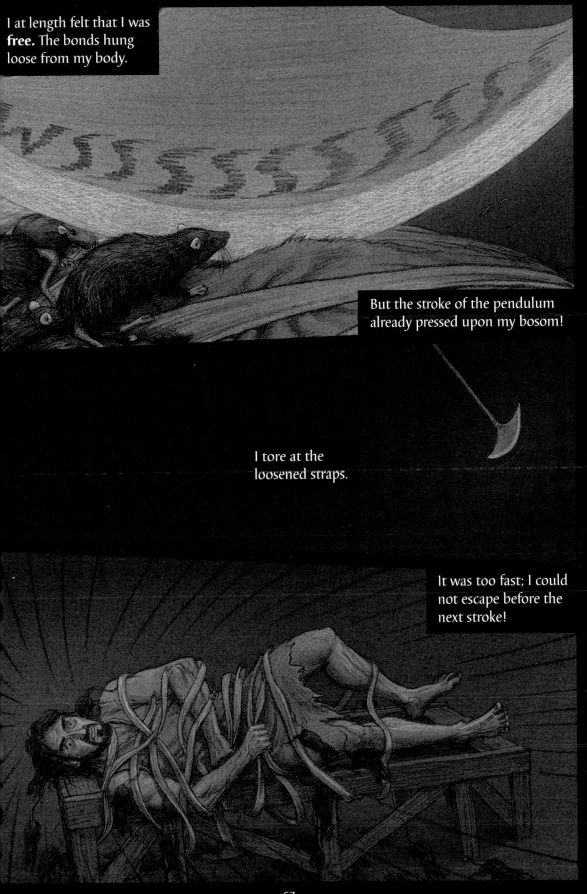

I at length felt that I was **free.** The bonds hung loose from my body.

But the stroke of the pendulum already pressed upon my bosom!

I tore at the loosened straps.

It was too fast; I could not escape before the next stroke!

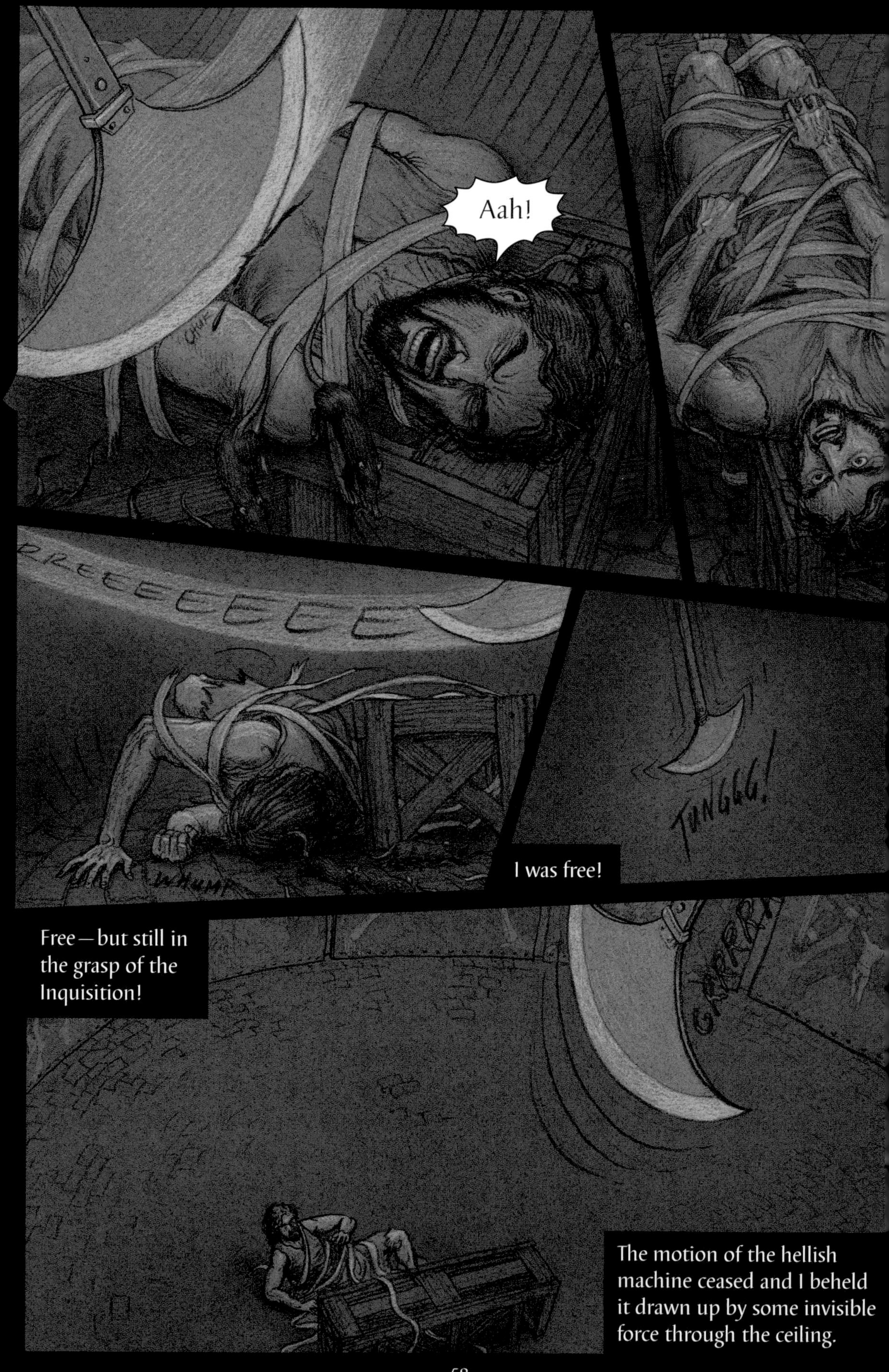
Aah!
TUNGGG!
I was free!
Free—but still in the grasp of the Inquisition!
The motion of the hellish machine ceased and I beheld it drawn up by some invisible force through the ceiling.

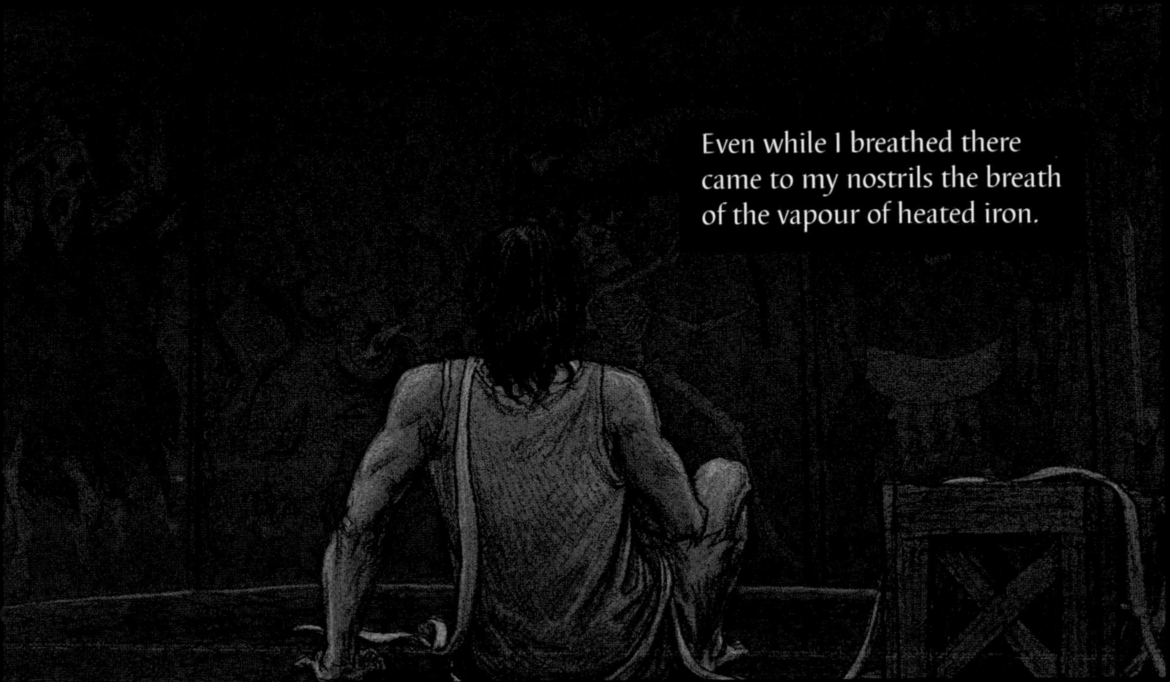
Even while I breathed there came to my nostrils the breath of the vapour of heated iron.

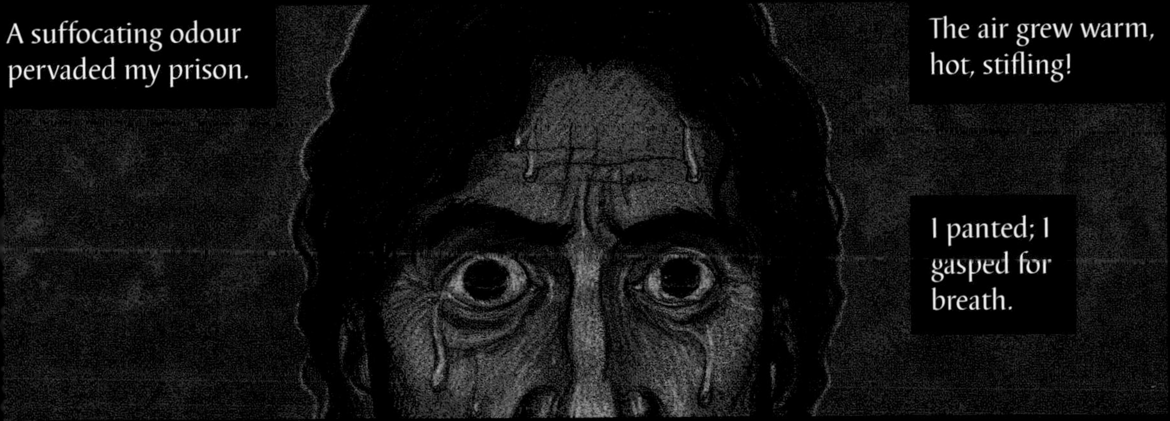
A suffocating odour pervaded my prison.
The air grew warm, hot, stifling!
I panted; I gasped for breath.

I thought of the coolness of the well. I stepped to the brink and looked into its depths.

The dull glare now illumined its inmost recesses. Yet, for a wild moment, did my spirit refuse to comprehend the meaning of what I saw. At length it burned itself in upon my shuddering reason. Oh, horror! Oh, any horror but this! With a shriek I threw myself back.

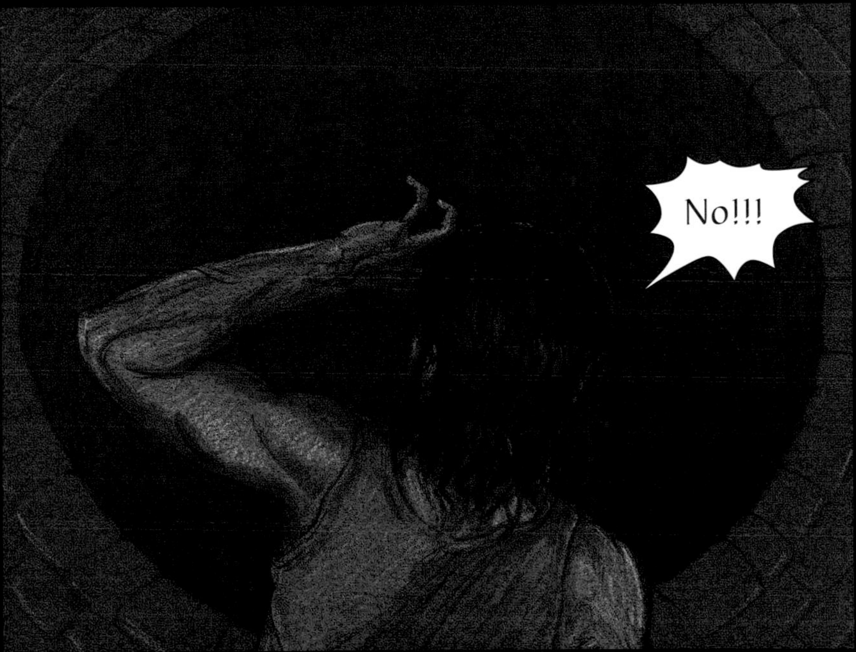
No!!!

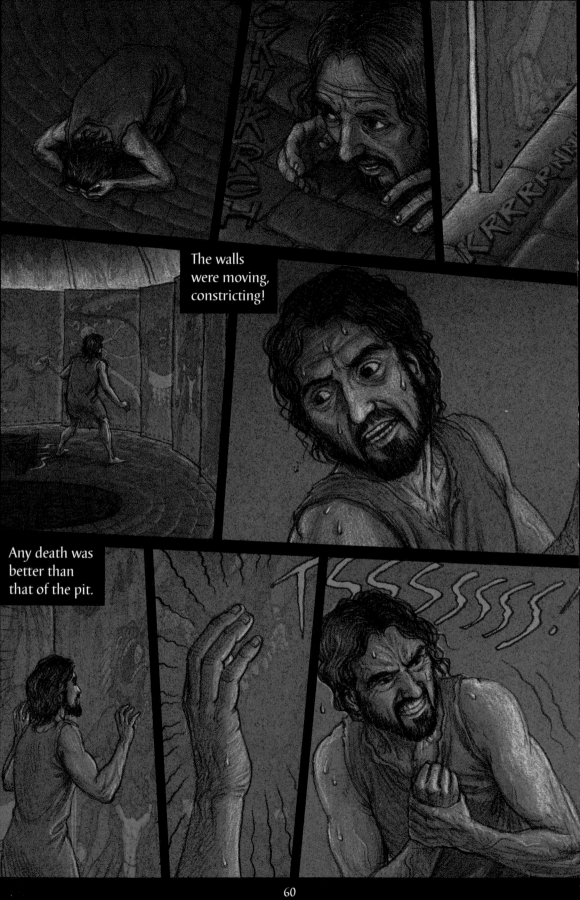

The walls were moving, constricting!

Any death was better than that of the pit.

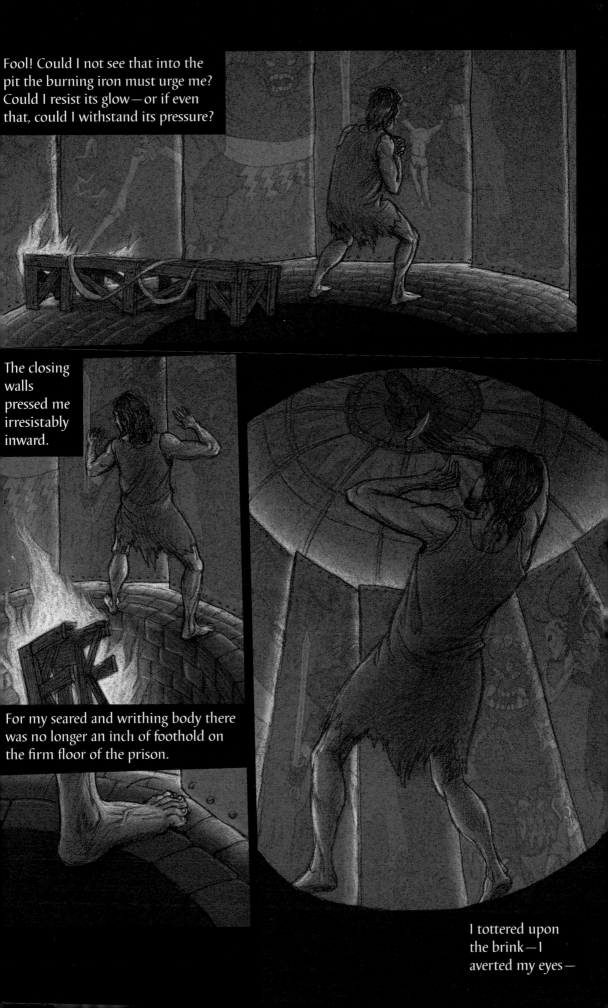

Fool! Could I not see that into the pit the burning iron must urge me? Could I resist its glow—or if even that, could I withstand its pressure?

The closing walls pressed me irresistably inward.

For my seared and writhing body there was no longer an inch of foothold on the firm floor of the prison.

I tottered upon the brink—I averted my eyes—

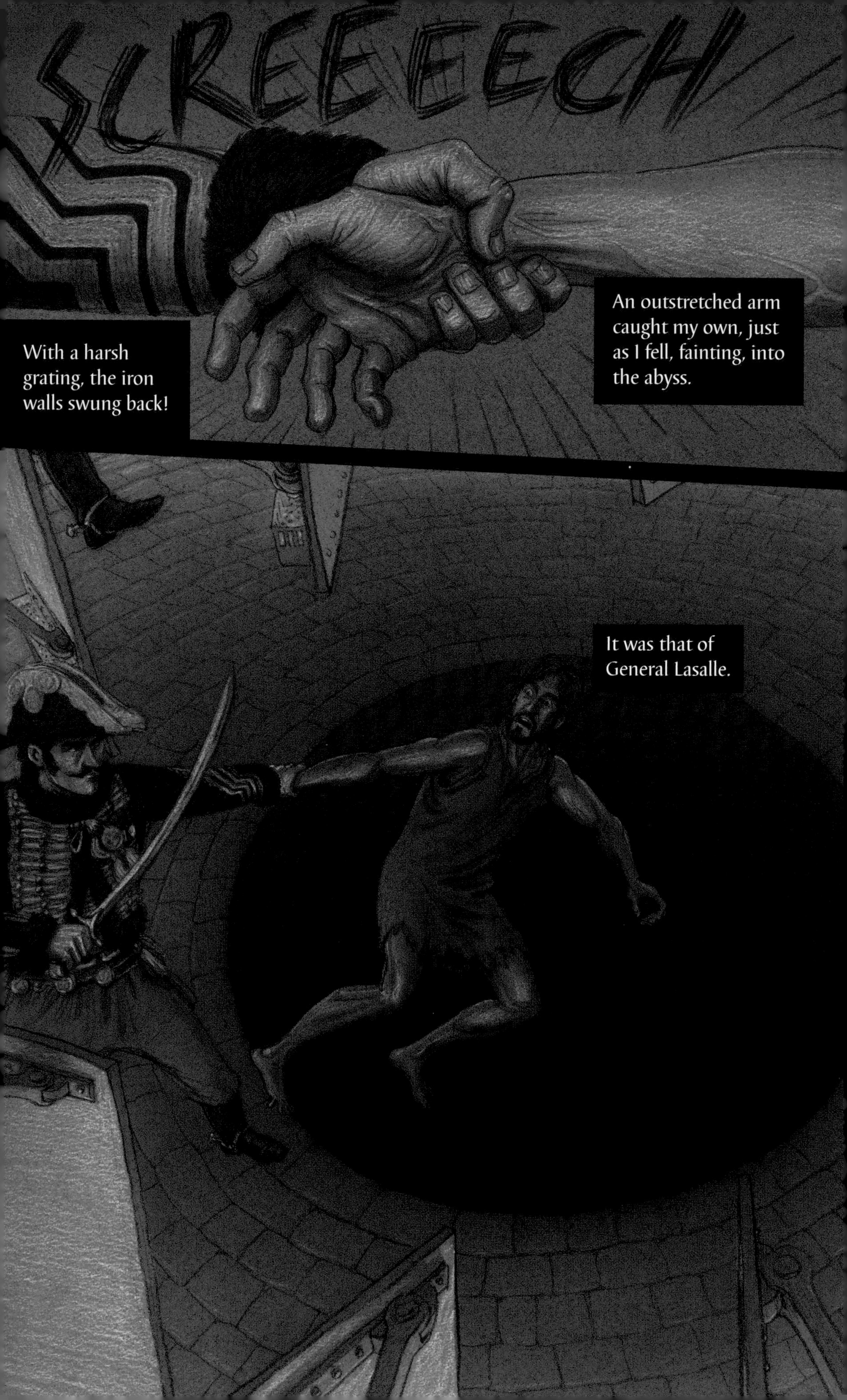
SCREEEECH
With a harsh grating, the iron walls swung back!
An outstretched arm caught my own, just as I fell, fainting, into the abyss.
It was that of General Lasalle.

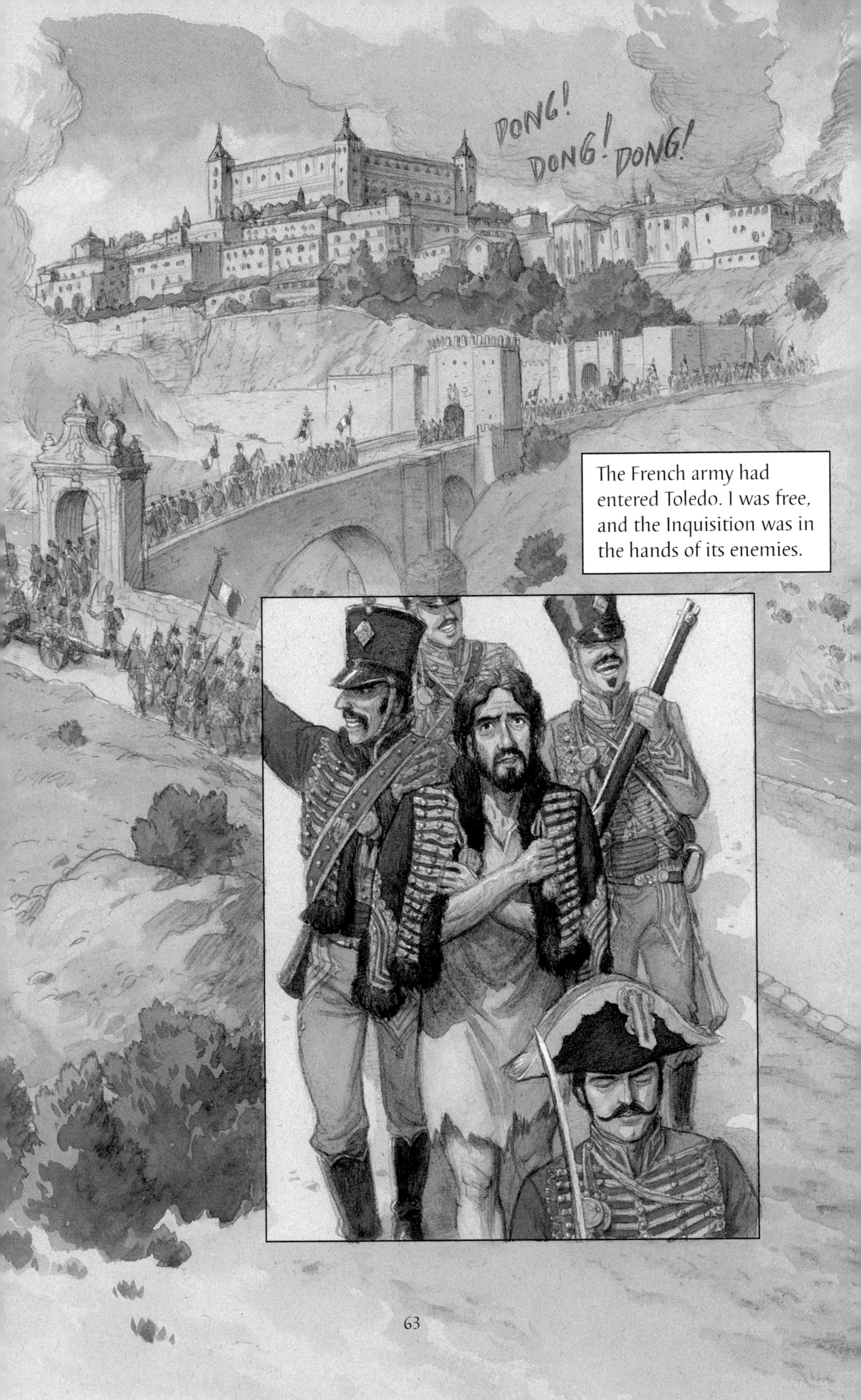
DONG! DONG! DONG!
The French army had entered Toledo. I was free, and the Inquisition was in the hands of its enemies.

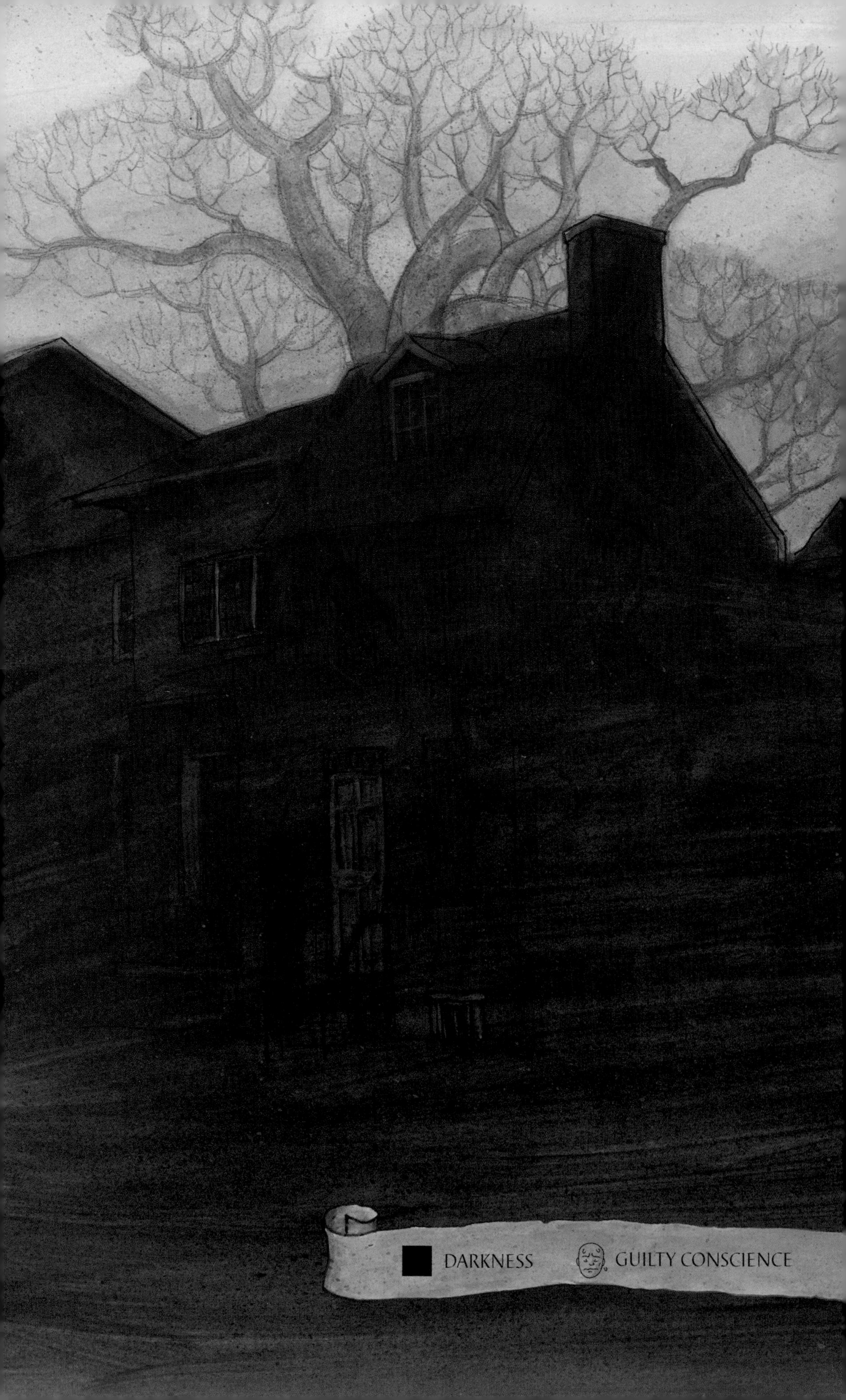
DARKNESS
GUILTY CONSCIENCE

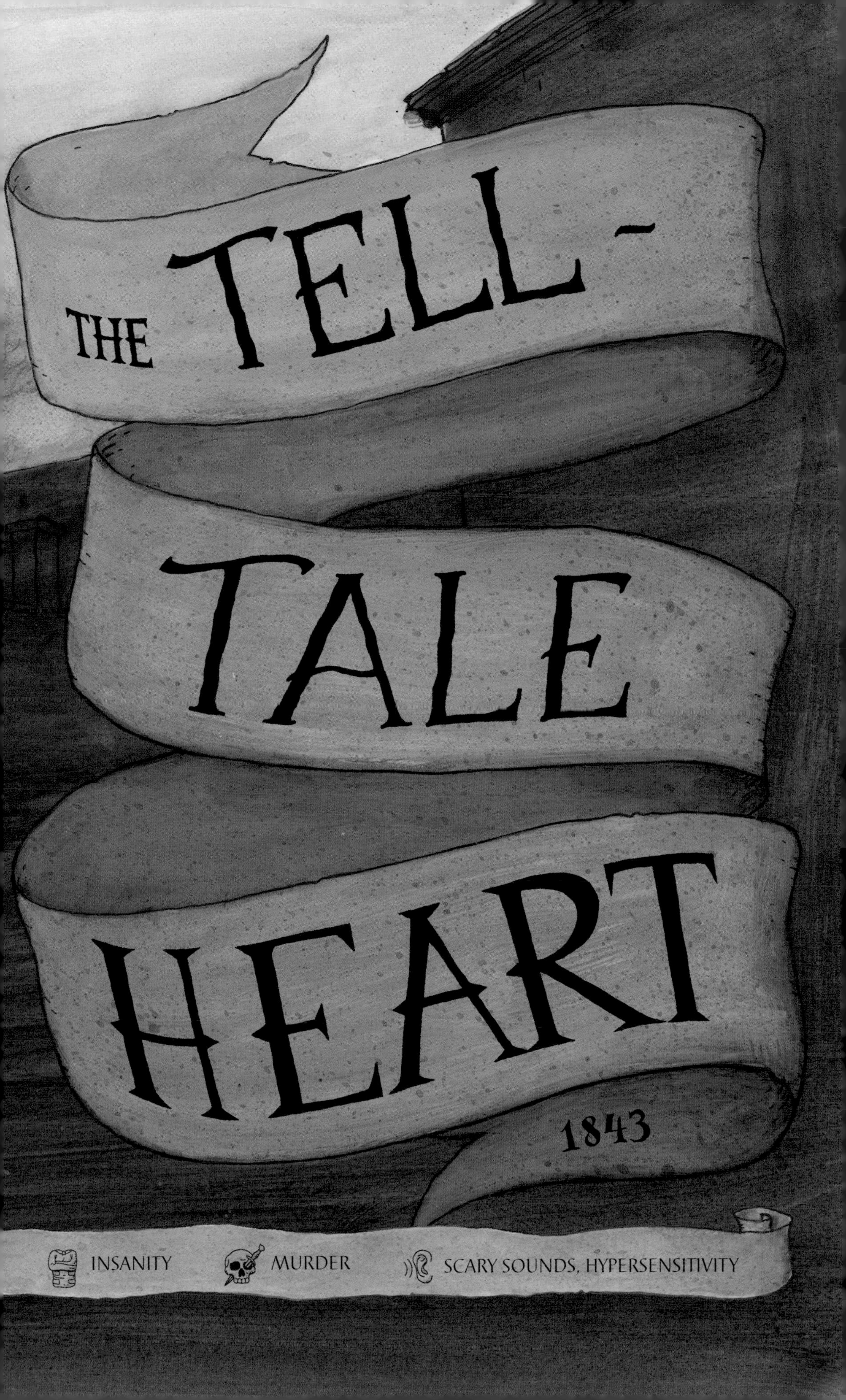
THE TELL-
TALE
HEART
1843
INSANITY
MURDER
SCARY SOUNDS, HYPERSENSITIVITY

It is true that I am nervous. But why will you say that I am mad?

Hearken, and observe how healthily, how calmly, I can tell you the whole story.

It is impossible to say how first the idea entered my brain; but once conceived, it haunted me day and night.

I loved the old man. He had never wronged me.

It was his eye. Yes, his eye!

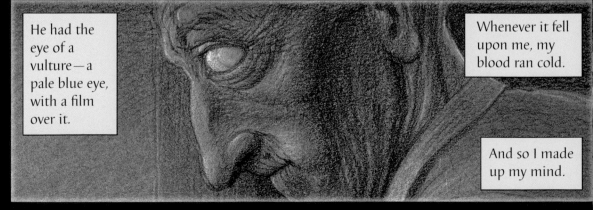

He had the eye of a vulture—a pale blue eye, with a film over it.

Whenever it fell upon me, my blood ran cold.

And so I made up my mind.

Each night, just at midnight, I went silently to his door.
I turned the latch and opened it—oh so gently!

When I had made an opening sufficient for my head, I put in a dark lantern, all closed so that no light shone out, and then I thrust in my head.

Oh, you would have laughed to see how cunningly I thrust it in! I moved it slowly— very, very slowly, so that I might not disturb the old man's sleep.

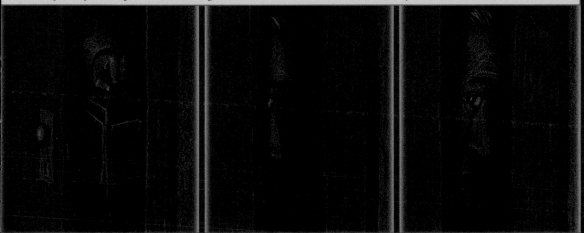

It took me an hour to place my whole head within the opening so far that I could see him as he lay upon his bed. Could a madman have been so wise?

Then, when my head was well in the room, I undid the lantern cautiously—oh, so cautiously (for the hinges creaked)—I undid it just so much that a single thin ray fell upon the vulture eye.

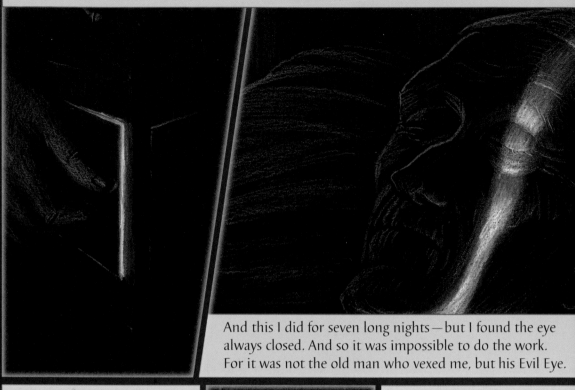

And this I did for seven long nights—but I found the eye always closed. And so it was impossible to do the work. For it was not the old man who vexed me, but his Evil Eye.

Upon the eighth night I was more than usually cautious in opening the door. A watch's minute hand moves more quickly than did mine.

I could scarcely contain my feelings of triumph.

I had my head in, and was about to open the lantern, when my thumb slipped upon the tin fastening.

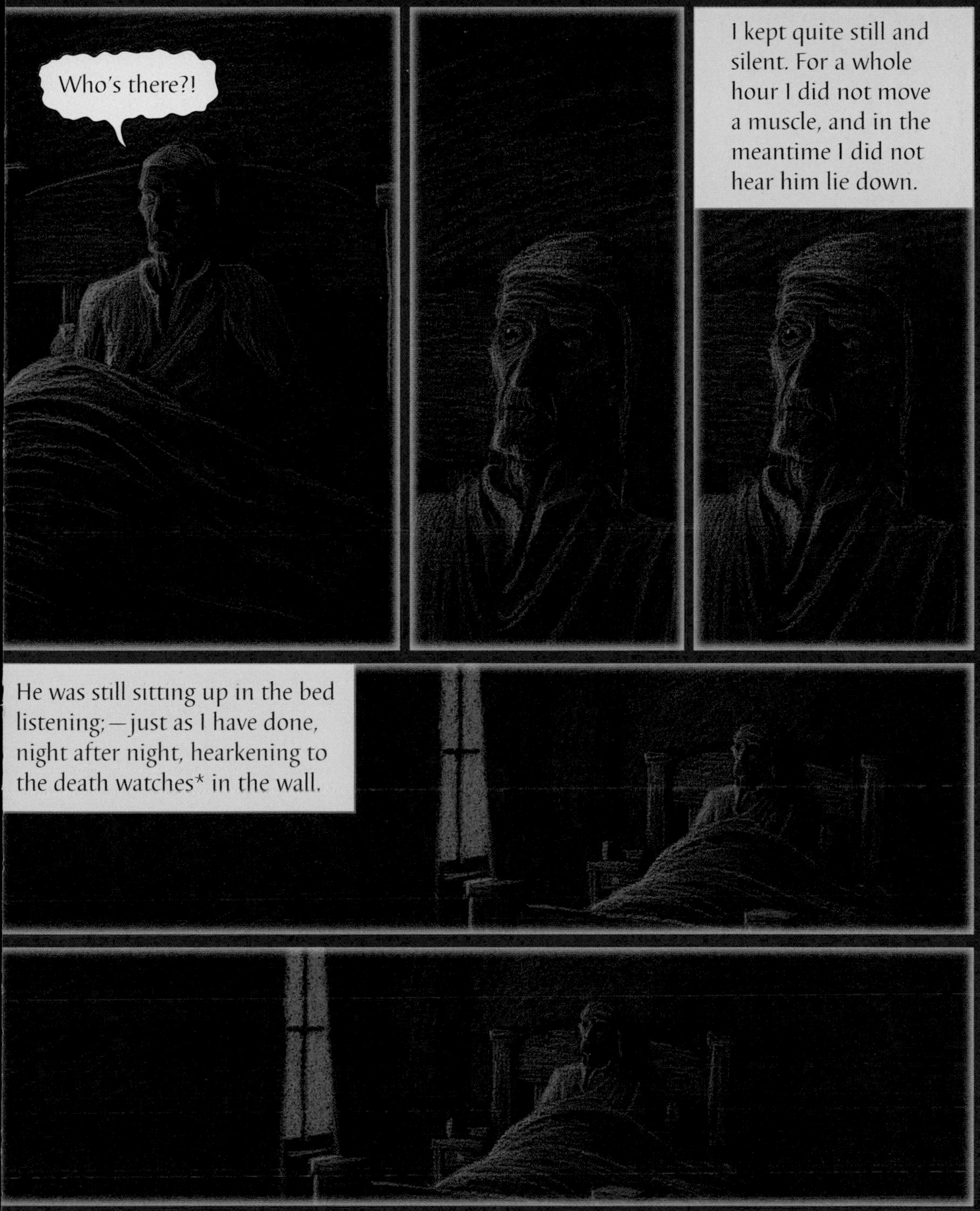
Who's there?!
I kept quite still and silent. For a whole hour I did not move a muscle, and in the meantime I did not hear him lie down.
He was still sitting up in the bed listening;—just as I have done, night after night, hearkening to the death watches* in the wall.

*death watch beetles, which tap their heads against the inside of walls to attract mates

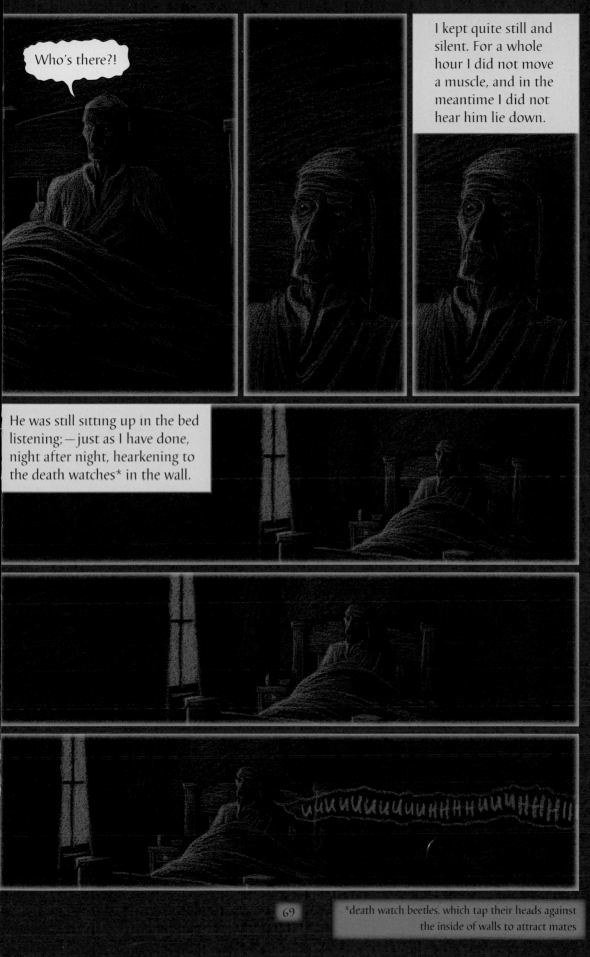

I knew that sound. It was not a groan of pain or of grief—oh, no! It was the low stifled sound of mortal terror.

Ahhhuuuuuuuu......

I knew that he had been lying awake ever since the first slight noise, his fears growing upon him.

You cannot imagine how stealthily, stealthily, I opened the lantern shutter, so that it cast a single dim ray, like the thread of the spider, exactly upon the vulture eye.

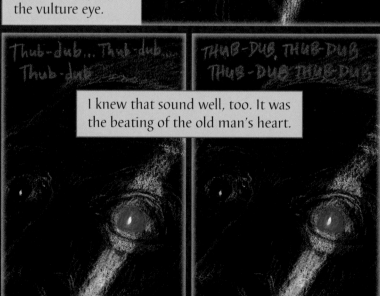

Thub-dub... Thub-dub...
Thub-dub

THUB-DUB, THUB-DUB
THUB-DUB THUB-DUB

THUB-DUB THUB
THUB-DUB, THU

I knew that sound well, too. It was the beating of the old man's heart.

I held the lantern motionless.

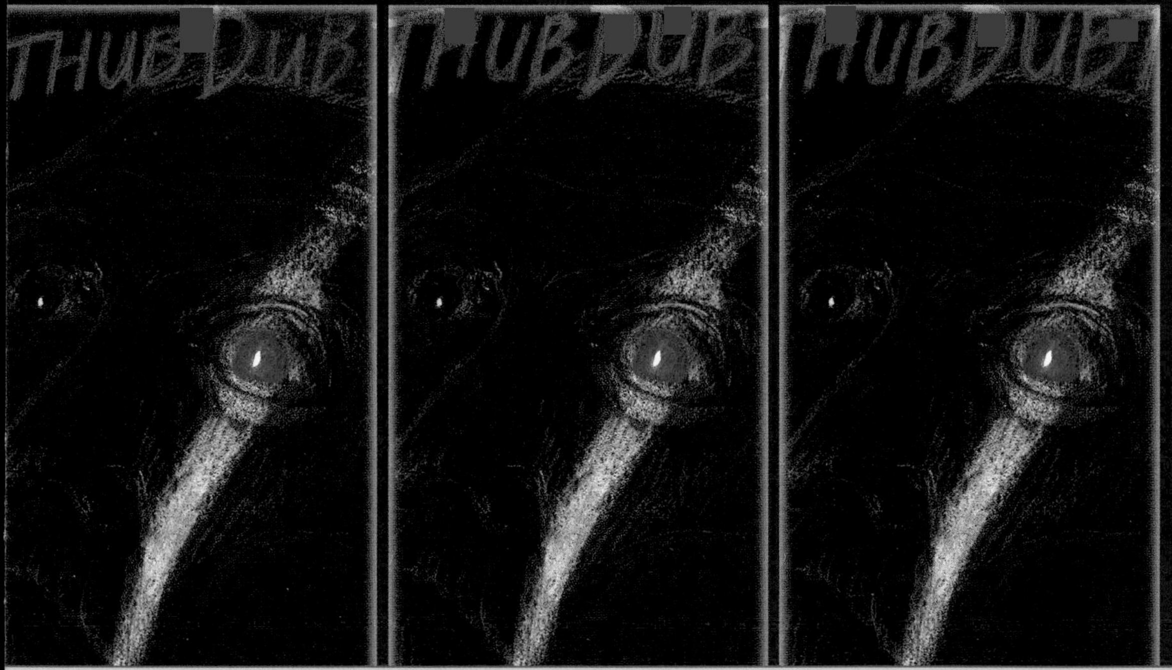
THUB DUB
THUB DUB
HUB DUB

I thought the heart must burst. And now a new anxiety seized me—the sound would be heard by a neighbour! I threw open the lantern and leaped into the room.

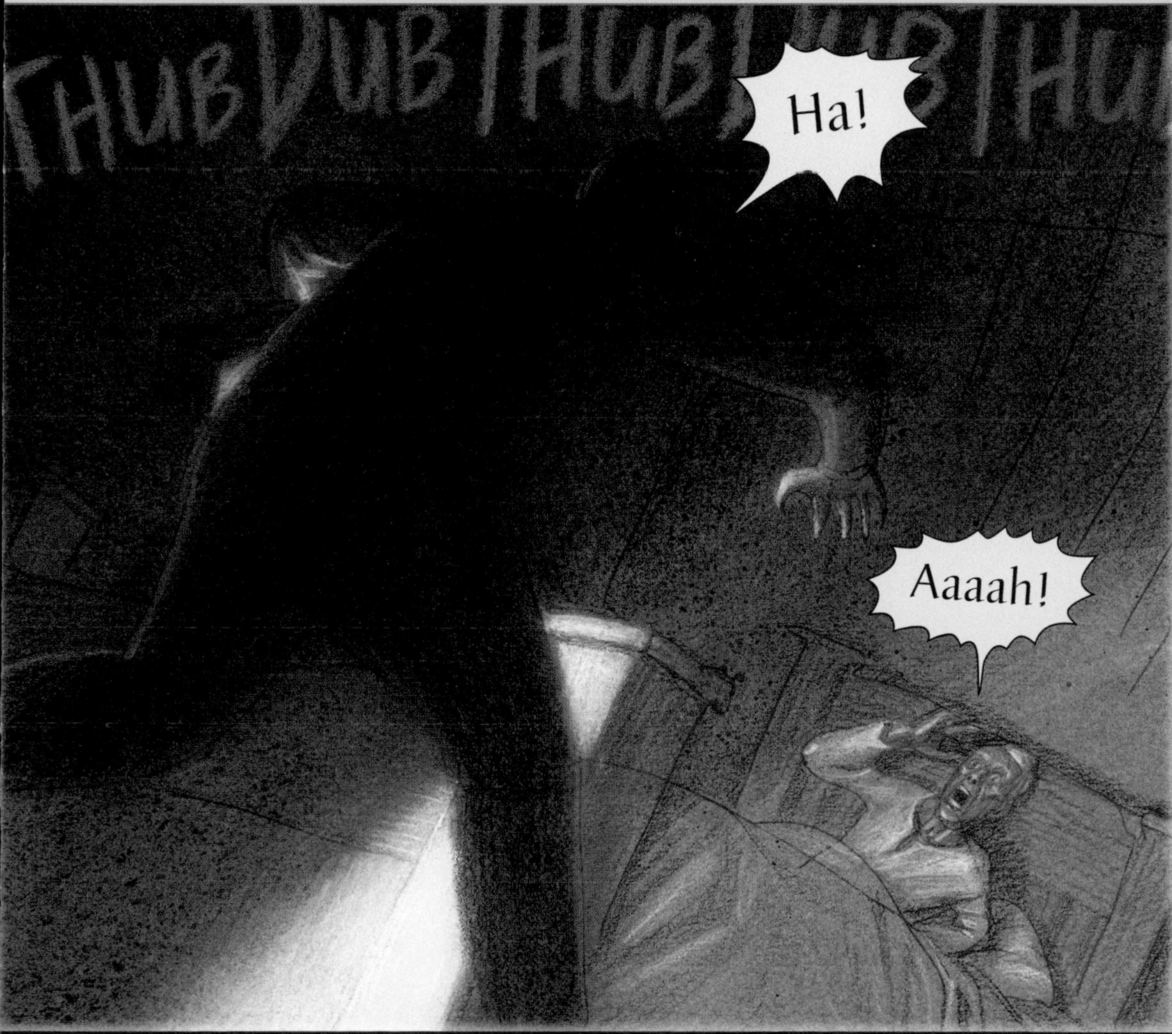
THUB DUB THUB
Ha!
Aaaah!

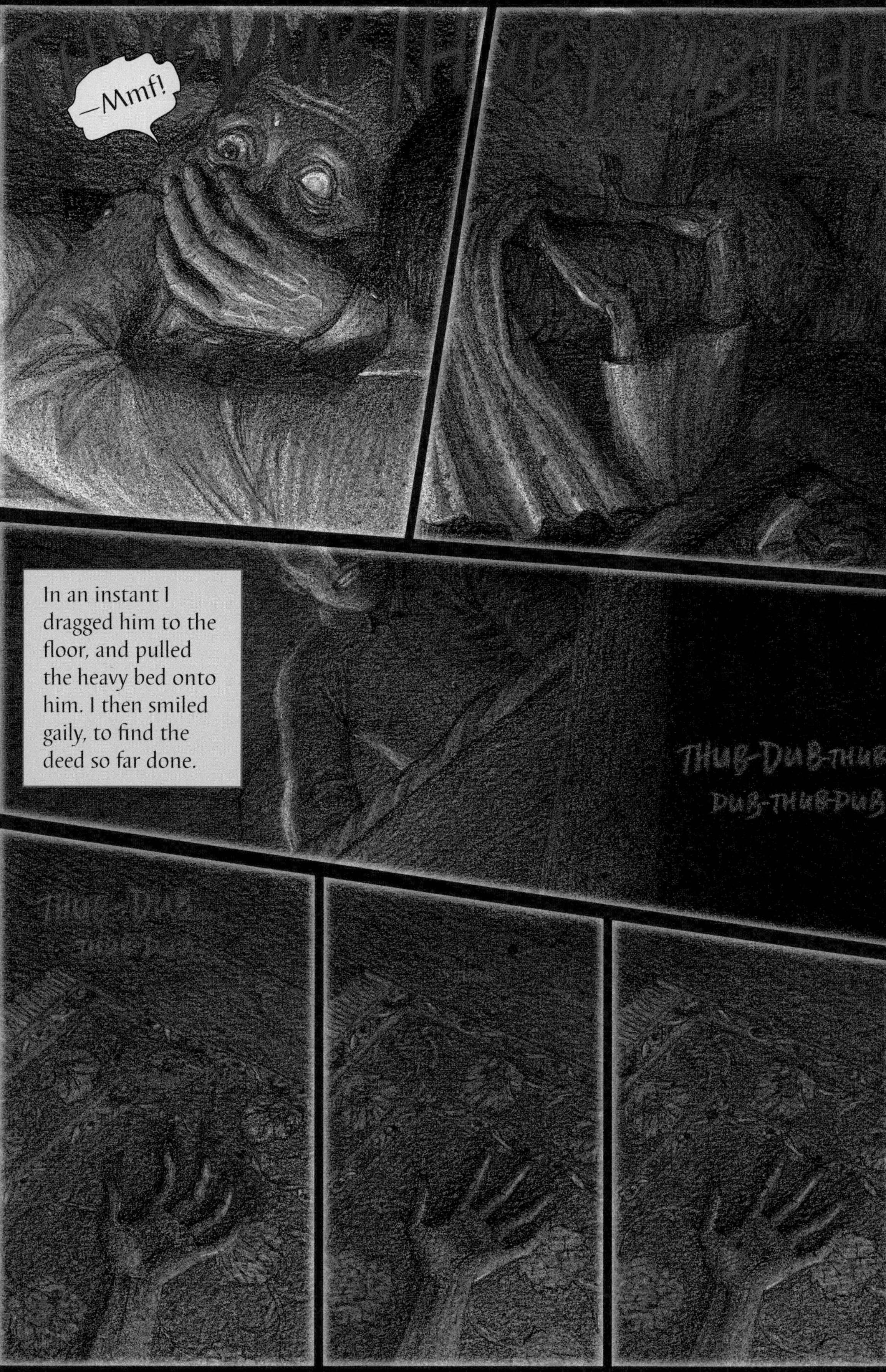
—Mmf!
In an instant I dragged him to the floor, and pulled the heavy bed onto him. I then smiled gaily, to find the deed so far done.
THUB-DUB-THUB
DUB-THUB-DUB

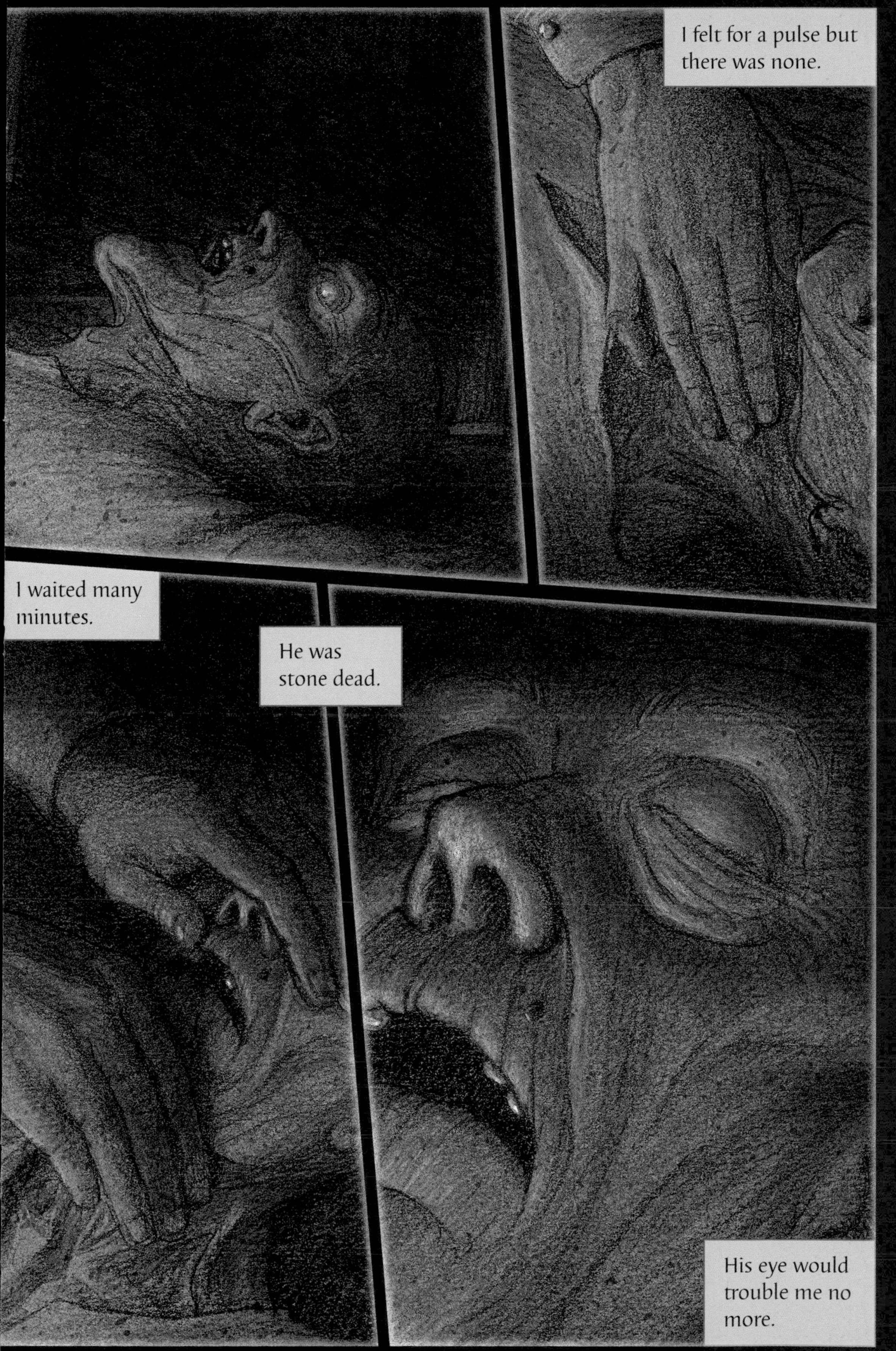
I felt for a pulse but there was none.
I waited many minutes.
He was stone dead.
His eye would trouble me no more.

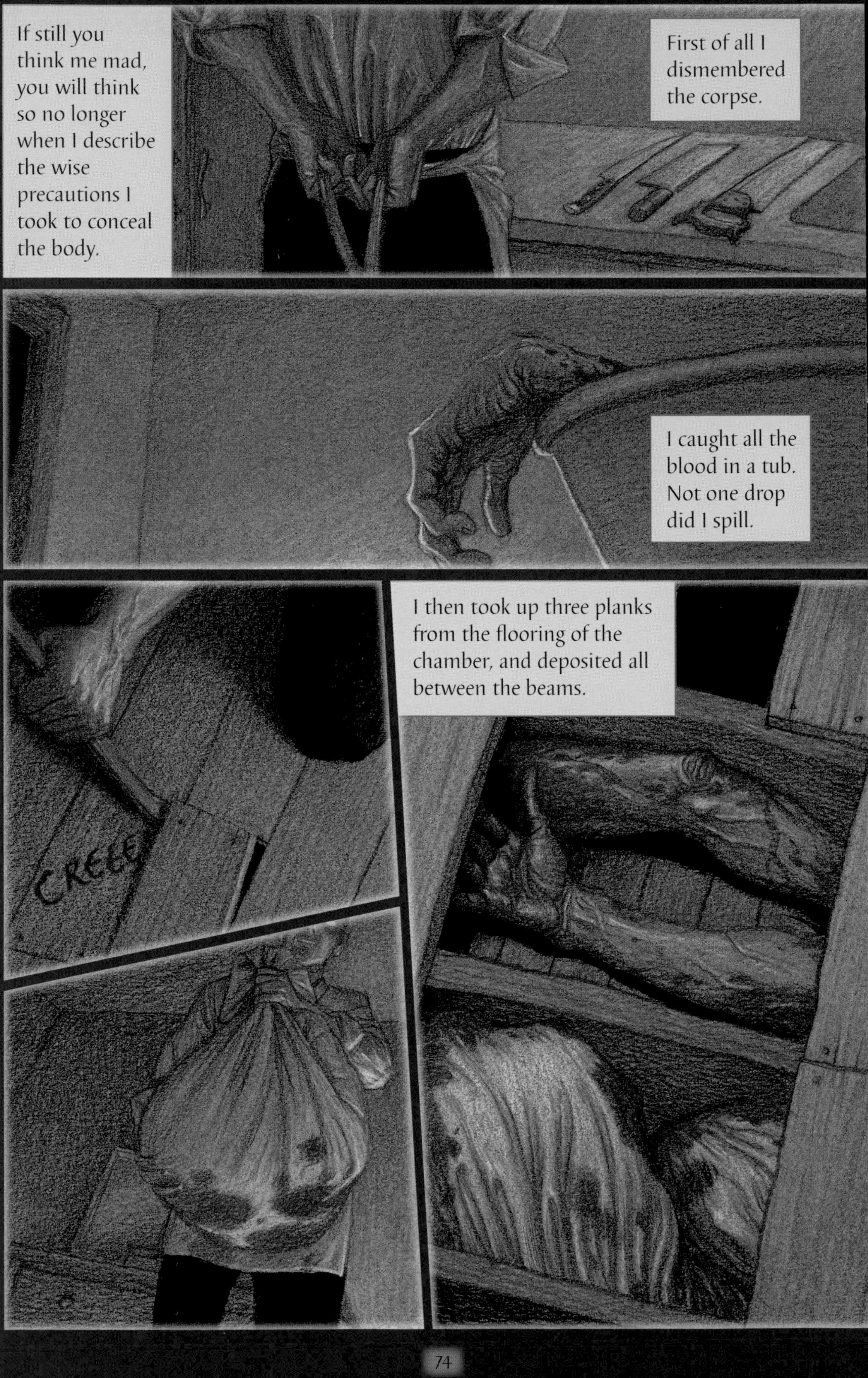
If still you think me mad, you will think so no longer when I describe the wise precautions I took to conceal the body.
First of all I dismembered the corpse.
I caught all the blood in a tub. Not one drop did I spill.
CREEE
I then took up three planks from the flooring of the chamber, and deposited all between the beams.

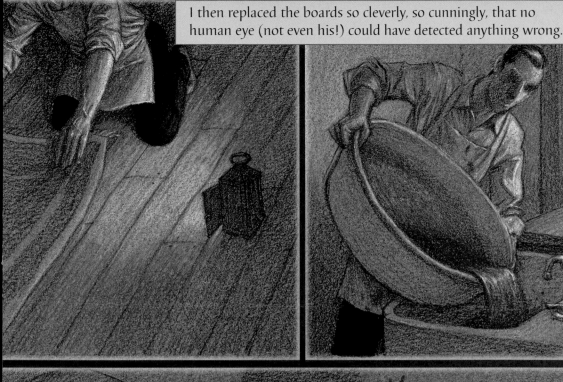

I then replaced the boards so cleverly, so cunningly, that no human eye (not even his!) could have detected anything wrong.

DONG
DONG
DONG
DON

KNOCK KNOCK KNOCK!

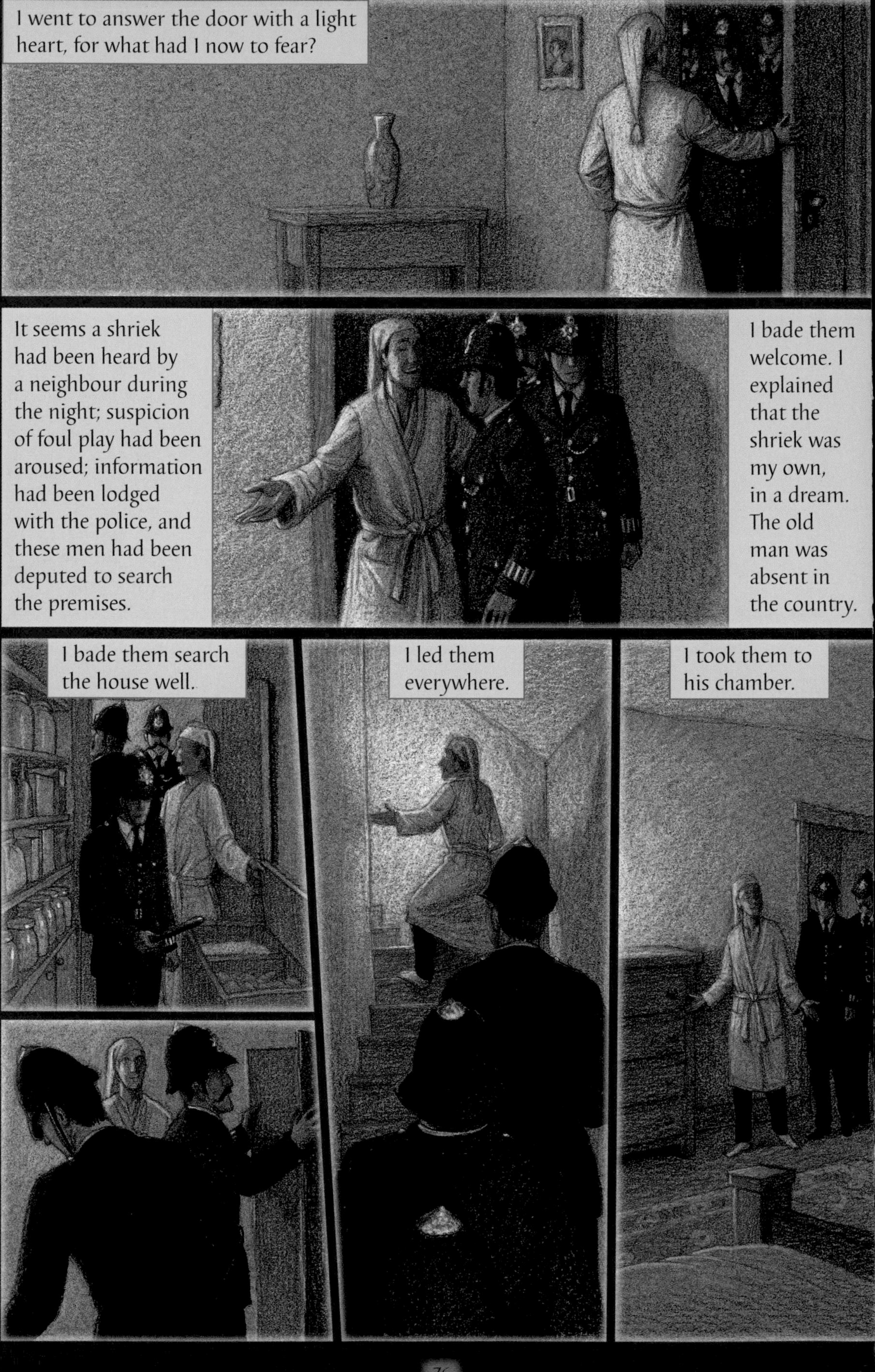
I went to answer the door with a light heart, for what had I now to fear?
It seems a shriek had been heard by a neighbour during the night; suspicion of foul play had been aroused; information had been lodged with the police, and these men had been deputed to search the premises.
I bade them welcome. I explained that the shriek was my own, in a dream. The old man was absent in the country.
I bade them search the house well.
I led them everywhere.
I took them to his chamber.

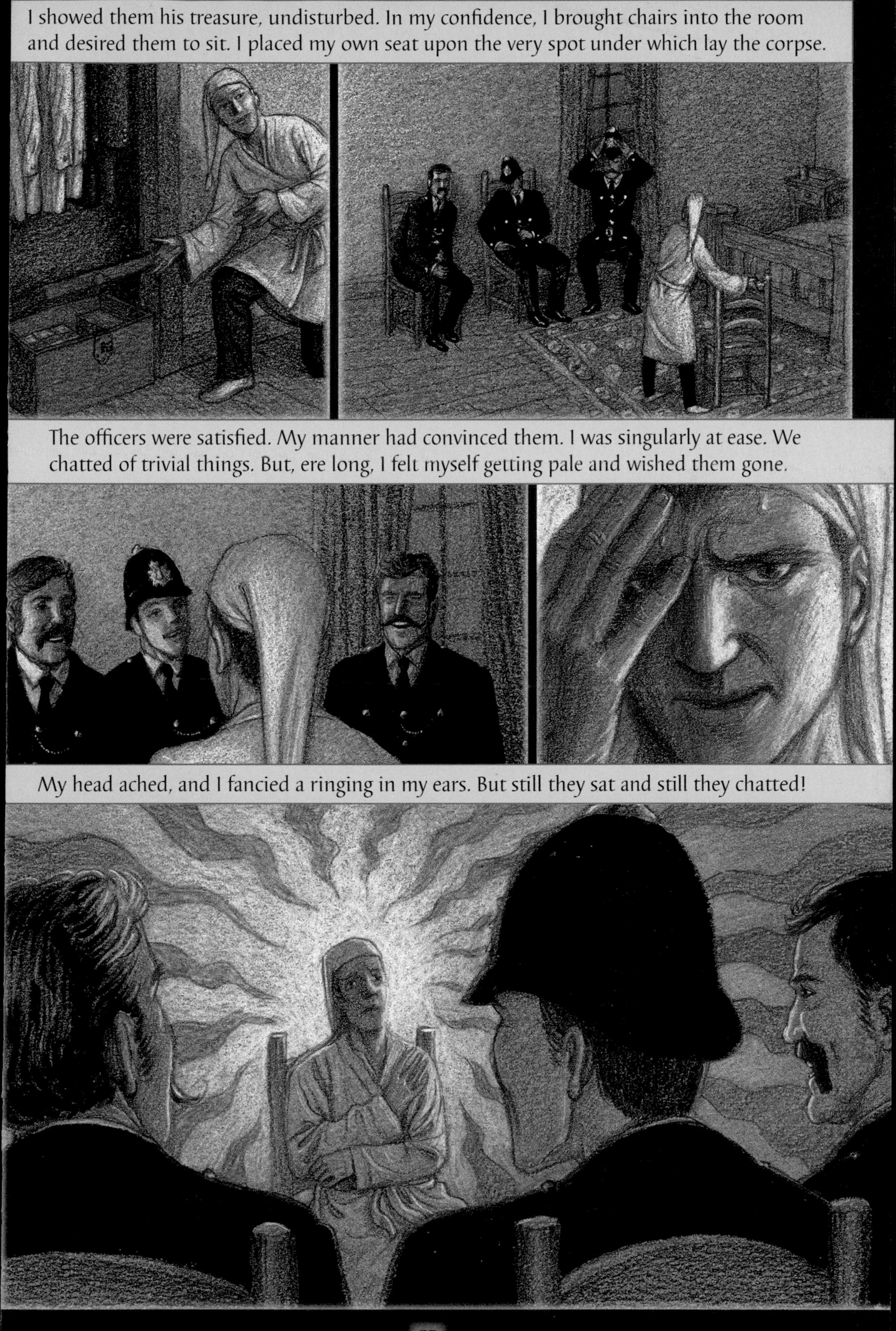
I showed them his treasure, undisturbed. In my confidence, I brought chairs into the room and desired them to sit. I placed my own seat upon the very spot under which lay the corpse.
The officers were satisfied. My manner had convinced them. I was singularly at ease. We chatted of trivial things. But, ere long, I felt myself getting pale and wished them gone.
My head ached, and I fancied a ringing in my ears. But still they sat and still they chatted!

The ringing continued, and grew more distinct. I talked more freely to get rid of the feeling, but still it grew louder . . . until, at length, I found that the noise was not within my ears.

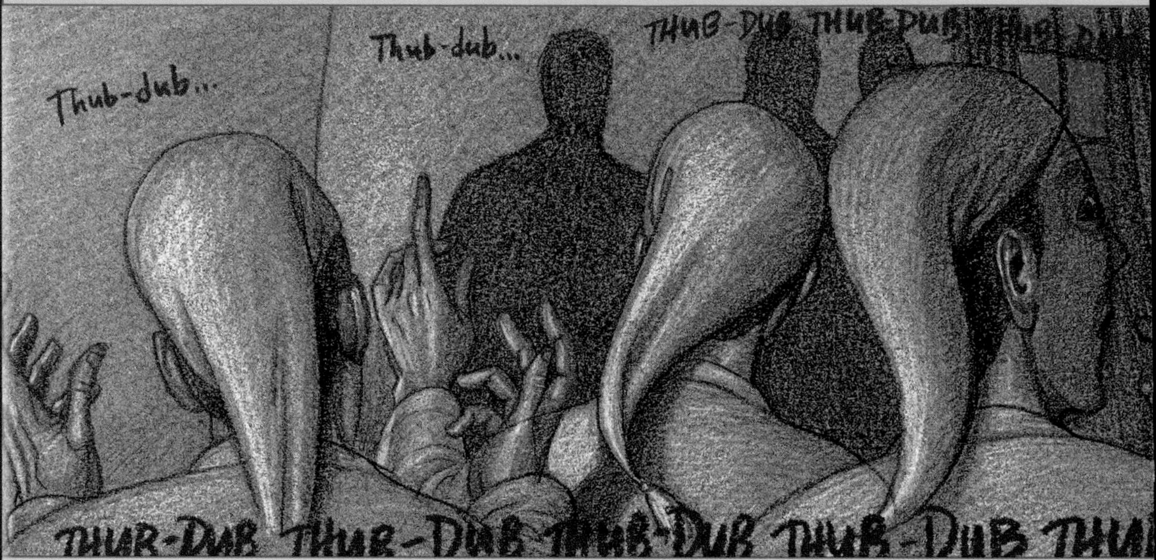

Thub-dub...
Thub-dub...
THUB-DUB THUB-DUB THUB-DUB THUB-DUB

No doubt I now grew very pale. I talked more fluently, and with a heightened voice. Yet the sound increased—and what could I do? I gasped for breath—and yet the officers heard it not.

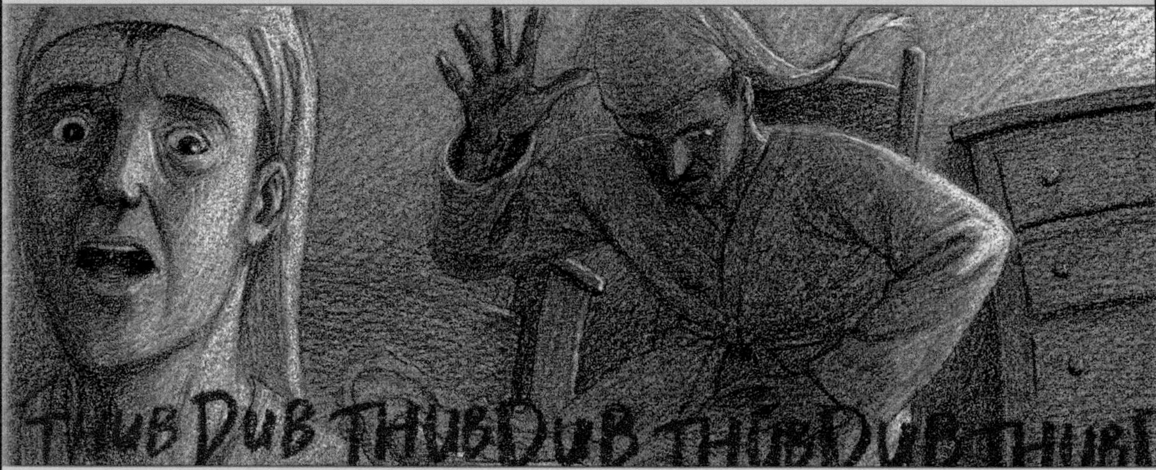

THUB DUB THUB DUB THUB DUB

I talked more quickly—more vehemently; but the noise grew louder and louder!

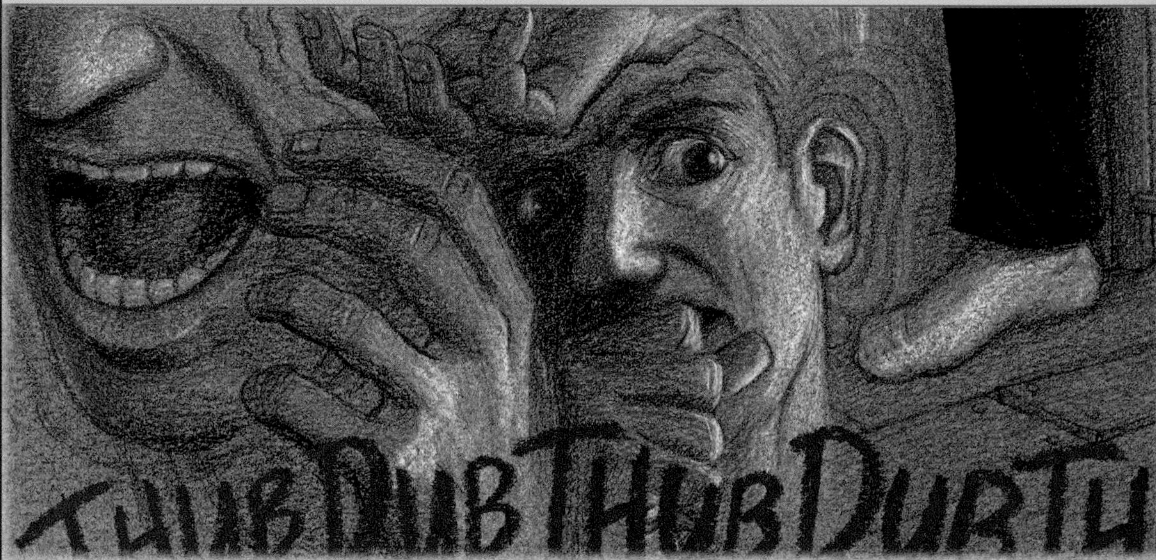

THUB DUB THUB DUB

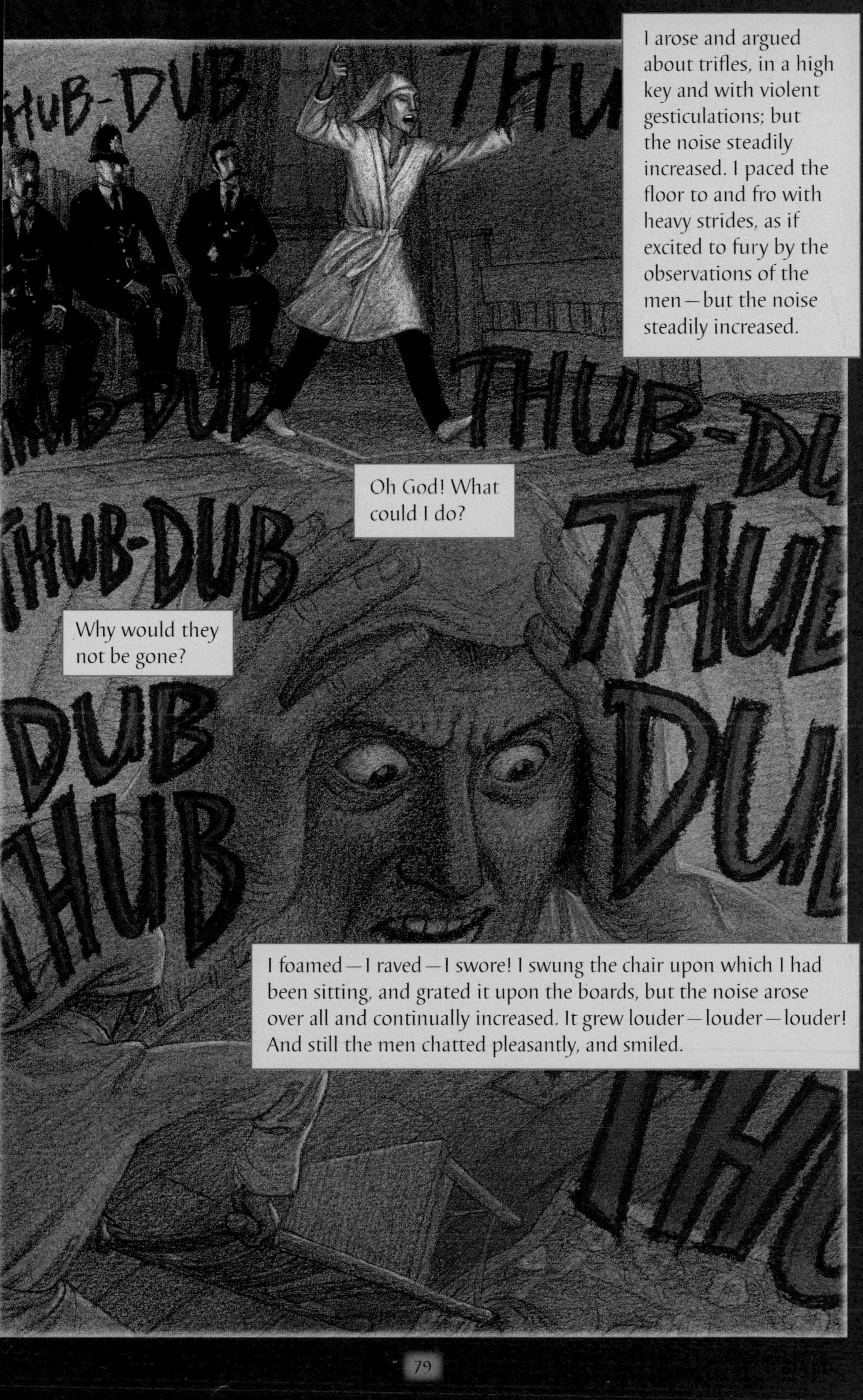
I arose and argued about trifles, in a high key and with violent gesticulations; but the noise steadily increased. I paced the floor to and fro with heavy strides, as if excited to fury by the observations of the men—but the noise steadily increased.
THUB-DUB
THU
THUB-DUB
THUB-DUB
Oh God! What could I do?
THUB-DUB
THUB
Why would they not be gone?
DUB
THUB
DUB
I foamed—I raved—I swore! I swung the chair upon which I had been sitting, and grated it upon the boards, but the noise arose over all and continually increased. It grew louder—louder—louder! And still the men chatted pleasantly, and smiled.
THU

Was it possible they heard not? Almighty God!—no, no! They heard!—they suspected!—they knew! They were making a mockery of my horror!

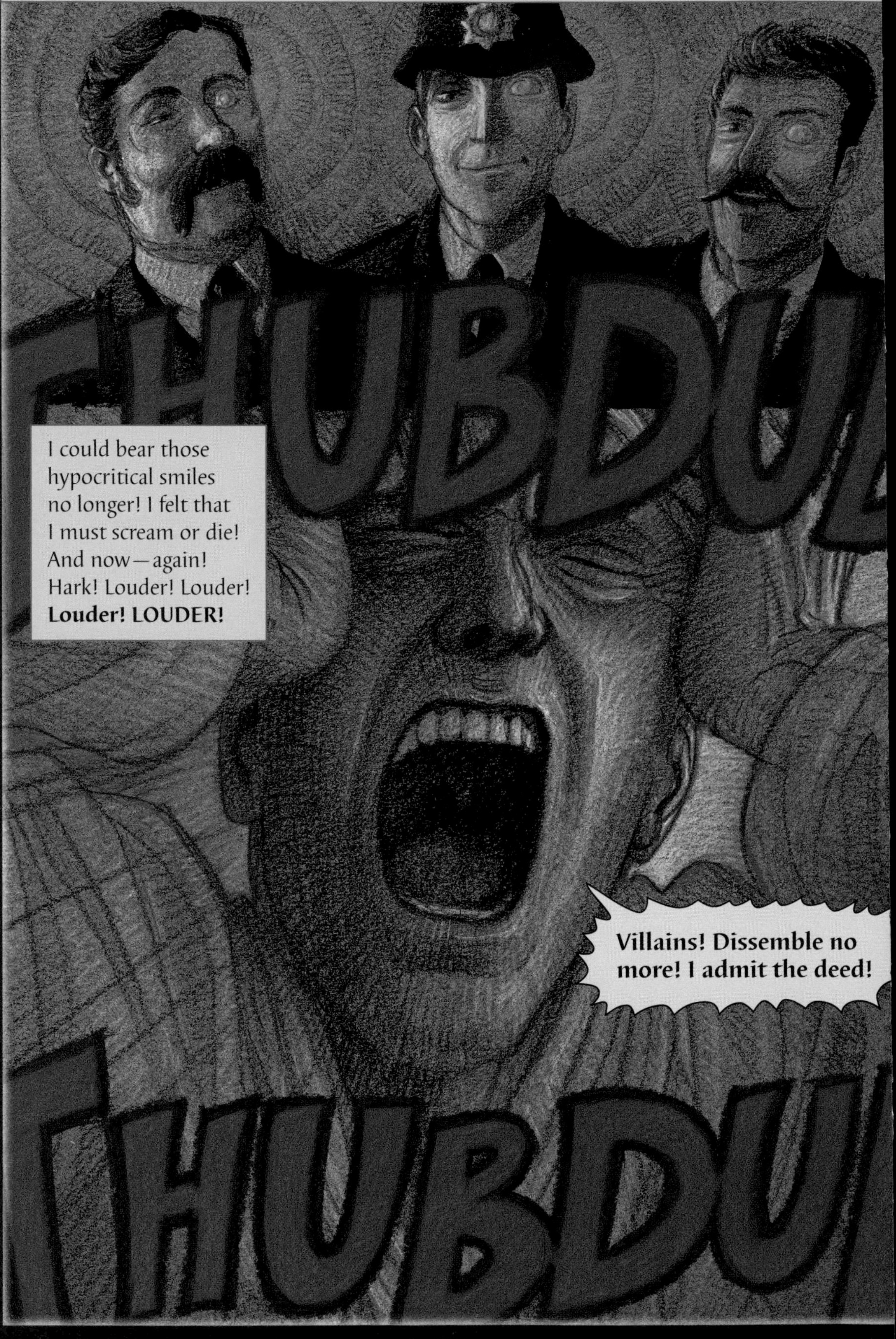
THUBDUB
I could bear those hypocritical smiles no longer! I felt that I must scream or die! And now—again! Hark! Louder! Louder! **Louder! LOUDER!**
Villains! Dissemble no more! I admit the deed!
THUBDUB

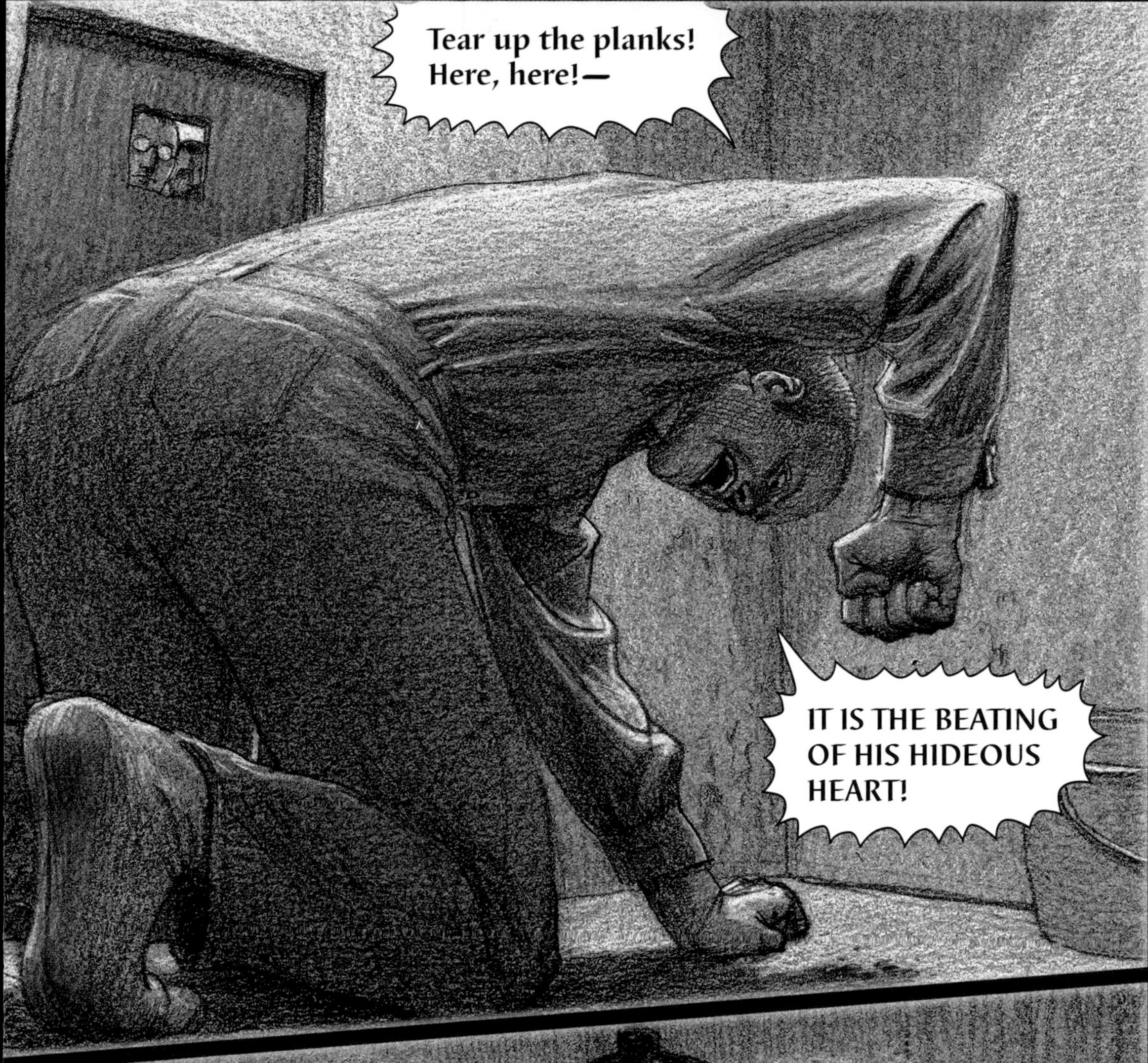
Tear up the planks! Here, here!—
IT IS THE BEATING OF HIS HIDEOUS HEART!

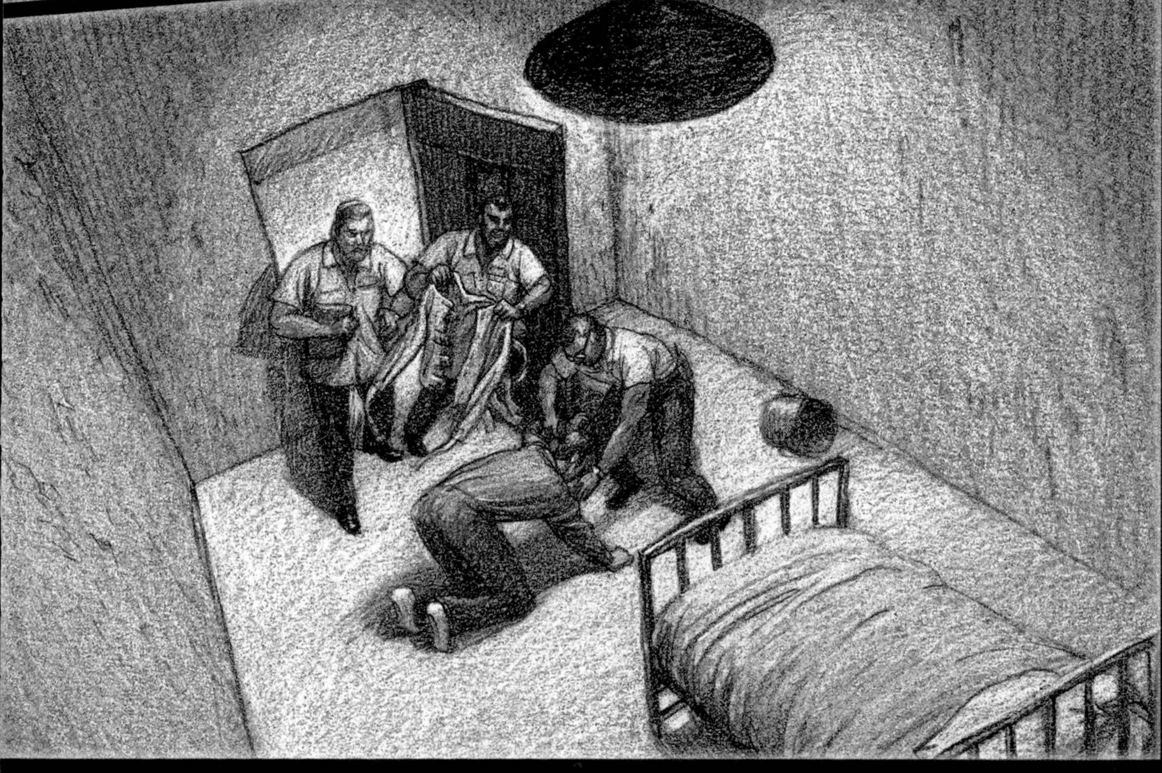

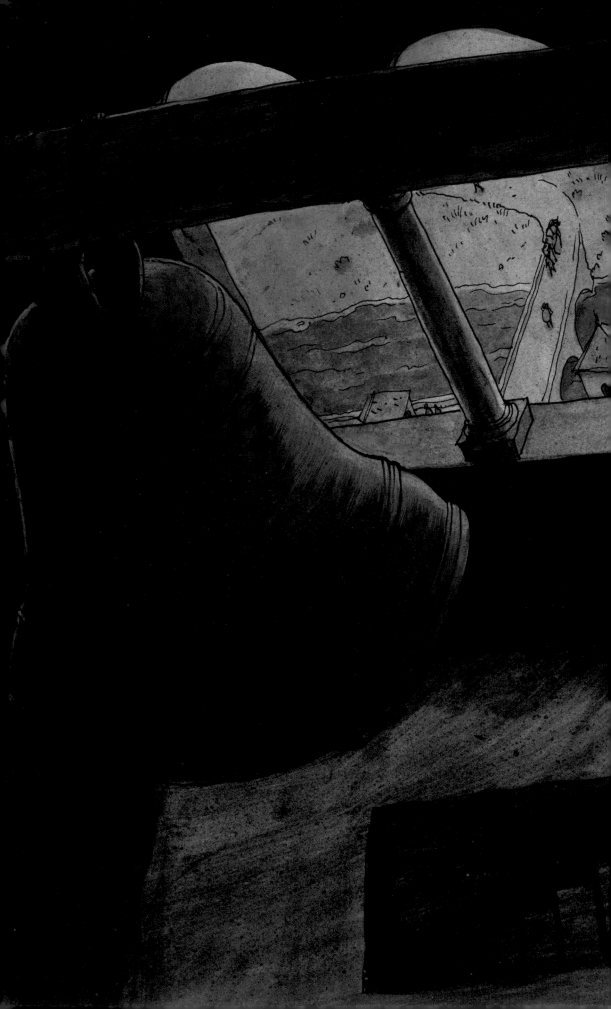

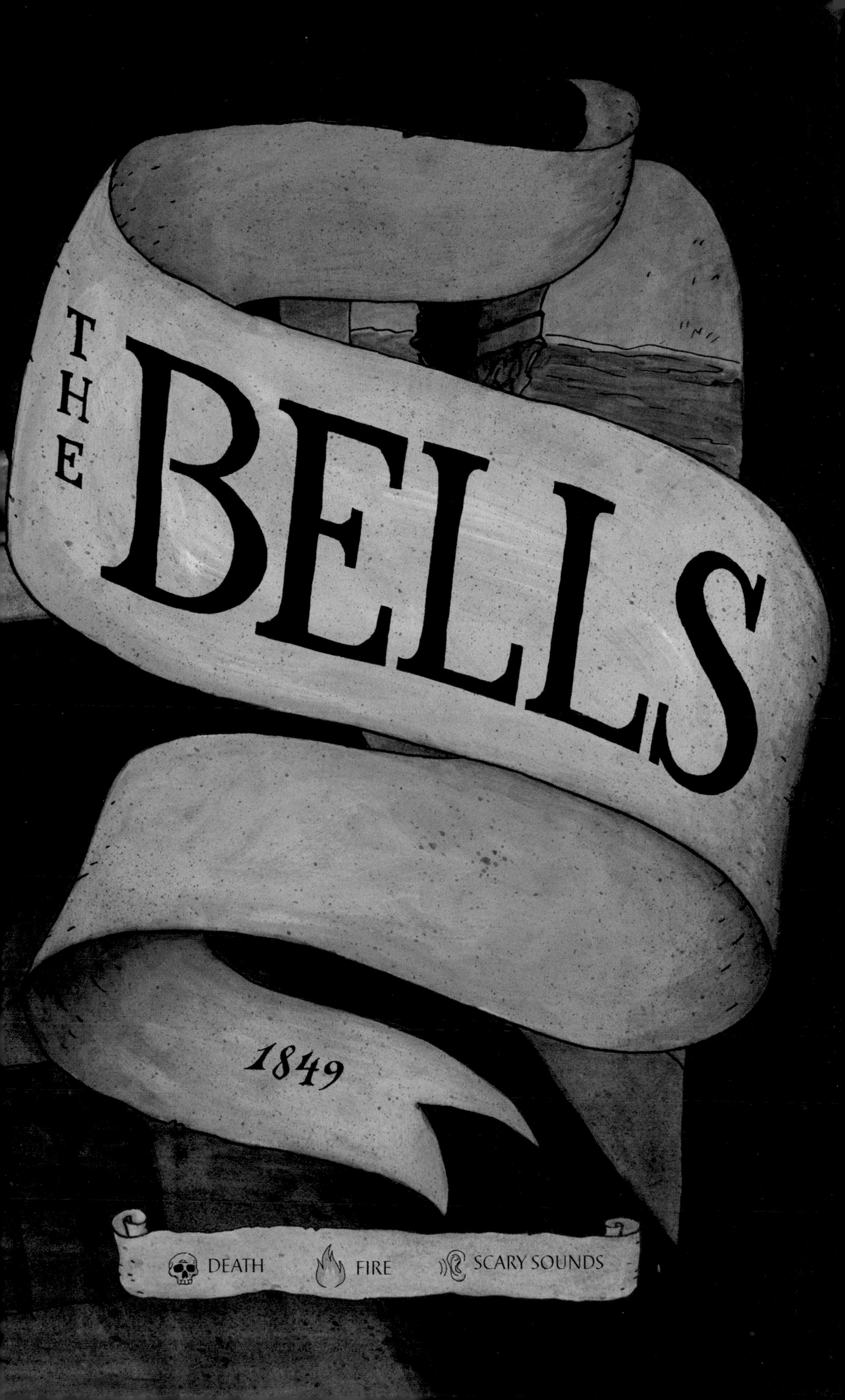
THE
BELLS
1849
DEATH
FIRE
SCARY SOUNDS

Hear the sledges with the bells,
Silver bells!
What a world of merriment their melody foretells!
How they tinkle, tinkle, tinkle,
In the icy air of night!
While the stars, that oversprinkle
All the heavens, seem to twinkle
With a crystalline delight;
Keeping time, time, time,
In a sort of Runic rhyme,
To the tintinnabulation that so musically wells
From the bells, bells, bells, bells,
Bells, bells, bells—
From the jingling and the tinkling of the bells.

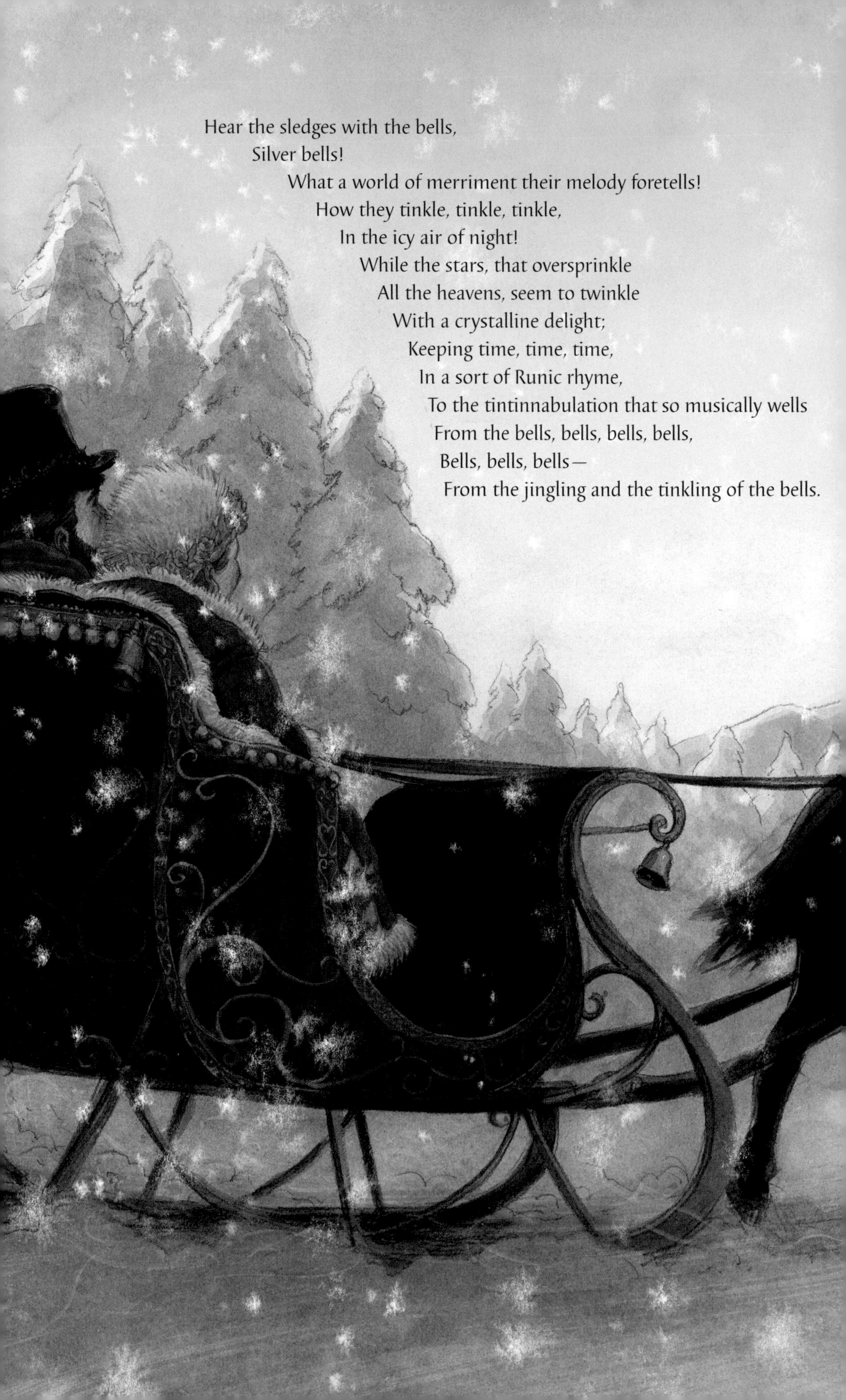

Hear the mellow wedding bells,
Golden bells!
What a world of happiness their harmony foretells!
Through the balmy air of night
How they ring out their delight!
From the molten-golden notes,
And all in tune,
What a liquid ditty floats
To the turtle-dove that listens, while she gloats
On the moon!
Oh, from out the sounding cells,
What a gush of euphony
voluminously wells!

How it swells!
How it dwells
On the Future! — how it tells
Of the rapture that impels
To the swinging and the ringing
Of the bells, bells, bells,
Of the bells, bells, bells, bells,
Bells, bells, bells —
To the rhyming
and the chiming
of the bells!

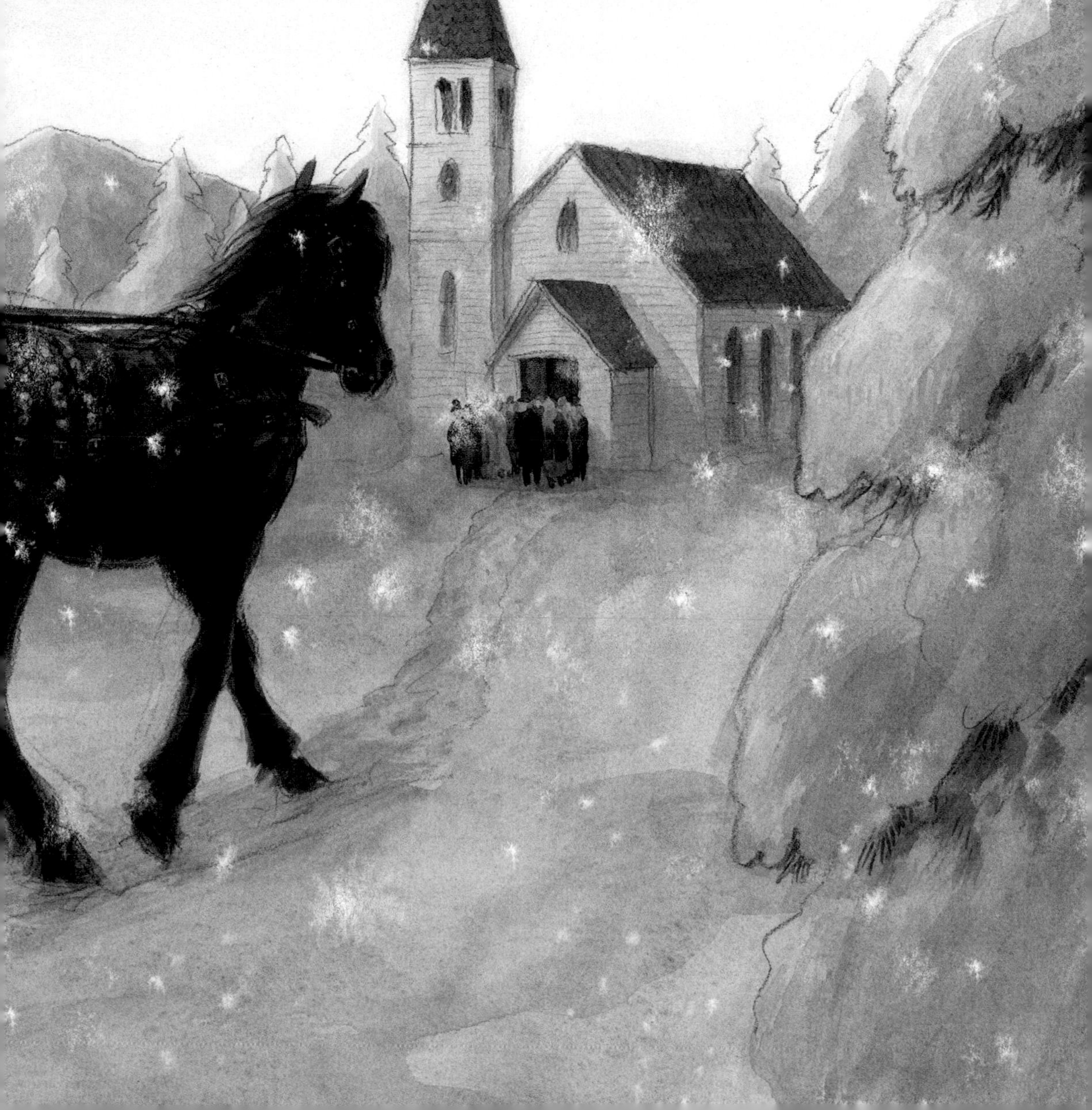

Hear the loud alarum bells,
Brazen bells!
What a tale of terror, now, their turbulency tells!
In the startled ear of night
How they scream out their affright!
Too much horrified to speak,
They can only shriek, shriek,
Out of tune,
In a clamorous appealing to the mercy of the fire,
In a mad expostulation with the deaf and frantic fire,
Leaping higher, higher, higher,
With a desperate desire,
And a resolute endeavor
Now—now to sit, or never,
By the side of the pale-faced moon.

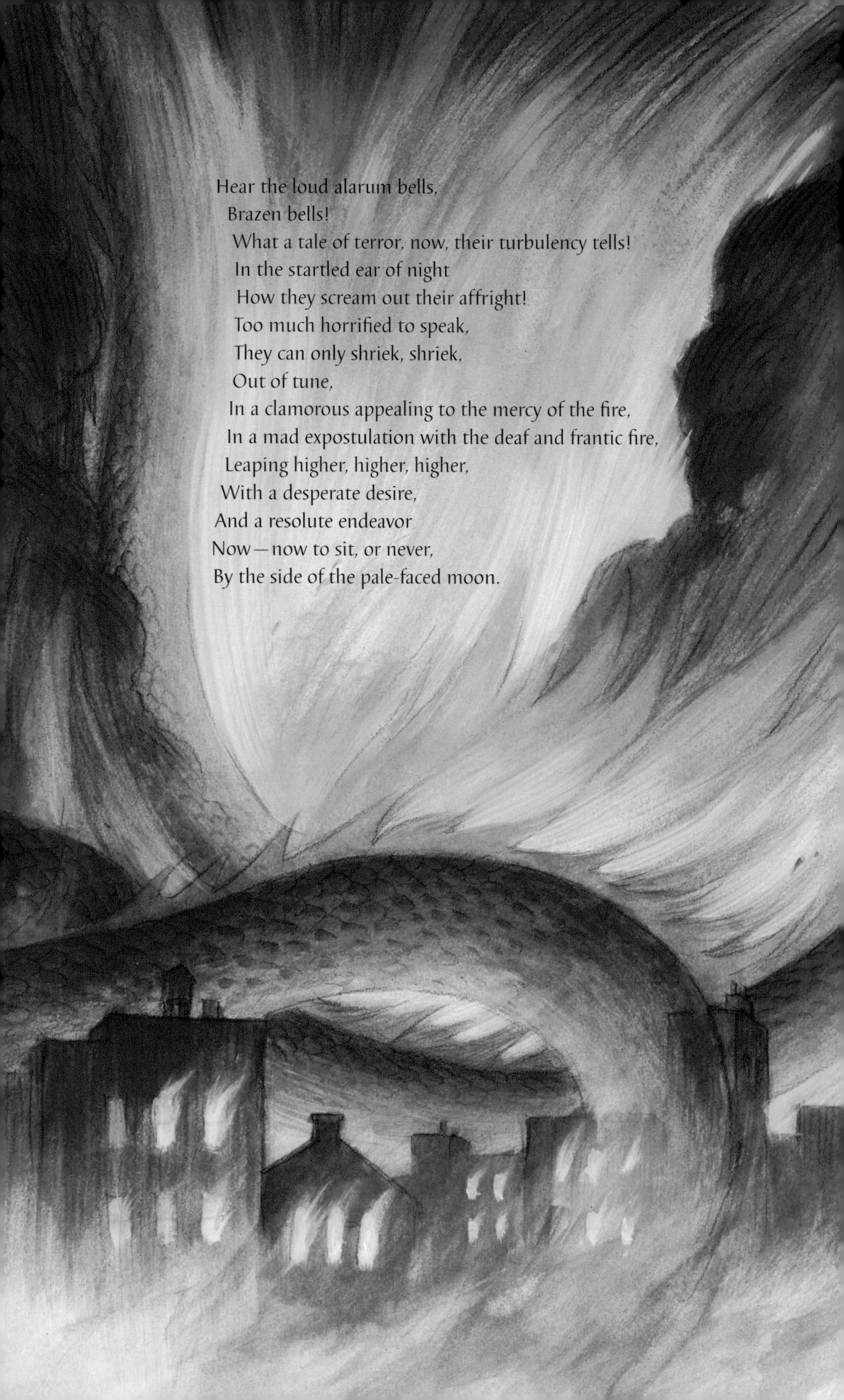

Oh, the bells, bells, bells!
What a tale their terror tells
Of Despair!
How they clang, and clash, and roar!
What a horror they outpour
On the bosom of the palpitating air!
Yet the ear it fully knows,
By the twanging,
And the clanging,
How the danger ebbs and flows;
Yet the ear distinctly tells,
In the jangling,
And the wrangling,
How the danger sinks and swells,—
By the sinking or the swelling in the anger of the bells,
Of the bells,
Of the bells, bells, bells, bells,
Bells, bells, bells—
In the clamor and the clangor of the bells!

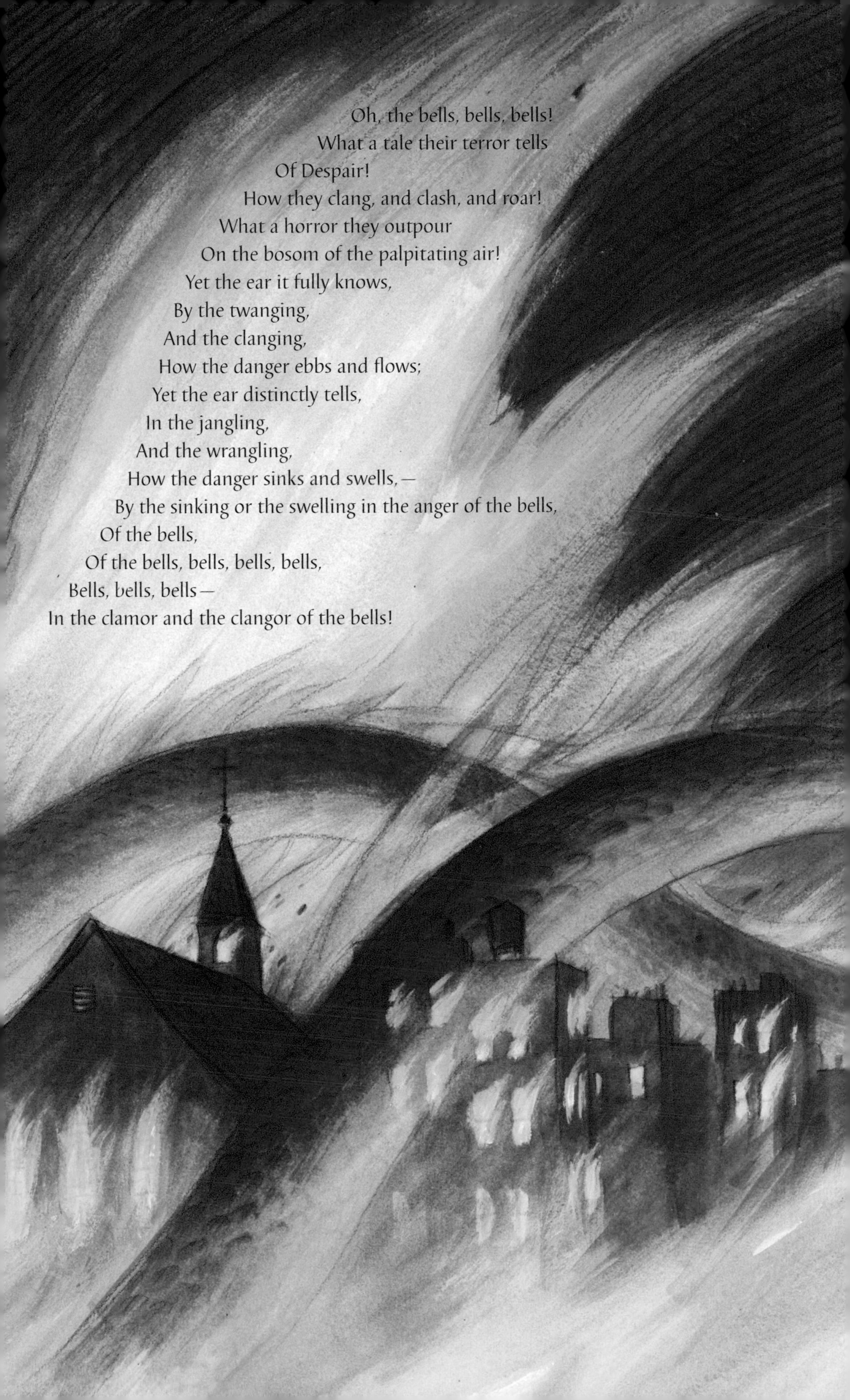

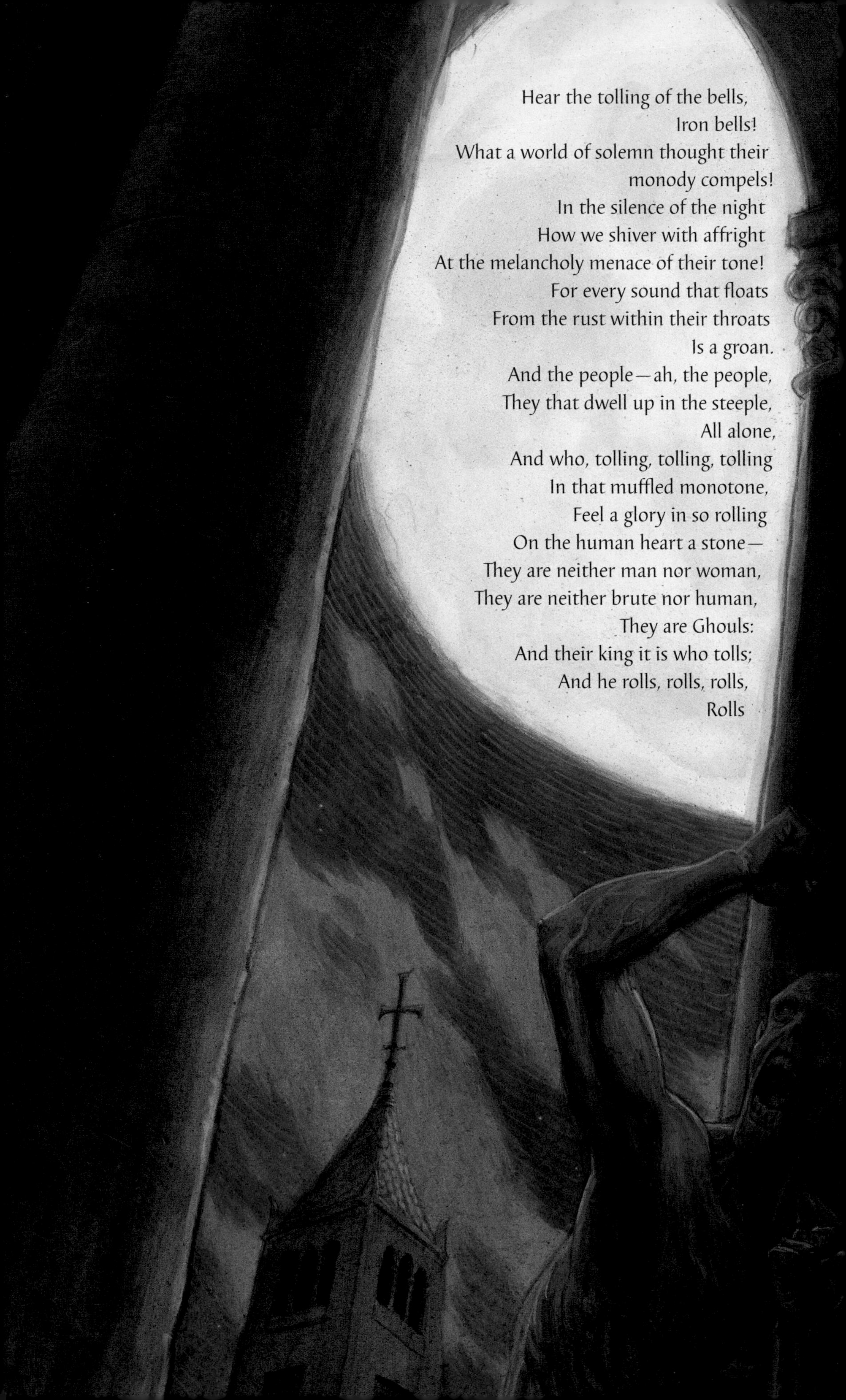

Hear the tolling of the bells,
Iron bells!
What a world of solemn thought their
monody compels!
In the silence of the night
How we shiver with affright
At the melancholy menace of their tone!
For every sound that floats
From the rust within their throats
Is a groan.
And the people—ah, the people,
They that dwell up in the steeple,
All alone,
And who, tolling, tolling, tolling
In that muffled monotone,
Feel a glory in so rolling
On the human heart a stone—
They are neither man nor woman,
They are neither brute nor human,
They are Ghouls:
And their king it is who tolls;
And he rolls, rolls, rolls,
Rolls

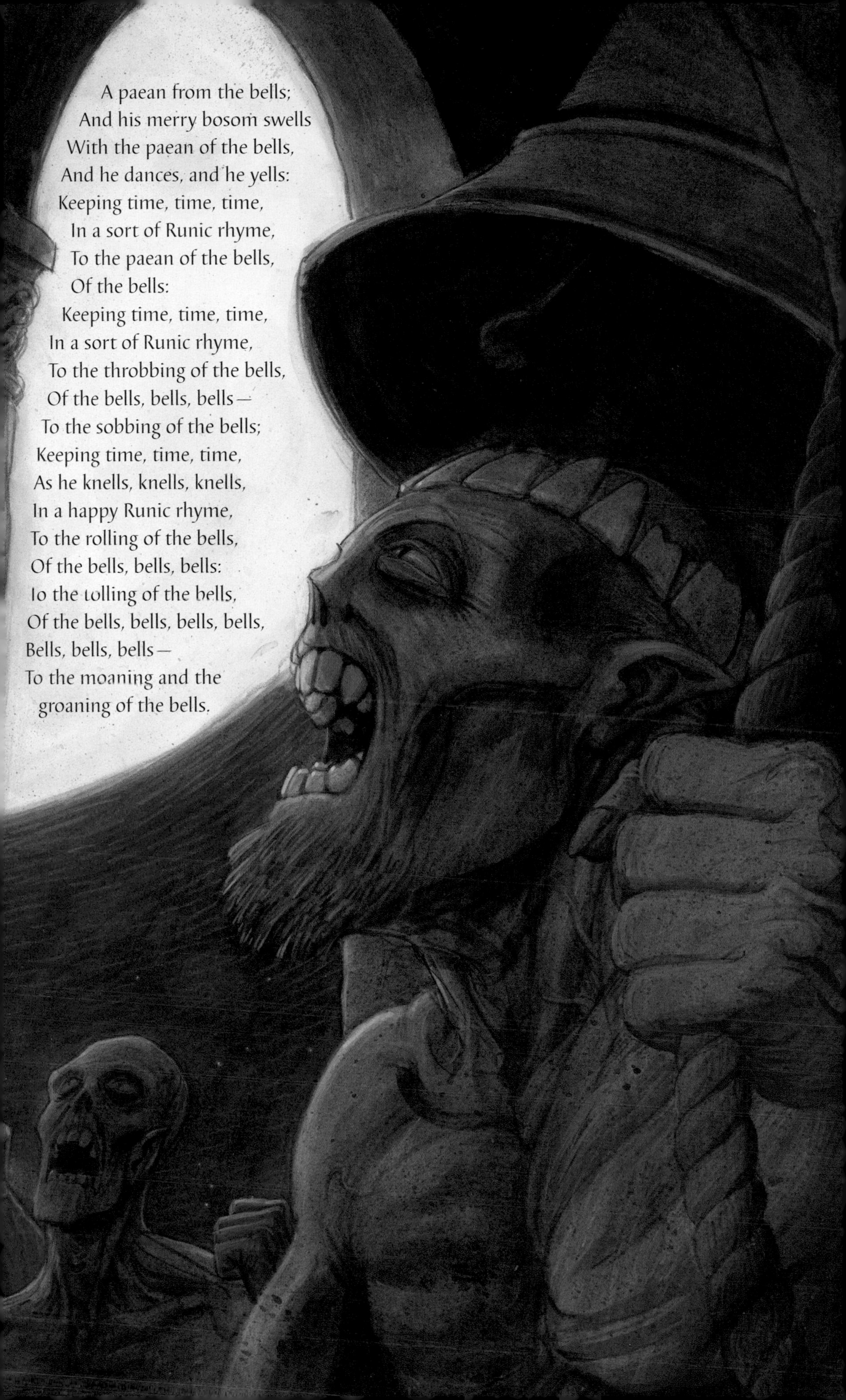

A paean from the bells;
And his merry bosom swells
With the paean of the bells,
And he dances, and he yells:
Keeping time, time, time,
In a sort of Runic rhyme,
To the paean of the bells,
Of the bells:
Keeping time, time, time,
In a sort of Runic rhyme,
To the throbbing of the bells,
Of the bells, bells, bells—
To the sobbing of the bells;
Keeping time, time, time,
As he knells, knells, knells,
In a happy Runic rhyme,
To the rolling of the bells,
Of the bells, bells, bells:
To the tolling of the bells,
Of the bells, bells, bells, bells,
Bells, bells, bells—
To the moaning and the
groaning of the bells.

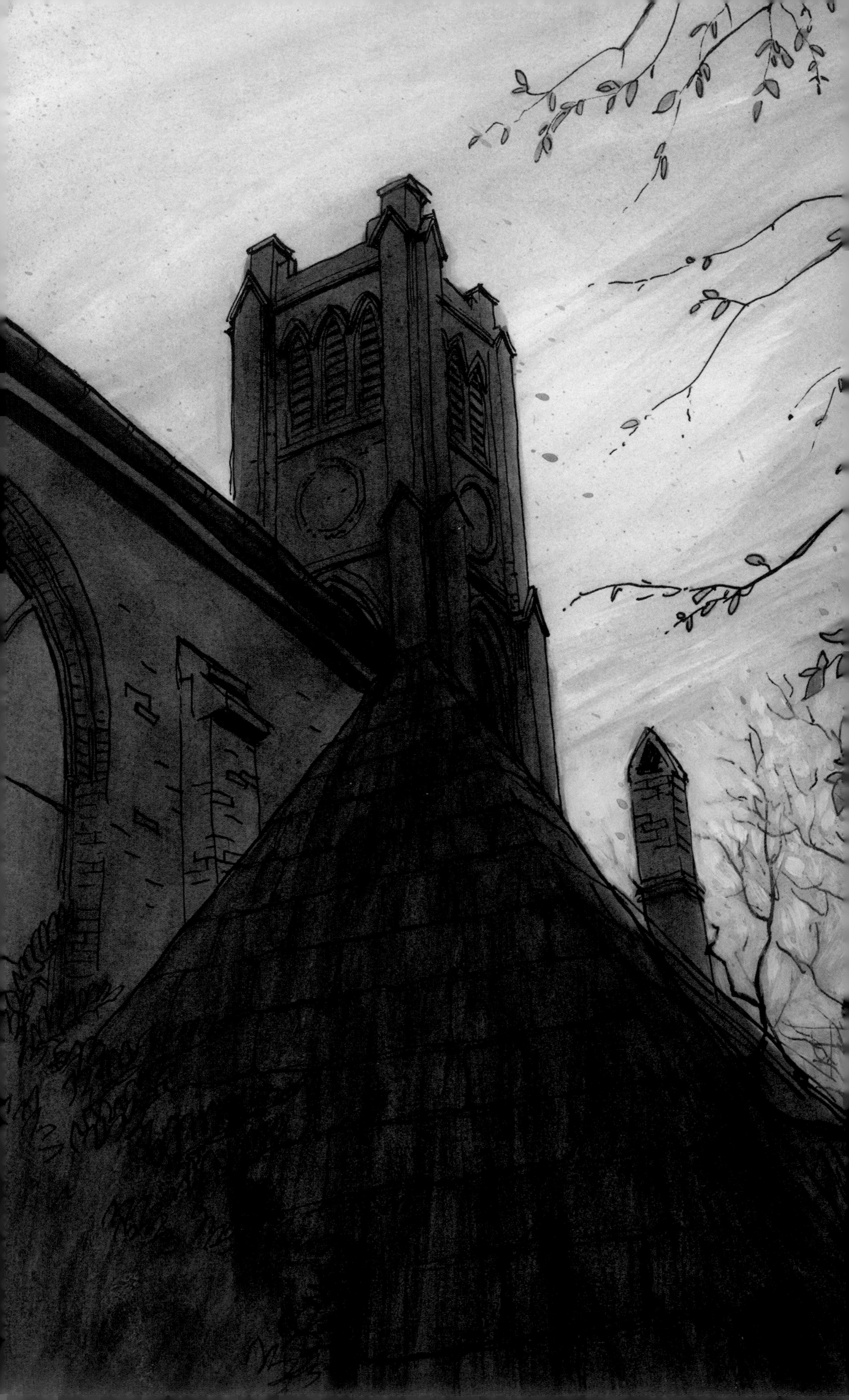

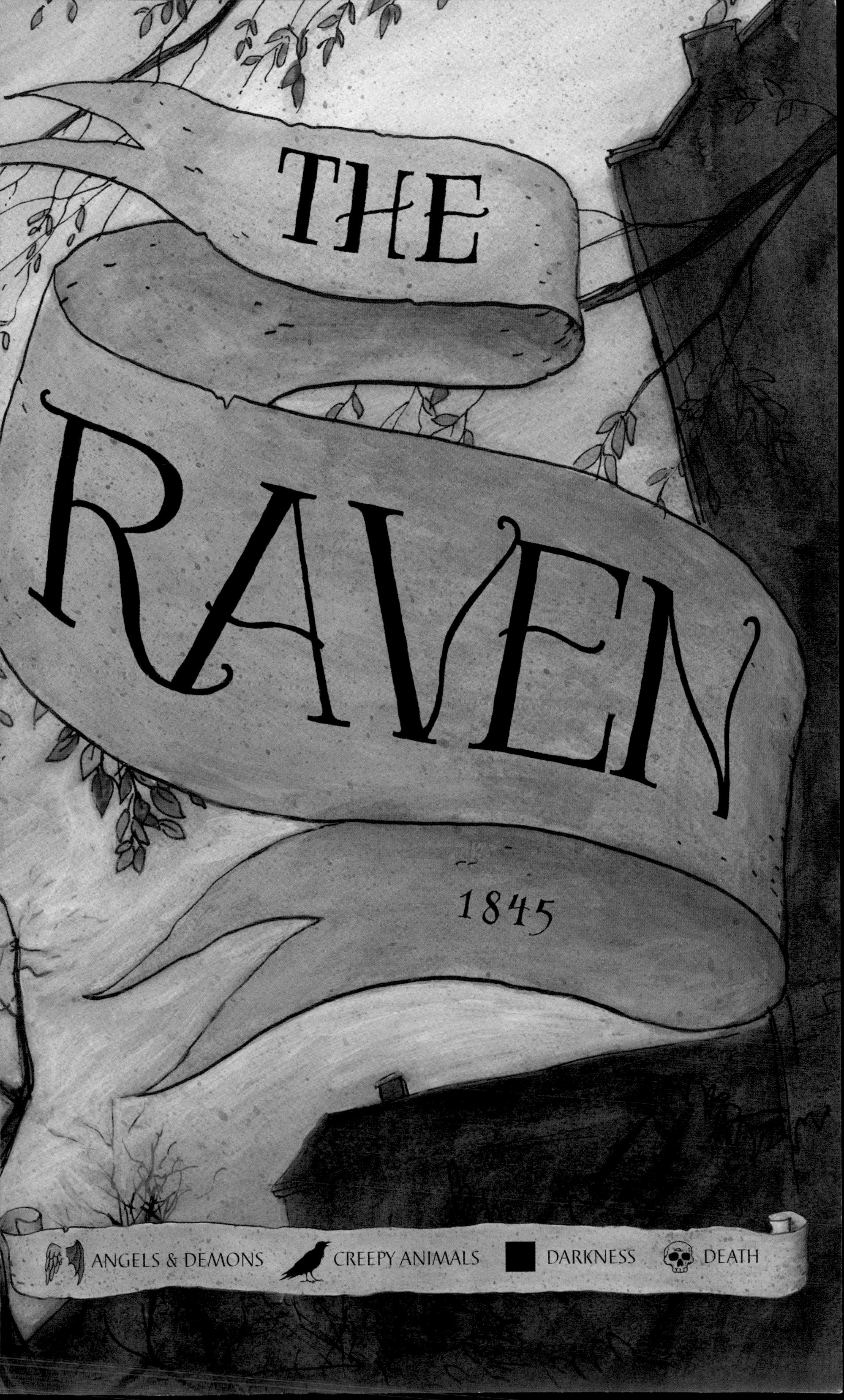
THE
RAVEN
1845
ANGELS & DEMONS
CREEPY ANIMALS
DARKNESS
DEATH

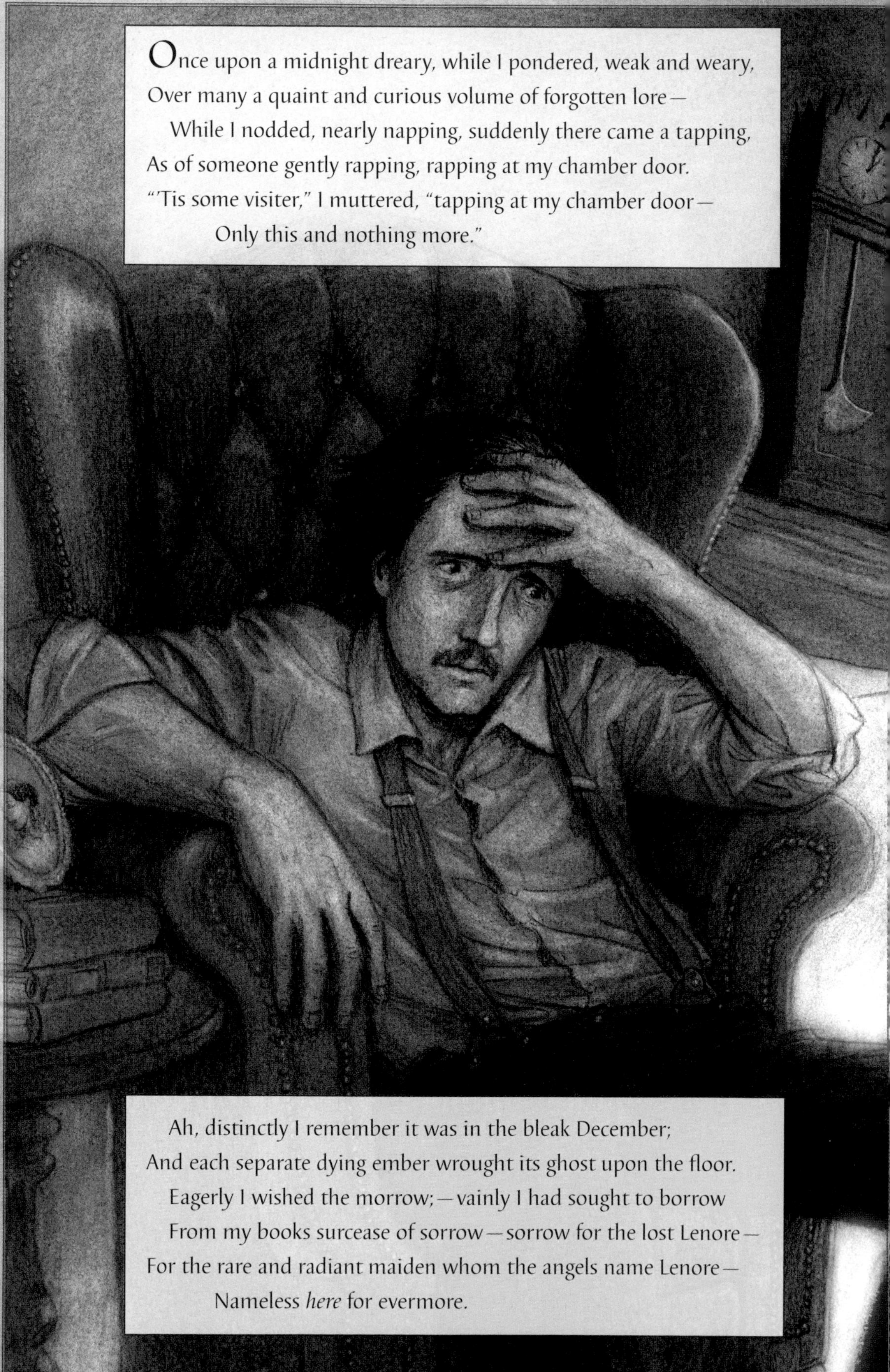

Once upon a midnight dreary, while I pondered, weak and weary,
Over many a quaint and curious volume of forgotten lore—
While I nodded, nearly napping, suddenly there came a tapping,
As of someone gently rapping, rapping at my chamber door.
"'Tis some visiter," I muttered, "tapping at my chamber door—
Only this and nothing more."

Ah, distinctly I remember it was in the bleak December;
And each separate dying ember wrought its ghost upon the floor.
Eagerly I wished the morrow;—vainly I had sought to borrow
From my books surcease of sorrow—sorrow for the lost Lenore—
For the rare and radiant maiden whom the angels name Lenore—
Nameless *here* for evermore.

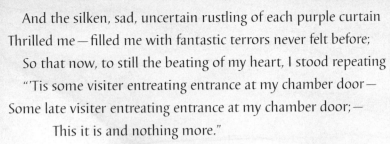

And the silken, sad, uncertain rustling of each purple curtain
Thrilled me—filled me with fantastic terrors never felt before;
    So that now, to still the beating of my heart, I stood repeating
    "'Tis some visiter entreating entrance at my chamber door—
Some late visiter entreating entrance at my chamber door;—
        This it is and nothing more."

Presently my soul grew stronger; hesitating then no longer,
"Sir," said I, "or Madam, truly your forgiveness I implore;
    But the fact is I was napping, and so gently you came rapping,
    And so faintly you came tapping, tapping at my chamber door,
That I scarce was sure I heard you"—here I opened wide the door;—
        Darkness there and nothing more.

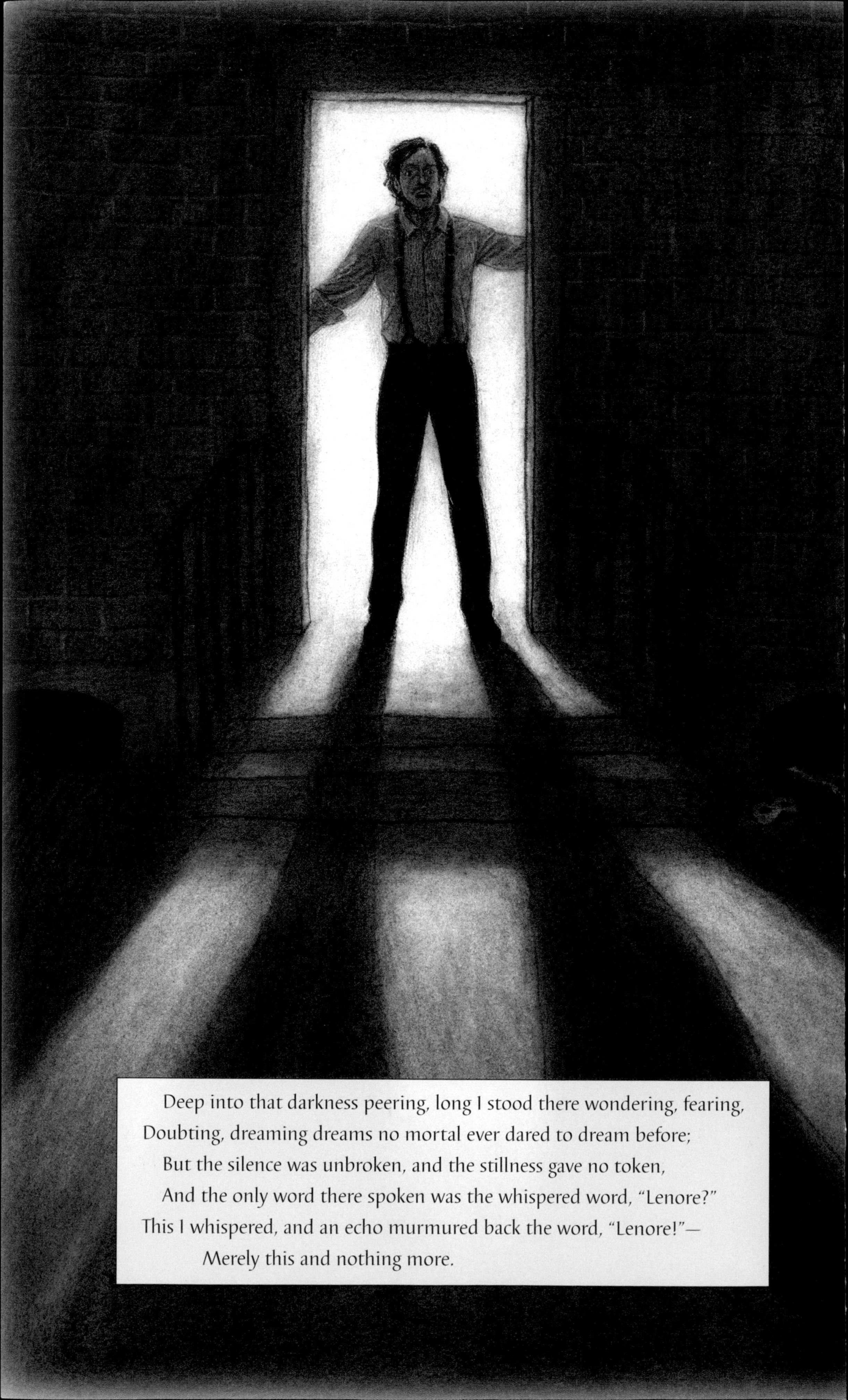

Deep into that darkness peering, long I stood there wondering, fearing,
Doubting, dreaming dreams no mortal ever dared to dream before;
But the silence was unbroken, and the stillness gave no token,
And the only word there spoken was the whispered word, "Lenore?"
This I whispered, and an echo murmured back the word, "Lenore!"—
Merely this and nothing more.

Back into the chamber turning, all my soul within me burning,
Soon again I heard a tapping somewhat louder than before.
"Surely," said I, "surely that is something at my window lattice;
Let me see, then, what thereat is, and this mystery explore—
Let my heart be still a moment and this mystery explore;—
'Tis the wind and nothing more!"

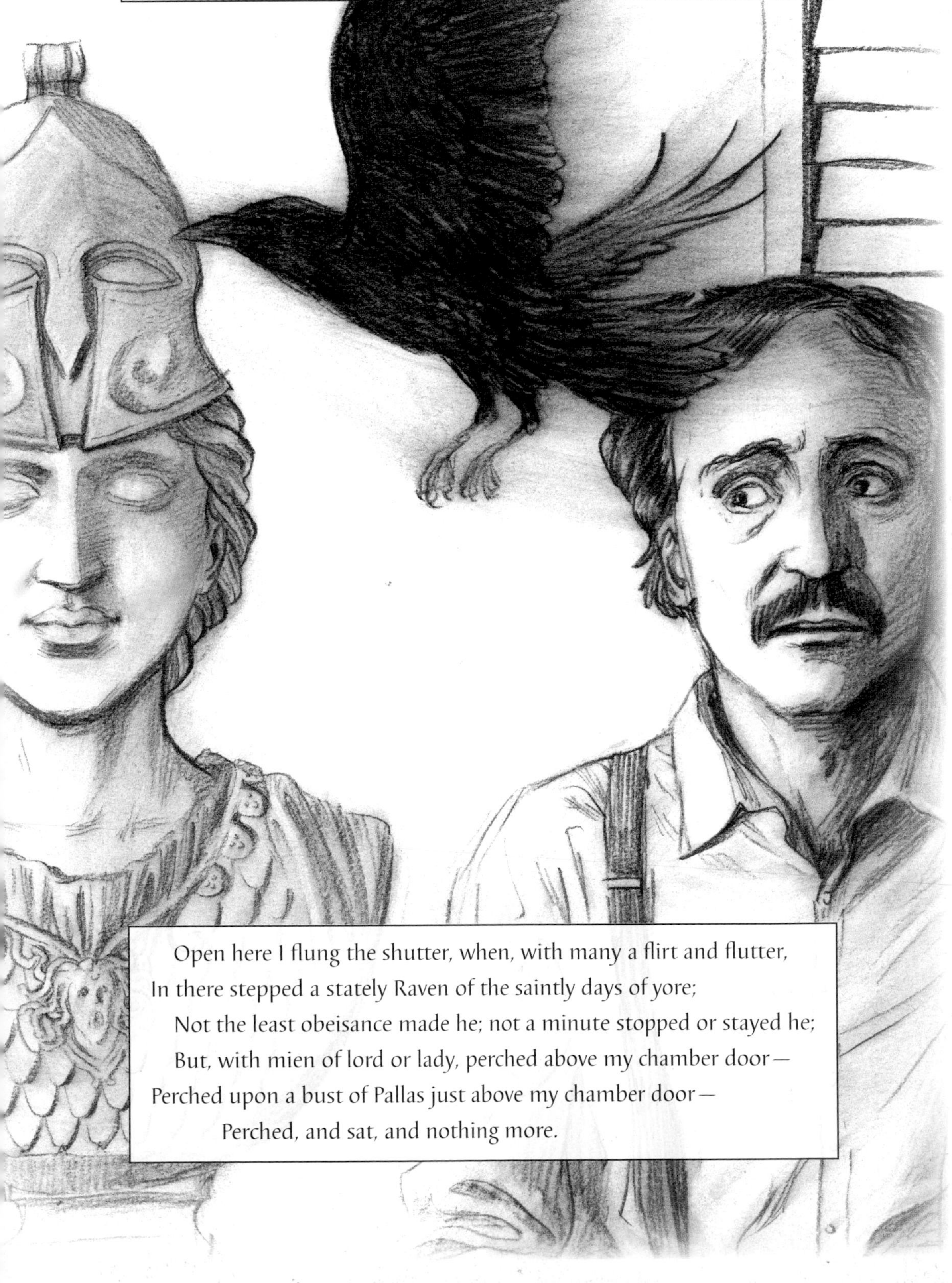

Open here I flung the shutter, when, with many a flirt and flutter,
In there stepped a stately Raven of the saintly days of yore;
Not the least obeisance made he; not a minute stopped or stayed he;
But, with mien of lord or lady, perched above my chamber door—
Perched upon a bust of Pallas just above my chamber door—
Perched, and sat, and nothing more.

Then this ebony bird beguiling my sad fancy into smiling,
By the grave and stern decorum of the countenance it wore,
"Though thy crest be shorn and shaven, thou," I said, "art sure no craven,
Ghastly grim and ancient Raven wandering from the Nightly shore—
Tell me what thy lordly name is on the Night's Plutonian shore!"
Quoth the Raven, "Nevermore."

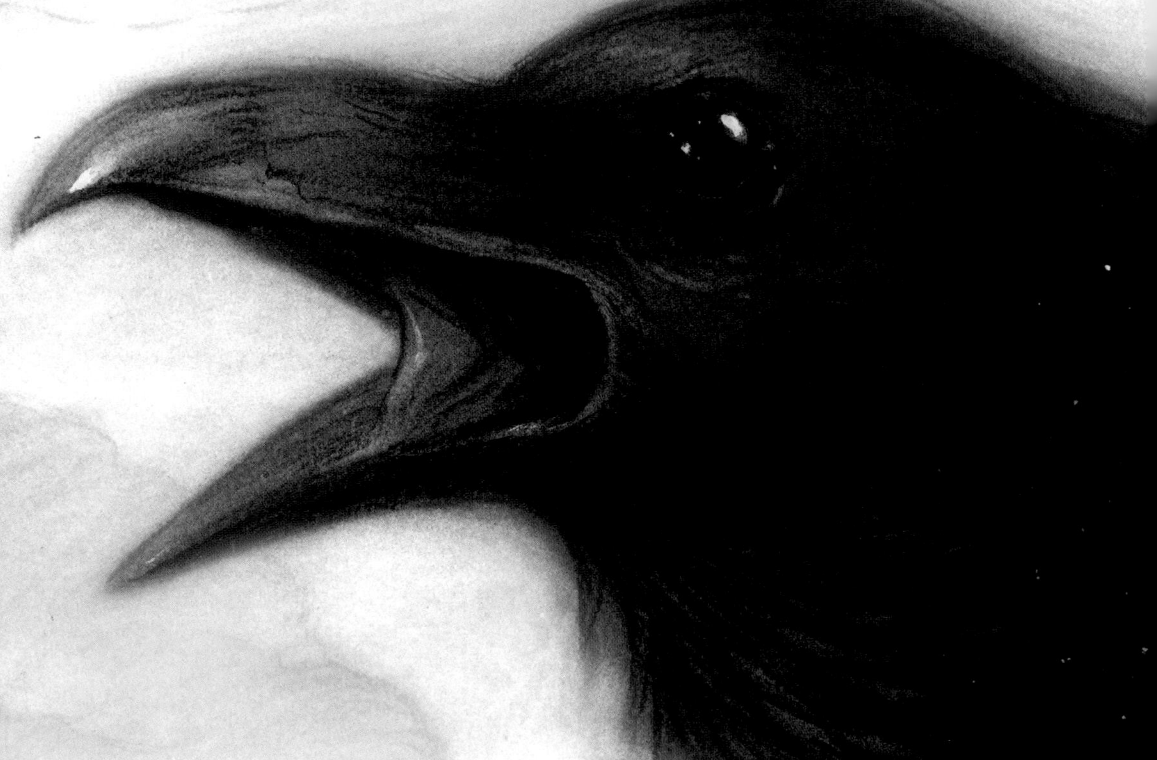

Much I marvelled this ungainly
fowl to hear discourse so plainly,
Though its answer little meaning—little relevancy bore;
For we cannot help agreeing that no living human being
Ever yet was blessed with seeing bird above his chamber door—
Bird or beast upon the sculptured bust above his chamber door,
With such name as "Nevermore."

But the Raven, sitting lonely on the placid bust, spoke only
That one word, as if his soul in that one word he did outpour.
Nothing further then he uttered—not a feather then he fluttered—
Till I scarcely more than muttered "Other friends have flown before—
On the morrow he will leave me, as my Hopes have flown before."
Then the bird said, "Nevermore."

Startled at the stillness broken by reply so aptly spoken,
"Doubtless," said I, "what it utters is its only stock and store,
Caught from some unhappy master whom unmerciful Disaster
Followed fast and followed faster till his songs one burden bore—
Till the dirges of his Hope that melancholy burden bore
Of 'Never—nevermore.'"

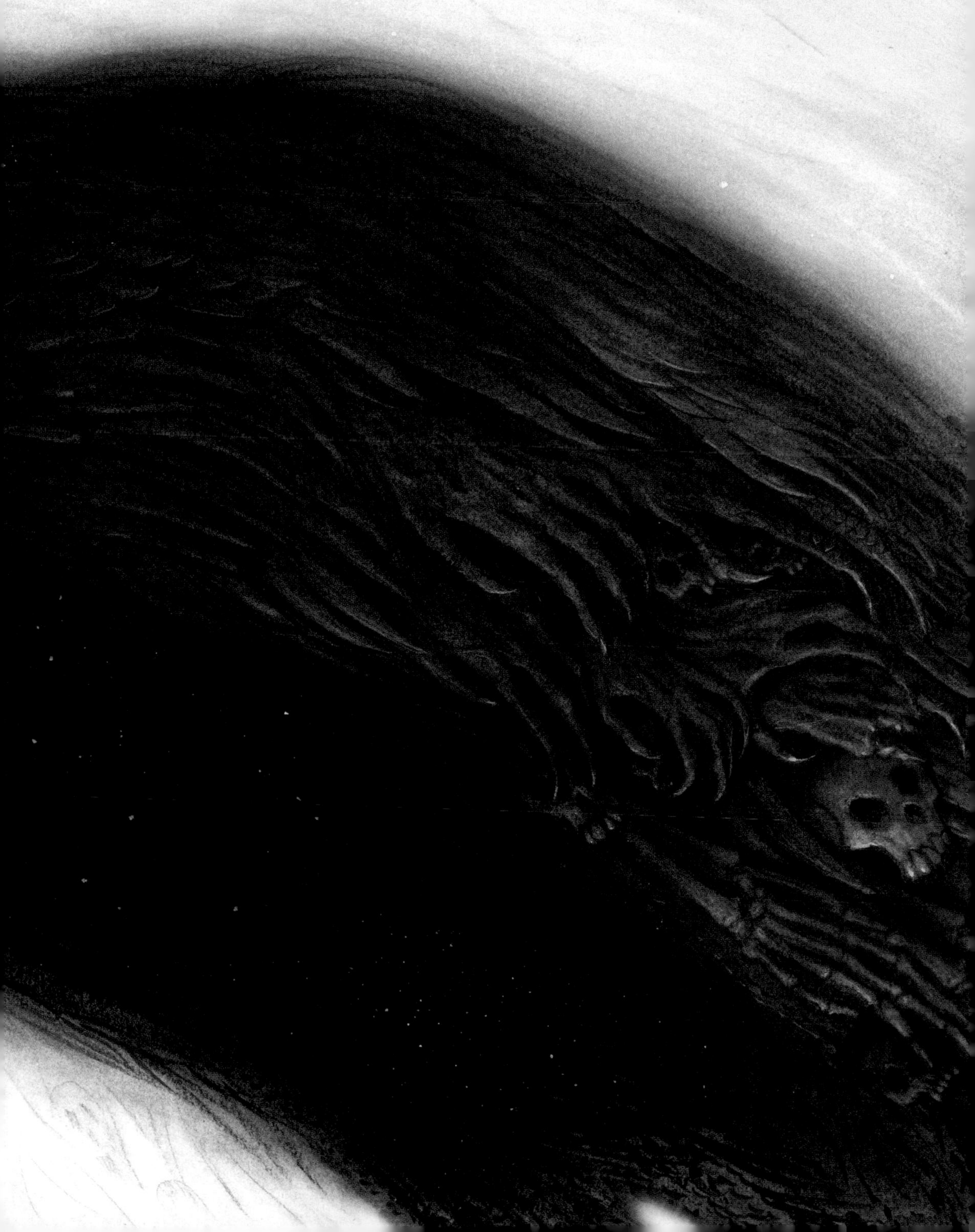

But the Raven still beguiling all my fancy into smiling,
Straight I wheeled a cushioned seat in front of bird, and bust and door;
Then, upon the velvet sinking, I betook myself to linking
Fancy unto fancy, thinking what this ominous bird of yore—
What this grim, ungainly, ghastly, gaunt, and ominous bird of yore
Meant in croaking "Nevermore."

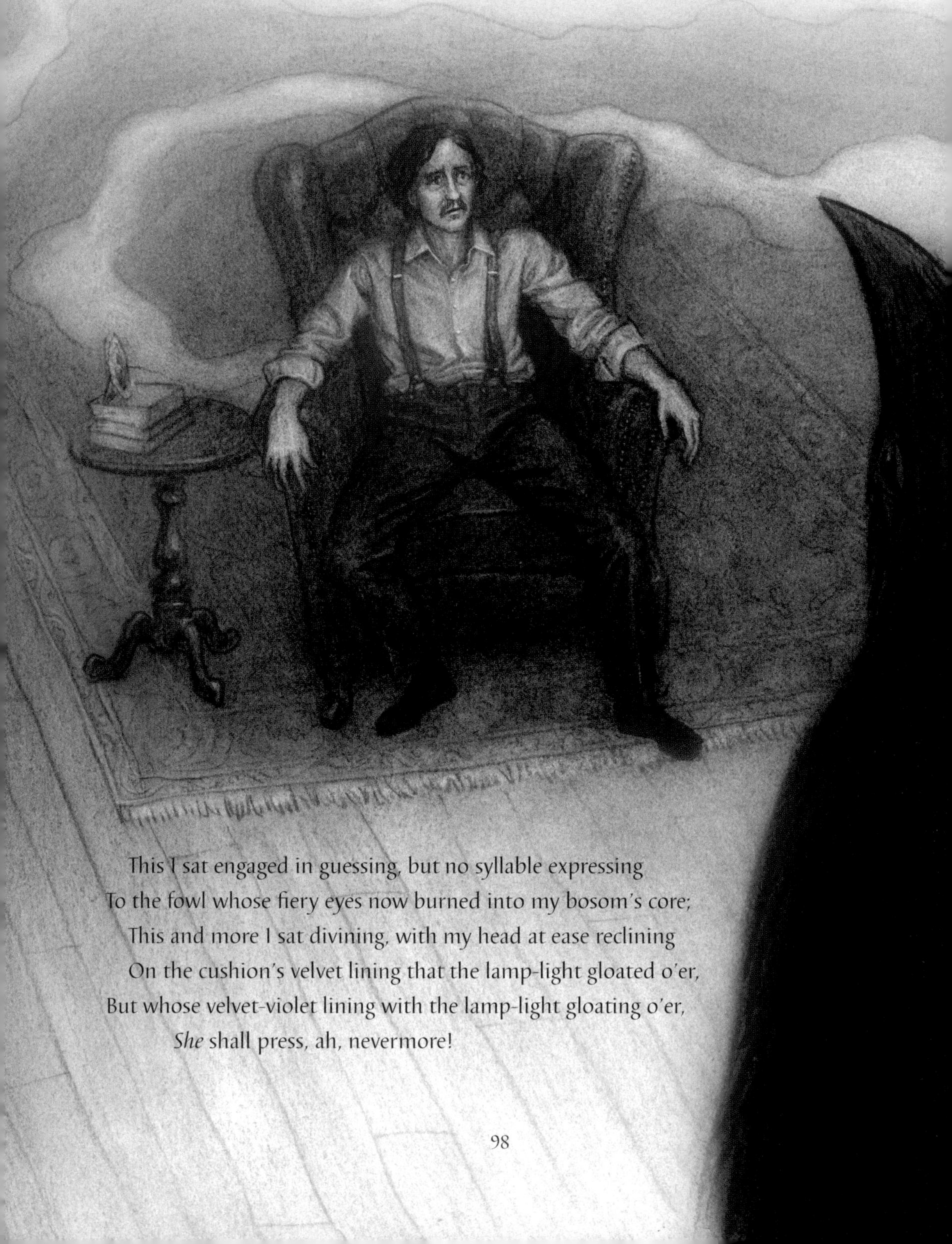

This I sat engaged in guessing, but no syllable expressing
To the fowl whose fiery eyes now burned into my bosom's core;
This and more I sat divining, with my head at ease reclining
On the cushion's velvet lining that the lamp-light gloated o'er,
But whose velvet-violet lining with the lamp-light gloating o'er,
She shall press, ah, nevermore!

Then, methought, the air grew denser, perfumed from an unseen censer
Swung by seraphim whose foot-falls tinkled on the tufted floor.
"Wretch," I cried, "thy God hath lent thee—by these angels he hath sent thee
Respite—respite and nepenthe from thy memories of Lenore;
Quaff, oh quaff this kind nepenthe and forget this lost Lenore!"
Quoth the Raven, "Nevermore."

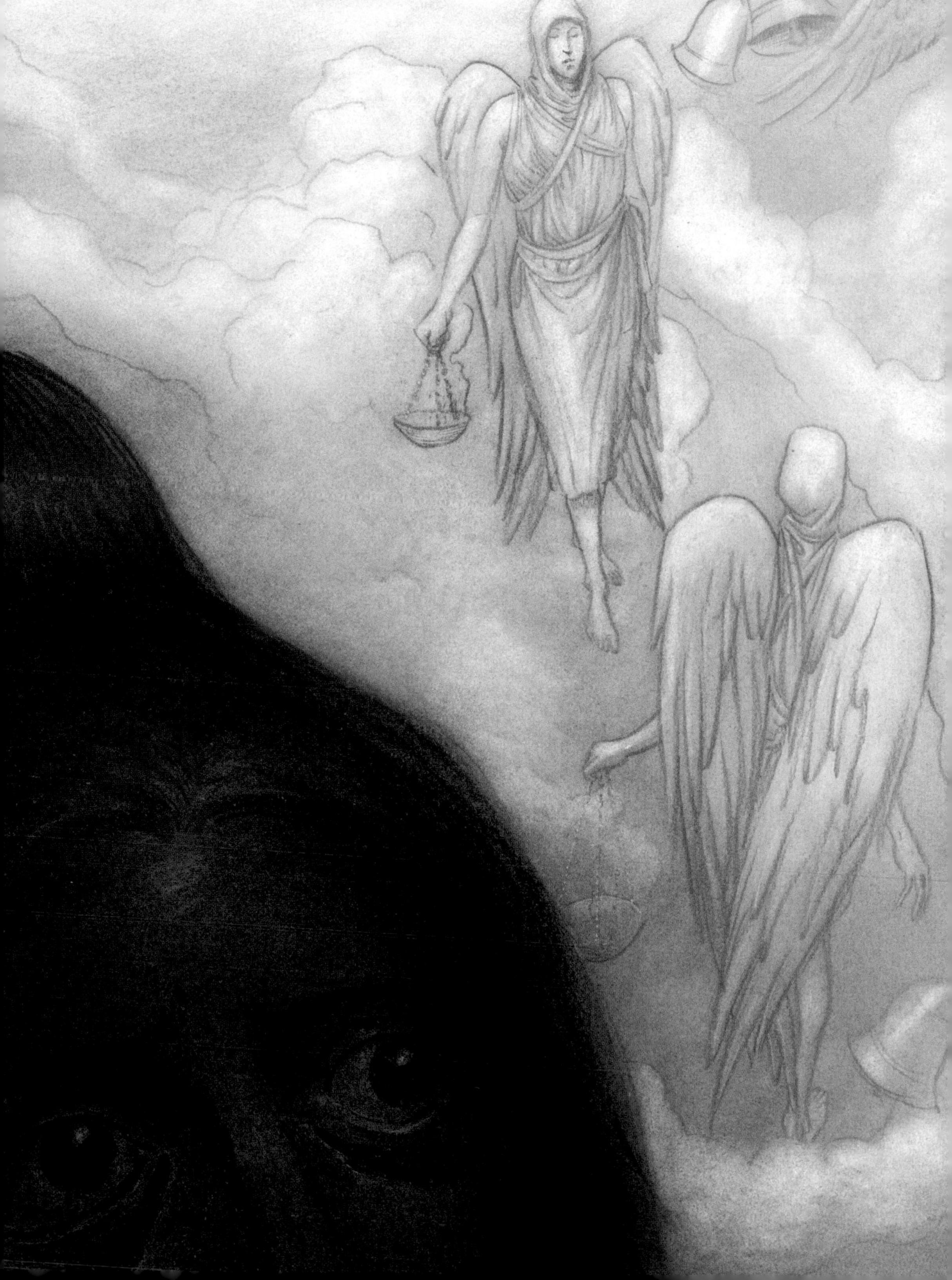

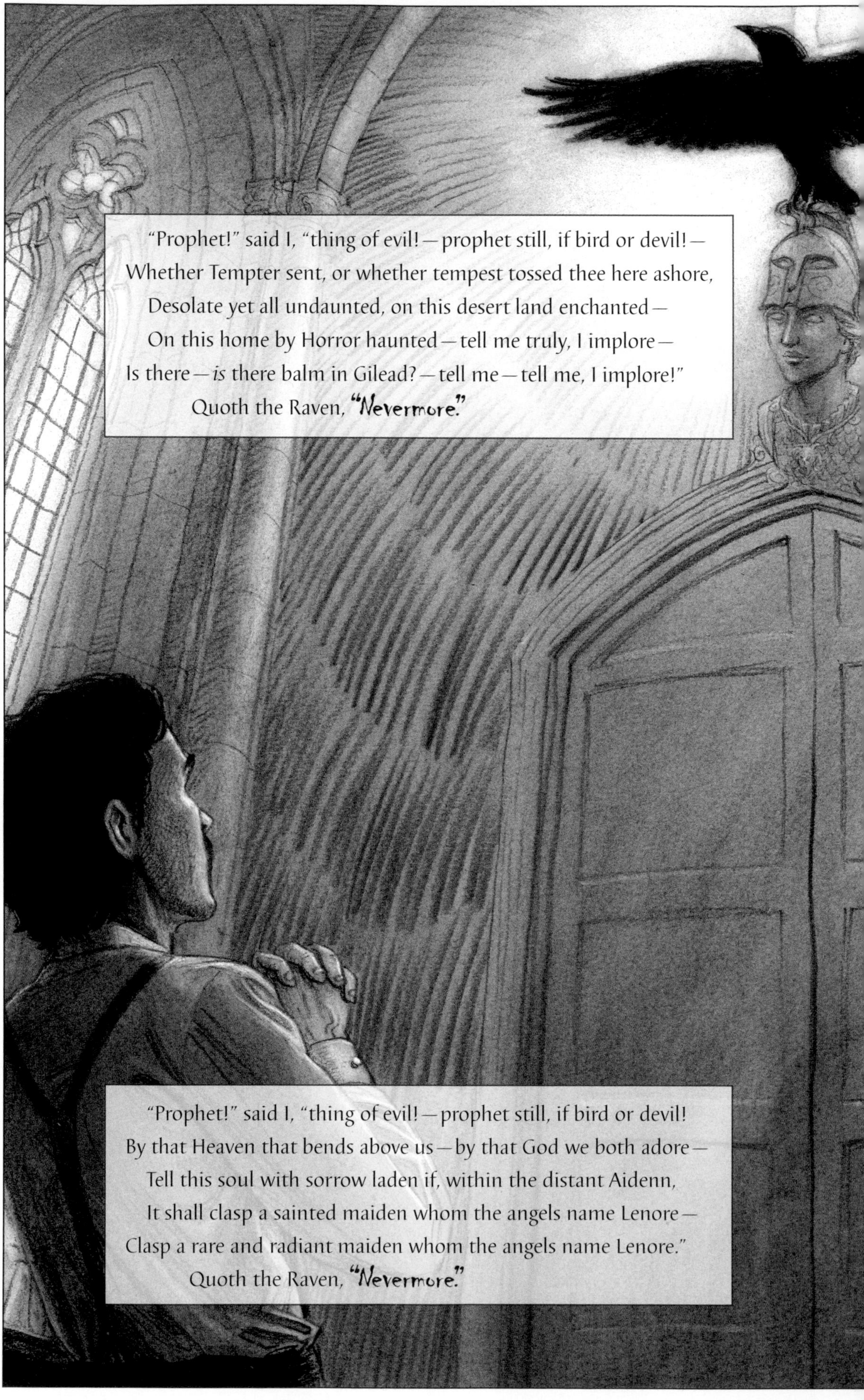

"Prophet!" said I, "thing of evil!—prophet still, if bird or devil!—
Whether Tempter sent, or whether tempest tossed thee here ashore,
Desolate yet all undaunted, on this desert land enchanted—
On this home by Horror haunted—tell me truly, I implore—
Is there—*is* there balm in Gilead?—tell me—tell me, I implore!"
Quoth the Raven, "Nevermore."

"Prophet!" said I, "thing of evil!—prophet still, if bird or devil!
By that Heaven that bends above us—by that God we both adore—
Tell this soul with sorrow laden if, within the distant Aidenn,
It shall clasp a sainted maiden whom the angels name Lenore—
Clasp a rare and radiant maiden whom the angels name Lenore."
Quoth the Raven, "Nevermore."

"Be that word our sign of parting, bird or fiend!" I shrieked, upstarting—
"Get thee back into the tempest and the Night's Plutonian shore!
Leave no black plume as a token of that lie thy soul hath spoken!
Leave my loneliness unbroken!—quit the bust above my door!
Take thy beak from out my heart, and take thy form from off my door!"
Quoth the Raven, "Nevermore."

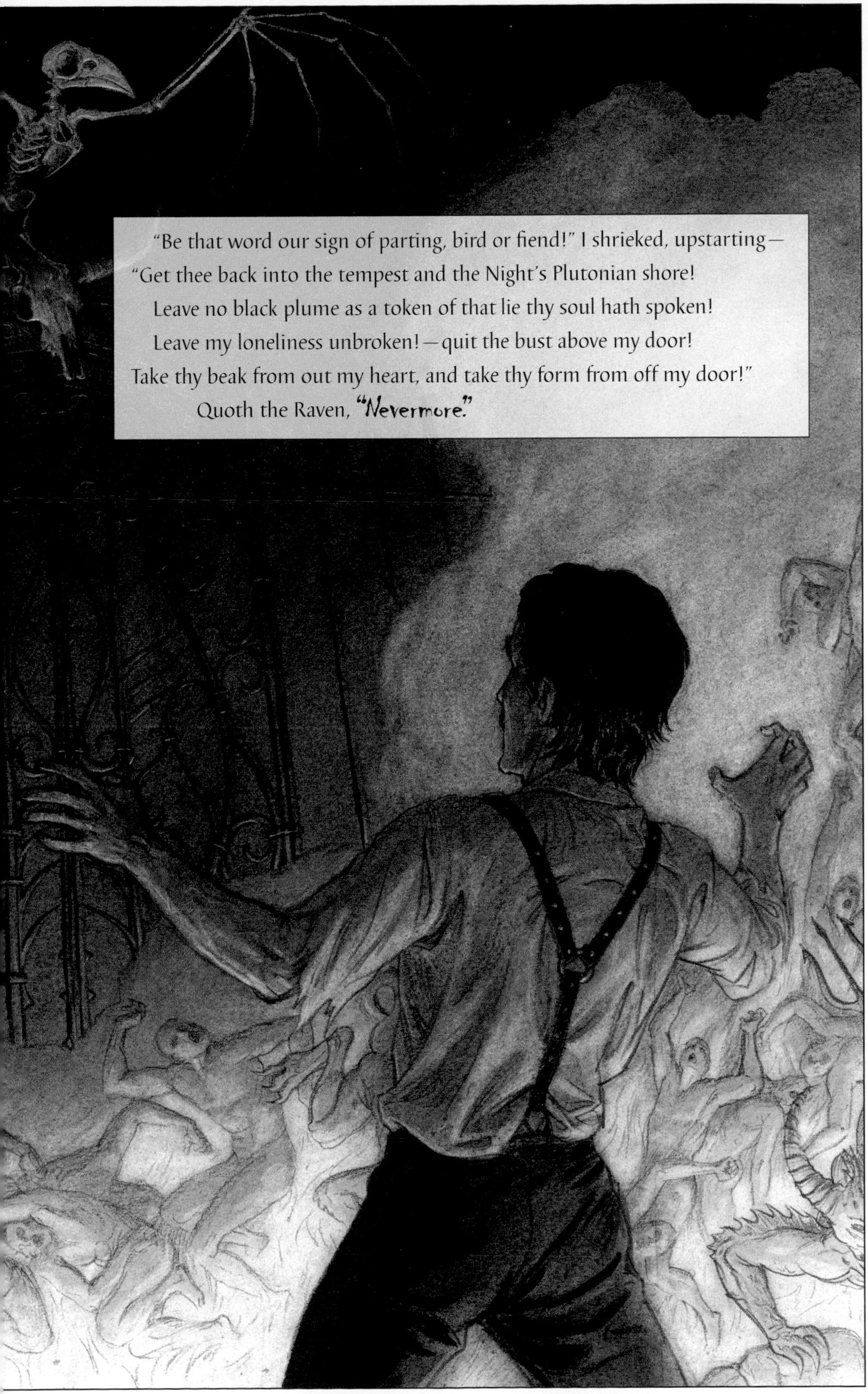

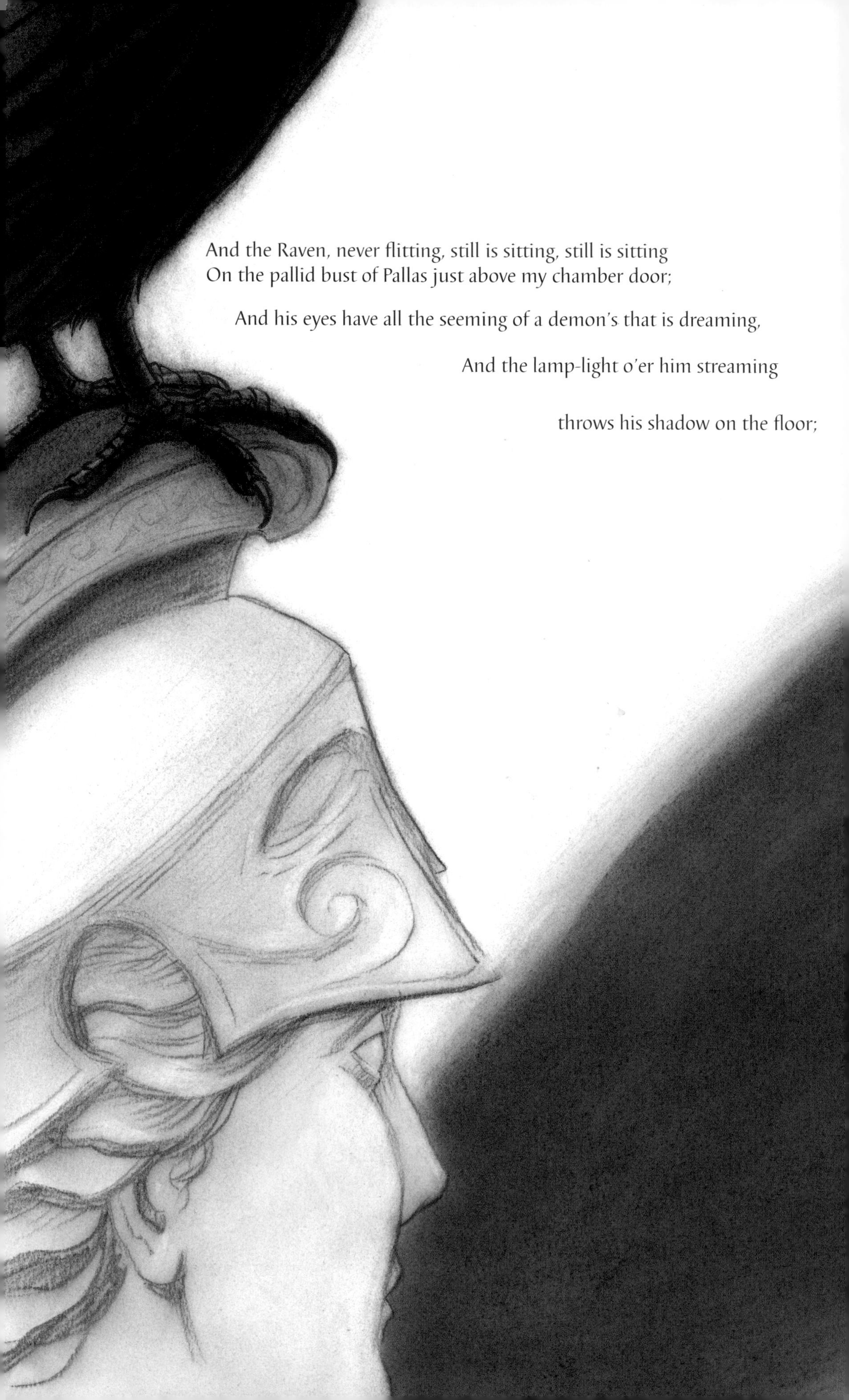

And the Raven, never flitting, still is sitting, still is sitting
On the pallid bust of Pallas just above my chamber door;

And his eyes have all the seeming of a demon's that is dreaming,

And the lamp-light o'er him streaming

throws his shadow on the floor;

And my soul from out that shadow

that lies floating on the floor

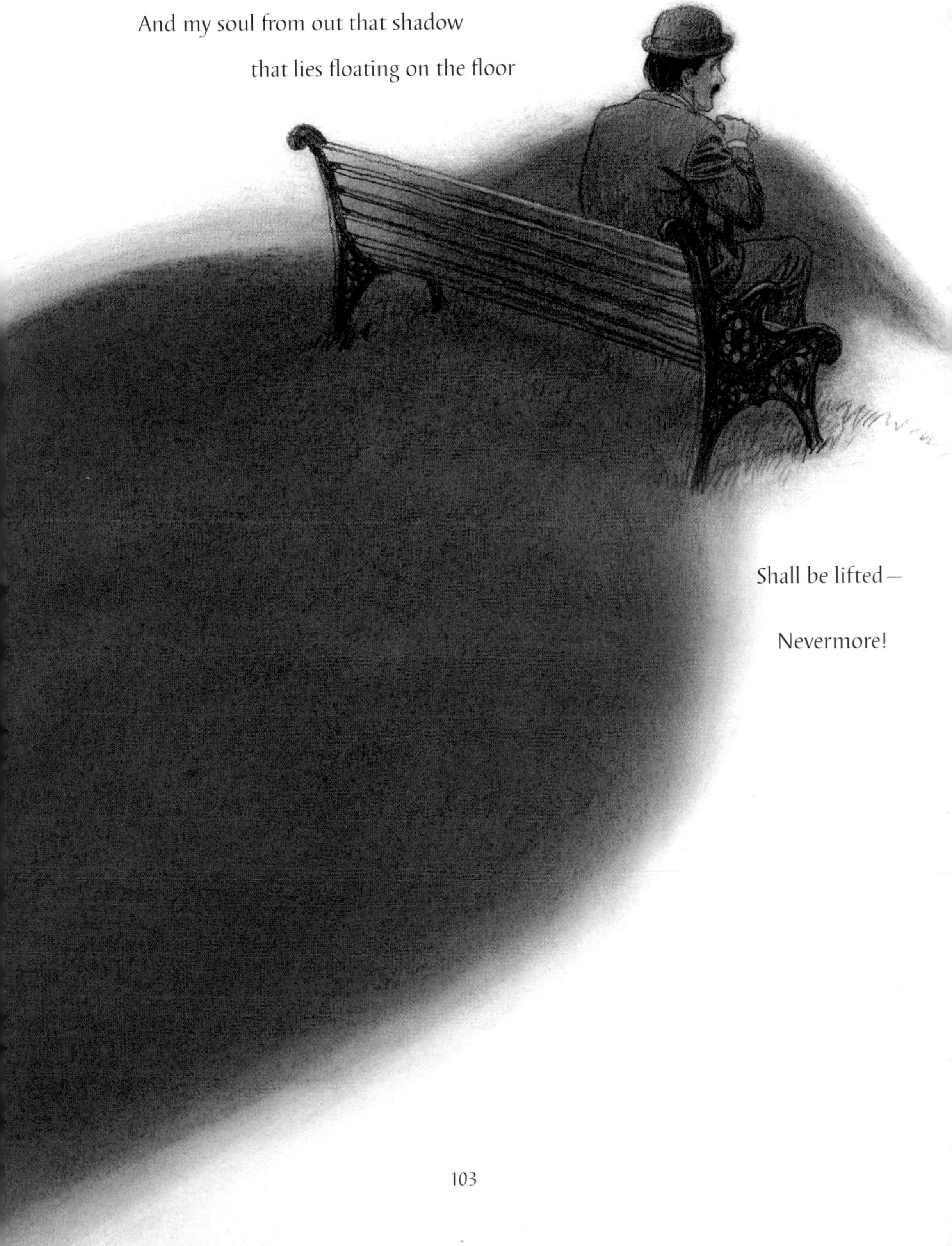

Shall be lifted—

Nevermore!

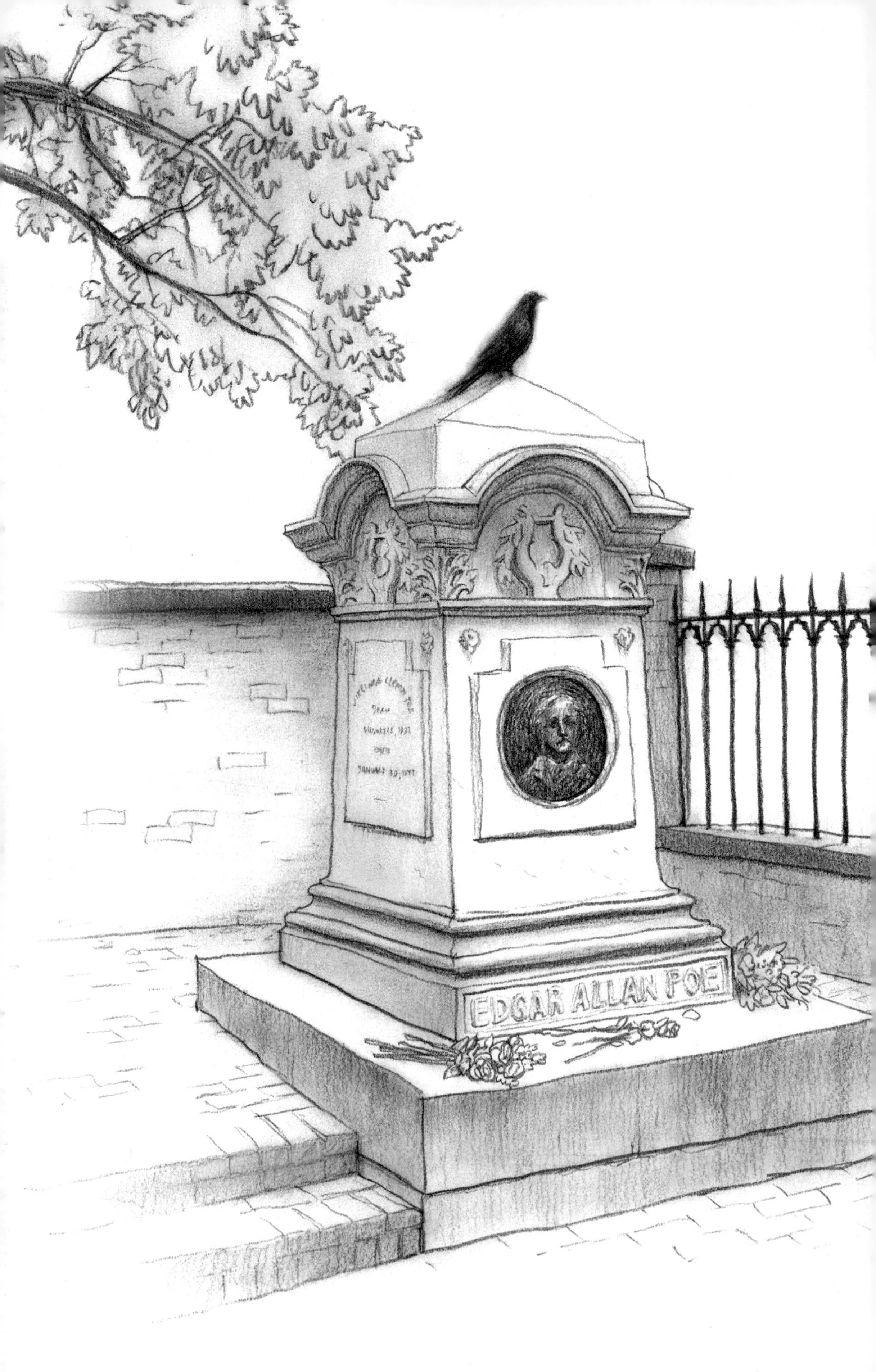
EDGAR ALLAN POE

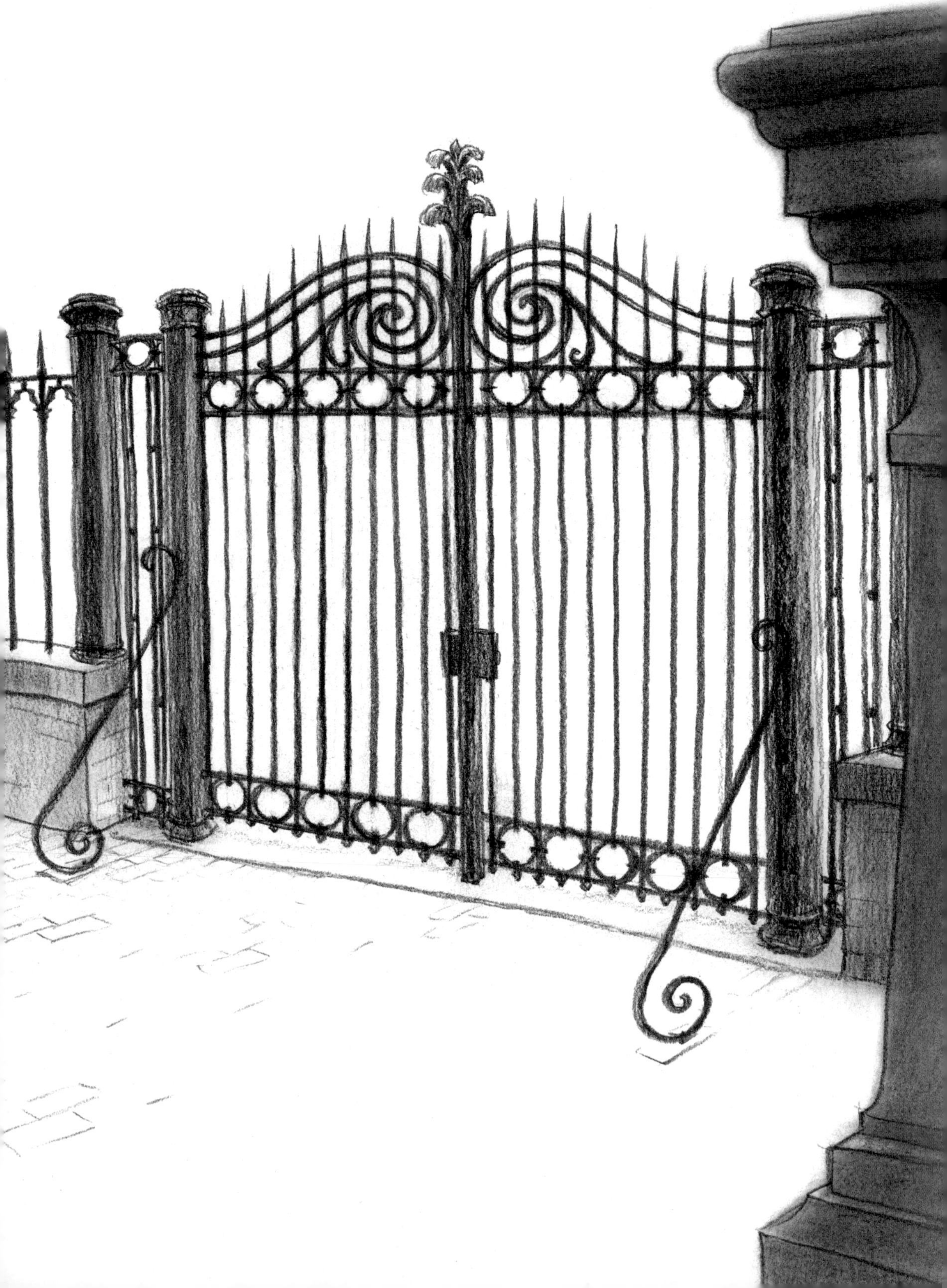

AUTHOR'S NOTE

Edgar Allan Poe was born in Boston in 1809. His father disappeared soon after he was born, and his mother fell ill and died when he was three. Edgar was informally adopted by a Richmond merchant named John Allan, who raised him and provided for his education. Poe's relationship with his adopted father became quite strained as he grew up, and when he went to college at the University of Virginia he fell into gambling and amassed large debts over which he and Allan quarreled. Poe withdrew from school and enlisted in the army, but was discharged early to attend West Point. He evidently did not care for West Point and was court-martialed for failing to attend classes or religious services. John Allan disowned him, and Poe struck out entirely on his own and tried to make a living as a writer.

He self-published a collection of his poems at the age of eighteen and showed a talent for editorial work, managing to get jobs proofreading, editing, and writing reviews and essays for various magazines to (barely) make ends meet. In addition to Boston and Richmond, he lived at various times in Baltimore, New York, and Philadelphia. Each of these cities has monuments or museums that proudly claim him as a native son.

By the time of his death at the age of forty, he had amassed a body of several hundred stories, poems, reviews, and essays, and his name was linked prominently and inextricably with several genres, most notably the gothic horror story and the detective fiction story.

Although Poe never became wealthy, or even comfortable, the stamp he left on the world of literature is enormous and enduring. Poe is beloved in a way few authors can ever hope to be. His work buries itself in the psyche and, though it horrifies, it also thrills and delights.

Pictured on the preceding page spread (pages 104–105) is the grave of Edgar Allan Poe. His remains lie in the burial ground of Westminster Hall in Baltimore, Maryland, alongside his wife, Virginia, and mother-in-law, Maria. The shadow of Virginia's death in 1847 lay over him for the rest of his life (as suggested by the image on pages 102–103). Arguably, so did the popularity of "The Raven," his most popular work, published in 1845 while Virginia struggled vainly with tuberculosis.

Poe died in 1849 under mysterious circumstances. He was found on the streets of Baltimore, dazed and incoherent, far from his home, wearing clothes that were not his own. He was taken to Washington University Hospital, where he died a few days later without ever regaining full lucidity, leaving both the exact cause of his death and the explanation for its bizarre circumstances unknown.

The stories and poems I have selected for this volume are among the most creepy, powerful, and highly regarded of Poe's works. Notes on each piece follow.

"THE MASQUE OF THE RED DEATH"

"The Masque of the Red Death" is probably the least well-known story in this collection, and I chose it primarily for its visual appeal and the fact that it is literally the most colorful of Poe's stories. Color is, in fact, almost a character in its own right—as is time. I also like how the seven rooms motif relates to the seven stories and poems in this collection. As I write this, the story still seems quite topical, as the specter of a global pandemic or antibiotic-resistant disease hovers in the background and the Doomsday Clock stands just three minutes from midnight.

"The Masque of the Red Death" was first published in *Graham's* magazine in 1842. Like many of Poe's stories, it takes place at an unspecified point in history. The disease is fictitious, although Poe may have been inspired by tuberculosis or the Black Death. Perhaps because I have Shakespeare on the brain, it made me think of the periodic closures of the theaters due to plague in Shakespeare's time, so I chose to set the story roughly in the early 1600s.

"THE CASK OF AMONTILLADO"

"The Cask of Amontillado" was published in 1846 in *Godey's Lady's Book* (which was, at the time, the most popular periodical in America). It's my personal favorite of Poe's works.

It is likely that the story was inspired by several existing tales, most notably Joel Headley's "A Man Built in a Wall," and by a legend Poe heard while stationed at Castle Island in Boston about a soldier who met a similar fate (though this legend has been shown to be fiction). He was also taking a jab at a rival author, Thomas Dunn English, with whom he had a long-standing feud. English had published a novel that ridiculed Poe in the same year, so Poe modeled the character of Fortunato on English and fictionally bricked him up in a wall.

I modeled the Montresor vaults after the amazing catacombs of Paris. The bones there are stacked in layers, with the skulls and large thighbones displayed most prominently.

Unlike "The Masque of the Red Death," "The Cask of Amontillado" and all the rest of the stories in this book are narrated in the first person. Poe never identifies his narrators, leaving the reader to decide their appearance, gender, age, style of dress, and so on. One problem with adapting Poe to a graphic medium is that I've had to choose a specific physical appearance for Montresor and the other anonymous narrators. However, I encourage you to try the thought experiment of re-imagining each of these stories with an entirely different narrator, to see how that might change the feeling of the story.

"ANNABEL LEE"

When Poe's wife, Virginia, passed away in 1847 after a five-year battle with tuberculosis, Poe was devastated. "Annabel Lee" was written two years later, and may well have been inspired by Poe's grief and enduring love for his wife. It was published posthumously. Although it is very much a poem about death, it is less dark and macabre than most of Poe's work. It is certainly the lightest in this collection, in large part because the narrator believes that he can never be "dissevered" from Annabel. (Again, I've had to choose a visual representation for each of Poe's anonymous narrators. Annabel Lee could be narrated by anyone, of any gender or ethnicity.)

One of the key images in the poem is the "sepulchre by the sea." (*Sepulchre* is another word for "tomb.") I thought of children playing with sand castles, and hit on the unlikely but romantic idea of the narrator building Annabel a fantastic monument out of sand. Of course, sand isn't a structural building material, but a little research showed me that you could build such a thing if you had the patience and know-how to construct a primitive kiln and bake batches of limestone or seashells in it. This would produce quicklime, the key binding component of cement, which could be mixed with sand and gravel to produce concrete.

"THE PIT AND THE PENDULUM"

"The Pit and the Pendulum" was first published in the literary annual *The Gift: A Christmas and New Year's Present for 1843*. (The publication date is sometimes given as 1842 and sometimes as 1843.) Although it makes use of historical elements such as the Spanish Inquisition and the French invasion of Spain, Poe was not writing for historical accuracy. Although General LaSalle was one of Napoleon's generals in the Peninsular War of 1808–1814, he was not in command of the invasion of Toledo, and the Peninsular War took place long after the height of the Inquisition. Likewise, the tortures depicted do not reflect known activities of the Inquisition. Nevertheless, this story gained great popularity for Poe's vivid descriptions of the terrifying tortures imposed upon its narrator.

"THE TELL-TALE HEART"

"The Tell-Tale Heart" was first published in 1843 in *The Pioneer* literary magazine, and it became one of Poe's best-known stories. It shares many qualities with "The Cask of Amontillado," most notably a confessional format and a murder without a compelling motive. It also contains a dismemberment, which I found was too gruesome if shown graphically (double meaning intended), and only slightly less horrifying when implied. I added the framing element of the mental institution to give the ending a bit of a twist. I based the institution on Eastern State Penitentiary, a wonderfully creepy prison-turned-museum in Philadelphia that's well worth a visit. (Don't miss the excellent audio tour narrated by Steve Buscemi.) The house depicted on the title page is based on the Edgar Allan Poe House and Museum in Baltimore.

"THE BELLS"

Like "Annabel Lee," "The Bells" was not published until after Poe's death in 1849. He wrote an initial version while living on the outskirts of New York City and is said to have been inspired by the bells ringing at St. John's College (now Fordham University). At the time, his wife, Virginia, was receiving nursing care from a woman named Mrs. Shew, who is credited with suggesting to Poe the idea for "The Bells," and perhaps the opening lines of each stanza as well. Her name appears on the manuscript of the first version, which is only two stanzas/seventeen lines long.

Poe purportedly said that his goal was "to express in language the exact sounds of bells to the ear." To this end he accentuated repeating rhythms and onomatopoeia. Perhaps the most prominent example is the word *tintinnabulation* (based on the Latin word for "bell," *tintinnabula*), which "The Bells" popularized (some sources actually credit Poe with inventing it, but prior uses of the word have been found).

A quick personal anecdote: When I first encountered "The Bells," read in class by my wonderful high-school English teacher Joyce DeForge, one of the other teachers, Tom McKone, came bounding in partway through, claiming that whenever "The Bells" was read aloud, he could hear its unique, sonorous rhythm from anywhere in the school. I think of that every time I read it.

"THE RAVEN"

"The Raven" was first published in 1845 and was a runaway success, appearing in numerous magazines and eventually becoming one of the most famous poems ever written. It made Poe a household name practically overnight, although it never brought him much wealth. (Sources say he was paid nine or ten dollars for its first publication, worth perhaps a few hundred dollars today.)

The poem contains a number of classical references that may be confusing:

- **Nepenthe:** a mythical drug, mentioned in *The Odyssey*, which brings forgetfulness to ease sorrow.
- **Balm in Gilead:** a medicine mentioned in the Bible (Jeremiah 8:21, "Is there no Balm in Gilead?"), or figuratively, divine healing (for which the narrator hopes).
- **Aidenn:** a poetic spelling of "Eden," referring to Heaven.
- **Night's Plutonian shore:** the mythical shore of the Underworld (ruled by Hades in Greek myth, Pluto in Roman).

I've made the narrator of "The Raven" look like Poe himself, since in some ways it seems very much like a reflection on his personal grief; but I've set it in a somewhat ambiguous time period because it's so timeless. I've also tucked a few visual ingredients from the other stories and poems into the illustrations.

This book is for Henry Isaacs and Ashley Bryan, my painting family; and for Deb Noyes, faithful editor and gothic horror aficionado.

I'd like to thank the wonderful team at Candlewick Press for their support and hard work making my books look good and sending them out into the world. Thanks to Michael Johnson, who checked my notes on Poe's life, and to Todd Krueger and Steve Barrows for additional feedback on the Author's Note. Thanks to Michael Bergman and Mark Millman for answering vintage menswear questions. I'd also like to thank those who maintain all the historic Poe landmarks and keep them available to the public — in particular, the Edgar Allan Poe House and Museum in Baltimore, the Edgar Allan Poe National Historic Site in Philadelphia, and the Westminster Hall burial ground.

Above all I'd like to thank my beloved wife, Alison Morris, for her love, support, and expert editorial eye.

Copyright © 2017 by Gareth Hinds

All rights reserved. No part of this book may be reproduced, transmitted, or stored in an information retrieval system in any form or by any means, graphic, electronic, or mechanical, including photocopying, taping, and recording, without prior written permission from the publisher.

First edition 2017

Library of Congress Catalog Card Number pending
ISBN 978-0-7636-8112-8 (hardcover)
ISBN 978-0-7636-9509-5 (paperback)

17 18 19 20 21 22 APS 10 9 8 7 6 5 4 3 2 1
Printed in Humen, Dongguan, China

This book was typeset in Barbedor.
The illustrations were done in mixed media.

Candlewick Press
99 Dover Street
Somerville, Massachusetts 02144

visit us at www.candlewick.com

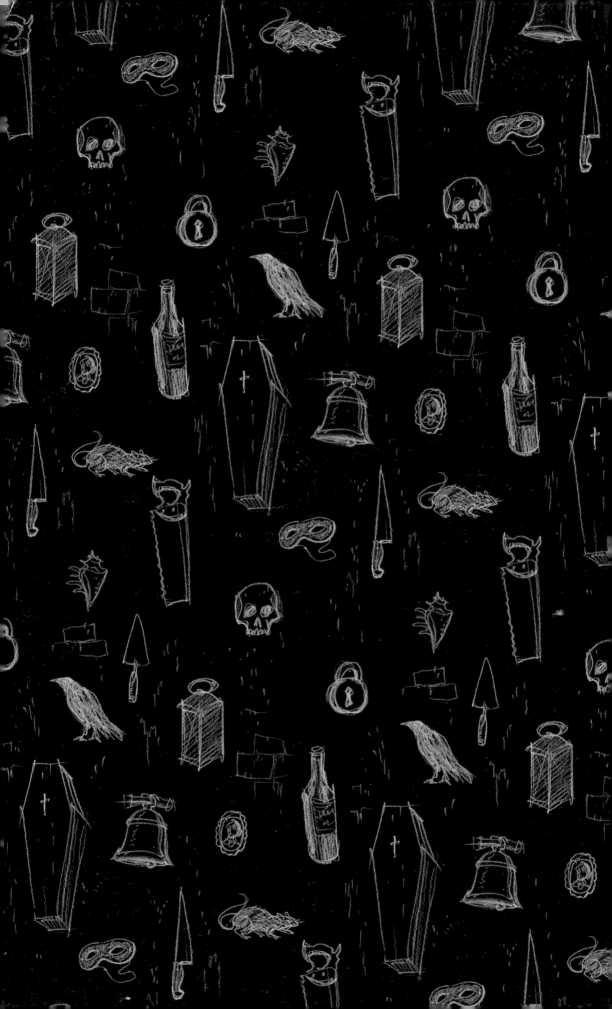